For my Parents

"Born again from the rhythm..."

Jeff Buckley

VINYL

PROLOGUE: THE DEVIL IS IN THE DETAILS
Roark

Heads. Tails. Heads. Tails.

The two familiar faces flared in the rain-soaked sun as the boy rolled them between his fingertips. The alloy was slick with his anxiety, yet their haughty expressions remained unsympathetic.

"Are you listening to me, boy?"

Roark started, his tailored suit coat squeaking against the leather seat of the auto. Victor Westervelt II glowered at him from across the compartment, his wolfish head backlit by the window.

"Yes," Roark replied, hastily pocketing the coin.

"Repeat it back to me."

"Passion is perilous. Emotion is treacherous."

"I have allowed you to grow up without the crutch of a Singer because I believe you are better than *these* people," his father said, gesturing at the dilapidated houses slinking by. "Nevertheless, you must learn to govern your emotions. If you cannot control these outbursts, I may need to reconsider."

Roark cast his eyes down to his forearms, sheathed by the silk-threaded jacket. Beneath the finery was a growing constellation of cigarette burns.

The auto lurched to a halt. Roark rocked in his seat, peered out at the dingy avenue.

His father reached forward with his oak walking stick and rapped the sealed privacy partition. "Why are we stopping?" he demanded loudly. "The shipment is due in less than an hour."

There was no response. Roark shuddered internally, reached for the talisman in his pocket. There would be harsh repercussions for the driver if he did not answer soon.

"Go have a word with the driver," Victor ordered.

"But the rain . . . " Roark began, disguising his reach for the coin as an itch at his thigh.

Victor gave his son a blistering look.

Restraining a sigh, the boy donned his bowler hat and opened the door on the driving rain. It was colder than he expected, and he wrinkled his nose at the pungent blend of fish and sewage characteristic of the outer ring. Slamming the door as hard as he dared, Roark started toward the front of the auto.

He had not taken half a step when a pair of monstrously large arms wrapped around his chest, lifting him from the soaked cobblestones.

Roark screamed, kicking wildly. His foot connected with the door at an angle, and a bolt of pain shot through him. His hat fell and rolled away down the street.

"Dad! DAD!"

The towering assailant hardly seemed fazed by his writhing as he pitched Roark over his shoulder and hurtled down the street. The boy continued to scream for help, his voice cracking, but the avenue was empty. The boarded windows of the houses looked on with vacant eyes; the gas lamps regarded him somberly.

Roark reached back desperately as the auto grew smaller behind them. He could see his father's silhouette through the rivulets of water slithering down the glass. The man was utterly still.

The kidnapper rounded a corner into an alleyway and skidded to a halt, reaching into his jacket. Roark squirmed, trying to see what he was doing.

"Hold still," the man hissed.

Before Roark could tell him to pitch off, a needle was jammed into his leg and a dose of searing fluid flooded the boy's bloodstream.

Roark gave a final, defiant twist and went limp.

The man dipped again into his coat and withdrew a black, palm-sized radio. He extended the spindly antenna, then clicked a button with his meaty thumb. Static spouted forth.

"This is Sphinx. The devil is in the details."

He waited in the fog of the static that returned. The freezing rain darkened his gray brushed hair and soaked his stolen Off uniform. He might have been shivering were it not for the adrenaline charging through his veins.

Three words shattered the white noise.

"This is Harpy," a female voice replied, losing its clarity somewhere over the waves. "The crows are flying."

A brief smile dusted the lips of the phony Off. He jabbed the button again and brought the radio to his mouth.

"Understood. I have the package and am bringing it home."

The man let the radio slip from his fingers and clatter to the ground. Hefting the boy higher on his shoulder, he slammed his booted heel into the device. It splintered, revealing copper entrails. He swept it into the gutter with his leather boot, then tore off down the alley, his prisoner thumping against his back.

Roark did not know if it was the throbbing ache in his head or the harsh words that awoke him. He had been propped up in a hard-backed chair. He did not try to move. He could feel the cold bite of manacles at his wrists and kept his eyes screwed shut, listened.

"—he can't be more than twelve, Wilcox," a woman was saying in a thick, rusty voice. She sounded as if she had been crying. "We can't just kill a child."

Roark felt the blood drain from his face as he struggled heroically not to move, to scream.

"What use is he to us now?" a man demanded.

A shudder ripped through the boy as he recognized the voice of his kidnapper.

"What good will killing him do?" the woman asked.

"His father massacred twelve of ours, *we* will eliminate his heir."

There was a jarring clang as the woman slammed something against a metal surface.

"No!" she bellowed. "There has been enough death today!"

"Wait," the man said, his voice abruptly lowered.

"No! I will not—!"

"He's listening."

Roark's muscles seized. He ceased breathing, hoping he could somehow bleed into his surroundings.

The man advanced on him, his steady footfalls thudding

across damp stones. He leaned in close to Roark, who kept his eyes closed, struggling not to inhale the hot, foul breath of his warden.

"I want you to hear me, boy," the man hissed. Roark twitched, but managed to keep his eyes locked shut. "We were banking that your father would send the Offs guarding the shipment after *you* and leave the warehouse ripe for the taking."

"Wilcox—" the woman warned.

"When our team arrived . . . Every. Single. Off. Remained. Your father couldn't even spare one man to save you."

"That's *enough*, Tristen."

"He couldn't even be bothered to take one of our agents prisoner. He had them all beheaded, left their heads sitting real polite-like next to their bodies. Right now, I'll bet you anything he's sleeping sound, knowing his fresh Singers are safe. He must *despise* you."

Roark smashed his teeth together. His eyes flew open. Wilcox's slate eyes were narrowed, rimmed with red. His mouth was twisted into a snarl born of agony, not true malevolence.

Roark knew the difference.

"He can keep his damn Singers," the boy growled. "I *hate* him."

Wilcox jerked back, appraising Roark calculatingly, then gazing over his shoulder at the woman. She was tall and willowy with a shock of dyed orange hair. The skin around her eyes was swollen, but she radiated undeniable strength and elegance.

For a split second, Wilcox whipped around to view Roark, his expression now inscrutable. Then he spun on his heel and stalked from the room. "Do what you will," he spat as he passed the woman. He slammed the iron door on his way out, shaking dust from the low, stone ceiling.

As soon as Wilcox was gone, the woman crossed the room in four strides and knelt before Roark, digging into her pocket. The boy twisted away at first, but stilled when he saw what she had produced. A key.

"I was bait, then?" he asked quietly as the woman freed his left wrist.

She inclined her head without looking up from her task.

"My father sent no one," he went on, more to himself than to her.

The woman nodded again as she sprang his other wrist and climbed to her feet, staring down at him with a vaguely absent expression.

Roark massaged the sore rings on his wrists, wincing as he accidentally brushed one of the burns his father had given him.

The woman caught his hand. Roark flinched, peered up at her fearfully. Instead of striking him as he had expected, she knelt before him and turned his palm to the ceiling. Slowly, carefully, she rolled back the sleeve of his damp shirt, revealing discoid wounds, some white, others red and oozing.

She sucked in a deep, trembling breath through her nose, closed her eyes, then released him. Roark shoved his sleeve down, embarrassed.

"There has been so much suffering," she murmured.

Roark fidgeted uneasily in his stiff chair. He was highly unaccustomed to anyone showing so much emotion, least of all pity.

"Victor—" the woman began.

"I go by Roark."

She dipped her chin in understanding.

"My name is Ito, Roark," she said, her bleak gaze mirroring the dim light of the room. "I think we may be able to help each other."

1: THE TUNNELER

Subtrain station 42 was drenched in a sickly green hue and reeked of vomit. Even through the sealed windows of her driver's cabin, Ronja could smell it.

She yanked her scarf higher over her nose, inhaled the sweet musk of wool. The stubborn odor still crept through the knit fibers.

Ronja huffed exasperatedly, let her head loll to the side. Her pale green eyes roved across the station. It was deserted, save for the barefoot man who sprawled across the benches each night. That is, until the 4 A.M. Off patrol threw him out mid-snore.

Ronja's gaze lingered on the bedraggled man for a moment. He lurched violently in his sleep, flung his fist out in a pitiful strike. His arm fell limp, swinging back and forth like a pendulum.

The girl turned from the pathetic sight. She folded her legs to her chest, rested her chin on the crest of her knees.

She was halfway tempted to invite the bum to board her train free of charge, just so she could have a new passenger to deliver someplace.

Her train seated a hundred. She now carried seventeen passengers.

The subtrain had once been the pinnacle of Revinian public transportation. In recent years, however, the tunnels had deteriorated. The constant redirection of routes made it an incredibly inconvenient way to travel. The once robust sea of rail riders had dwindled to just a few scant customers. The rest took to the streets, preferring the torrential autumn rains to falling rock.

Ronja herself wasn't keen on plunging headlong through the crumbling caverns, but wasn't likely to find better employment above ground.

She shoved back her sleeve, squinted at the cloudy face of her watch. 2:26 A.M. Wasserman had instructed her to wait at least ten minutes at each station on the late shift just in case any straggling customers needed shuttling.

Then again, her boss was not here. He was probably in his office, shoveling canned beef into his face.

Ronja glanced about the station, craning her neck to survey the furthest corners of the room.

No late-night passengers awaited her.

I could leave early, she mused. *Cram in a few extra minutes of sleep.*

The thought snapped in two.

Ronja winced, clutching her right ear as The Night Song spiked. The cool, metal Singer grafted into her skin tightened its grip on her cartilage, forcing her to listen. The listless, curling notes of The Music sharpened each time the smallest defiant notion flickered in her mind. A warning born of a pounding rhythm.

The driver screwed her eyes shut, waiting for the frantic notes to subside.

After a few minutes, The Night Song lulled. Ronja released her knees, rubbed the exhaustion from her eyes.

Disobedience is destruction.

The phrase, plastered across the faces of buildings and the undersides of bridges in massive red block letters, flared in her psyche each time The Music condemned her actions.

Ronja tucked her chin into her chest, nestled deeper into the furls of her scarf.

Waited.

It seemed an age before her departure time rolled onto the face of the clock. Ronja had been too tired to open her book, so she amused herself by tracking the flow of The Night Song. It was a game they were taught as children; to unravel the pattern stitched into The Music. Her schoolmates had insisted one existed, but Ronja could never find it.

She shook the fog from the valleys of her mind, cracked her stiff knuckles, then slid to the edge of her oversized chair and began to wake the train.

The engine yawned, purring beneath the soles of her boots. A cloud of steam built outside the windshield and was inhaled by the hungry vents above.

Ronja let her gaze slip out into the station. The false luminescence of the electric lights swelled as their gears were spun by the excess steam from the train. Fully powered, the lights were more yellow than green. The atrium seemed less desolate saturated by the friendly glow.

The girl refocused on her task.

She yanked the lever dangling from the ceiling, releasing a shrill, warning blast. The bum stirred in his sleep. A terrified rat scampered into its hole. With the push of a button, Ronja sealed the doors on her scant riders.

She shoved the joystick forward with a grunt of effort. The steamer groaned and began to roll forward, quickly gathering speed.

Yawning, Ronja flipped a brass switch, and the headlamps flickered to life, illuminating the gaping tunnel. The light struck a reflective surface and catapulted back, momentarily blinding her.

"Skitz!"

Ronja slammed her boot into the brake, choking down the scream in her throat. The train lurched to a halt with a hiss and a sickening clang. Black smoke peppered with white sparks seeped from the dashboard.

Ronja waved her hand, coughing into the crook of her elbow. The smoke dissipated slowly, leaking through the vents.

She squinted through the singed windshield.

Standing rigid in the arch of the tunnel was a boy not much older than herself. He was tall, with tawny skin and dark hair knotted at the base of his skull. His eyes refracted the glare of the headlamps so powerfully that Ronja was seized by the urge to blink, but it was the silver pendant resting against his chest that had blinded her. He was garbed in plain dark clothing, not the stark white uniform of a maintenance worker.

That meant he could be only one thing.

A tunneler.

Ronja swore colorfully. She leaned forward and punched a button. The intercom shrieked to life, rebounding off the walls of the cavern. The tunneler grimaced and clapped his hands over his ears.

"Oi!" Ronja roared into the com. "Off the tracks! You think you're just gonna bounce off the front of a steamer?"

The boy shook his head, a slow grin sweeping across his face. His shoulders trembled and Ronja clenched her teeth. He was *laughing*.

She jabbed the button again.

"If you don't pitch off, I'll report you."

"I'm not afraid of the Offs," he called back.

The intercom crackled with his laughter. Ronja swallowed, glad of the glass between her and the obviously unbalanced tunneler.

"Leave now and maybe I'll let you off—"

The Night Song screeched in her ear. Ronja winced.

It was against the law to aid the tunnelers, who lived in the bowels of the city and stole from obedient citizens aboveground. Ronja tugged at her ear as if she could peel away the Singer burrowed in her skin. The boy squinted at her through the glare, curiosity etched into his features. Ronja realized she had been staring at him blankly. Blushing fiercely, she punched the intercom again.

"Look, I'm leaving," she said, hoping her voice was steady. "With or without you on the tracks."

The boy sneered. His teeth were as white and straight as the capitol building's marble bricks. He raised both hands in mock surrender. Ronja's lips curled into a snarl.

"All right, you got me," he drawled. "I'm leaving. You can get back to your precious schedule."

He turned around to leave. The headlights bathed his sharp profile in yellow light.

Ronja sucked in a shallow breath. The microphone picked up her inhalation, projecting it down the tube. She pressed her hands to her mouth as if she could retract the sound.

The boy paused. He turned his face back to hers, sneer now a genuine grin. He winked blithely and melted into the black.

Ronja sat petrified in her chair. In her right ear The Night

Song roared, the notes wordlessly bidding her to drive forward, to report the incident, then to forget.

In her left ear was the frantic tick of her watch, warning her that she was behind schedule. The image of the boy played like a moving picture on the gritty face of the windshield. His straight jaw, his sly grin . . . and his naked right ear.

The boy did not have a Singer.

2: CUT

By the time she revived the ancient engine an hour later, her train was nearly empty, and she was elbow deep in black grease.

Stripped down to her tank top, her cap backward on her damp curls, Ronja rolled into the final station with heavy lidded eyes and a fresh collection of burns on her callused fingers. With any luck she could get her hands on some salve, but luck did not appear to be on her side this week.

Charged by the final hysterical stage of exhaustion, she hopped from her cabin to coax her few remaining passengers homeward. She slid her stingring onto her forefinger in case they were agitated. The ring was cool, but snapped with violent electricity upon contact with an assailant's skin.

Fortunately, these commuters were the quiet sort. A few exhausted businessmen in rumpled pinstripes, a handful of bums reeking of the sap, and a call girl with smeared makeup puffing a slim.

They were worlds apart, but all were united by their silver Singers implanted at birth. The tiny, identical devices curled about their cartilages, plunged and snaked into their ear canals, pouring out whatever Song The Conductor deemed appropriate for the hour.

The tunneler's exposed ear leapt to the front of her mind, but she forced it back.

Later, she promised herself. Or perhaps she was promising The Night Song, which flared as she suppressed her unwitting knowledge of the crime.

Ronja paced along the railcars, peeking through the windows in search of any lingerers. Finding none, the girl sighed gratefully and returned to her cabin. She applied the emergency brake, gathered her bag, and locked the door behind her.

Ronja took the stone steps to the surface at a jog, eager to feel the splash of the cool, 5 A.M. air. She broke out of the tunnels like a moth bursting from its cocoon.

The city unfurled around her, steel and brass and layer upon layer of brown brick. The Conductor's words sprawled lazily across the soot-tarnished blocks in red letters:

PASSION IS PERILOUS

EMOTION IS TREACHEROUS

DISOBEDIENCE IS DESTRUCTION

The buildings around her were simple and dull, but in the distance glowed the core. The gold-trimmed capitol building was illuminated by electric power even in the pre-dawn gray. The mammoth clock at the tower's crown peered at Ronja from afar, stealing her seconds with a warm smile.

Wine-red airships pregnant with helium roamed the bleary skies, whirring softly. They shed their behemoth shadows on the glimmering upper ring.

Ronja ripped her gaze from the core, a brief crescendo of The Night Song reprimanding her jealousy.

She trotted across the empty street to the subtrain office, the hour she'd lost to the tunneler itching her. The worn soles of her boots slapped against the wet cobblestones, spraying murky water across the tail of her overcoat.

Georgie's plants needed water, she'll be glad it rained again, she thought as she approached the office.

The subtrain office was pinched between a bicycle shop and an abandoned tenant home. It was a squat building with a single, square window and a gated door. A kind word for it might be "rustic," but "dilapidated" was more appropriate. A wooden sign above the locked door read:

SUBTRAIN: ROARING TOWARD THE FUTURE

Ronja's fingers trembled as she rummaged through her bag for her keys. It was not long ago that Wasserman had entrusted her with her own set. She imagined him snatching them from her hands, enraged by her incompetence. Her fingers closed around the cool teeth of the gate key.

The door burst open in a flurry of light and sound. Ronja stumbled backward, fumbling with her keys and dropping them.

A man of immense size loomed in the doorway. He was almost as wide as he was tall. His neck boiled over the lip of his tight collar. The top button of his shirt strained heroically against its burden. His eyes were hooded by thick pockets of fat, though his lips were surprisingly thin.

"You're late," Wasserman rumbled.

Ronja arranged her face into an apologetic mask, twined her fingers behind her back to still them. "There was a disturbance in 42," she replied.

"You shoulda dealt with it, I didn' give you steamies them stingrings for nothin'."

Ronja spun her weapon around its axis.

"It wasn't that kind of disturbance. I had to stop suddenly and my engine choked."

"You sure took your time dealin' with it, then."

"I apologize, Mr. Wasserman."

The man grunted, itched his ear. A shower of dead skin rained down like dirty snow, dragging Ronja's eyes to his Singer. The machine was caked with rust. The skin around it looked raw, sick.

"You got somethin' to say, girl?" Wasserman snarled.

"No sir, it's just—"

"What?"

"I think your ear might be septic."

A telltale sheen built on Wasserman's bloated face, followed by a creeping, violet blush. Ronja could imagine The Night Song building in his infected ear, imploring him to discipline his employee for her impudence.

Ronja dropped her eyes and face, but the man caught her chin with two beefy fingers, forcing her to look at him.

"You think you're smarter than me? You think that *mutt*

mother of yours gave you some kinda smarts the rest of us don' know about?"

Ronja sighed internally, felt her muscles go lax. They had arrived at her mother, as they always did. Wasserman never missed a chance to remind her of her inferior status.

"No, sir," she heard herself say.

"Bein' a mutt ain't something to be proud of. Bein' a mutt's kid ain't any better."

He spat bitterly at her boots.

"No, sir."

"Good. Wouldn't want you gettin' any delusions in that punkass little head."

Wasserman shoved Ronja back with his swollen hand. She tripped, catching herself on the open gate. Her stingring struck the metal and a shower of blue sparks leapt from it, flitting harmlessly to the ground.

"That's my time you're spending, understand? I can't leave till the last train's in."

Ronja swallowed the bitter lump in her throat, nodded mechanically.

"You're goin' home with twenty-five," her boss hissed through his stained teeth. He reached into his threadbare waistcoat, withdrawing a wad of cash. He peeled six bills from the mass and thrust them at her. "I'll throw in an extra note—remember, I'm generous."

"That won't last a week," Ronja whispered hoarsely.

"Twenty-five would last less," Wasserman replied unhelpfully.

"I've got a family."

"So do I, punk. 'Sides, don' mutts just eat outta the garbage, anyway?"

Wasserman guffawed to himself. Ronja felt her ears grow hot. Her boss's blubbery neck loomed so close.

The Night Song soothed her anger with a heavy barrage of notes. Ronja breathed in through her nose, exhaled through her mouth, and snatched the bills from Wasserman. She stuffed them into the deepest pocket of her overcoat.

"Scram, mutt. I'm lockin' up."

Ronja whirled and careened into the empty street. Her path bled in and out of view in the puddles of light cast by the gas lamps.

When she reached her street, Ronja slowed to a jog. The sun had been roused behind the rows of cramped houses. It stretched its luminous, pink arms over the rooftops, but in their wake the shadows only lengthened.

Ronja settled into a walk, her legs heavy with dread. Georgie and Cosmin would be stirring soon, but it was her mother's rising she feared.

She never knew what it might bring.

3: THE GAP

By the time she reached her row house, a languid drizzle had given way to a downpour. Ronja stood immobile on the gum-spotted sidewalk, the curls that peeked from beneath her hat growing dark with rain. Black grease slithered down her arms and face, ferried by the cool water. The burns on her palms sighed with relief.

Her front door had once gleamed red to match the airships drifting overhead, but it had long since faded to a tired gray. In fact, everything about the house was weary. The crumbling bricks were smeared with soot. Georgie's winter squash had withered in the polluted air. Even the cast iron railing lining the steps sagged with an unseen burden.

Ronja steeled herself at the base of the stairs, stroking her stingring with a callused thumb. The Night Song had faded to a sigh. Soon it would disappear altogether, only to be replaced by The Day Song.

The girl hitched her bag over her shoulder, tapped up the steps, and unlocked the door.

The tilting entry corridor was uncommonly still and dark. Stale air seeped out into the rain like a slow exhalation.

Ronja tiptoed across the threshold, now clutching her bag to her chest to keep it from jostling. She closed the door softly, pausing when the hinge moaned, cringing when the lock clicked.

She stilled, listening.

Only the dying thrum of The Night Song and the patter of rain greeted her.

She trudged to the kitchen, placed her knapsack on the table. Resting her palms on the surface, Ronja peered around through drooping lids.

Dust motes swirled lazily in the air. The hands of the clock trudged in steady circles. A portrait of The Conductor, Atticus Bullon, regarded her from above the icebox. Bullon was a beefy man with a mustache like a squirrel's tail and small, beady eyes. Though he was not attractive, he radiated undeniable prowess and grace.

Prickling beneath The Conductor's acrylic gaze, Ronja moved to the sink where last night's dishes lay waiting. She made a mental note to smack Cosmin for neglecting his chores. Too exhausted to bother with the soggy food and curdled milk, Ronja moved to the squat icebox and crouched before it.

Once she popped the stubborn door, her stomach plummeted. The shelves were nearly empty, save for a hunk of cheese and half a quart of milk. There was bread in the cabinet, a few of Georgie's vegetables might be salvageable, but . . .

"Ro?"

Ronja spun and rose quickly, shutting the icebox with a soft clap.

A slight form stood in the door, hair frazzled from sleep, nightgown equally rumpled. Remi, the child's plush rabbit, dangled from her fist by a ragged ear.

Ronja felt a smile budding on her lips despite the emptiness in her gut, and she opened her arms to her cousin.

"Morning, Georgie," she called quietly.

"Why are you covered in grease?"

"Engine choked. Come here."

Georgie shuffled forward, bare feet whispering on the wooden floor, and leaned into Ronja's embrace. The younger girl was all elbows and knees. Her shoulder blades jutted out like the wings of an aeroplane, and her Singer was cold and unforgiving against Ronja's neck.

"How did you sleep?" Ronja asked into her mussed hair.

"Bad," Georgie yawned, her voice muffled.

"Why?"

"Night Song was too loud."

"You know you could fix that if—"

"I stopped dreaming so much, I know."

Ronja released her cousin and held her at arms length. Georgie met the elder girl's tense stare with irritable hazel eyes.

"Georgie, I'm serious," Ronja reprimanded in a low voice.

"This is the third night this week your dreams have raised your Song. If you cross the threshold too many times, the Offs will be notified, or worse you'll trigger The Recovery Song."

"But *I'm* not a mutt, they don't watch me as close as you and Aunt Layla," Georgie grumbled.

Ronja swallowed, her nostrils flaring.

"You're close enough," she said flatly, releasing Georgie's arms as if they stung her. "You've got a mutt Singer. Doesn't really matter if you have the genes or not, The Music's still stronger."

Georgie looked down, her teeth gritted. Ronja sighed wearily and returned to the icebox. She wrenched it open, snatched the hunk of cheese from the top shelf, then sealed the door with a dull thud.

"Ro—" Georgie began, wringing the ears of her rabbit.

"No, *I'm* sorry," Ronja said, waving off the pending apology.

She set the cheese on the table absentmindedly and rested her elbows on the wood. The rain ceased.

"I didn't mean to sound harsh, you just need to be more careful."

Georgie nodded sharply.

"Passion is perilous."

"Emotion is treacherous," Ronja replied in the customary format.

She drew the kitchen knife from its block and plunged it into the firm cheese.

A ray of sunlight passed across Ronja's knuckles as she sliced. She paused and glanced up in time to see the shaft peeking through the half-curtained window. She followed the beam as it tumbled across the floor, exposing every scratch and scuff left in the wake of their lives.

The clock caught up to the sun, striking five-thirty with a satisfying click.

Georgie's eyelids flickered shut. Ronja watched her, their breakfast abandoned.

Waited.

The Night Song ceased in a flurry of high-pitched notes.

The wall clock was impossibly loud. The creak of the

floorboards twined with the rattling of a passing motorcar. A pigeon cooed from a streetlamp, a sound she could hear but never quite grasp beneath the veil of The Music.

The world was deafening in The Music's absence, but Ronja's mind was quiet.

Her breathing slowed; her heart rate followed. Her senses unfurled. Her fingertips brushed the rough surface of the table, feeling the scar left there by the knife lying before her. The deep gash sparked the wick of a memory she did not wish to recall. Ronja shook her head, shifted her attention back to Georgie. The way the sunlight perched itself upon her unruly locks. The way she always clutched Remi by the same worn ear, worrying it until the fabric was in tatters.

Feeling abruptly overstimulated, Ronja shut her eyes and waited for the ear-splitting silence to end.

The quiet cacophony lasted sixty-three seconds. Then The Day Song stirred in her caged ear. It was faster than The Night Song. More urgent, and just as persuasive.

Ronja shivered as she settled into the anxious flutter of notes. The surrounding world fell back into its usual muted state. The sounds, the sights, lost their potency. What was seconds ago laced with memory was now hollow. The sunlight was just sunlight. The mark on the table was just a mark, not a scar.

"Sit down," Ronja ordered briskly, gesturing to the chair opposite her with the knife.

She recommended hacking away the tainted bits of the cheese as Georgie clambered into the chair. It sagged even under her slight weight.

"Where's your brother?" Ronja asked.

"Sleeping."

"And my mother?"

"Sleeping."

"Do you know if she . . . slept well?"

Ronja paused and glanced up, waiting for an answer. Georgie's eyes slid up to meet her cousin's. The girl pursed her lips thoughtfully. Even Remi was somehow quieter.

"I don't know," Georgie admitted.

"How was she last night?"

"How she usually is."

"Vegetable-like?"

Georgie nodded.

"Good, with any luck she'll stay that way."

Georgie regarded Ronja from behind wisps of ashen hair.

"Did something happen, Ro?" she asked.

Ronja sighed, resting the blade on the table. Georgie had always been insightful beyond her years. She was almost as hard to lie to as a Singer.

I can't tell her about the boy, Ronja decided. *But she needs to know about the money.*

"My paycheck got cut," she admitted. "I was late checking in, Wasserman and I both got pissed. Actually my Night Song rose too, so I guess I'm a hypocrite."

As if on cue, The Day Song swelled. Georgie and Ronja cringed in unison. It was not unusual for their Singers to sync when in conversation. Dangerous thoughts seemed to grow between them.

"How much did we lose?" Georgie asked when the spike ended.

"Not much," Ronja lied. "We'll be fine, but I'll have to take up an extra job this week."

"Ro," Georgie leaned across the table, eyes like searchlights. The rabbit slipped to the hardwood, forgotten. "We have to turn the heat on soon. You gotta let me and Cos help."

"Absolutely not." Ronja returned to flaying the cheese with increased ferocity.

"You started working when you were my age."

"I was ten, you're nine."

"Yeah, and I'm already more mature than you."

Ronja tossed an irritated glance across the table, but Georgie only grinned, exposing her missing front teeth.

Ronja returned to her task, but froze a moment later. Georgie stretched down to the floor for Remi's ear.

Even through the curtain of The Day Song, Ronja registered the significance of the large, bare feet trampling down the wooden staircase.

She swallowed her nonexistent saliva.
"Good morning, Layla," she called.

4: SPIKED

D amn," Georgie muttered.

"Language," Ronja hissed back, glancing toward the empty doorframe. "I thought you said she was in her usual state!"

Georgie shrugged helplessly.

"I can't predict when she's gonna have a fit!"

Ronja's eyes darted from the open door to the cheese, the slices so thin they resembled cloudy windowpanes. She dropped the knife and hurried toward the cabinet where the bread was housed.

Georgie joined the hustle, leaping from her chair and beginning to scrub the dirty dishes in the sink.

Layla's bare heel struck the second step from the bottom. The wood shrieked. Ronja flew to the icebox, kicking herself internally, and grabbed the last of the milk.

"Georgie, cup," she whispered urgently.

The girl tossed a dripping mug at Ronja. She caught it, pried the cork, and poured the last of the frothy drink into the waiting cup.

"Do you *know* what time it is?"

Ronja tensed. Georgie paused mid-scrub, lip curled in helpless disgust. Ronja sniffed the air discreetly and grimaced, empathizing with her cousin's discomfort.

"I asked you a question, Georgie, *Ronja*."

Ronja turned, plastering a smile to her lips.

"It's five-thirty. The Day Song just started."

Layla Zipse stood in the arching doorway, hirsute arms folded before her worn bathrobe, feet bare and filthy, perpetual growl hanging on the corner of her mouth. Her matted gray hair hung limply around her shoulders. She grabbed her right ear and tugged. The dull glint of silver flashed in the morning light.

"I heard it start, Ronja—do you think I'm a pitching idiot?"

"No," Ronja began carefully.

She set the mug on the table and slid it toward her mother, who was already trembling.

"But you asked the time, and since The Day Song always starts at five-thirty—"

"I know what time it starts," Layla spat. Even the frayed ends of her hair seemed to shudder with anger. "My question was rhetorical."

"Then why did you expect an answer?" Georgie asked.

"I didn't want an answer," she replied, her voice abruptly low.

The mutt prowled forward, reaching out with clubbed fingers for the milk. She lifted the glass in her left hand and reached into her dressing gown pocket with her right. She pulled out a metallic flask, popped the lid, and poured half the contents into her milk.

Layla sipped the drink and smacked her lips, smiling sweetly.

"I didn't want an answer, I wanted an *apology!*"

Ronja closed her eyes, sucking in the oxygen and The Day Song.

Passion is perilous. Emotion is treacherous.

"I'm sorry, what did we do to upset you?" Ronja asked, keeping her voice level.

"You woke me with all your jabbering," Layla gulped her mug ferociously. "I was up late with The Night Song going yak yak *yak,* then I wake up to hear you two skitz-heads jabbering about Ronja's check getting cut. Why were you late, hmm? Out kissing boys on your shift?"

"I'm sorry you didn't sleep well, and that we woke you," Ronja replied evenly. "I forget your ears are more sensitive than ours. I'm sorry my check was cut, but I have it under control."

"I've decided to take up a job after school, to help Ro out," Georgie broke in. "She works so hard."

Ronja shot a withering glance at Georgie, which she tactfully ignored.

Layla paused, puffy lips pressed to the rim of her mug, then snorted into the repellent concoction.

"If she's working so hard, why are we out of milk again?"

Ronja felt her ears grow hot. She dropped her gaze to her hands, which were pressed palms-down on the table. The knife caught a shard of sunlight, glinted in her peripheral vision.

Emotion is treacherous.

"Georgie," Layla barked.

The mousy-haired girl nearly dropped the plate she was polishing.

"Yes?"

"You can get a job after school, but *just* after school. Can't have you droppin' out like this pitcher." Layla gestured at her daughter with a tilt of her head.

Ronja's composure snapped. She slammed a fist into the table. The bread shuddered, the blade rang against the wood. The Day Song started like a frightened rabbit, wailed in her ear. Hot white lights ruptured in her vision, but she ignored them. She leaned toward her mother, whose jaundiced eyes narrowed to slits.

"I left school because you were too lazy to get off your ass and work, you useless *mutt*."

Layla lunged forward and seized Ronja by the front of her sweater. Her spiked milk crashed to the floor, shattering and splashing across their legs. Georgie screamed and grabbed Ronja by the shoulders, trying to yank her away. The older girl shoved her off with ease, matched her mother's snarl.

"Don't you ever talk down to me, girl," Layla spat. She drew Ronja closer, licked her rotten teeth. "If I hadn't been too sick to work, you'd have flunked out anyway."

"I'm smarter than you ever were," Ronja insisted, her voice climbing higher than she thought it could.

"Then why can't you get a better job?"

"Because my mother's a pitching *mutt*, and they think I'm one too!" Ronja shrieked.

Layla released her jumper and shoved her away with a gnarled hand. She dug into her dressing gown again, retrieving her flask. Ronja was reminded of Georgie grasping her rabbit's ear for comfort.

"That ain't true," her mother growled, fiddling with the cap.

"It is!" Ronja shouted. "They *bark* at me when I walk down the street," her voice cracked. Her eyes glazed over and she blinked them into focus. "If you could just *tell* them I'm not a—"

"What?!" Layla roared, lobbing the metal cap across the kitchen. It sang against the wall, then bounced across the floor before vanishing beneath the icebox. "Not a mutt?! You're skitzin'. Mutt genes are passed with the rest of 'em. You've been sayin' for years you ain't one, but you *are* and you'd best get used to it."

Layla swiped a slice of stale bread from table and, ripping off a portion with her teeth, marched from the kitchen. She paused in the doorframe, her muscles taut beneath her sagging skin.

"Just listen to The Music, girl, you'll hear the truth. No one hears The Music like us mutts."

Ronja swallowed the stone in her throat. It landed in her stomach, nearly dragging her to her knees.

She was about to turn away when Layla loosed a gasp, drawing Ronja from her stupor. The mutt flicked her gaze to The Conductor's brooding portrait. Her papery lids fell like curtains over her twitching, yellow eyes.

"The Music hears me. The Music hears me. The Music hears me. The Music—" Layla's words bled together beneath the scalding gaze of the mute painting.

A minute passed, choked by the string of words. Ronja felt Georgie watching her, but she ignored it. She looked on as her mother's rage unraveled into nothingness and tried to feel relief.

When Layla opened her eyes, they were still and flat. She no longer seemed to register their presence. The mutt turned on her heel and trudged toward the door, her hands feeble at her sides.

Neither Georgie nor Ronja spoke as Layla retreated up the staircase.

The Conductor was vividly present in their kitchen and their ears.

A door squeaked open, then clicked shut above them.

Ronja sank into a chair and exhaled deeply, forcing her anger out with her breath. Generally, The Music was enough to maintain her composure, its tune wringing the rage from her mind. Today, it was not sufficient. She knew she would feel the repercussions of her temper later.

"You know she's wrong, right?" Georgie asked.

Ronja fell back into the kitchen. Georgie was sweeping the

shattered glass into a dustpan.

"About?"

"You. You *are* smart, and I know you're not a mutt."

Ronja laughed dryly.

"One thing's for sure, it doesn't make sense. She was made a mutt before I was born. I checked our papers."

Georgie paused and leaned on the broom handle heavily, her wide eyes roving. Ronja could tell she was seeing far beyond the kitchen.

"It doesn't have to make sense," the girl finally said. "Just be grateful you're not like her."

Ronja allowed her head to sag onto the table. She wrapped her arms around it as if to protect it from a bomb blast.

A soft hand kissed her shoulder.

"It isn't your fault, Ro," Georgie whispered in her free ear.

"She shouldn't be like this," Ronja murmured, her forehead pressed to the cool, scrubbed wood. She screwed her eyes shut, drew her arms tighter around her curls. "She should be like the rest of them."

"She usually is," Georgie replied, beginning to knead her cousin's stiff shoulders. "She's just—"

"A time bomb," Ronja finished.

"The Music gets her before she goes too far," Georgie said soothingly, moving her fingers up to massage Ronja's neck.

The older girl chuckled mirthlessly from beneath her tent of hair.

"Not always. I prefer her as a vegetable."

"No you don't," Georgie admonished gently.

Ronja rose abruptly, knocking away the tender hands. She shoved a piece of bread into her mouth. It was stale and tasteless on her tongue, and it stuck in her throat. She reached for the milk bottle, then swore when she found it empty.

"I'm going to sleep," Ronja said through her mouthful of food.

She slammed the bottle down on the table.

"When should I wake you?" Georgie asked calmly, leaning on the broom.

Ronja sighed, passing an apology to her cousin through her

gaze. "Eleven . . . no . . . ten-thirty, please," she replied in a milder tone, gathering her coat in her arms and starting toward her bedroom. Her limbs were leaden. Her train of sleepless nights was gaining on her.

"Wake Cosmin in a half-hour, would you? And get him to finish the pitching dishes."

Georgie nodded, mustered a weak smile.

Ronja's heart tightened. Georgie looked like a paper doll. She clung to the broom like a life raft. Her eyes were rimmed with dark circles, and her lips were cracked.

"Finish that," Ronja commanded, pointing at the loaf as if to prove a point. "Just leave a bit for Cos, he always gets extra from his friends."

"What about Aunt Layla?"

Ronja glanced up the quiet stairwell where her mother had disappeared.

"Don't call her that," Ronja replied. "Just Layla."

She turned on the heel of her boot and strode toward the basement door.

5: HOME

It was a relief to shut the door on her mother's erratic rage, on Georgie's aching expression.

Ronja stood at the crest of the basement stairs with her back pressed against the door. The weight of the world bulged against the wood.

She peeled away from the barrier and started down the stairs. The aroma of must and dry soil settled in her nose. She inhaled deeply. The knots in her shoulders loosened.

Home for Ronja was not the house; it was her bedroom.

Her basement chamber was nearly pitch black, save for the silvery light that crawled in through the narrow street-level window. Each day, the glass was caked with sludge from trampling boots and revolving wheels. Each day, she took a rag to the mess. It was a hopeless task, but she liked to watch the pairs of feet go by and imagine the lives attached.

Her room was sparsely furnished. It housed a twin bed; a plain, ancient desk; an oil lamp; and a chair with an uneven leg. A smaller rendition of Bullon's portrait regarded her from the shadows above her headboard.

Ronja tossed her hat and coat onto her desk. Her cap tumbled to the floor, but she ignored it. Her limbs like anchors, she flopped onto her bed face first and sank into her blankets.

Despite the comfort, dark memories swirled behind her eyelids. Not even The Music could drown out the creeping sense of dread that accompanied them.

Layla had been a mutt since before Ronja was born, but she knew her mother had not always been so demented.

She had proof.

Ronja let her fingers drip over the edge of her bed. They skimmed the underbelly of her mattress, pausing when they brushed the sharp edge of the photograph lodged between the rusted springs. She tugged it into the muted light.

In the photograph, Ronja's father had swept Layla off her feet. She could not see his face, it was hugged by the shadow of his hat. His Singer glinted hollowly in the sunlight. The camera portrayed him as a sturdily-built man with a smudge of gray for a face.

Ronja had never known her father. He had died when she was a baby. He sometimes slipped into her dreams, a splotch of gray in a trench coat. She trailed him through the tilting city streets, losing him around corners only to rediscover him behind her. His footsteps tapping on the bricks, nearly loud enough to overcome The Music. She would awake to a cold sweat and an aching skull.

Ronja brushed her forefinger across her mother's static face, which was bitingly clear in comparison to her father's.

In the past, Layla was neat, pretty without being beautiful. Her hair was spun into tight pin curls, her dress was pressed, her toes pinched into dainty heels. Although the photograph was black and white, Ronja could see that a hint of color had been applied to her cheeks and lips. Her teeth were stark white, her eyes scrunched with laughter.

Ronja let the snapshot fall from her fingers. She pressed her face into her pillow, breathing in the cool, dry cotton.

It was against the law for mutts to keep photographs of themselves pre-procedure. Ronja did not know how it had escaped the furnace. She had discovered it when she was seven, tucked between two quilts in the attic. She had been too fearful to ask if its presence was purposeful.

Despite the roar in her head, Ronja had not been able to burn the illicit photo.

She rolled over onto her side, careful not to crumple it.

No one really knew what was in the serum that created mutts. It was a tangle of nefarious genetic material laced to a carrier virus that chewed through healthy human DNA and filled the gaps with recombined sequences. In the end, it did not matter what it was made of, but what it did.

The mutt virus opened the minds of citizens previously deaf to The Music. Criminals, traitors, enemies of The Conductor and

His regime. Their fiery brains were numbed, their erratic emotions plateaued. They were made soft, malleable, and highly susceptible to The Music.

At least, they were supposed to be.

Layla spent days, weeks at a time, in the foggy stupor where she belonged. She wandered the house, mumbling to herself about the flow of The Music, nursing her flask. Occasionally, the mutt would sink into a coma that spanned days. Ronja suspected these episodes were signs of the virus beginning to wear her down, especially since they seemed to grow worse with age. She often wondered when her mother would go to sleep and never wake up.

Then, there were times when Layla's rage erupted, shattering The Music like a brick through a window.

It was against the nature of a mutt to feel rage. It was against their nature to be anything but obedient and docile. Regardless, Ronja had the marks to prove her mother's violent outbursts.

Ronja reached up and brushed the jagged scar puckered on her collarbone with the pads of her singed fingers. She closed her eyes, shoved her hand under her cool pillow.

If Layla kept fighting her nature, she would doubtlessly go into The Quiet.

But did she deserve to?

That was the question Ronja had wrestled with since the day her mother gave her her first black eye. Was Layla a naturally violent person barely restrained by her numbing mutt genes? Or had something gone wrong with her procedure, altering her brain and making her—?

Ronja winced as The Day Song pinched her.

The Music Hears You.

She grabbed the spare blanket folded neatly at the end of her bed and wrapped it around her shoulders. She laid down and tucked herself into a ball, her knees curled to her chest. She tried to close her eyes, but found her lids were painted with both her mother's faces. Human and mutt. Old and new. Worse and . . . better?

Ronja snaked her hand out from beneath her pillow and rubbed the bridge of her nose.

In the end, Layla was right.

Mutt DNA was transferable. It was designed as a mark of shame that lived on through generations. Ronja should have inherited her coarse features, harsh voice, and muddled brain.

But Ronja knew damn well she was human.

In her youth she had spent hours staring into the hazy bathroom mirror, nose pressed to the glass in search of a hint of yellow in her irises. They had always remained the same pale shade of green, flecked with gray. Her fingernails were not clubbed, but long and slender. She was not plagued by listlessness and lethargy. By age ten, she was convinced she did not house a sliver of mutt DNA.

Such logic did not affect the minds of the Revinians. Ronja had never understood it, and had long since given up trying. Each and every person she encountered seemed to inherently recognize her genes though she knew in her bones they were invisible. It was as if they could smell the virus festering beneath her skin.

Since the first grade, Ronja had been shunted into corners. Teachers averted their gazes, ignored her questions. Her peers shied away from her, cringing if their skin happened to brush hers. Her naturally quick mouth stilled when she realized that her words were discounted.

By all but one.

Ronja smiled feebly at the thought of Henry. Her best friend was blissfully unaware of the consequences of his actions. He had doubtlessly lost friends in order to maintain their relationship, but he never complained.

Ronja fell asleep as the rest of the city was beginning to stir.

She dreamed of driving a steamer through a ceaseless, linear tunnel punctuated by unsavory fluorescent bulbs. The vision was perfectly dispassionate, until a familiar silhouette appeared in the arch of the catacomb.

6: SAPPED

Ronja," a voice called from somewhere in her dream. Ronja groaned.

"Ro!"

Ronja blinked sluggishly. A blinding shaft of sunlight shot through the window above her bed. She flung her forearm across her eyes.

"You gotta get up," the voice implored.

Two hands shook her shoulders roughly.

"I'm up, Cos, I'm up," Ronja muttered.

She yawned and propped herself up on her elbows, squinting wearily at her cousin.

Cosmin beamed at her, his arms folded over his chest. He was tall for a twelve year-old, and thin as a rail. He had the same mop of dark curls Ronja was burdened with, and an easy smile. He wore spectacles while he read, which magnified his grayish-green eyes.

"I wish I had a camera, Ro. You're a train wreck."

Ronja stretched, her muscles creaking like the scaffold of an old house. "Is that supposed to be a pun?"

Cosmin laughed good-naturedly and offered his hand. Ronja clasped it, and he yanked her out of bed. She was still wearing her boots, trousers, and sweater.

"What time is it?" Ronja yawned again, stretching her arms toward the low hanging ceiling.

"Nearly eleven," Cosmin replied, stepping back.

Ronja opened her mouth to yell at him, but the adolescent threw his hands up.

"Hey, I wanted to get you up, but Georgie said you needed to rest."

Ronja huffed in vexation, but let it be. It made no difference, anyway. Her day job did not start until 1:00, and she had little hope of finding a week's work before then.

"I'll let you tame your hair, then," Cosmin said, backing toward the steps. "Do you want some shears, or do you want me to just hack it off with a knife?"

Ronja yanked off her boot and lobbed it at Cosmin, but he was already halfway up the stairs, cackling.

"Do the pitching dishes!" she shouted after him, but the door cracked her words in half.

Ronja went to her dresser, a reluctant grin on her mouth. She grabbed a clean sweater, loose trousers, and underwear from the dresser. She slid out of her remaining boot and scooped up its mate on her way up the stairs.

The kitchen and hallway were empty when she emerged from her room. The house was still, as if holding its breath. Georgie was likely outside tending her garden. Cos was bound to be studying, never mind the fact that it was Saturday morning. Layla, with any luck, was comatose.

Ronja crept up the staircase and into the single bathroom.

Brittle autumn air leaked in through the poorly insulated window above the bath. Ronja leaned across the tub and drew the curtain on the little portal, then spun the knob all the way to the left. Freezing water spewed from the faucet, stinging her fingers.

It took nearly three minutes for warm water to be coaxed forth. When steam finally began to billow, Ronja plugged the drain. Shivering, she climbed out of her clothes and clambered into the steadily-filling bath.

She sat quickly and leaned back against the porcelain, forcing herself to become accustomed to the intense heat. She wrapped her svelte arms around her legs, rested her chin on her knees. Dirt and grease were already sloughing off her body, though the water had barely reached her midsection. Her messy curls were teased into wilder waves by the ballooning steam. Goose pimples rose on the backs of her arms where the warmth had not yet enveloped her.

When the water reached her shoulders, she slipped beneath its lip.

It was nearly silent beneath the waterline, save for the hum of the stream. Even The Day Song was less potent. The water provided a cushion against the incessant, meandering tune. Ronja allowed her eyelids to part slowly. She blinked against the dull sting, sending twin shoots of air bubbles to the somehow distant surface. The gleam of the naked bulb hanging from the ceiling danced through the lens of the water.

Tangled thoughts bobbed to the surface of her mind. The tunneler, her sliced paycheck, Layla, Georgie, Cosmin . . . the tunneler.

The Day Song prodded her lightly through the liquid barrier.

I have to report it today, she thought with a wave of decisiveness. *It's the right thing to do.*

One thing at a time, advised a tranquil voice in the back of her head. The voice sounded far too much like Georgie's to ignore.

Okay. First, I have to find a job.

Henry's bright face materialized in her mind's eye, his signature grin clicked into place.

Ronja shot up from beneath the seal, her drenched mane slinging droplets onto the walls and mirror.

"Henry," she said aloud.

Henry would help her. He always knew how to get her out of a pinch. A subtrain driver himself, he had probably already heard of her misstep. Wasserman gossiped more than a teenage girl and was always eager to diminish Ronja in Henry's eyes. Like the rest of Revinia, he strongly disapproved of a mutt-human friendship.

This had not deterred Henry thus far.

Hope bulging in her throat, Ronja snatched the bar of soap from the windowsill. She began to scrub her body furiously, desperate to scrape away the remains of the night.

By the time Ronja had bathed, made an attempt to comb her hair, and dressed, the world outside was pulsing with life. The rain had recommenced. Throngs of Revinians struggled against each other, traveling in innumerable directions. Shouts rang out when feet were crushed, when shoulders were jostled. Black umbrellas and sopping white newspapers peppered the writhing crowds.

If the subtrain were working, the streets wouldn't be nearly this clogged, Ronja thought with vague annoyance.

She drew a deep breath, shoved her cap over her already damp curls, and plunged into the fray.

Ronja kept her elbows out as she walked, ready to jab anyone who came at her. She had seen too many people engulfed by the treacherous mobs, then spat out with bruises the size of oranges and bags half their original weight. She did not intend to become an unfortunate casualty of a traffic backup.

Around her, shops were open for business. Customers cycled through the swinging doors like bees revolving through hives. Street vendors raised their voices, hoping in vain to penetrate both The Day Song and the metropolitan cacophony.

Ronja ducked down one alley, then another, working her way from the overwrought avenues into the shady maze of backstreets. Following an internal map impossible to sketch, she eventually reached a narrow, unassuming passage between two decrepit tenant homes. A bum slouched against one of the walls, cradling a flask similar to her mother's. His eyes were closed, and a rumbling snore stirred his beard every few moments.

She turned to the wall the man faced and let her eyelids fall shut.

For a moment, she stood static in the lazy rain, allowing it to wring the babel from her mind. She breathed in deeply though her nose, then exhaled through her mouth. She counted her heartbeats, tapping them out against her thigh with her index finger.

1-2-3

2-2-3

3-2-3

Beat by beat, The Day Song was pacified. Sensing her muted mind and falling vitals, it loosened its grip, believing she had reached placidity.

Ronja opened her eyes. A small smile built on her lips. She forced it away and focused her mind. She ran her index finger along the face of the wall, counting seven bricks to the left of a vacant doorway. On the seventh brick she stopped, and pried the loose stone from its nook. It was far lighter than it appeared, its core chiseled out.

A rustling from the belly of the hollow brick pricked her ears.

She sent out a silent thank you to her friend, and dumped the contents of their secret mailbox into her hand.

A note, scrawled on a clipping from the *The Bard*, tumbled into her palm. Ronja unfolded the fragile paper carefully.

Heard you pissed off W — Nice — Got a job for you — Good pay but the whole thing is skitz — Office at noon — Ask for A. — morning herring

Ronja reached into her pocket and produced her matchbook. She tore one of the sticks from the cardboard and scuffed it against the scratchpad. A feeble flame coughed to life. She pressed it to the crumpled note. Energized, it devoured the clipping. She tossed the remains into the air before the fire could lick her palm.

She replaced the brick, spun around, and froze.

The bum was watching her, his eyes like foggy windowpanes. He fingered his Singer doubtfully. Ronja swallowed a wad of nonexistent spit and touched her own Singer, which had begun to fidget, sensing her fear.

The Music Hears You.

Ronja dug into her bag and withdrew three of her remaining six notes. She advanced on him, waving the bills like flags of surrender. His eyes latched on to the gray and green notes. He licked his stained, cracked lips with a blackened tongue. Ronja glanced at his fingers, which were also bruised black.

He's on the sap, she realized.

The sap was the cheapest drug on the market. Popular, and easy to make. It could be shot, but was usually chewed. Needles were as expensive as they were rare. The drug turned the mouth and fingers black, and corroded the users organs until he or she was a tent of skin held aloft by a skeleton.

But it stimulated the senses, made everything sharp, while suppressing The Music.

"Hey, you're out, yeah?" Ronja whispered urgently, crouching before him. She gave the bills a shake. They whispered against the humid air.

The addict's eyes darted to Ronja's own Singer. His stained

finger tapped nervously against his tin flask.

"You can have the cash if you promise not to tell about my box."

The man grabbed at the notes, but Ronja held them out of his reach.

"Swear you won't say a word."

"I swear," he rasped, his voice limp in his blackened mouth.

"On?" Ronja pressed, fighting against her churning gut and throbbing right ear.

"The sap."

Ronja thrust the man his notes, then faded into the rain.

7: BALANCE

T he Office crouched in the basement of a pawn shop toward the edge of the outer ring. It was guarded by a barrel-chested man robed in tattoos who dosed himself daily with minute amounts of the sap. The tiny hits muffled the nagging cries of The Music, which crescendoed with each illegal endeavor. The trouble was, if The Music got too loud without him knowing, the Offs would be notified, and the Office discovered.

It was a tricky balance, but the scales had yet to tip.

The legality of the Office was questionable, to say the least. It provided short notice, temporary employment for the people of the outer ring. Most available jobs were hard labor, and all had dubious sources.

The Conductor mandated that all businesses had to be registered, approved, and surveyed by the government. The process could take months, even years depending on the profession. Some would starve before they received their permit.

The Office was one of the only secrets the Revinians kept from The Conductor. Even The Music could not quell hunger.

Ronja's throat constricted as she stepped across the threshold of the pawnshop. Her skin prickled when the tinny bell over the entryway announced her presence. She loosed a resolute sigh as she shut the door on obedience.

Ronja worked her way through the maze of overflowing shelves. Dolls and stuffed animals wilted with neglect watched her with milky eyes. Mismatched shoes, empty bottles, bent silverware, cracked plates and bowls, costume jewelry, and innumerable stacks of useless files lined the racks. The only thing the shop lacked was customers.

Ronja rounded the end of the aisle, and nearly smashed into the guard.

Her eyes met his torso. A swollen lattice of black veins trickled down his thick biceps, flaring against his pallor. A bandage was wound tightly around his right forearm. She supposed it hid the branching wound that spread each time he shot up. Ronja craned her neck to view his face, wondering how much they paid the guard to ravage his body this way.

He peered down at her with blackened eyes, his lip curling as if he could smell the mutt genes festering beneath her skin.

"Morning herring," she said loudly.

The man sighed audibly and motioned for her to shut her eyes. She did so slowly, her fingers wound tightly around the strap of her bag.

Two sausage fingers pressed against her neck, seeking her pulse. Ronja shivered, then stilled herself. The Office could not allow emotional patrons to enter. If her vitals betrayed fear, she would be sent away.

Ronja inhaled meditatively. Her heartbeat slowed, and The Music deflated.

The guard removed his fingers from her neck. Ronja cracked an eyelid.

The man regarded her skeptically, searching for a hint of deception. After a tense moment, he rolled his eyes and turned his back on her. He shoved a pair of books aside, revealing a brass lever.

Ronja shuffled backward as the guard pulled the lever and pried the hinged cabinet from its recess, unveiling a stooped doorway framed by a stone arch.

Rippling voices swelled from below, and a warm glow crawled up the rickety, wooden stairwell.

Ronja nodded at the man and stepped toward the portal, but he swung out a massive arm to stop her.

"What?" she snapped.

The guard rubbed his thumb and forefinger together, eyebrows high on his bald head.

"I don't have any pitching money, why do you think I'm here?"

Ronja did not wait for an answer. She ducked beneath the brawny arm and strode down the staircase. A shock of stale air blasted her from behind as the sentry closed the door.

The odor of sweat and anxiety crept up to meet her as she

descended. Voices mingled with the thick stench. Doing her best to refrain from holding her nose, Ronja stepped from the stair and rounded a tight corner.

Pipes oozing steam and suspicious fluids decorated the walls and ceiling like road maps. A dozen desks lined the walls, manned by exhausted employees with green armbands. Customers swarmed around the desks, ignoring the hand-painted sign that begged them to form a queue.

Ronja slipped into one of the clusters, her fingers knotted behind her. She hung toward the back, listening to the patrons vie for attention. A part of her wondered why the guard bothered to check their pulses at all. As soon as they crossed the threshold tensions mounted. Ronja could sense despair leaking through the dam of The Music.

"Oi, oi!"

A young employee leapt to his feet and raised his hands soothingly. Ronja recognized his face and knew he ran in Henry's circle, but could not place his name.

He must be A, she realized, but her thoughts were cut short when the boy spoke again.

"You're all going to get jobs so kindly *shut it* and wait your turn."

He's lying, Ronja realized with a surge of anxiety.

The falsehood glinted plainly in his murky brown eyes.

Sudden resolve shocked her muscles into motion. Ronja lunged into the crush of the unemployed, her sharp elbows jabbing into protruding ribs, triggering cries of pain and surprise.

Ronja tumbled from the mob with a final grunt of effort. Her palms slammed onto the aged wooden desk, stirring the papers and rocking the inkpot.

The employee lurched back on his chair, the legs scraping against the dirt floor. His nose wrinkled distastefully as he looked her over.

"Henry Romancheck sent me," Ronja called over the knot of voice.

The irritated sheen over A's eyes melted. An understanding smile snapped into place on his mouth.

"Oh yeah, he dropped by earlier. You Ronja?"

Ronja dipped her chin.

"He said you work the subtrain, yeah? What shift?"

"Nine to three."

"A.M. to P.M? P.M. to A.M?"

"P.M. to A.M."

A grunted sympathetically.

"What happened?" he asked as he rifled through his papers.

"My paycheck got cut," Ronja explained sheepishly. "Henry found out, sent me to you."

A whistled through the gap in his teeth.

"Good friend you've got there, especially for a . . . " He trailed off.

"Yeah," Ronja replied blandly.

A fell silent and continued to thumb through his files methodically. Ronja waited, painfully aware of the growing disquiet behind her.

1-2-3

2-2-3

"Ah, gotcha."

Ronja's attention switched back to A. The boy licked his index finger and pried a thin manila envelope from the stack.

"Private delivery to some kid up in 45. Package has to ride in the front with you."

"That's not possible," Ronja snapped, abruptly on edge. Her right ear and temple began to throb dangerously. "Cargo's gotta ride in the back."

3-2-3

A shrugged blithely. He tossed the envelope onto his overflowing desk and reclined in his chair, his fingers knit to support his curly blond head.

"No skin off my back. You want the job, better take it now. People are getting antsy."

Ronja glanced over her shoulder and was greeted by a sea of disgruntled faces. She turned back to A, grimacing.

"How much?" she asked resignedly.

"Thirty, even."

"Thirty?" Ronja balked, her eyebrows shooting up her freckled forehead. "What *is* it?"

A shrugged again.

"I'll take it," Ronja said.

"Fine."

A unlaced his fingers and passed her the envelope. It was lighter than she had expected. Ronja eyed the employee, her query written plainly on her face.

"Those are the delivery instructions. Henry's holding the package, said he knew you'd take the job."

"Of course he did," Ronja grumbled.

She thanked A and wormed back through the crowd, mumbling apologies and keeping her eyes trained on the exit.

1-2-3

2-2-3

3 · · ·

Ronja took the stairs two at a time, the envelope tucked snugly in the crook of her elbow. She rapped the door with a fist, perhaps too ferociously. When the guard threw it open, he was scowling at her.

The girl dropped her gaze to her boots. She sprinted past the sentinel and out of the shop.

8: THE VOICE OF REASON

The slim envelope grew heavy as Ronja trudged through the steady rain. It was as if the paper cloaked a slab of lead. Her mouth was dry, and her stomach writhed. Her head pulsed to the irregular beat of The Day Song.

"Desperation is apt to muffle The Music's voice of reason," she recalled an Off explaining at an assembly in grade school.

The woman had worn the finest clothes Ronja had ever seen. A royal blue dress that dusted the floor, sheer stockings, and pointed heels. Pinned to her lapel was The Conductor's insignia: three concentric white rings. Her Singer was threaded with gold, and diamonds drooped from her earlobes.

"You must not give in to your trials," the woman continued. "The Conductor knows best. His wisdom is transmitted to you directly, children. The Music knows when you are naughty. It will strengthen until it has you back in the proper place. This is for the best."

As if in reply, The Day Song bucked again.

Pain ripped through her skull, and Ronja stumbled into a broad-shouldered man lugging a crate of wilted vegetables. He shoved her off with a grunt.

Ronja stood hunched in the middle of the bustling road, gathering her wits. White spots like bullet holes flared behind her eyelids. She pressed her rain-slick palms to her sockets to smother the pain.

"Ro!"

The familiar voice pricked her free ear and Ronja smiled through the agony. She uncurled her spine and forced her eyes open.

"Henry! Over here!"

Henry Romancheck's grimy face slid into view between an age-crumpled woman and a man leading a goat. Ronja raised her hand in greeting. Her friend beamed and lifted a thick hand in return.

"Hear you've gotten me into trouble," Ronja whispered, tapping her Singer emphatically. "Visits to the Office are *strictly forbidden.*"

Henry laughed and drew her into a rough embrace, which Ronja returned enthusiastically. It had been nearly two weeks since they had last seen each other. They both worked tirelessly, especially in the winter. Like Ronja for her family, Henry was the sole provider for his sister Charlotte, who was a year older than Georgie.

"A simple thank you would suffice," he muttered in her free ear.

Ronja drew back from the embrace and rolled her eyes toward the gray clouds, still holding her friend by his forearms.

"Thank you," she drawled. She sobered. "How'd you figure out I was in trouble so fast?"

The boy shrugged nonchalantly.

"You know Wasserman, he gossips more than Tahlia Davidson. Remember her?"

"I remember you making out with her in the broom closet seventh year," Ronja replied dryly.

Henry squinted into the distance for a moment, then a spark of recognition lit his face.

"Oh yeah! I forgot about that."

Ronja shook her head in mock disgust.

"I hear you have a package for me," she said.

"Yeah, it's back at the office, come on."

Henry grabbed her hand and began to lead her through the crowd. Warmth immediately spread from Ronja's fingertips to the rest of her body, melting the white patches in her vision.

Ronja and Henry had been like kin since their first days of primary school. Their peers suspected some scandalous romance, but the pair knew better. Henry had tried to kiss Ronja in the fourth grade. She had broken his nose, and they had been best friends since.

Ronja squeezed the boy's hand. He returned the gesture automatically.

Henry led her through the maze of streets, tossing greetings at friends and family as they wandered past. Their replies dissolved when they saw who Henry towed in his wake. The word "mutt" slithered through the avenues like a snake through tall grass. Henry was oblivious, as usual.

As they navigated the city, the rain trickled to a halt, but the humidity was still dense in the air. Ronja's curls stuck out at all angles, protruding from her cap like twisted strands of ivy. The midmorning light shivered as it fell through the lifting steam.

They reached the subtrain office at noon when the sun crested the sky, illuminating the cracks in the building's foundation and the rust that crept up the bars of the gate.

"Wait," Ronja wrenched her hand back and scraped to a stop.

Henry peered back at her, arching a thick brow.

"Problem?"

"Wasserman," Ronja hissed.

"He cut your check, Ro. It's not a big deal."

Ronja crossed her arms, Wasserman's hateful words pooling in her memories.

"Look. I just . . . don't think I should go in before my shift, okay?"

Henry sighed deeply and ran a hand over his cropped hair.

"It'll be fine, just say you forgot something."

Ronja made a noise close to a growl, then threw up her hands in defeat. "Fine," she muttered.

Henry's mouth quirked into a smile, which he quickly smothered to avoid her wrath.

Ronja stalked forward, one hand curled into a fist, the other clenched around the envelope. The sweaty silhouette of her palm bled into the yellow paper. Henry chuckled dryly and followed.

Wasserman was snoring in his leather-backed armchair when they slipped in through the front door. His great breaths rattled the windowpane he slumped against.

Ronja flicked an obscene gesture at the behemoth, drawing a scarcely muffled snort from Henry.

The boy ushered Ronja toward the back room, which served as an office for the three junior managers. The trio consisted of Henry, a sinewy man called Pete, and an elderly woman named

Doris with hair liked dried brambles and an even drier wit. Henry was the only one who had been awarded his position sans bribery. Ronja knew her friend thought little of Wasserman, yet he continued to show him every respect.

It drove her mad.

Still, Ronja figured she could not complain. If Henry were not so good natured, she would be entirely friendless.

The office of the junior managers was little more than a collection of three desks drowning in stacks of papers hip high. Henry's desk crouched in the far corner beneath the street-level window and was by far the best kept.

Ronja dropped her bag and tossed the damp envelope onto the desk. She cleared away a bundle of alphabetized papers, then perched on the polished wood. She knew Henry hated it, but this time he did not reprimand her.

Henry sank into his chair, which creaked dangerously beneath his weight. He leaned back, observing Ronja with quiet eyes. "What happened?" he asked after a moment.

"My engine choked," she snapped, thrusting out a burnt hand for him to see.

The image of the tunneler's naked ear hit her harder than a wave of The Day Song. She shivered and swept the memories away.

"That's not what I meant," Henry said gently. "What happened with your m . . . with Layla?"

"Oh."

Ronja's gaze fell to her lap. She wanted to sink into the folds of her coat, to pull the brim of her hat down over her filling eyes.

"How'd you know?" she asked.

"I always know. What was it this time?"

"The usual."

"Pitch."

"Yeah," Ronja agreed. "Still not worth talking about. Doesn't change what she is. A mutt's a mutt."

"You shouldn't call her that."

"What *should* I call her?" Ronja inquired vehemently. "I shouldn't deny it, they don't." She thrust a finger at the narrow window, through which the worn boots of the populous could be seen. "They think I'm like her," Ronja said softly.

"*I* know you're not."

"You're *you*."

Henry cocked his head, considering.

"I don't care what they think of me," Ronja assured him. "But it's hurting Georgie and Cos. You know, some kids in Georgie's class cornered her in the bathroom, dunked her head in the toilet until she barked?"

Henry looked queasy.

"What did she do?"

"What do you *think*?"

"It's not fair," Henry said after awhile. "You don't even know what your mother did."

Ronja snorted mirthlessly and reclined against the wall. She closed her eyes. The gray light from the window seeped through her translucent lids along with her friend's heavy gaze.

"Just leave it, Henry. Please," she begged.

Henry inhaled, preparing a chiding speech. Ronja tensed. Thankfully, her friend swallowed his comments. His chair groaned as he shifted uncomfortably, but all else beyond the constant rustling of The Music was quiet.

After some time, Henry changed the subject.

"How long has your head been hurting you?"

Ronja's eyelids fluttered open. Her thumbs had started massaging her temples of their own volition. She screwed up her brow.

"It started to get bad last night after . . . " She bit her tongue.

"After?" Henry prompted.

Ronja shook her head, perhaps too forcefully.

"Nothing, just a headache. Where's my package?"

Henry parted his lips, but his words died on his tongue when he saw her expression. He sighed heavily and reached into the knapsack at the foot of his desk. He withdrew a slim, square package. It was slightly larger than a dinner plate and was swathed in newspaper.

Ronja frowned as she took the cargo with careful hands. It was heavier than she had expected. She laid it in her lap and ran her rough hand across its level face. The paper whispered beneath her palm.

"What do you think it is?" she asked, curiosity dripping from her voice.

Henry shrugged.

"No idea. Not a book, is it?"

"No, you'd be able to feel the pages around the edges," Ronja murmured.

She flipped the package lightly in her hands. Henry hissed and reached out to catch it.

"Relax," Ronja said, laughing softly.

"Getting this for you cost me breakfast, and it'll cost you more if you break it," Henry whispered harshly.

"Sorry," Ronja muttered. She looked up, eyes flickering earnestly. "I'll be careful."

Henry started to make a comment about her apathy, but Ronja's mind had turned from her friend. She bent toward the face of the package, squinting at the familiar symbol sketched over the mind-numbing words of a fashion column. She grazed it with her thumb. Something was strange about it.

"Are you listening to me?"

Ronja's head snapped up.

"What?"

Henry made an exasperated noise, sank further into his chair.

"Henry, look at this." Ronja offered him the package. He took it, glaring at her across its rim. "*Look,*" she implored.

Henry perused the box for a moment, then glanced up at her dubiously. "It's a package wrapped in *The Bard.*"

"Yeah, look at the fashion column."

"You'd like me to start wearing pearls?"

"No, skitz-head."

The radiator hummed in the corner. The paper crinkled as Henry turned the parcel upside down. Ronja's impatience swelled.

"I don't—" Henry began.

"Look!"

Ronja snatched the package and jabbed her index finger at the emblem. Henry squinted.

"It's The Conductor's emblem, may the ages hold His name," Henry said, tossing up his hands.

"No, it isn't."

"Yes, it is. Three concentric circles. Did you learn anything in school?"

"But it's *black*."

The symbol always appeared in white. The rings represented the three districts of the city: the core, where The Conductor resided, the middle ring, and the outer ring. They were always inscribed in white, symbolizing the purity of Revinia and its leader.

Henry shrugged indifferently.

"So? Who has a white pen?"

"They should have just stuck one of the official stamps on it. Come to think of it, why mark it at all if they're sending it through the back channels?"

"What are you getting at?"

"I'm not sure," Ronja admitted, itching the bridge of her nose contemplatively. "It's just strange."

Henry massaged his eyes with his palms. The triplet lines that appeared between his brows when he was stressed had surfaced.

"Just let it go, please."

"But—"

"Ronja, you're looking for something that isn't there."

Ronja's jaw bulged. She dropped her gaze to her rolled fists. Henry thrust the wrapped item back at her and rose.

"I have to go," he said curtly.

Ronja nodded without looking up. Henry grabbed his bag from the floor and draped his coat over his shoulders. She scarcely registered his movement.

Then he was kneeling before her, his dark hands clasped around her small, clenched fists. "If you go looking for trouble, you'll find it," he warned, his voice low. "Running a package is one thing, but if you start asking questions, you'll end up with The Quiet Song in your ear."

Ronja finally looked up from her lap, but she did not see. She smiled feebly.

"Don't worry. I won't do anything stupid. Like think. Or feel."

"Ronja—"

"I'm gonna be late," she said tightly.

She wrenched her hands away and swiped her pack from the floor. She jammed her hat lower on her head, flipped up her collar, then shouldered past her friend and out the door.

9: PRESSURE POINTS

Ronja's day job paid less than her graveyard shift as a driver. Half a note per hour. The task, at least, was simple. From one to eight she manned the shabby news kiosk at the corner of East and Crane. For seven hours she stood behind the plywood counter and sold stacks of crisp, white *Bards* delivered each morning from the core.

Some years ago gossip and specialty magazines had been available for purchase, but they had since been discontinued. Bankrupted, The Conductor had reported, though Ronja recalled them selling well. She still had some of the nature magazines stashed in the depths of her desk, as they had not technically been outlawed.

It was a six-block trek from the subtrain office to East and Crane. The optimistic sun that had shown up at noon had bundled itself away behind another pregnant cloud. An airship branded with the massive, golden WI for Westervelt Industries powered into the thunderheads, doubtlessly headed for one of the many factories and warehouses beyond the wall. The groan of the propellers filtered into the streets, filling the cracks between old cobblestones and the spaces between the notes in their ears.

Ronja tore her gaze from the airship and walked briskly, spurred by the damp wind at her back. Her conversation with Henry had taken longer than she had expected, and had gone in an unexpected direction. Even in the cold, her cheeks still burned.

Ronja had known Henry for nearly eleven years. She knew things about him no one else knew. She would do anything for him, and knew he felt the same way.

Still.

Ronja hugged her shoulders against the mounting chill.

There were pieces of Henry that eluded her, parts of him that were paradoxical, incongruent. He would risk his reputation and safety just to snag her a run, but invalidated her most pressing questions.

He's probably right, she thought dully. *But . . .*

Ronja glanced down at her sling bag. The corner of her charge poked out innocently. She brushed its edge with her fingertip, trying to smooth the waves of anxiety that radiated from it. The dark variant of the crest glared at her, its central ring a scrutinizing pupil.

Ronja tugged her collar higher around her neck and pressed forward, doing her best to ignore the black gaze.

By the time she reached the news kiosk, a fresh drizzle had begun to seep from the fat clouds. Soot-blackened puddles burgeoned. Shops locked their shutters. Gas lamps were lit reluctantly. Umbrellas bloomed, and those without made for the pubs.

The weather could not deter the news-seekers, though. They huddled around the bare-bones newsstand, nestled deep into their coats, shawls wound around their stringy hair. *The Bard* was their only connection to the core, especially now that the subtrain was scarcely functioning.

"Afternoon, Joe," Ronja called over the babel.

Joseph looked out over the small crowd and smiled blandly when he spotted her approaching. He waved, then turned back to a woman rummaging through her handbag for coins.

"Hurry up," the man behind her grumbled.

"Haven't got all day," another cut in.

One of the men, his face dappled with grime and stubble, shoved her roughly from behind. The woman gasped. Her coins scattered, singing against the cobblestones. She cried out and clambered for them, making a boat in the folds of her dress.

She did not notice her assailant stoop and pocket three of her silver pieces.

"Oi!" Ronja barked.

The man whipped around, his pupils dilated.

"Hand them over, pitcher," Ronja ordered, stalking toward him with her hand outstretched.

The crowd parted for her. Their whispers filled the gap.

Mutt.

Disgusting.

Look at it.

Ronja halted before the crook, her expectant palm catching the quickening rain.

The thief's apprehension dissolved when he heard the murmurs rippling around them. He sneered, revealing rotting teeth and gums. Ronja curled her lip in revulsion.

"My Singer agrees. You a mutt. You got no right to tell me what to do."

"Maybe," Ronja said softly, her eyes fixated unblinkingly on his shifting gaze.

She came to a halt a breath from his pockmarked face, her jaw slightly unhinged, her breath coming out in short pants. The man swallowed, his Adam's apple bobbing. He took a small step backward.

"I would still give her back the money, though," she growled under her breath.

The thief shuffled from foot to foot, looking anywhere but the thunderous face of the mutt. The gawking crowd made no move to assist him, unwilling to risk touching the revolting creature he faced.

Ronja growled again at his prolonged hesitation, her teeth gnashed together.

He flinched, then jammed his hand into his pocket and retrieved the coins he had lifted. He dropped them into her palm, careful not to let their skin brush.

"Interest," Ronja said, adopting a sudden air of professionalism.

The crook dug into his pocket again, glowering at her through the rain. Slowly, deliberately, he pinched two coppers between this thumb and forefinger and let them fall to the slick street. Ronja did not look down when they bounced off her boot and ran away down the cobblestones.

The thief turned, and with a reverberating guffaw to mask his fear, melted back into the crowd.

The ring of onlookers dispersed as Ronja glanced around for

the twin coppers. She caught sight of one glinting dully in the gray daylight, but the second had either been snatched or had rolled into the gutter.

Ronja retrieved the coin, then turned back to the victim. She stood still, her lips parted slightly, her dress still a cradle for the runway coins.

Ronja dumped the money into the waiting fabric and the woman shuddered, averting her eyes. She whirled and took off down the avenue, her cash clinking, her sopping dress slapping against her bare legs.

Ronja watched the woman retreat, then wrenched her gaze away, abruptly hot in the frigid downpour.

She set her bag on the newsstand countertop with a soft thud. Joseph, who had watched the scene unfold, sought her eyes, but she kept them firmly on her hands.

Joseph had always been kind to her. Rather, he had never been unkind.

Ronja boosted herself up onto the rough counter, swung her legs around, and dropped into to the kiosk. The loose floorboards below her rattled like chattering teeth.

"You'd better go. I don't think this thing can hold both of us," she muttered, grabbing her bag and tucking it in the belly of the stand.

"You sure? I can stick around for awhile," Joseph offered half-heartedly.

Ronja did not respond, only rummaged through the front pouch of her bag for something she was not looking for.

Joseph stood watching her, toying with his Singer absentmindedly. After a long moment, he grasped the straps of his rucksack, flung it over his shoulder, and sprang across the counter with a shriek of wood.

Ronja only got to her feet when she was certain he had gone. Now, a man in a woolen sweater stood before her, thick arms folded menacingly.

"Haven't got all day, mutt," he growled.

Ronja held out her hand for the cash. He dropped it into her palm. She reached beneath the counter for a *Bard*, drawing out the most rumpled copy she could find. The man snatched the paper from her and stalked away, muttering under his breath.

"Next," Ronja called politely.

10: SPLIT

The library was only a block from the newsstand, and since her lunch break would not be filled with food, Ronja decided to fill it with words.

The library was by far the most splendid building in the outer ring. Unlike most of the structures far from the core, it was maintained by an army of white-clad government laborers. They never spoke to the visitors and went about their work viciously. They scrubbed the marble floors until they gleamed like mirrors, dusted each shelf with clinical precision, and thumbed through newly-returned volumes with suspicious eyes, hunting for tears in the fragile pages.

The Conductor's official position on literature was that it was valuable in healthy doses, on specific subjects.

"Words are powerful," Ronja recalled his robust voice booming through her Singer during one of his monthly addresses. "They are the muscles that move ideas. Uncaged ideas can be dangerous, even deadly. However, if you read the proper, approved literature, your minds will be expanded in beautiful ways."

As Ronja pushed through the massive oak doors of the library, she found herself wondering if the looming shelves had once been full. Revinia was not a wasteful society, yet the stacks were not a tenth stocked. Pristine volumes with titles like *The History of Revinia, Vol. 34* and *A Brief Review of Post-War Culture in Revinia* and *The Great Crescendo* stood like solitary trees in the maw of a vast desert.

After being forced to drop out of school at fourteen, Ronja had promised herself that she would not forgo her education. Each evening she copied Cosmin's mathematics exercises and solved them by lamplight after dinner. Cosmin was a night owl, so he often walked her through the more difficult problems. On rare holidays, she went to Henry's house to copy from his history textbooks, but usually they ended up talking instead.

Most importantly, Ronja dutifully made the journey to the library four times a week and spent an hour reading. For lack of a better option, she had decided to read the entire library in alphabetical order. Despite the sparseness of the available texts, this was a considerable undertaking. It had taken her a year just to make it through the A's, and even longer to struggle through the B's, which were present in inexplicably tremendous quantities.

Nodding briefly at the birdlike librarian perched behind the front desk, Ronja made her way toward the back of the building, where the titles beginning with F were located.

Running her callused finger along the spines of leather and cloth, Ronja felt some of the tension leech from her body. Her muscles unwound, and the constant ache in her head receded somewhat.

The rough pad of her fingertip caught on the lip of a leatherbound volume entitled *Flora and Fauna of the Revinian Countryside.*

Ronja pried the book from its niche and hugged it to her chest like a child. The promise of words humming against her ribcage, she strolled toward her armchair.

Her chair was upholstered with cracked leather. It crouched with stubborn pride on squat legs in the furthest corner of the library. Tucked away between two nearly vacant stacks, Ronja could watch the movements of the knowledge-seekers undisturbed over the rim of her book.

Ronja flopped into the pliant armchair and felt the material mold to her form. A vague smile on her lips, she kicked off her boots and tucked her stocking clad feet beneath her. She flipped through the pages of *Flora and Fauna* until she reached her mark, then sank into the text.

With each word she consumed, The Day Song shrank a decibel.

Ronja remained folded in the same position for nearly an hour. She shifted only to turn the page, or to track down a word she did not know in the fat dictionary lying open on the adjacent shelf. Certain words and their definitions were blotted out with generous blotches of ink. Many pages were torn out completely.

When the long hand on her watch timidly clicked into place five minutes before the hour, Ronja yawned and stretched. She rolled her neck, snapping a wayward vertebra into place. The Day Song leaked back into her consciousness, as potent as ever.

Ronja took *Flora and Fauna* under her arm, then slammed the dictionary shut. She shouldered her bag and trekked across the library to the front desk, the polished marble squeaking beneath her soles.

The librarian smiled wearily at Ronja as she handed her the volume.

"I'd like to check this out," Ronja said unnecessarily, glancing down at her watch.

She would have to run to make it back East and Crane.

"Are you enjoying it?" the librarian asked Ronja as she took the book and wetted the date stamp.

"Sure."

"Your kind can't leave the city, right?"

Ronja felt her gut cinch.

"No," she replied curtly.

The librarian smashed the date stamp into the back of the book and shut the cover with a resounding thwack.

"Don't get this dirty. Understand?"

Ronja agreed blandly and took the book back under her arm. She exited the library with leaden arms and heavy feet.

Ronja completed the remainder of her shift without a hitch. After closing down and shooing away a handful of belated customers, she made the four-block trek to station 34, where she was scheduled to start her night. By the end of the walk, she sorely regretted checking out such a substantial volume.

When she descended into the station, Ronja found it bustling with a hint of its former glory.

On Saturday nights, the people of the outer ring scraped their cash together, donned their least-worn clothes, and rode the subtrain to the middle ring. There, the casino Adagio floated atop the central channel. Its spotlights of red, green, and violet were nearly as bright as the face of the great clock tower, and the lure was even stronger.

When one stepped onto Adagio, it was said, The Night Song morphed, flowering into The Calm Song. It was rumored that The Calm Song filled the body with unimaginable warmth and pleasure, that it could cure hunger, sickness, and even sadness as long as it was in your ear.

When Adagio closed at sunrise, the gamers were corralled and forcibly ejected from the floating palace. Gambling was a privilege that was not to interfere with their working lives.

Ronja could not say if these words held truth. She had never possessed the funds or the desire to visit the casino. It was grounds for trouble.

I'm in deep enough already, she thought, glancing at the package jutting from her bag. Her paranoia swelled and she thrust the parcel deeper into her pack.

Ronja numbered her heartbeats as she waited on the platform alongside the Revinians preparing to deal away their time. The trick failed, so she focused on the people. The women's eyelids glittered, their hair piled atop their crowns and pinned with brass masquerading as gold. The men's jackets and waistcoats had faded from black to gray, but they looked proud. Still, it was all too easy to see through their facades.

A keening flooded the atrium, tugging the crowd toward the tracks like moths to a flame. The steamer roared into the station with a blast of hot air, stirring Ronja's tangled curls. The station blazed momentarily brighter. A baby screeched as the brakes locked. Her mother petted her soft head and cooed. The passenger doors yawned, exhaling a cloud of white-clad cleaners on their way home from the middle ring.

"Coming through!" Ronja bellowed. "Excuse me!"

The grumbles that followed her shouts quickly dissipated when people turned and spied her driver's cap bobbing toward them. They split a path to the front car. For once, no insults filled the space they created. They respected her when they needed her.

The previous driver was exiting when Ronja reached the foremost car.

"Brakes are pitch on this one," the old man said as he hobbled down the stairs. He swiped off his hat and rubbed the sweat from his balding head. "Ease into your stops."

"I'll keep that in mind," Ronja said, mounting the steps. "Thanks."

Ronja waited until he had disappeared to slam the door and rip open the manila envelope containing the delivery instructions. She let the casing flit to the floor. In her hands was a single sheet of paper, smooth and rich as silk against her rough skin. In formal black type it read:

```
The runner will be in sight of your train with
his back to the third column from the left.
Handle the package with care.
```

Ronja crumpled the note and pressed a match to it. It caught fire quicker than expected, and her fingers were singed before she could release the wad. Cursing creatively, she stamped out the seething ashes. Sitting heavily, she yanked the whistle three times.

Time moved slowly that evening. While her train roared along its tracks, night crawled toward morning with infuriating lethargy. A nervous tick had settled into her fingers, drumming out a beat that did not quite match the one in her ear. Sweat beaded on her forehead, stained the fabric of her sweater.

All the while, The Night Song threatened to rupture the walls of her skull. The irregular notes and swooping pulses rattled her brain, honing the persistent ache.

"When you have been naughty, The Music can tell. It will strengthen until it has you back in the proper place."

How long until I'm back in my place? she wondered, staring blankly into the near total darkness of the tube. *Until I deliver the package? Until I turn in the tunneler? Until I stop thinking about...?*

Electric light shattered the dark.

Ronja yelped and wrenched back the brake. The train screamed to a halt in station 45, white sparks flying from its paralyzed wheels.

Ronja leapt to her feet, rattled head throbbing. She released the passenger doors with trembling fingers and drew the package from her bag. She clutched it to her chest gingerly. It seemed to shiver against her ribcage. Sucking in a deep breath, Ronja donned her coat and hat, then stepped into the station.

Her commuters were grumbling as they shuffled from their cars, massaging banged heads and elbows. Ronja stood by, apologizing lamely. She could hardly hear them cursing her genes over the clamor of The Night Song and her heartbeat.

Ronja lingered by her train as the disgruntled passengers filtered out. She kept her back to the engine, her arms folded across the package. Her eyes darted about the emptying station wearily. There was no one waiting by the third column. She rose up on her tiptoes, peering into the far corners of the atrium. Was he running late? Was she early? She returned her gaze to the indicated pillar, and stiffened.

He stood with his spine to the column, head thrown back and pressed to the stone. His hands were burrowed in the pockets of his long, leather overcoat. A pair of riding goggles flecked with sludge were draped about his neck. His dark hair was drawn into a knot at the base of his skull.

"The tunneler," Ronja murmured.

As if he had heard her across the platform, the boy's eyes flicked toward her. A wry smile tugged at the corner of his mouth, pulling in turn at her insides.

Ronja braced herself and started toward him, pocketing her cap as she went. It was the longest walk of her life. She kept her eyes trained on her boots, counting each step, mindful of the acute gaze tracking her progress.

When she reached the boy, she lifted her chin. Her stomach turned over. He was far more attractive than she might have guessed from their first meeting in the tunnels. At first look his eyes were nearly black, but a second glance exposed traces of honey. His features were strong and regal, but there was something about his countenance that seemed . . . wild.

The boy spoke first.

"You have something for me?"

"Nice coat for a tunneler," she replied.

"I wouldn't know what you're talking about," the boy said.

A hint of mirth gleamed behind his professionalism.

"Of course not," Ronja said, holding out the slim package with two hands. He grabbed for it, but she did not relinquish her end. "You wouldn't know much about Singers either."

To her indignation, the boy laughed loudly. Ronja glanced around fearfully, her throat constricting.

"No, I would not," he admitted.

"So that's a fake then," Ronja nodded at the convincing silver piece that now clung to his ear.

"Indeed."

"If you tell anyone I was here, I'll report you," Ronja threatened icily.

"They won't get far without my name. You've an empty hand, and I've nothing to fear."

Ronja clenched her jaw and tightened her grip on the package.

"What are *you* so afraid of?" the boy asked, leaning toward her across the flat face of the cargo.

He smelled like gasoline and rain.

"I'm not afraid."

"Even if the Offs discover you delivered an unauthorized package, it's not exactly a capital offense."

Ronja snorted, imagining what sort of punishment the Offs would have in store for *any* crime committed by a mutt. The boy peered down at her curiously, as if trying to see into her mind.

"Easy for you to say," Ronja retorted.

"The key is in the mask, love."

It was her turn to eye the boy inquisitively. She gave the package a brief shake. "What is this?" she asked.

The boy arched an eyebrow. "I'm not at liberty to say, nor are you at liberty to ask."

"Lucky for me, I was never here, so I never asked," Ronja shot back. "Is it dangerous?"

"What makes you think it is?" he asked, cocking his head like a dark-feathered pigeon.

"That," Ronja jerked her chin at the alternative symbol.

The boy blanched. His expressive eyes flattened, and he strengthened his grip on the parcel.

"What are you talking about?" he asked in a low voice, speaking as though he walked barefoot over shattered glass. "It's The Conductor's emblem, may the ages hold His name."

"See, that's what my friend told me, but it's *not*. Anyone could see that."

"Except no one does."

The boy stepped closer, forcing the sharp edge of the package into her stomach. Ronja inhaled sharply, but refused to back away.

"How many are there?" the boy growled.

"How . . . what?"

"How many of your *friends* are here?"

"What do you—?"

The tunneler grabbed her faster than her eyes could track. His fingers were curled around her wrist before she could jerk away. They were tan and strong juxtaposed with her papery complexion.

"Cut the pitch," he growled, tugging her toward him. Ronja snarled back, though she felt as though her bones were about to crumble. The station was completely empty. Her train idled on the track without a care, puffing a thin trail of steam into the weary lamps overhead. "You'll be stuffed before you can signal them, understand?"

"You think I'm an *Off*?" Ronja asked with a panicked laugh. "That's the stupidest thing I—"

Before she could finish, the boy whipped out a pistol and smashed the butt into her skull.

Only the dim headlights of the steamer bore witness as he heaved Ronja over his shoulder and carried her into the tunnels, the delivery tucked safely beneath his arm.

11: ASHES

P *ing. Ping. Ping.*
The delicate sound of dripping water was like a militant march. The noise came from somewhere near her head. Her mouth was parched and sour, and she yearned to taste the drops. Her head throbbed to the rhythm of the drip. Her limbs were leaden, and she had lost feeling in the tips of her fingers and toes.

A low, angry rumble shook the room. The wooden chair she had been placed in creaked as the sound waves rattled it.

I'm underground, she thought vaguely. *Near the subtrain.*

"She's got to be fifteen pounds under weight," a female voice was saying. "Strange for an Off."

"Maybe they're getting creative," a familiar, male voice replied.

"I think she's coming around. How hard did you hit her?"

"Not hard enough, evidently," the boy answered darkly.

"I don't think it'll scar."

"Everyone down here has scars. Maybe I should hit her again, even the score."

"Trip, are you sure about her?"

"She recognized the record, Harrow. Someone tipped them off. If they know about me *and* it, who knows what else they know?"

Ronja's muscles coiled as Trip's booted footfalls approached, then wrapped around her chair. The skin on the back of her neck prickled. She smothered a shiver.

"I know you're listening," he whispered, his breath hot in her ear. "Open your eyes."

Ronja forced her leaden lids open. Slowly, her vision ate into the blinding sting of her migraine.

The room was cramped, smaller than her basement chamber. Its walls were stone behind a sheen of groundwater. Rusted steel filing cabinets fortified with combination locks lined the walls floor to ceiling.

A woman stood before Ronja, her arms folded anxiously over her bleached lab coat. She was squat and rotund. Even sitting, Ronja was almost taller than her. Her hair was blond and lusterless, but her eyes were a brilliant shade of blue.

"Harrow, leave us," Trip ordered.

Harrow glared at the boy, who still stood behind Ronja. She was still for a moment, weighing her options. Then she nodded, accepting the command.

Ronja found herself shaking her head frantically. She felt desperation clawing its way into her expression. If Harrow saw the fear in her eyes, she elected to ignore it. She whirled and slammed the iron door on her way out. Ronja heard her brief footfalls tapping down the corridor almost as fast as her heartbeat.

"Congratulations, you've found us," Trip said after a pause.

"I've already seen your face, want to stop hiding?" Ronja snapped, cringing when her voice cracked.

The boy breathed a humorless laugh.

Trip stepped back around her chair. Ronja squinted into the glare of the light bulb that crowned him. He had shed his jacket and goggles, trading them for a knit sweater. He had also cleaned the grime from his face, and the shadows made his cheekbones jagged.

"Sorry about the restraints, love. Can't have you running off on us."

Ronja looked down, dread thick in her stomach. Between her terror and the lancing pain in her skull, she had failed to notice that her wrists and ankles were locked to the chair with leather straps. "No problem," she said bitingly, meeting his piercing gaze again. "It'll save you a black eye."

Trip cocked his head, considering her.

"You're still green, aren't you? Believe it or not, there *are* ways to overcome The Music."

Ronja swallowed her nonexistent saliva.

Trip reached into his back pocket. Ronja recoiled fearfully, but to her surprise he withdrew a pack of cigarettes and a matchbook. He sighed deeply, regarding the white cardboard pack with disdain.

"I *hate* smoking."

The wound on her forehead pulsed as Ronja furrowed her brow.

Trip tapped a slim cigarette from the half empty pack. He clenched it between his teeth and struck a match. "It's a horrible habit," he continued through his teeth.

He cupped his fingers around the tip and pressed the shivering flame to it. Wincing as it licked his finger, he tossed the dying match at his feet and inhaled. The cigarette smoldered beneath the electric light. "But for the sake of this evening, I'll indulge myself," he went on. "If you don't answer my three questions by the time I finish this cigarette, it's going in your eye."

Ronja tried to speak, but when she opened her mouth she found that her words had dried up along with her spit.

"One," Trip inhaled slowly, then blew a cloud of smoke at the ceiling. It struck the damp stone and scattered. "How long has The Conductor known about my involvement here?"

Ronja's stomach clenched. "I don't . . . I don't even know who you are."

"Unfortunately, I don't believe you."

"I'd never seen you in my life before yesterday."

"I'm supposed to believe that in a city of six million we just happened to meet twice in less than twelve hours?"

"Yes!" Ronja exclaimed. "Yes, because that's what happened! I didn't tell anyone about your Singer, and I won't say anything about the package or the symbol. Please just let me go, I have a family. They need me."

"Didn't I tell you to cut the pitch?" The boy hissed a cloud of smoke through his teeth. They were stark white. He could not be a heavy smoker. "This will be considerably less painful if you just answer the question."

"I can't, because I don't know! I swear I was just running a package. I didn't know you'd be receiving it. Honestly, I hoped I'd never see you again. I didn't even want to think about you, because every time I do—"

A bolt of pain ruptured her words. The Night Song roiled in her skull, so loud it muted the rumble of the subtrains burrowing through their tunnels. The oxygen was thin, the smoke dense. Ronja screwed her eyes shut, trying to snuff the agony.

"Half gone. You might want to rethink your answer."

A glob of ash plummeted from the cigarette and landed on her thigh, smoldering on her trousers.

"I swear I don't know anything!"

"Wrong."

Ronja screamed as her captor drove the scorching tip of his cigarette into her exposed forearm. She was hoarse by the time he lifted it. She forced her eyes open, but refused to look at the bloody burn that marred her skin.

"I'm just a subtrain driver, I swear," she insisted through gritted teeth. "I've got two younger cousins. I dropped out of school because my mother was too lazy to get off her ass and—"

Ronja bit back another scream as The Night Song knifed through her brain. Black bled into her line of sight. Her head wilted on her neck. Her curls drooped forward to form a protective curtain around her face.

"You're not a bad actor, Off. I've never seen one of your kind fake emotion before. I'm almost impressed."

"Not . . . acting," Ronja panted.

Her mouth felt fuzzy, like her words were made of cotton. The Night Song was louder than a train engine, louder than the roar of a crowd, louder than anything she had ever heard. She wanted to tear off the metal vice like a scab.

"I don't know how The Conductor found us," the boy said in her free ear. "But what's more important is how *long* he's known. Speaking of time, yours is about up."

Ronja was not listening.

The Night Song had shifted.

The rambling notes leveled, like a clump of butter smoothed over a slab of toast. The new Song was a ceaseless, winding ribbon that curled around her brain, her body, her heart. It was almost comforting, the smoothness, the consistency.

Ronja's head lolled over the back of her chair. Her sightless pupils expanded. Something warm oozed from her nose, pooled in her mouth. It tasted like metal. Then it tasted like nothing.

The boy's cigarette plummeted from his teeth, rapidly dying on the damp, stone floor.

"Skitz . . . HARROW!"

12: QUIET
Trip

Footsteps sang down the corridor, then the steel door flew open on his shouts. For half a moment, Caroline stood rigid in the doorframe, jaw unhinged.

"What the *skitz* did you do?"

"Confirmed she's not an Off," Trip said lamely.

Caroline smashed the door shut and stalked forward. She knocked Trip out of the way with a broad shoulder and put her fingers to the girl's neck, hunting for her pulse beneath clammy skin. The doctor swore colorfully. "She's in The Quiet," she said, jerking her hand back and raking it through her mousy hair. "What triggered it?"

"I may have told her I was going to stick a smoke in her eye."

"Trip!"

"I thought she was an Off. When was the last time you saw one of them go into The Quiet?"

"Except she's *not*! This is why Wilcox doesn't want you gallivanting around on your own!"

"The day Wilcox tells me what to do is the day I die."

"No, it's the day she dies."

Trip's retort froze on his tongue. The girl's labored breathing swallowed the silence. "What do you mean?" he asked warily.

"It means she's too far gone."

"It hasn't even been two minutes!"

"*Look* at her."

Trip turned slowly. Dread dragged his stomach to the floor. The girl was twitching erratically. Her skin was gray beneath a sheen of sweat. Her swollen corneas glinted like black marbles in their sockets. Dark blood drained from her nose and ears.

"How is this possible?" Trip asked, touching the back of his wrist to her forehead. It was blistering. "It should take at least an hour."

"If The Quiet Song needs to be this strong to take her down, she must be something special."

"I'm going to get Iris," Trip said, starting toward the door.

Caroline caught his arm, her grip surprisingly firm.

"Trip," she said quietly. "There's no time. She'll be dead in minutes."

The girl retched behind them, but her stomach was empty. She vomited acid, staining her worn sweater. Her back arched and her coiled muscles fought against their restraints. Still, she was utterly silent. She did not scream or cry. She only struggled to breathe.

Trip's legs moved without his permission. He crossed the room to a supply cabinet, unlocked the combination with several flicks of his wrist. He flung open the door to reveal a waning hoard of medical and surgical supplies. From the top shelf he grabbed a small, gleaming instrument. He spun on his heel.

"Caroline," he said, voice painstakingly calm.

"Don't—"

Trip shouldered past the doctor. He braced his right hand on the girl's restrained forearm and twirled the surgical knife in his left hand. Her convulsions had slowed. Her irises were almost completely devoured.

Her execution was drawing to a close.

"I'm sorry," he said to the unraveling girl.

He was not sure if he hoped she heard him.

Trip brought the knife to her right ear.

"Wait!" Caroline screeched.

She flew forward and snatched the blade from him. Trip straightened, preparing to challenge her.

"Let me do it," Caroline hissed. "Get me some gauze. *Now.*"

Trip rushed to the indicated cabinet and grabbed the last roll of gauze from the shelf. He unspooled it, then crumpled it into a sponge. If memory served him well, it would not be enough.

"Hold her steady," the doctor commanded.

Trip used one hand to rake the girl's abundant curls from the right side of her head and the other to still it. Her skin had started to cool, and was morbid beneath his hands.

Not a good sign. She was nearly gone.

"Do *not* let her move, do you understand me?"

Trip nodded.

Time slowed as Harrow took the girl's caged ear in her hand, pulled it taut, and sliced the blade clean through the tissue. Blood oozed from the maw, thick as oil, and dribbled to the floor in sickening plops. The knife struck metal with a soft clink. Thin wires peeked out from the flesh, flashing like coins in a murky river.

Trip wondered vaguely at the strangeness of it all. That a small bouquet of copper could control an entire city.

Gingerly, Harrow began to saw.

The girl woke when the first wire snapped. Her pupils pulled in on themselves. Her labored breathing sped. Trip felt the veins branching across her right temple bulge beneath his fingers.

"Trip," Caroline growled.

Trip tightened his grip on the girl, forcing her shoulders back into the chair with his elbows.

Another wire split.

A stream of tangled words began to crawl from the girl's mouth, trailing the blood. He could not discern their meaning, but caught "peace" and "Conductor" more than once.

Caroline severed another wire. Sparks snapped from the angry metal. The Singer was fighting back.

The girl gasped. She was nearly lucid. Harrow cut with increased ferocity. Trip put all his weight against the prisoner, fighting her convulsions with all his strength. Tears were leaking from her eyes. His stomach twisted. He had to do something.

Without thinking, Trip leaned toward her free ear and began to sing.

The last two wires gave way as one. The knife slipped through the remaining tissue. The ear and the Singer came off in one final motion. There was left a gaping hole, from which uncoupled wires jutted like broken branches. Trip crammed the wad of gauze into the wound, pressing down with all his strength.

The last words of the song left him, ending on a soft note that clashed with the jarring scene.

The sudden silence was louder than any Trip had ever heard. Bodies and minds froze, even the wall clock seemed still. Caroline, who still grasped the limp ear, slid her gaze toward Trip. The doctor did not speak, but she did not need to. Her words were clear on her face.

That was when the girl began to scream.

13: WARPED

The following days were fractured, warped.

Ronja passed out moments after Dr. Harrow amputated her ear. Mercifully, she remained unconscious for a majority of the procedures that followed. The yawning wound was sterilized. A surgeon removed lingering Singer debris. The bleeding was dammed with a series of sutures and a wreath of bandages.

Then withdrawal hit her with the full force of a steamer.

The medicine that muted the pain of her wound did nothing to fill the cavity left in the wake of The Music. Her body rejected its absence. She had been twined with the bewitching notes since birth, and could not function without them. She may as well have been deprived of water or air.

Lurching nausea bombarded her stomach. Blurred figures with sympathetic words pressed food and water to her cracked lips, but nothing stayed in her stomach for long. Somewhere in the tangle of hours she stumbled into consciousness to find an IV pumping saline into her veins. Her nose oozed a slow stream of blood and mucus. Her body was racked with chills, though her muscles brimmed with heat. Someone kept her forehead damp with cool rags.

Ronja began to lose track of time. On one occasion, she gathered enough of her wits to ask the date, but found that words seared her throat. She let out a raspy squeak and was immediately shushed by one of her guards.

When the sickness took brief respite, she hung in a gray place between wakefulness and sleep. In those moments, she was aware enough to fear, to wonder about her family, about Henry, if they were looking for her or not.

Worse than the nausea and the weakness, was the noise. She had once thought that life would be quiet without The Music. She was wrong.

The world was deafening.

Her remaining ear was hyper-attuned to every sound. Whispered conversations shared between her guards sounded like screams. Her own breaths were small hurricanes. Her heart was a fish writhing on a dock. The whir of electricity pouring into the lamp at her bedside was the thrum of an auto engine. The roar of the subtrain manifested physically, rattling her nerves and teeth.

Her silence was all she could control, so she kept it dutifully.

Slowly, steadily, the nausea dulled.

Her nose and eyes dried. The ache in her right temple receded. Someone wiped the brown crust from her upper lip and the sweat from her brow. The rag felt as it should, like cotton rather than sand. The ache abandoned her muscles, the chills crawled from her skin.

Relief flooded her, and for a day she slept so deeply her captors feared she might have succumbed to withdrawal or infection.

It was not so. Beneath the shroud of sleep, Ronja was coming alive.

Memories took shape in her slumbering mind. The boy taking her from the station. Strapping her to a chair, interrogating her. The smoke slithering from his cigarette, the ring of pain on her forearm. He thought she was an Off because she had seen the symbol, as if it were somehow invisible. No, not invisible. Dangerous. Why? What did it mean? He was so scared. Terrified of her and the knowledge he thought she held.

Then there was nothing but The Quiet Song. It must have been The Quiet Song, she now realized.

It was so peaceful, so different than what she had envisioned. An easy death, like slipping into a warm bath and never surfacing. Then, a knife and a voice punctured her tranquility. The former brought agony. The latter . . . something else. Something she could not name.

Be still, my friend
Tomorrow is so far, far around the bend
Cast your troubles off the shore
Unlace your boots, and cry no more
For today, my friend, I promise you are on the mend

He did not speak. He did not scream or whisper. His words rose and fell like boats cradled on gentle waves. Though they came from his mouth, they took on their own meaning when they struck the air. Through the sickening sound of her own flesh peeling away, the screech of the knife against the wires, the monotonous roar of The Quiet Song . . . she heard him. Each word was heavy with significance, light with grace.

It stole her breath in a way pain never could.

Now, Ronja lay in her bed as her endless sleep fell away. She turned the gory scene over in her mind like a coin between two fingers.

The memory of her amputation was weighty in comparison to the ones preceding it. Her life was crystalline in her memory. Meals eaten, smiles shared, steps taken. All moments were accounted for. Yet, they were inexplicably lighter, as if made of tissue paper.

The patter of approaching footsteps bucked Ronja from her contemplation.

Her chest tightened. Her stiff fingers rolled into defensive fists beneath her starched bedsheets. A blip of pain at her wrist reminded her of the IV plugged into her veins.

The footfalls tapped up to her bedside. They ceased in a whisper of skin against stone and a soft metallic clink. Ronja's muscles coiled. Handcuffs? Did they plan to restrain her again, even while she slept? Curiosity implored her to open her eyes, but panic glued them shut.

"Breakfast," announced a whispery voice.

Ronja's hands relaxed slightly. She struggled for a moment against the weight of her eyelids, then blinked her surroundings into focus.

She had been removed from the dank room flanked by filing cabinets. Her chair had been exchanged for a small cot, which was draped in surprisingly fine linens. They clashed with the corroded bed frame and the dingy stone ceiling overhead. To her right stood a coat rack, its wooden arms extended politely to hold her IV bag, which was plump with clear fluid.

The room had only one true wall, which rose behind her head. The other barriers were thick, dusty curtains that drooped from the ceiling. They were the same wine red as the airships that wheeled through the skies. Through their folds, Ronja could hear the drone of human activity. Her remaining ear was beginning to adjust to the workings of the world, and the sounds were almost bearable.

"You shouldn't eat anything heavy for at least another three days, so I just brought you some broth. I hope that's okay."

Ronja switched her gaze to the girl at her beside. She was so small, her voice so soft, she could easily dissolve into the curtains. Her strawberry-blond hair spiraled to her shoulders in loose curls. Her face was sweet and round behind a layer of grime, and she wore a timid smile on her pink mouth. She bore a tray laden with a steaming bowl and a perspiring glass of water.

"It's chicken, is that okay?"

Ronja's stomach rumbled.

The girl smiled knowingly and perched on the edge of the bed. A spoon quivered on the tray as she set it down beside her, the sound Ronja had pegged as shackles.

"Can you sit up?" her caregiver inquired.

Ronja nodded against her pillow. Wincing, she propped herself up on her elbows. Her muscles groaned in protest, uncurling from dormancy. Her head felt strangely light as she raised it.

The girl clasped Ronja's cold hands in her own, hauling her upright. She reached around and fluffed the sweat-drenched pillow.

"Sorry," the redhead apologized, motioning toward the dirty cushion. "I would have changed the case, but I didn't want to disturb you. I changed your sheets a few times, though. You had some troubles."

Ronja felt heat flare in her cheeks, but the girl appeared utterly unembarrassed. She opened her mouth to apologize, but the words dried up on her tongue. She pointed helplessly at her burning throat.

"Oh! I'm so sorry, here."

The girl grabbed the glass of water from the tray and handed it to Ronja. Snatching it, she swallowed half the contents in one gulp.

"Slowly! You'll make yourself sick."

Ronja did not heed the warning, but finished the drink in three gulps. She sighed contentedly, though her stomach moaned.

"Thanks," Ronja said hoarsely, passing the empty glass back to the girl.

She took it in a petite hand and smiled ruefully.

"Of course. It's the least I can do. I'm Iris, by the way. Iris Harte."

"Ronja," Ronja replied, wiping her lips with the back of her wrist.

Iris made a noise of surprise, and her fingers flew to her lips. Ronja arched an eyebrow beneath her bandages.

"I'm sorry," Iris apologized again, fluttering her hands dismissively. "I'm just surprised. They said you wouldn't say."

"Oh," Ronja glanced down at her knees, which poked through the sheets like craggy peaks. "Guess I forgot to care."

"No! I'm glad you told me. I don't like not knowing people's names. It's like reading a book without a title."

"How long was I out?" Ronja asked, prodding the bandages that encompassed her head gingerly.

"Four days, plus this morning. You were awake for some of it, though. I'm assuming you don't remember?"

Ronja shook her head, unnerved.

"It's better that way, you mostly just cussed us out and vomited. Not that I blame you. You should have seen Evie when she got her Singer off."

Ronja itched the bridge of her nose, unsure how to respond.

"I'm sorry this happened to you," Iris went on after a pause, clasping her hands in her lap. Her skin was dry and cracked, the nails cropped short in their beds. "You have to understand that this has never happened before."

"Which part?" Ronja asked.

"All of it," Iris replied, shifting the spoon on the tray so it aligned with the cooling soup.

"Want to explain a little more?" Ronja asked through gritted teeth. "I'm getting really tired of being in the dark."

Iris did not reply. She lifted the tray from the edge of the bed and set it on Ronja's thighs delicately, as if worried she would snap under the slight weight.

"I'll leave you to eat, then. Please go slowly, or you'll vomit."

Ronja let out a harsh laugh of disbelief, which Iris tactfully ignored. The slight girl stood collectedly and padded from the room on bare feet.

Ronja glowered at her murky reflection in the soup. Her gut was in tumult, but her jutting bones begged for food. Steeling herself, she lifted the utensil from the tray and plunged it into the broth.

The curtain flew aside as Ronja put the spoon to her lips.

"*You*," she spat.

14: COMPENSATION

Trip stood in the gap, robed again in his overcoat. His muddied riding goggles ringed his neck, and dark circles rimmed his eyes. The smirk he had worn in the subtrain station had evaporated.

"Me," he replied mildly.

He let the curtain fall and strode into the room, his hands deep in his pockets.

"How are you feeling?" he asked.

"You skitzing son of a bitch!" Ronja bellowed.

She launched the tray from her legs and it landed on the floor with a deafening crash. Ronja gasped as the sound ricocheted off the walls of her skull.

As the pounding in her head receded, she shoved back the linens. Bracing herself with quaking arms, she swung her legs off the bed and planted them firmly on the floor.

"Don't—"

Ronja shot to her feet and immediately cascaded to the ground, knocking into the coatrack with a thwack. The wooden stand and accompanying bag of hydration teetered. Trip lunged forward and steadied them.

He knelt next to Ronja cautiously. She tried to scramble away, but was tugged back by the needle in her arm.

"Here," Trip said, moving to take her wrist. "Iris told me I could take this out."

Ronja flinched away, her face pinched into a snarl and her arm curled to her chest. Trip held her caustic gaze as he took her wrist with gentle hands. Slowly, he unwound the gauze that held the needle in place and slid the catheter from her vein. A dome of blood bubbled up on the soft tissue, but he stoppered it with a fresh wad of linen.

"Better?" he asked.

Ronja nodded blackly.

"Let's get you back to bed."

Ronja moved to stand, but in one swift motion Trip's arms were around her, and she was swept from the ground like a child. Even through his jacket, she could feel the warmth of his skin radiating, his heart thumping in his ribs.

Trip placed her on the bed and shook out her sheets, which were miraculously dry. Most of the soup had splattered against the far curtain. The boy tucked the linens up to her chin, then unfolded the extra blanket at the foot of the cot and smoothed it over her. Ronja was not cold, but did not protest. Trip stepped back, his arms hanging loosely at his sides.

"Why did you do this to me?" Ronja whispered after a pause.

"It was a mistake."

"A mistake?" Ronja said, hysteria creeping into her voice. "A mistake? Kidnapping me and torturing me was a mistake? Cutting off my Singer was a mistake?"

"Please," Trip spread his hands before him. "Let me explain."

"*Please*, give it a go."

"You saw me without my Singer that night in the station," he began, running an anxious hand through his black hair. "I was worried of course, but you didn't seem to know who I was. Even if you brought it to the Offs, as I assumed you would, you didn't have my name, or any means of finding me. Then you showed up with my parcel."

"You thought I was following you," Ronja interjected.

Trip bobbed his head.

"Why not take me out right away?"

"I wasn't sure, until you mentioned the rec . . . our emblem."

"If you're so pitching secretive about this symbol, why the hell would you put it on a package?"

"Because nobody with a Singer can see it."

Ronja's brow wrinkled beneath her bandages. She opened her mouth to reply, but her words froze on her tongue. Trip went on.

"Well," he said, dropping onto the foot of her bed with an exhausted sigh. "They can see it, but they think nothing of it—at least, that's what usually happens. Obviously, that wasn't true in your case."

"What do you mean they think nothing of it?" Ronja asked carefully.

Trip craned his head back to view the ceiling. His eyes flicked from stone to stone as he considered her question. He snapped his gaze back to her abruptly.

"Do you remember what your third grade instructor looked like?"

"Wha . . . vaguely. Why?"

Ronja's third grade instructor was a spindly old man with salt and pepper muttonchops and a stiff knee. He walked with a gnarled cane, which doubled as an instrument of punishment.

"Can you tell me what color their eyes were? If their ears were large or small? How long their nose was?"

"Uh, no."

"Exactly, because it doesn't really matter what your third grade teacher looked like."

"Do you have a point, or is this a new form of torture?"

Trip smiled grimly.

"Despite what you might think, The Conductor is not all powerful. He can't reach into your mind and obliterate a thought. But," Trip held up a long finger, "He can make that thought seem obsolete. If He determines something is . . . " he trailed off, weighing his words " . . . *troublesome*, He writes it into The Music. People unconsciously begin to avoid that thing like the plague."

"Like mutts," Ronja muttered under her breath.

"Sorry?"

"Never mind. So, He wanted people to forget the symbol existed?"

"Precisely. But if they do notice it, they tend to believe it's an alternate take on His crest."

"Yeah, that's what—"

Ronja caught herself before she spilled Henry's name. She could not involve him in this. Trip was watching her expectantly, but she fluttered her hands dismissively.

"So, what about any of this made you think I was an Off? Wouldn't they be more prone to ignoring your symbol?"

Trip beamed and leaned toward her. Ronja felt her heart stutter in her chest. She could scarcely hear its damp palpitations now, which she took as a good sign.

"Well spotted. Off Singers are even more powerful than common ones. Clever girl. That also means that they run on a different frequency. And who controls all these Singers? Those without. The Conductor and his shinys. People who can see our symbol."

The bed frame creaked as Ronja reclined against it, considering the claim.

"Oh," she exclaimed after a moment, sitting up. "You thought they changed the frequency."

"And that they were attempting to infiltrate our ranks, yes," Trip replied.

Ronja could not smother a dark chuckle. Trip arched a questioning brow.

"I'm sorry, it's just so ridiculous," she said, whisking away her humor. "Anyone can see I'm not an Off."

"How?"

"Your doctor friend had it right when she said I was underweight. Off rations are way higher than ours. Half of them are twenty pounds overweight, the other half are thirty."

"True enough, but it could have easily been a ruse."

"Yeah, but I wasn't wearing an Off Singer."

Trip's other eyebrow followed its mirror up his forehead. He appeared to be fighting a smile, or more likely a grimace.

"They're a bit bigger than common ones," Ronja explained. "Come on, you didn't know? Typical shiny."

Trip barked a laugh. Ronja's sensitive ear throbbed, but she could not resist a smug smile.

"Shiny? What gave me away?"

"Where should I start? For starters, you talk too pretty. You cleaned your face not long ago," Ronja said, gesturing at his spotless, if drained features. "Anyone who lives in the outer ring knows as soon as you clean up, you're dirty again. But mostly it's your name. Trip. Stands for 'the third,' if I remember right. You're named after your father and his, which means two things. One, your family has been together more than a gen. More importantly, it means your father was an honorable man, worth remembering. Put it all together? You've got a pitch ton of cash."

Trip was silent for a long time. His eyes were as flat and unreflective as dry bricks. His jaw worked beneath his skin, and Ronja wondered if she had gone too far.

Suddenly, the boy brightened. He shook his escaped hair from his face. A black feather was twined with the cord that gathered it at the base of his skull.

"Not bad," Trip commended. "Only, I'd call my father more memorable than honorable."

"I see," Ronja said.

She rubbed her nose with her index finger and stared at her knees, abruptly apprehensive. She was in no position to insult these people. Trip said her capture had been a mistake, but did that mean she could trust him? Her Singer was gone, along with her ear and her migraines. For anyone to be found without a Singer was a severe crime, but for a mutt, even a second gen, it meant certain death.

"I don't have a Singer," Ronja murmured, as if it had only just occurred to her.

"You're quite welcome."

"No, they'll kill me," Ronja said, panic squeezing her voice into a higher octave. "They'll kill you. My family . . . what have . . . what have you done?"

The ceiling pressed down on her from above, the floor up from below. Cold sweat beaded on her skin, tracing patterns down her spine. The lights were too bright. The world was pounding on the door of her mind. If she let it in, she was lost. Ronja buried her face in her knees.

A hand on her shoulder. Ronja gasped and jerked backward, abruptly alert.

Trip shifted away and threw his hands up, as if she were a wild animal.

"Your family will be fine, okay? We've brought people in from the outside before and removed their Singers. Granted their experiences are generally less traumatic, but same concept. Some had families."

"What . . . what happened to them?" Ronja croaked.

Trip smiled gently.

"They were questioned by the Offs, just questioned, not tortured. Then they were sent on their way. No one can lie to an Off under The Music. Your family knows nothing of your circumstances. They may be worried, but they are safe. I promise."

"My family isn't . . . "

Normal.

That was the word she was looking for. But she could not tell Trip her mother was a mutt. That by all accounts, she should be one as well. Genetics went beyond The Music. What if she told him, and he did not accept her? He did not seem to have an inkling as to her true identity, unlike the rest of Revinia.

She wanted to keep it that way.

"We've had some trouble with the law in the past," Ronja finally said. "What if they were . . . taken?"

To prison. Or to be made into mutts. Or to their deaths.

Trip snorted.

"A rebellious streak, huh? That might explain your ability to overcome The Music. Regardless, that shouldn't affect this kind of issue."

Ronja breathed a sigh of relief. She felt the walls recede slightly as her breaths lengthened and slowed.

"Why did you do it?" she asked when she could speak again.

"You were dying, I had to—"

"No," Ronja cut him off. "Why did you take off *your* Singer?"

Humor flared in Trip's gaze, igniting his easy grin.

"Now that is a very complicated and fascinating question, one that I am not at liberty to answer."

"Oh, come on," Ronja groaned, flopping back against the bed frame dramatically. She crossed her arms over her hospital gown. "You can't be serious."

"I am," Trip replied dryly. "You'll have your questions answered soon, though. My superiors will want to speak with you."

Ronja chuckled bitterly and rubbed her sore eyes with the heels of her palms.

"I'm sorry."

Ronja dropped her hands. Technicolor splotches pulsated in her vision. She blinked them away to find Trip regarding her earnestly.

"I'm sorry for the burn, for your ear, for taking you from your family, and for the pain of these last days. I don't expect your forgiveness, but I do have something to offer you as a means of compensation."

"What?" Ronja asked blackly.

"Freedom."

Ronja opened her mouth to reply, but the boy had risen and was making his way toward the exit.

"Wait," she called, stretching out her arm as if to pull him back.

Trip halted and peered back over his shoulder.

"What's your real name?"

The boy smiled crookedly. "I don't use my first name," he said after a moment. "But if you don't want to call me Trip, you can use my middle name."

"Which is?"

"Roark."

"Roark," Ronja repeated, testing the name on her tongue. It was an old, wealthy name, certainly not native to the outer ring. "I'm Ronja."

"Ronja," Roark echoed softly. "It is a pleasure to meet you."

Roark turned from her without another word and disappeared through the curtained door. The fabric swayed in his wake. Ronja watched it until it was utterly still, turning the name over and over in her mind.

15: KNOTS

Curiosity coaxed her to step beyond the curtains, but fear kept her rooted on the spot. Ronja did not know if she was truly a prisoner, but got the sense that she would be stopped if she attempted to leave.

She felt as if she had slept for months, though her limbs remained numb and cumbersome. Her joints twanged and popped like those of an old woman as she threw back her sheets and hefted her legs from dormancy. Wincing, she twisted her body and let them droop to the cool floor.

It took several frustrating minutes and the assistance of the coat rack for her to stand, but eventually she managed to stay on her feet without swaying. Walking was even more trying. Her muscles burned as she worked the knots from them, but in a way, she welcomed the pain. It meant she was healing.

Ronja staggered back and forth across the room half a dozen times, rolling the kinks from her neck and kneading her shoulders. The exercise worked the hitches from her mind. For the first time in her life, her thoughts were bitingly clear.

Everything that had happened over the course of the last few days was impossible. A shiny without a Singer. A makeshift hospital underground. A symbol invisible to an entire city that she alone could see. Her Singer, ripped from her skull just before The Quiet Song could drag her under.

Ronja halted, her heart writhing in her ribs.

The Conductor tried to kill me, she thought dimly. *Why?*

She racked her brains, fighting through the lingering smokescreen of withdrawal back to the chair. Back to Roark, standing over her with a cigarette. What had she felt that her Singer had not been able to subdue?

Fear. Undeniable terror. But she had felt fear before, had she not?

Fear of her mother, of the Offs. Fear of failing Georgie and Cosmin. Fear for her own life and safety.

A cigarette in the eye?

There was nothing in Revinia worth seeing.

Her hand drifted to the bandages that swaddled her head. Ronja dug her fingernail beneath the adhesive that held them in place, then began to tug at the rings of linen.

Something else had wormed into her consciousness that night. It had always lurked in the corners of her mind, but had never been able to sink its claws into her.

The bandages were spiraling off her crown, layer after layer. They draped over her shoulders like cobwebs. Many were stained with crusty brown blood.

The feeling had first manifested in her hands, begging them to clench into fists. It slithered up her arms, charged her heart, filled her lungs with so much heat she thought they might burst. Her skull threatened to crack not from the pain of The Music, but from a far more potent agony.

Ronja knew the word. She had never spoken it. Was not sure if she could speak it, even without a Singer.

The last of her bandages slipped from her head, dusting her shoulders like snow.

The word was *rage*.

Ronja felt a scream build on her tongue. She clapped her hands over her mouth, smothering it with all her strength.

Roark had thought her an Off. One of her own tormenters. One of the men and women who carried out the orders of The Conductor, who placed her and her family at the foot of society. *Beneath* the foot of society. Why? Ronja had no idea. All her life she had paid for the mistakes of her mother, mistakes she could not begin to comprehend. She had been starved, assaulted, discriminated against for a crime she did not commit. For nearly two decades, she had been exposed to mutt Music, and for all she knew corrupted genetic material, based solely on the chance that she might follow in her mother's footsteps.

Her entire world was the pain The Conductor inflicted upon her.

How *dare* Roark lump her in with his lackeys?

Ronja let her hand drift to the wound on the side of her head. She flinched when her fingertips brushed the raw, lumpy flesh and sutures that formed a rough headstone for her ear. Lacking a mirror, she imagined her appearance and her heart sank. She must look repulsive.

It was then she realized she could hear nothing on her right side.

Ronja snapped her fingers several times before the wound. Nothing. She was completely deaf on that side. Of *course* she was. Between the thick gauze and her conversations with Roark and Iris, she had not stopped to think about it.

The feeling was simmering in her gut again. The rage. She gritted her teeth, tried to keep it from clawing up through her throat. It was not directed toward Roark, or even the doctor who mutilated her.

All at once she could not hold it back anymore.

The scream ripped from her like a leech pried from skin. It was long and animalistic, a sound she did not know she was capable of making.

When she quieted, Ronja found herself on her knees. She did not remember falling. She looked around, half expecting the world to have crumbled beneath her piercing cry.

The curtains were still. The curving ceiling and the wall behind her bed did not yield. Not even a speck of dust had been dislodged from its place.

A sudden, hysteric laugh bubbled up on her chapped lips.

Passion is perilous, they had always said, but it seemed to have little impact.

"What the hell was that? Are you all right? Why did you take off your bandages? Get back in bed, now!"

Ronja whipped around, but Iris was already at the bedside. She carried a stainless steel tray laden with various medical instruments and bottles of pills. She set it on the nightstand as Ronja climbed to her feet, embarrassed.

"You shouldn't be out of bed yet," Iris scolded, moving quickly to take her elbow. "You were uncoupled mid-Quiet Song. That's about as bad as it gets, and to top it off you didn't even have a proper operation. If Trip had just *mentioned* to me that there was a possibility that you weren't a . . . "

Iris cut herself off with a huff, fluttering her hand dismissively. Ronja sat down on the squeaky cot again.

"Nothing to be done now," Iris continued, throwing the blankets over Ronja's twig legs. "I just wish I could have been there to see you through a proper surgery."

"You mean they didn't have to cut off my ear?" Ronja asked, her fingers wandering toward the wound.

Iris smacked the wayward digits away.

"They *did*, unfortunately. From what Trip tells me, you went into The Quiet in about three minutes. Usually, it takes a person an hour to die from that. So the answer is yes, they had to take your ear. However," Iris grabbed a tin cup from the tray. She offered it to Ronja, who accepted it uncertainly. "I could have made a cleaner cut. Harrow may have two decades on me, but she's not a Singer surgeon," Iris placed a graceful hand over her heart. "I am."

"You're pretty young," Ronja commented mildly. She took a sip of the water Iris had handed her. It tasted like metal, but soothed her throat.

"I'll take that as a compliment," Iris replied tartly. The surgeon took an amber bottle of pills from the tray and gave it a shake. The tablets rattled like chattering teeth. "Take two a day until they're gone. One in the morning, one in the evening."

"How do I know which is which?" Ronja asked sarcastically, taking the offered bottle. She unscrewed the lid and dumped one of the white tabs into her palm. "What is it?" she inquired suspiciously. She pinched the pill between her thumb and index finger and held it up to the light. It did not appear particularly menacing, but then, neither did Singers.

"Antibiotics. They'll keep your wound from festering. I won't force you to take them, but you'll be begging for them later if you don't. Also," Iris tossed her a smaller bottle made of the same dark glass. Ronja caught it in her free hand. "Pain pills. Take them as needed, but no more than three a day."

Ronja nodded and laid the bottles beside her on the mattress.

They clinked hollowly against each other as she shifted. They reminded her of sleeping children, tucked into bed side by side.

"Are you going to take it?" Iris asked, jerking her chin at the white tablet locked between her fingers.

Ronja answered by placing the pill on her tongue and washing it down with the remainder of her water.

Iris beamed, flashing her dimples. "Brilliant! Mind if I give you a checkup? That's not really a question. Sit up straight so I can check your heart."

Iris examined her heart and lungs, a procedure she was forced to remain silent for. For everything that followed, however, the girl chattered incessantly.

"Don't get the wrong idea about me and Harrow," she said, prodding Ronja's stomach through her thin gown. "She's wicked smart, a fantastic doctor, but she's got no experience taking off Singers. That's a very specific skill that my father passed down to me and I've done dozens. I just don't understand why Trip didn't call me! Probably because he knew I'd put a stop to torturing you. I'm really sorry about that, by the way. How's your—?"

"You've taken off dozens of Singers?" Ronja asked.

Iris paused. She put her hands on her hips, glaring at Ronja down her button nose.

"Evie always says I talk to much. You weren't supposed to know that." Iris smiled cheekily and waggled a finger at Ronja. "I like you. I hope we get to keep you."

Before Ronja could remind the girl she was not a dog, Iris tucked her strawberry-blond curls behind her right ear. The cartilage was pierced five times. However, it was not crowned by a Singer. It looked as though it never had been. There was no scar tissue. She was born *free*.

Ronja felt a tendril of senseless jealousy take root in her stomach. The lumpy swath of skin where her ear used to be prickled, vividly present.

"Don't worry about your scar," Iris soothed, reading her mind. "You aren't the only one down here who lost their ear in the process. I can't always be around to save the day. It won't look so bad, especially with those pretty curls of yours."

"Who are you people?" Ronja wondered aloud, shaking her head.

"I'm sure you can figure it out," Iris said, twisting to grab an otoscope from the tray. She twirled it thrice in her hand and held it at the ready. "I've said too much, so you'll just have to wait for my superiors to get back. Now, sit up and be quiet."

Iris finished her examination without spilling any more secrets, as hard as Ronja tried to pry them from her. She did, however, continue to ramble about a string of incongruous topics Ronja could not begin to follow. Eventually, Ronja fell silent and allowed herself to be lulled by the meandering tales.

Iris checked her heart, lungs, reflexes, blood pressure, eyes, throat, and her remaining ear before she was satisfied. Ronja, who was highly unused to being labored over and had never been to an official medical appointment, was somewhat relieved to see her go.

"You need to stay here and rest, okay?" Iris said as she replaced her tools on the tray.

Ronja nodded compliantly, which seemed to all but make her caretaker's day. The surgeon spun on her heel and flitted from the room on her bare feet, tossing farewells over her shoulder.

When she was gone, Ronja debated sneaking from the room, but something held her back. She did not think she would be hurt if she left, but it seemed as though Iris genuinely wanted her to heal.

"Five days and I'm already soft," Ronja grumbled to herself.

She reclined into her pillow and let her eyelids sink shut. Drowsiness came with unprecedented swiftness, and when sleep took her she did not fight it.

She dreamed of running through an open field. It was a dream she had started many times in her life, but it was always burst open by a bolt from The Music. She moved forward in the scene, further than she had ever gone. Raindrops the size of baseballs fell around her, landing with uncanny softness on her hair and shoulders.

She paused. The grass brushed against her knees. She held out her palm to collect the rain. Upon closer examination, she found what was falling was not water, but tiny, translucent words. She could not see them, but she could feel them. She could hear them.

For today, my friend, I promise you are on the mend.

16: TWO CITIES

W ake up, love."
   The familiar voice dragged her from her dreams. Her lids were heavy with imaginary raindrops. Or words. She had forgotten which.

"Ready for some answers?"

Ronja snapped her eyes open. Her pupils retracted painfully quickly.

Roark stood above the bed, his hands shoved deep into his pockets. Her eyes latched onto the pendant swinging from his neck, the same one that had blinded her in the subtrain tunnels. Upon closer examination, Ronja saw it was a coin with a hole drilled through the mirrored profiles of The Conductor and Victor Westervelt I. She wondered at its significance, but was distracted by its wearer.

Roark seemed to have aged several years since the last time they had spoken. His mouth was tense and his jaw bulged in his cheek.

Ronja sat up, ignoring the stars that crackled her gaze. The boy offered his hand. She grabbed it with her own calloused one and rose haltingly. She swayed for a moment, but he anchored her.

"It can get a bit cold, down here," the boy said, gently withdrawing his support.

"I *had* a coat," Ronja grumbled, running her fingers through her tangled mane.

"You should be a bit more trusting," Roark replied, squatting and opening the large drawer beneath the bedside table.

"Forgive me for not trusting my kidnapper to keep my bloody . . . oh."

Folded in the belly of the drawer were her overcoat, sweater, pants, and undergarments. Roark pulled the coat from the compartment and shook it out. It was as frayed and patched as ever, but seemingly free of stains.

"I had everything washed for you, even had one of the buttons replaced."

Ronja accepted the coat from Roark. Its texture and weight was familiar, but it had lost the musky scent she loved.

"What's wrong?"

"Nothing," Ronja lied quickly.

"Liar."

"Kidnapper."

Roark rolled his eyes.

"Your shoes are at the end of the bed," he said, jerking his chin toward them. "I'll let you change."

Ronja nodded, and the boy slipped from the room with a fleeting smile.

It was a relief to strip off her sweaty gown and don her familiar woolen sweater and soft trousers. Roark had been right about the chill, so she shrugged on her coat. It settled on her slim shoulders like a comforting embrace.

Ronja moved to the end of the cot and found her boots waiting for her. They had been scoured of dirt. The leather was much lighter than she remembered. She shoved them over her bare feet, wriggling her toes into their familiar indentations.

She looked down at herself. She appeared utterly unaltered, but beneath the layers of cloth and skin, she knew everything was changing.

"Can I come in?"

Ronja looked up. Roark was already through the curtained doorway. She glowered at him.

"You look fantastic, love."

"Ronja."

"Of course, Ronja, love."

Ronja narrowed her eyes.

"What's going to happen?" she asked, fiddling with a button on her coat to keep from socking him in the jaw.

"My superiors are going to ask you a lot of questions. Then, if they like your answers, they're going to answer *your* questions."

"How do I know the correct answers?"

"Just be honest."

"You're about as helpful as a square tire."

Roark smiled crookedly and offered his elbow. Ronja took it, her heart thudding like a ball bouncing down the stairs. The pair ducked through the drapes.

Ronja blinked.

A city sprawled around her, bathed in both electric light and fire light and cocooned in arching stone walls. Its buildings were more like huts, constructed from swaths of multicolored cloth and plywood. Some were tents, others were built from privacy partitions. Where the domed ceiling drooped low, drapes were hung from hooks, encircling their occupants in thick, dusty arms. Ronja felt a rush of unprecedented affection for her own little room just behind her.

Decrepit furniture too large for the ramshackle homes littered the cavernous space. Bum-legged chairs and dressers with missing drawers were stacked high with books, their spines frayed with use. The aroma of home-cooked stew rested heavily on the air, mingling with pungent body odor and the sharp tang of underground cold.

Through the veins of the makeshift city, its citizens roamed. The walls of the impermanent homes shook as they rushed past, arms laden with food and other goods. Shouts rang out across the expanse, bouncing off the concave ceiling and firm walls.

None of them wore Singers.

Ronja was about to comment on this when the walls began to tremble. She squeezed her eyes shut, as though this would somehow quell the pain of the deafening sound. Plumes of dust cascaded from above, settling on her hair and shoulders. The rumble faded.

Suddenly, Ronja opened her eyes. She squinted at the ceiling, the walls, the floor.

"Wait . . . we're in the subtrain tunnels."

Roark looked at her wryly.

"What gave us away?" he drawled, stroking his chin sardonically.

"I know, but . . . " Ronja glanced around, a grin unfurling across her cracked lips. "The tunnels aren't really decaying, are they?"

Roark echoed her mischievous smile, his marble teeth flashing in the warm light.

"You pitchers almost put me out of work!" Ronja said with a disbelieving laugh.

"We rigged some explosives and brought the roof down at every entrance to the station," the boy explained, running a sheepish hand through his black hair. "The platform extends all the way in either direction," he gestured left and right.

Ronja stood on her tiptoes to peer over the sagging rooftops. The ocean of cloth and plywood extended as far as she could see in either direction. She had forgotten how massive some of the older stations were.

"The tunnels go even further," Roark continued, jerking his thumb over his shoulder.

Ronja followed the digit to the edge of the crowded platform, where a brick canyon housed two sets of parallel tracks. The wooden planks had been ripped up, but the metal rails remained, corroded from disuse. Twin archways on opposing sides of the ravine marked the entrances to the tunnels. Multicolored flags, chains of dried flowers, and strings of electric lights decorated them.

"You can walk about a quarter mile in each direction before you hit the cave-in," Roark told her, a hint of pride ringing in his voice.

"How do you get out?" Ronja asked, twisting around toward him.

"There's a service elevator that dumps out in an abandoned above-ground station," he explained. "It's safe, but pretty small. We won't be bringing in any new furniture for a while. I don't think Evie thought of that when she blew all the other exits."

Ronja nodded; she knew exactly what he was talking about. The lift was in the same place in every station, and always smelled of sweat and motor oil.

"I keep hearing about Evie—is she your girlfriend?" she asked.

Roark barked a laugh. "I'll tell her you said that, she'll have a fit. Come on, they're waiting for us."

Ronja allowed him to lead her through the meandering streets of the village. She wished she had three extra sets of eyes to take in her surroundings. Her head swiveled left and right, making her look rather bewildered. Her overt awe drew a few chuckles from passersby, but the laughter was good-natured, void of malevolence. She was accustomed to attention from strangers, but it was generally negative.

Roark pulled her away from the nucleus of the city to the far end of the atrium. Despite the unusual decor, Ronja knew where he was taking her. Every subtrain stop had an identical control room at its rear. With a fireproof door and sturdy walls, it seemed a likely place for a gathering of "superiors."

Her assumption quickly proved correct. They came to a halt before the familiar steel door. A hint of rust licked the base of the metal, but it was still impregnable. Ronja did not find this comforting, despite her steadily growing awe.

I don't know these people, she reminded herself. *They kidnapped me. Tortured me.*

But it was The Conductor that nearly killed you, a voice countered from the back of her mind.

Roark rapped on the door three times with a knuckle.

"Enter," a sharp voice called.

Ronja swallowed dryly.

If Roark sensed her anxiety, he did not address it. He turned the knob and put his shoulder into the door. With a grunt from the boy and a shriek from the metal, it caved. Ronja peered around her guide into the chamber.

The room was robed in dense shadows. The dark was diluted by a naked electric bulb that dangled precariously from the ceiling. A long oak table consumed most of the limited space, and a projector was mounted on a cart beyond. It spat a grainy, colorless spray at the far wall.

The table was manned by a dozen men and women ranging in age from their late teens to their late sixties. All eyed Ronja with varying degrees of curiosity and distrust. She attempted to keep her expression neutral, but her mouth was pinched into a taut line and cold sweat was beading on her back.

Two chairs at the head of the table stood empty. Ronja regarded them grimly. They were situated furthest from the door, making it impossible for her to bolt if things turned sour.

Movement to her left drew her gaze.

A woman had risen from her seat at the opposite end of the table. She was tall, considerably taller than Ronja, who stood at five feet eight inches, with a wiry, but not scrawny, frame. Her shockingly orange hair was piled atop her head and held in place by twin wooden rods. Her hooded eyes looked nearly black under sharp brows whose brown color suggested naturally dark hair. A smattering of freckles littered her porcelain nose and high cheekbones.

She was not beautiful, Ronja decided. She was striking.

The woman rounded the table at her leisure, her willow-branch finger tracing her path along the table. As she approached, Roark moved out of her way, leaving Ronja to catch the burden of her gaze. As much as she wanted to, the girl refused to drop her stare.

The fiery woman scuffed to a stop a few inches from Ronja, who had to lift her chin to hold eye contact.

"You've caused quite a disturbance in the Belly, Ronja," the woman said. Her voice was a stone pillar supporting a broad roof. It did not sway, waver, or question.

"Maybe you ate something weird," Ronja replied stiffly.

A collective laugh pooled behind the pair. Roark snorted loudly.

"I was referring to our home, not my stomach. We call this place the Belly."

"Feels more like a prison to me."

The woman arched a brow, which disappeared beneath her ragged bangs.

"Prison?" she inquired.

"Well, I can't leave, can I?"

"That depends entirely on you," the woman replied.

She motioned toward the vacant chairs with a quick jab of her chin, then spun and strode back to her seat.

Roark grabbed Ronja by the hand and tugged her toward the

indicated seats. The door swung shut behind them. Ronja had not seen anyone close it. Was there a guard outside the door?

The occupants of the table watched the girl silently as she sat. An elderly woman coughed into her gnarled hand, then continued to regard Ronja with curious owl eyes. A man with a paunchy gut stroked his jowls and appraised her with a condescending smirk. Ronja felt a snarky comment rise in her throat, but she swallowed it and lifted her chin.

The woman with orange hair broke the awkward hush.

"State your full name," she commanded from the opposite pole.

"Why don't you tell me yours," Ronja demanded flatly.

The woman sighed audibly and looked to Roark.

"Is she always this difficult?"

Roark was leaning back in his chair, his fingers laced to form a pillow behind his head. He shrugged and flashed his signature grin. The woman returned her focus to Ronja.

"Ito Lin, second in command of this operation," she said, placing her hand over her heart.

"Ronja Fey," Ronja replied.

"You're lying."

It was not a question.

"I'm not."

"You're withholding."

"Not as much as you are."

Ito bowed her head as if to hide the quirk of her mouth.

"If you cooperate with us," Ito began, bringing her head up. "We will answer all of your questions."

"And if not?"

"If not, you'll be sent back into the world."

"What's the catch?" Ronja asked, narrowing her eyes.

"That is the catch."

Ronja could not resist a smile at that. As anxious as she was to return home to her family, Ito was right. Nothing but pain awaited her on the surface. Her unwitting smile evaporated. "Wait, that doesn't make sense," she said. "How do you know I won't just go to the Offs?"

Whispers erupted around the table, but Ronja ignored them. Ito silenced the babble with a bored wave of her hand.

"Roark was right, you're sharp," Ito said, more to herself than to Ronja. She crossed her arms on the table and leaned forward. "You wouldn't last a week up there. As soon as you were caught you'd be administered a new Singer, and would subsequently forget everything that happened here."

"What's to stop me from telling them beforehand?" Ronja asked.

Ito shook her head slowly, a smirk worming its way across her full lips.

"You wouldn't do that," she said. "It's written all over your face."

Ronja rubbed her nose with her forefinger and looked away, studying the blank wall to her right. Every pair of eyes in the room bored into her, as if trying to see the gears revolving in her head.

"Let's try again," Ito suggested. "Your full name?"

"Ronja Fey Zipse," Ronja said, meeting the penetrating gaze flatly.

"How old are you?"

"Nineteen."

"Circle?"

"The Ninth."

Ito stared at her uncomprehendingly. Roark chuckled to himself.

"You know," Ronja said, gesturing helplessly at the intangible. "Like the Ninth Circle of Hell?"

"Hilarious," Ito said dryly. "Circle?"

"Outer."

"Family?"

"Fractured."

Roark nudged her in the ribs. Someone further down the table coughed to mask a snort.

"Fine. My father died when I was an infant, my mother is incapable. No siblings, two cousins."

"The names of your parents?"

"I'm not sure about my father," Ronja replied honestly. Roark peered at her sidelong, but she ignored him. "My mother's name is Layla."

"How did you find us?" Ito asked.

"Well—" Ronja looked to Roark, who shook his head, signaling she should talk.

The radiator in the corner hummed. The projector continued to devour the quivering, gray road. Ronja exhaled her anxiety.

"I work as a subtrain driver, or at least I did," Ronja began.

She recounted the night she caught sight of Roark on the tracks and snatched a glance of his free ear. She described her subsequent tardiness, her cut paycheck, her trip to the Office, and the run she had been saddled with. She left Henry out of the tale for his safety. She went on to detail her shock upon discovering Roark waiting for her at the end of the run.

"Then the bastard knocked me out," she said, shooting Roark a withering glance.

"And why was that, exactly?" Ito interjected.

"Ask him," Ronja said, jerking her head at the boy and folding her arms.

"Well," Roark clapped his hands together and sat forward. "She saw our emblem."

Another plume of whispers rose from the bodies crowding the table. Ito and Ronja remained silent, watching each other like dogs preparing to brawl.

"She understood the significance?" Ito asked, flicking her eyes back to Roark, who shook his head.

"No. She knew it wasn't The Conductor's, and suspected it might be dangerous. The fact that she realized that on her own is more than the rest of Revinia can say."

"That's impossible," a reedy voice cut in.

Ronja craned her neck to locate the speaker. He was a wisp a man with abnormally sharp nails, which he was currently using to scratch his rather bulbous head.

"In two generations no one under The Music has been able to see our record," he continued, poking a spindly finger at Ronja, who was seized by the urge to reach out and snap it. "For better and for worse The Conductor made sure of that."

"Which led me to believe she was an Off. Yes, that was my first reaction, too, which gave Ronja here a massive headache," Roark gestured at her forehead, which was still bore the shadow of his pistol. "That is, until The Quiet Song nearly killed her an hour later."

The silence deepened. The waifish man flapped his lips mutely, then settled back into his chair with arms crossed tight. Ito broke the quiet by blowing a whistle through her teeth.

"Now there's something you don't hear every day," she said. "How long did it take her to go under?"

"About three minutes," Roark said with a slightly manic grin.

"I see," Ito's eyes flashed like steel in sunlight. "Ronja, tell me, were you plagued by migraines before you were freed?"

"Yeah," Ronja said, her heart stumbling.

"At what age did they start?"

"I don't know. Four, five?"

Ito nodded. She did not look surprised.

"What were they?" Ronja asked, sliding her gaze from Roark to Ito questioningly. Ito opened her mouth to explain, but the boy beat her to the punch.

"When The Music can't control you, it resorts to inflicting pain. The pain is intended to, what's the phrase? 'Put you back in your place.'"

Ronja's mouth quirked darkly.

"In your case, it didn't work," Roark finished.

"Indeed," Ito agreed, resting her chin in her hand and staring into space contemplatively. "A nineteen year old from the outer ring resistant to The Music, nearly killed by The Quiet Song in under three minutes. This *is* intriguing."

"The nineteen year old is right here," Ronja reminded her, waving a hand dramatically.

Ito's gaze snapped back to her.

"Ronja, there is something inherently wrong with this society. You knew that in your gut, but not in your mind. If you want, we will tell you everything. If not, the door is waiting."

Ronja studied her hands, which were clenched tightly in her lap. The wound on the side of her head pulsed rhythmically. All that she had ever felt, but could never prove, lay before her just waiting for her to reach out and accept it.

"Show me," she said.

17: A HISTORY LESSON

"Teller," Ito said, nodding toward the middle aged man to Ronja's immediate left.

Teller stood wordlessly and roused the projector. The whirling gray blur stuttered to a halt, and an aerial view of Revinia materialized on the wall.

It was far from the Revinia Ronja knew. Even from 100 feet above, it was vastly different. There was no distinction between the rings. The entire metropolis was awash with vibrant hues. Red, green, blue, and gray rooftops winked like sea glass. Autos wove through the veins of every ring. The thick cloud of smog that constantly lingered above the city had evaporated, replaced with clear, sharp air Ronja could almost taste. The great wall still encircled the city like a black eye, but it was studded with pinpricks of white.

Exits.

The image faltered in the silence of the room, then changed.

Ronja's jaw went slack.

"Revinia, circa 65 PC," Ito narrated, rising from her high backed chair and moving to stand beside the makeshift screen. She leaned against the wall, slinging one ankle across the other. The edge of the moving picture played across the left half of her body, warping with each angle and curve. "Strange, isn't it?"

Ronja nodded mutely, her unhinged jaw bouncing slightly.

If 65 PC Revinia was different from above, it was unrecognizable at eye level.

The buildings, though less dilapidated, were fundamentally the same. They were clearly situated in the outer ring. Ronja would recognize the plain, squat structures anywhere. The streets winding between them were paved with the same drab cobblestones, newly damp with rain.

It was the people who were beyond recognition.

At first Ronja thought that her ancestors had simply been taller, but she quickly realized that they merely carried themselves higher. Their spines were not bent beneath some unseen burden. Their faces were alive, constantly shifting between shades of emotion. Anger. Excitement. Aggravation. Pleasure. Even boredom.

Ronja could not imagine what they found so tedious.

They tossed smiles like seeds, exchanged frowns like small change. They were unabashed in the face of their emotions, and she knew why. She saw it replicated before her now.

"They," Ronja began uncertainly, afraid the words would cut her. "They don't have Singers."

She knew she should not have been surprised. Her sixth grade class had spent an entire month studying Pre-Conductor Revinia. Her instructors made it abundantly clear that Revinia had not always been guided by The Conductor and His Music. However, she was led to believe this society was plagued by violence.

The men and women that filtered through the ghostly avenues did not look particularly vicious. They were certainly more vibrant than anyone Ronja had ever seen above ground.

"Tell me," Ito demanded, snapping Ronja's musings in two. "What do you know of The Conductor. What do you know of Atticus Bullon?"

Ronja blinked, dragged her eyes away from the moving picture and focused on Ito, who was watching her calculatingly. She itched her nose as she weighed the question. "Well, he was elected mayor in 10 PC, when Revinia was still part of Arutia," she began, shifting uncomfortably under the collective gaze of the room. "He declared the city independent in 8 PC, took up the title Conductor in year 0 after he and Victor Westervelt I pioneered The Music."

"Do you know why he chose to break from Arutia?" Ito inquired, dipping her chin in approval.

"To avoid the war," Ronja replied automatically.

"Indeed."

As if on cue the familiar portrait of Atticus Bullon materialized on the wall. Ronja felt her fingers twitch feebly, aching to salute the photograph. She clenched the wayward digits into a fist and regarded the picture grimly.

"As you said, Bullon did not agree with the war Arutia had chosen to take part in. Not a poor position, truthfully. It was bloody in infancy and destined to be fruitless. Despite its unorthodoxy, most Revinians were initially happy with the secession. No one wants to fight an unjust war. Most of the Arutian army was across the ocean, so there weren't enough troops to put up a real fight. Eventually, Revinia was left alone."

"You sound like my history instructor," Ronja commented.

This drew a chuckle from the occupants of the table. Ito did not appear particularly amused.

"What if I told you that entire story was pitch?"

Ronja considered, regarding the photograph with her head tilted to the side. Days ago she would have called such a claim treason. "Honestly, there isn't much that would surprise me anymore," she said with an exhausted shrug.

"Smart girl," Ito praised her, rapping Bullon on his protruding nose with a sharp knuckle. "Bullon didn't give a skitz about protecting his people from the ravages of war. He was out for power—absolute power. When the war ended, he became paranoid that Arutia would try to reclaim the city, so he tightened security to the point that almost no one could enter or leave. As you might imagine, this did not sit well with the Revinians. They began to rebel. And that"—Ito nodded at Teller, and the image switched—"is when he sought the help of a confidant."

"Victor Westervelt I," Ronja named the man on the screen.

The industrial giant scowled down at Ronja from the wall, his expression simultaneously condescending and disgruntled. His nose was sharp, his eyes equally potent. Deep canyons carved by stress ran across his large forehead, and frown lines pooled around his mouth. Three aeroplanes wheeled through the sky behind him, leaving trails of pollution in their wake.

"Yes," Ito said. "Westervelt was a master inventor at the head of the largest company in Revinia. Bullon went to him seeking a way to control the rebellious population."

"Why are you giving me a history lesson?" Ronja demanded, her voice growing brittle with impatience. "Roark told me you were going to answer my questions."

"In order for you to understand who we are, you need to learn the true history of this city, and The Music," Ito replied levelly.

"Fine, enlighten me."

18: STIFLED

The Music was introduced to the public in 3 PC. Bullon declared himself The Conductor in year 0, and it was made illegal to be found without a Singer a year later."

Ronja bobbed her head, indicating she followed.

"What were you told is the purpose of The Music?" Ito asked.

"To keep people calm; to counteract violence."

"Not precisely." Ito peeled herself from the wall and slipped her hands into her pockets. She stepped into the eye of the projector, warping Westervelt's wolfish face with her own. "It isn't exactly a lie, is the funny thing. The Music *is* what keeps Revinia from plunging into chaos, but the reasoning is not as noble as it sounds."

"Not that there's anything noble about playing with people's emotions," Roark muttered darkly.

Ronja considered him out of the corner of her eye. His countenance was stiff, and a twitch had settled into his forefinger. It tapped against the table quietly, a rapid pulse nearly muted by the whir of the projector.

"I don't understand," Ronja admitted, refocusing on Ito.

The woman snapped her fingers at Teller, who exchanged the portrait of Westervelt for another moving picture.

The image was grainy. The camera lens was clogged with rain and mud. Through the haze, Ronja discerned a crush of bodies charging down a street. They were somewhere near the core, judging by the wide paved avenue and elegant marble buildings. Blotches of white glinted amid the gray scene, torches held aloft to scatter the dark. Though the sound had been sucked from the image, Ronja knew rage was thick in the air.

"Revinia was a city of artists, writers, musicians, creators," Ito continued. It was no longer only the glare of the projector that made her eyes gleam. She seemed to speak more to herself than to Ronja, who was now sufficiently lost. "It was not a city of soldiers, but of human beings of the purest form. They were not fools, though. When their rights were stolen, they were not blind to the injustice. So the artist became the soldier."

Ito fell silent. Most of the council members regarded the unsteady images bleakly. Others bowed their heads, including Roark. Ronja wondered if some of the older members had witnessed the riots first hand. The owl-eyed woman trembled as she gazed at her interlocking fingers. The room itself seemed to hold its breath. Through the fog of the lens, Ronja watched the Offs arrive on the scene.

She could not help but jump when the gunfire started. The protestors fell like dominos to the ballistics, and for a moment Ronja was thankful the images were so blurry.

"Together, Westervelt and Bullon crafted a plan to suppress the riots and to keep Revinians from deserting the city."

"The Music," Ronja murmured.

The moving picture shifted to a new scene. Ronja braced herself.

There were three men in the frame, two of whom had turned their backs to the camera. They were garbed in white lab coats. The third man was a prisoner. His wrists and ankles were fixed to a gurney with thick leather buckles. Ronja could not see his face clearly, but his muscles were twisted with fear.

The two white-clad scientists turned to face the camera in unison, gaudy smiles plastered across their faces.

The first man was Victor Westervelt I. He appeared much younger than when he sat for his famous portrait. His hair was black rather than gray, and the lines that mapped his stress were not so deep. He was almost handsome in his youth.

The other man Ronja did not recognize. He was younger than Westervelt, with light hair and nearly translucent irises. He held a device that was faintly reminiscent of a Singer, but much bulkier and far less refined. The earpiece was attached to a crown of adjustable leather straps.

"The first Singer," Ito named it.

Ronja was too engrossed to nod.

The bleached man handed the antique Singer to Westervelt at his request. Westervelt exited the frame, turning the device over in his hands almost tenderly as he left. The colorless man advanced on the prisoner, saying something to his partner out of view of the camera. The captive began to struggle against his restraints, but the man seized his head, steadied it.

Westervelt came back into the shot.

The prisoner thrashed with increased ferocity as Westervelt leaned over him, Singer in hand. Just as the machine was about to settle on his head, the prisoner did something Ronja would never forget.

He spat in Victor Westervelt's face.

Ronja felt her hands fly to her mouth of their own volition.

The Westervelt family was held in the highest regard, almost level with The Conductor. To see someone disrespect him in such a blatant way was unthinkable.

Westervelt withdrew. He closed his eyes. A vein in his temple twanged. He set the antique Singer on a nearby table with careful fingers, as if he were handling a child.

The man lashed to the table was screaming something, but his words were sucked away by the limitations of the moving picture.

Westervelt lashed out, striking the man once in the groin, once in the neck, then twice across his face. Blood spurted from his nose as he gulped for air, his back arching in agony.

Westervelt snatched the device from the table and launched forward, cramming it onto the subject's skull before he could twist away. His fingers slick with black Ronja knew was truly red, Victor fumbled with the chin strap that secured the Singer. Meanwhile, the pale man tightened the cranial buckles.

Victor and his partner stood back and regarded their handy work. The prisoner flailed and shouted, but the two men grinned at each other as if they had just been awarded a prize. Westervelt laughed soundlessly and wiped his bloody hands on a spare rag.

The pale man disappeared from view, only to reappear a moment later carrying a fist-sized box. He offered it to Westervelt, who cradled it with both hands and admired it like a rare trinket. He said something to the cameraman, who angled the lens toward his cupped palms.

Ronja squinted at the screen. It was not a box at all, but a small radio studded with a handful of switches and dials.

Westervelt turned his back on the lens, which redirected upward. His shoulders rose and fell as he took a steadying breath. He aimed the radio at the prisoner, and flicked a switch.

The man's empty screams halted. His eyes scattered, trailing different paths across the room. His jaw slackened, his tongue lolling inside his open mouth. Blood flowed generously from his nose and ears, showing no signs of stopping.

"The Quiet Song?" Ronja asked as the film came to a staggering halt. For half a moment Ronja wondered what she had looked like beneath the influence of The Quiet Song, but then she realized she did not want to know.

"No. The Day Song, before it was perfected," Ito corrected tonelessly. Her mouth was stitched into a grim line. "This is the same prisoner three months later."

A photograph sprang up onto the wall, coming into focus in a spray of black and white.

There were four men in the picture. One was Westervelt. He stood with his arms crossed and his chin high, his ego radiating. To his immediate left was Bullon, his faintly crossed eyes glittering triumphantly. Ronja did not recognize the third man, but he was forgettable juxtaposed with the two social giants.

The last man was the prisoner.

He knelt on the ground before the trio. It was undoubtedly the same man from the horrible film—his jutting nose and generous quantities of dark hair proved that—but Ronja would not have recognized him out of context.

In the first film, his hair had been matted, his eye sockets deep trenches, his nose spurting blood. This man was crisply dressed. His hair was slicked back, the ragged edges trimmed. Perched atop his head like a bizarre crown was another Singer, slightly less cumbersome than the prototype, but far less elegant than the current model.

The subject knelt on the floor before the trio and gazed up at them reverently.

Teller jabbed a button on the projector and the image disappeared. Another photograph slipped into its place half a beat later. Ronja felt her gut contort as the significance of the image soaked in.

The scene was fundamentally identical to its predecessor, with one major change. The prisoner was bent forward, his forearms pressed against the lush rug that blanketed the hardwood floor.

His lips were pressed to The Conductor's onyx shoe.

"The Music was not crafted to protect the people of Revinia from their demons. It is a muzzle, one that purges all powerful emotions and rebellious inclinations, prevents tumult in the face of Bullon's injustice. It exchanges your natural-born passions for a single thought: Be loyal to The Conductor."

Ito paced toward Ronja as she spoke. Her shadow elongated on the screen, obliterating The Conductor and his confidants.

"Every notion you have against Him and His laws is pulverized with a flourish of sound," Ito stepped around Ronja's chair and placed her hands on her shoulders. The girl flinched, but did not duck out. "Everything you ever felt besides strict loyalty—love of a partner, hate of an enemy, terror, excitement, anxiety—all are muted by The Music. Every time your passions spike, they are beat down. You have lived your life shackled to a weightless iron ball."

"No . . . " Ronja twisted in her seat to view Ito, who towered above her. She could not read Ito's expression. "I loved my cousins . . . my friend."

"Of course you did," Ito threw up her hands violently. "They can't take away everything. When they are completely drained of emotion, people become sloths. Can't work. Can't pay taxes. Most importantly, they can't feel devotion."

"But . . . I was . . . " Ronja trailed off.

The cords that anchored her mind to her body had been snipped. She was floating somewhere far above the claustrophobic chamber.

You have lived your life shackled to a weightless iron ball.

"But you . . . you were different, weren't you?"

The question yanked Ronja back into the room. Ito was

regarding her with piercing eyes.

"You felt anger toward Him, didn't you?"

Ronja turned toward the screen, which was now blank. Ito's gaze prickled on the back of her neck. Sweat beaded under her dense curls. Her heart bucked in her chest.

"You hated Him. Maybe you couldn't string the words together, or even write it down, but you despised Him."

"Not when I had a Singer. I was good, I tried to be good."

Oxygen was draining from the room. The walls were inching closer, pressing against her body, cracking her ribs.

"Most people under The Music react accordingly. They wander through life in a muted state, caring, but not loving. Disliking, but not hating. But you, *you felt more*. The Music is a beast, Ronja. A living, breathing beast that has its claws on your pulse. When your heart races, it clutches you harder. Pain is the secondary tool in The Conductor's belt. Unorthodox thoughts and sensations are smashed with blinding migraines. Usually the pain is enough to put people back in their place, and their resistance dies. But you kept fighting."

"I—"

"You fought it, why?"

"I don't—"

"You're a smart girl. You understood that the pain would fade if you simply stopped thinking so damn much. If you stopped noticing. So, why didn't you?"

Ronja slammed her fists into the table, sending a shudder rippling down the surface.

"I DIDN'T WANT TO, OKAY?" she roared, shooting to her feet. "I HATE HIM! I HATE THE CONDUCTOR NOW, AND I HATED HIM THEN, AND I DIDN'T WANT HIM TO WIN!"

19: OXYGEN

The room was silent save for Ronja's ragged breaths. Her shouts had replenished the oxygen, shoved the walls back into their rightful places. Her chest was empty, as though screaming had somehow dispelled the dust from her lungs, making room for much needed air.

"Well, I believe you have your answer, Ito," Roark drawled.

Ito smirked at Roark, a sardonic expression reminiscent of the one Ronja and Cosmin often shared. The pair quickly disguised their joking manner, and the solemn atmosphere was reinstated.

Ito paced back to her chair, surveying the room with unwavering eyes. Ronja remained standing, her spine rigid, her hands curled into fists at her thighs.

"You have two options," Ito said, coming to a stop behind her chair and staring Ronja down. "You may leave our compound and reenter Revinian society. You will go directly to a government hospital and receive a new Singer. We will tail you to ensure that is your intention. Then you will forget any of this ever happened. You will never hear from us again."

Ronja snorted disdainfully.

"What's my second option?"

"You stay in the Belly, and fight for us."

"You still haven't answered my question: who are you?"

"Have you really not guessed?" a new voice intoned.

Ronja tracked the disdainful words to a young woman seated at Ito's immediate right.

The girl had a forgettable, though not unattractive face. The left half of her skull was shaved, but the rest was heavy with thick blond hair. Her exposed ear was pierced many times, including a twisted copper rod through her cartilage. She rested her pointed chin in her hand, her expression a combination of distrust and vexation.

Ronja swallowed a scathing reply and shook her head.

"We're the resistance, love," Roark said, touching her elbow softly. "We call ourselves the Anthem. We're going to take down The Conductor."

Anthem.

The word was foreign to Ronja's ear, but the way Roark said it made her feel as though she already knew its definition. The word took root in her chest and made her shiver with inexplicable elation.

"Take your time, answer carefully," Ito warned her.

I can't go back.

Not after everything she had seen. Her world had been twisted beyond recognition. It seemed disrespectful, to wash away her knowledge of the past and present horrors. Her gut begged her to stay and fight. Her rage whispered, beckoned.

Still.

Her family awaited her aboveground, still suffocating beneath The Music. They probably thought she was dead. Had the Offs come to speak to them yet? Was it worse for them to believe she was dead, or a traitor? In their warped vision of reality it was probably better they thought she was dead than disloyal.

I am disloyal, she realized with an abrupt chill. *I am Singerless.*

"I have a family," Ronja finally said. "Two cousins. My mother can't care for them. I'm all they've got. I can't leave them."

Ito made eye contact with Roark across the table. Ronja saw him incline his head in her peripheral vision.

"Your cousins, can they pull their own weight?" Ito asked.

Ronja felt her heart stutter. She nodded vigorously, her curls bobbing like springs.

"Yes, yes! Absolutely. Cosmin's twelve, Georgie's nine. Cos is bright for his age and Georgie can . . . "

Ito raised a hand to silence her. Ronja bit the inside of her cheek to keep from talking.

"What of your mother?"

"She's . . . "

Could she confide in these people Layla's nature, in the strangeness of her own? Would they even believe her? She had never heard of a mutt giving birth to a normal child. They might think she was lying, or hiding something else.

"She's an alcoholic," Ronja finally said.

There. It was not a lie, but it was not the whole truth.

Ito sighed empathetically.

"Not an uncommon side effect of The Music, especially in the outer ring. When her Singer is removed, we can help her through rehab."

A screech of wood against stone forced Ronja to clutch her remaining ear.

"Hold up a pitching second!"

Ronja swallowed.

The girl who had spoken before was on her feet, her chair shoved against the far wall. An escaped blonde lock swayed like a pendulum before her rage stricken face.

"We know *nothing* about this girl," she hissed. "Ito, you're going to allow her and her entire skitzed-up family to just move in?"

The girl did not bother to look at Ronja as she spoke, which made her comments sting all the more.

"We know enough, Terra," Ito retorted firmly. "I trust Trip's opinion. Remember, our ultimate goal is to free the entire city. To do that, we need to take chances now and again."

"So, you admit this is a gamble," Terra growled.

Ito rolled her eyes.

"Stepping outside the Belly is a gamble," she sighed, massaging her temples. She dropped her hands and looked back to Ronja, signifying she was done with Terra. "Can your family survive the night alone?"

Ronja considered. There was some food remaining when she had disappeared five days ago. Cosmin knew where the emergency funds were. By her count, the pair could subsist for a week on their own. Layla ate very little these days, so Ronja hardly counted her.

"Yes, they'll be fine."

"Excellent. We will collect them tomorrow afternoon."

"You're sure they're okay, you know, since The Conductor tried to kill me?"

"At most, some lower level Offs will search your house, ask your family a few questions. They can't lie through their Singers, and as they know nothing of your disappearance, they are in no danger."

Roark beamed at her impishly, and Ronja gave him a shove.

"I'll stay," she said, looking Ito directly in the eye. "I'll stay and fight for the Anthem."

20: SMASH

"A re you okay?"

The meeting had disbanded ten minutes ago. At its terminus, Ito had swooped out with a flash of her artificially-orange hair and a brief nod toward Ronja. Terra followed moments later, her expression a broiling storm. The rest had filtered out at their own pace, talking amongst themselves, shooting curious glances and tentative smiles at Ronja. She'd returned them with as much fervor as she could muster while endeavoring not to hyperventilate.

Presently, she and Roark sat alone in the conference room. Roark eyed her anxiously. She appreciated his concern, but his gaze was not aiding her in her attempt to breathe normally.

"It's a lot to take in," Ronja replied, rubbing the bridge of her nose without looking at him.

"Do you believe it?"

Ronja let her hands fall, keeping her eyes fixed on the far wall.

"What?"

Roark gestured, as if "it" was omnipresent.

"All of it. The Conductor. The Music. The Anthem. It must be rather difficult to believe after a lifetime of being told the opposite."

"Was it difficult for *you* to believe?" Ronja asked, finally swiveling to view her companion.

Roark smiled, but it did not reach his eyes.

"Not at all, but my situation was rather different."

"How?"

He shook his head forcefully. A stray strand of hair flopped into his eyes. He flicked it back with an aggravated twitch of his fingers. "Another time," he said. "Right now, I want to hear about you."

Ronja leaned back in her chair, blew out a puff of air through her nose. "Yes," she replied, and was startled to realize that it was true. "I do. I have no real reason to doubt it and . . . it *feels* like the truth.

Maybe it helps that my head is so much clearer now that . . . " Ronja reached up and brushed the mangled remains of her ear. Pain prickled beneath her fingertips, but it was nothing compared to the brutal notes of The Music.

"You look like you need some of your pain meds," Roark noted.

"Yeah," Ronja replied, relieved he had changed the subject.

"I'll take you back to your room," he offered.

Roark got to his feet and stretched his arms above his head with a groan. He let them plummet with a crunch of leather. "You should take your antibiotics too, or Iris will start mashing them up in your food."

As soon as they exited the suffocating room, Ronja felt a good deal of her anxiety leak away. The Belly was full of exotic aromas and bizarre spectacles, but, more importantly, abundant space.

Word of her induction had spread like wildfire in the few minutes since the meeting ended. The people of the Belly kept their distance, but offered quick words of welcome as they passed. Ronja's stomach fluttered each time someone said "welcome" or "congratulations." She tried to respond each time by thanking them, but usually stumbled over her words.

"How can they be so sure of me?" she asked Roark after an elderly woman with a hunched back and hair like steel wool attempted to kiss her cheeks.

Roark had shooed her away gently, claiming Ronja's injuries were still bothering her. "They aren't," Roark said, waving at the woman over his shoulder. "They're just hopeful. It's not every day we get new blood down here."

"They don't know me."

"Good thing, too, or you'd have been topside days ago."

Ronja rammed the boy with her shoulder, nearly causing him to careen into a man balancing a ludicrously tall stack of books.

"You're stronger than you look, Ronja," he laughed, massaging his shoulder tenderly.

Ronja shrugged. "Had to be, I guess," she replied offhandedly, sidestepping a barrel-chested man toting a toddler. "Did you just call me by my *name*?"

It was Roark's turn to shrug. "You're the only one who calls me by my real name. I figured I could return the favor once and awhile."

"Why don't you use your first name?" Ronja asked, stepping around a couple entwined in a rather compromising embrace.

"I hate it."

Ronja eyed the boy sidelong. His jaw was abruptly stiff, and he stared ahead blankly. "Why?" she prodded carefully.

Roark blinked. He snapped his gaze back to Ronja, and the fog clouding his pupils dispersed. He forced a laugh through his stiff mouth. "It's about a century old and a syllable longer, you'd hate it."

It was a weak excuse, but Ronja let it be. She was not being completely honest about her own past, so why should Roark feel obligated to be? They had known each other for less than a week, and she had been comatose for most of it.

The thought nearly made her stumble. She felt as though she had known Roark as long as her own reflection. Perhaps it had something to do with her newly-uninhibited emotions.

That's right, she realized dimly. *I can feel whatever I want.*

A streak of color fractured her thoughts. Ronja came to a grinding halt as two children, a boy and a girl barely hip high, tore across their path. She watched them as they darted down the walkway. The girl was faster than the boy, her coarse braids always an inch out of his reach. Both the children and their shrieks of delight were swallowed by the crowd as quickly as they had emerged.

"What?" Roark asked.

Ronja blinked rapidly. "I don't remember the last time I saw kids playing like that."

Ronja had played games as a child—or rather, she had been *used* in games. A class favorite was mutt and catcher. That usually ended badly.

"Here you are," Roark said, nodding at the curtained doorway to her room.

Ronja looked up in surprise. She had not noticed they had arrived.

"You should get some sleep; you look like you could use it."

"You expect me to sleep?" she inquired doubtfully. "I just

joined a highly illegal revolution in an abandoned subtrain station and you expect me to take a nap?"

"You're still recovering," Roark said seriously. "Trust me, when you lie down, you'll be able to fall asleep."

Ronja nodded, but remained skeptical. The boy gave her a lazy salute and started to back away.

"Where are you going?" she called after him.

"I have an errand to run. I'll be back later tonight," he reassured her.

"What happens tonight?"

Roark grinned, and the laden air of the Belly was suddenly thin.

"You'll see. Get some sleep."

Ronja ducked into the bedroom. For a time she stood still, gazing at the cot with dull eyes. As inviting as it looked, she could not bring herself to succumb to sleep.

Instead, she rinsed her face in the basin of clean water that had been placed beside her bed. She washed down one of the antibiotic tablets and two pain pills with water and a hunk of sourdough, which someone (presumably Iris) had left at the foot of the bed. She reminded herself to thank the surgeon for the bread, which was some of the best she had ever tasted.

Her stomach full and her pain preparing to subside, Ronja began the arduous task of untangling her matted locks with the comb she discovered in the drawer. Ten minutes later her hair was still winning the battle, so she surrendered and twisted it into a knot. The bun perched atop her crown in victory.

Feeling somewhat revived, Ronja ventured out into the Belly.

There was something invigorating about the handmade city. It reminded her of the moving pictures of old Revinia that Ito had shown her, but it was even better.

It was real.

The mammoth platform appeared to be the heart of the miniature metropolis, though the tunnels also throbbed with activity. Narrow paths threaded between the squat homes. The platform was flanked by two rows of proud brick columns like shading trees. Some bore stunning murals: tranquil faces as tall as

Ronja, rural and urban landscapes, swaths of roiling color that served no purpose but made her shiver with strange delight. The dual flights of steps that once led to the surface now served as bleachers on which Anthemites relaxed in clusters. From afar they reminded Ronja of birds on telephone wires.

Members of the Anthem roamed freely, channeled by the winding walkways. The vast majority bore faint scars on their ears and temples, but some of the children and teenagers did not. They had never worn Singers. Never heard The Music. Their freedom was absolute, unquestionable. It was almost dizzying.

Iris was not lying when she told Ronja there were others who had suffered unconventional amputations. As she walked, Ronja came across a one-eared woman with cropped blond hair. She seemed to wear her puckered scar as a badge of honor, going so far as to shave the area around the old wound.

Ronja was watching the girl disappear into the crowd when she slammed into an elderly man lugging a potted plant. With a cry of shock he lost his grip on the foliage and its hollow home. The clay shattered on the floor, and a cloud of silence settled over the area.

Ronja closed her eyes, bracing her body and mind for the slough of insults.

"Are you all right?"

Ronja cracked an eyelid.

The man was peering at her with wide, concerned eyes, ignoring the clay shards and black soil at his feet.

"I . . . " Ronja looked about anxiously.

The onlookers had returned to their tasks after the brief hiccup. They appeared entirely unconcerned with the incident.

"Are you hurt?" the man prompted.

"N . . . no . . . I'm sorry, I didn't mean—"

The man waved her off and crouched before the mess, knees popping. A hiss of pain escaped through his teeth. Ronja knelt quickly and began to scoop the chunks of dirt into a more manageable pile.

"Don't worry about it," the man said, waving a wrinkled hand dismissively. "You young people are always moving so fast. Old men like me don't mind a slow task."

"It's no problem," Ronja replied hastily. She reached out and scooped the homeless plant from the flagstones. "The roots are all intact. If we get it back into soil, it should be fine," she assured him.

The man glanced up. He smiled at her as one might smile at an old photograph. "Are you a gardener, my dear?"

"My sister is," Ronja replied absently, brushing earth from the fragile leaves. "Do you have another pot?"

"Yes, right over there," the man pointed at a nearby tent with a sagging roof. "There's a crate by the entrance, could you get it for me?"

Ronja rose, swiftly brushing the dirt from her knees. She retrieved the wooden crate and set it before the man, then crouched alongside him again to help scrape the damp soil into the box.

"Where is your sister now?" the man asked, dumping a handful of black earth into the crate.

"Up there," Ronja gestured to the ceiling that cloaked the sky. "Hopefully at school."

"I find that hard to believe," he admitted with a glance at his watch. "Considering it's nearly seven-thirty in the evening."

"Really?" Ronja craned her neck to view his timepiece. It was of surprisingly fine make. The numbers were inlaid with gold, and the hands laced with silver.

The man chuckled, a sound peppered with nostalgia. "I nicked it when I was a boy," he said, admiring his watch. "Singer and all."

Surprise knocked a grin onto Ronja's face. "No skitz?"

The man mirrored her smile. His teeth were corroded and yellow, but his eyes were flush with youth. "I was a fantastic pickpocket, I'll tell you what. I could snag a wallet from a man's jacket and put it back without him feeling a thing. I would do that once in a while, get the wallet, snag the cash, then put it back empty just to see if I could." The man itched his balding head. "Of course, that's how the Offs got me in the end."

Ronja laughed. She rubbed her hands together to clean them. Most of the soil they had managed to scrape into the fresh container. The rest had tucked itself into the cracks between the flagstones.

"Thank you for the help, Ms . . . "

"Ronja," she said, shooting to her feet and extending her earth-stained hand for the old man to grasp.

"Very nice to meet you, Ms. Ronja."

He took her hand with his age-rumpled digits and allowed her to help him up. He smiled softly. "May I?" He gestured to her forehead with two fingers.

"Oh, umm . . . "

"It is a gesture of good fortune," the man explained, his fingers outstretched.

"Oh, okay. Sure."

Ronja dipped her head awkwardly. The elderly man touched the center of her brow with two fingertips.

"May your song guide you home," he said gently.

Ronja opened her eyes, a niche forming between her eyebrows. The man was already hefting the newly potted plant from the floor.

"See you tonight," he said cheerily.

Ronja nodded mutely, baffled.

When she saw that the old man had safely completed the fifteen-yard marathon to his home, Ronja continued to wander the Belly. Though it was tiny compared to the sprawling metropolis she had grown up in, it was infinitely more intricate. If Revinia was a bare-bones sketch, the Belly was an elaborate tapestry.

Cook fires, which dotted the landscape and radiated intoxicating aromas, seemed to be constant and communal. Each fire was ringed with Anthemites of every age and race. They passed dishes heaped with steaming food, read aloud from fat books, told stories animatedly. The vents that had once powered the station had been retrofitted to inhale smoke; she could hear their steady drone above the babel.

Ronja discerned that each family was allotted a plot of land on which they built their home from whatever materials they could scavenge. Many slept in large, drooping tents. Others had crafted huts from construction scrap. Underground, they did not need to be protected from the elements, so Ronja assumed the barriers were mostly to preserve privacy.

Though that seems rather pointless, she thought.

Life bled into life in the subterranean community. Ronja had already seen dozens of children in the Belly, something she found rather curious. Barefoot and lithe as cats, they darted from house to house, family to family, in packs of three or four. It was impossible to discern who was blood and who was not, and even harder to tell which children belonged to which parents, or if they had parents at all.

As Ronja watched, a group of three scrawny boys a bit younger than Georgie pounced on a woman stoking a fire, their sticky fingers grabbing at the bowl she had set on the brick hearth. The woman spun expertly and swatted them away with a rag. The boys bolted, cackling. The woman shook her head, but even from across the road Ronja could see she was smothering a chuckle.

An explosion of riotous laughter erupted to her left. Sudden panic knifed through her, and Ronja tripped backward over her feet.

When her spine struck the floor, she was no longer in the Belly.

She was six. She wore a jumper and nearly-matching stockings. It was lunchtime at school, but she did not have a meal. Layla had passed out on the couch in a virtual coma the night before, a bottle of vodka hollowed out on the floor next to her. Ronja had managed to find a hunk of bread in the cabinet, but had given it to Cosmin. She sat at the long table, drinking the milk provided by the school with fervor, sucking each calorie out of the soggy carton. Two girls with clean platinum braids snickered at her over the tops of their crisp sandwiches.

She was seven. Lying awake in bed, The Night Song roaring in her ear. She had been naughty that day, stolen an apple from a stall, eaten it in the alley next to her house.

Ronja crashed back into her body, gasping for air and steeped in sweat. A ring of faces orbited her tilting vision.

"Hel—" she gasped.

Her memories buried their hooks in her again.

Six months after the apple. Her first true migraine happened in the middle of history class. She had spoken out against something her teacher had said, something about The Conductor. White lights swarmed in her vision, and she had cried out. The other children laughed. The teacher averted his eyes.

She was ten. She had locked the bathroom door, crawled to the top of the sink. She sat cross-legged in the shallow basin, staring into the foggy mirror. The skin on her face was taut and pale as parchment. She was crying, tugging at her scalp. Chunks of her dark curls were coming out in her hands. She thought she was turning into a mutt. She had watched her mother's hair thin rapidly, her nails flake from their beds. She did not realize that these were also the symptoms of starvation.

She was twelve. Her right eye was swollen shut. Blood poured from her nose. Sharp pain ruptured in her ribs each time she inhaled. The boys had jumped her out of nowhere, pinned her to the brick wall. People trudged past, looked into her face, then away. The smallest boy stood guard at the mouth of the alley.

She was fourteen. She had turned in her textbooks and applied for a job as a driver. Scrawny though she was, she was tall for her age, and easily passed for the minimum age of sixteen. She cried as she exited the school, despite being relieved to escape the torment she had endured. She had seen far too many people abandon their education, and it never turned out well.

She was fifteen. She was dreaming of running through a field somewhere far away when The Night Song woke her with a series of stabbing notes. She choked down a scream by stuffing her face into her pillow. She did not know what she had done wrong.

She was sixteen, driving a steamer through endless branches of tunnels. A messenger tapped on the window of her car when she came to a stop in a station, telling her to go home immediately. She ran all the way across the city, abandoning her post and her paycheck, imagining the worst. When she arrived home, she found that Layla had discovered a library book under her pillow, wanted to know why she was wasting her time on such ridiculous things.

"Come back to us, mate."

Ronja blinked.

The world fell back into place. Each brick settled into the mortar, each tent flapped and stilled. The halo of faces above her stopped spinning. Half a dozen sets of eyes gazed down at her.

"I'm—" Ronja heaved, trying to force her apology through her tight chest.

"The memories will settle out with time," a voice to her left said.

Ronja shifted to view the speaker.

It was a girl about her age with thick black hair chopped at her cheekbones. Her features were plain, but her eyes were the color of dark honey and her skin was tan and smooth. She wore a green jumpsuit smudged with grease. The top was knotted at her waist, revealing a tank top and lean, muscular arms. The emblem of the Anthem was tattooed over her heart, and fine, intricate designs decorated her long fingers.

"A lot of us have been through it," the girl continued, kneeling next to Ronja and holding her stare as it attempted to reel back into the past. "Nothing to be ashamed of. You're seeing things as they were for the first time, bit of a skitzing shock if you ask me. You want to talk about it?"

Ronja rocked her head back and forth against the hard floor. She did not think she had the words.

"All right, but it does help. You ought to go get some sleep. Big night tonight."

Ronja nodded mutely.

The dark-haired girl gave a crooked smile.

"I'm Evie. You're Ronja, right?"

"Yes," she replied hoarsely, marveling again at the amazing speed at which news travelled around the Belly.

"You know your way back to the hospital wing?"

"I think so."

Evie stuck out a hand for her to take. Ronja gazed at it for a moment, then grasped it firmly. The black-haired girl tugged her to her feet, anchoring her as she swayed.

"You good?" Evie asked, slowly withdrawing her support.

"Yeah," Ronja lied, blinking rapidly.

Evie beamed, then reached up and pressed two fingers to Ronja's brow. This time, Ronja did not flinch away from the touch, but sank into it.

"May your song guide you home," Evie said brightly.

Ronja found herself bobbing her head again, unsure how else

to react. Was she supposed to reciprocate? To offer her thanks?

"I gotta go," Evie said, backing away before Ronja could determine the appropriate response. "Boss'll kill me if I'm late again."

"Okay. Um, thank you."

Evie raised her hand in farewell, flashing her dazzling smile, then dashed off down the curling road.

Ronja stood static for a time, attempting to gather her bearings. Her ring of gapers had disappeared, but she still felt like she was being watched. She looked around sheepishly and found a scrawny boy with large, inquisitive eyes regarding her. The boy blinked, cocked his head, as if to ask her what she had been doing rolling around on the floor.

Ronja offered him a feeble smile. For a moment his face was grave, then a sudden grin split his mask. Ronja did not have time to return it, because he was already gone, darting between the legs of adults with all the agility of an alley cat.

21: HARD FROM THE PAST

Once Ronja shook herself free from her flashbacks, she made her way back to her room and crawled under the covers. She tucked the sheets up over her head and curled her legs into her chest. Her cheeks still burned with embarrassment. Her head hummed with the remnants of those brutal memories, which had descended on her with the force and swiftness of a hurricane and now lingered like a storm's aftermath. Her panic was gone, but she was left utterly drained.

Ronja fell asleep with her forehead pressed to her knees. No sound or nightmare could puncture her shell of exhaustion.

Hours later, Roark was forced to shake her shoulders to rouse her. "Time to wake up, love," he said with a final jostle.

Ronja blinked lethargically. Her sheets were in a bundle around her legs. Roark stood over her, smiling widely and clutching a package wrapped in brown paper. The girl raised herself up on her elbows with a wince. She had managed to bruise her spine when she collapsed.

"That's not my ear, is it?" she asked, nodding at the package.

Roark tossed the parcel at her lightly. It landed in her lap with a crinkle.

"What is it?" she asked, tugging at the strings gingerly.

"A gift."

Ronja teased apart the wrappings and gasped. Her hand flew to her mouth in an overtly feminine fashion she had never thought herself capable of. In the discarded paper was a ludicrously fine emerald dress. She lifted it delicately, afraid it would disintegrate at her touch.

"Roark," she hissed.

"You don't like it?"

"It's not that."

"What, then?"

"How much was this?"

"That's not what you're supposed to say."

"I . . . I can't wear this."

"You have to."

"No, I mean, *I* can't wear this."

Roark narrowed his eyes.

"Why not?"

"It'd be pointless."

Roark let out a low groan and clapped his hand to his brow.

"You girls and your standards of beauty."

"This has nothing to do with my self-esteem," Ronja snapped. "I'm just being realistic."

"It's a gift, love. Accept it with grace."

"*Fine*. Thank you."

Roark shook his head, but his usual, lopsided grin had returned.

"I'll leave you to get ready, then. Iris will be in soon to show you where you can clean up."

"Is anyone going to tell me what's going on?" she called after him as he disappeared through the drapes.

"Nope," he shouted back with a ringing laugh.

Ronja sighed, then returned her attention to the dress in her lap. She handled it with the very tips of her fingers. She had never seen anything so beautiful, not even when she visited the middle ring as a child.

"Oh, that's lovely," a soft voice commented from curtained entry.

Ronja started, dropping the dress into its wrappings as if it had burned her. Iris stood in the gap, holding back the curtain with a freckled forearm. Her curls were drawn away from her face with a black ribbon, and she wore a navy dress that plunged low on her chest.

"It matches your eyes," Iris continued, flitting into the room on the balls of her bare feet.

"Thanks," Ronja replied.

"Trip feels bad, that's why he got it for you."

"Why on earth would he?" Ronja inquired dryly.

Iris smiled ruefully and perched on the edge of the bed. "You know, I was born down here," Iris said, peering past the confines of the room. "I've never had a Singer. I don't even know what The Music sounds like."

"Lucky you," Ronja said.

"Lucky you, too."

Ronja arched a skeptical eyebrow. The surgeon twisted to look at her. The light from the oil lamp rebounded off her hazel irises.

"I've been told it's hard at first," the girl continued. "Withdrawal, the memories you didn't know you had, the ones that are worse than you thought. But once you get past it, you're really free."

"I know," Ronja said, more to herself than Iris. "I can think for myself, but that's half the problem."

Iris laughed and bobbed her head. "Aptly put," she said. "Maybe it's time you stopped thinking and started feeling." The surgeon stood and clapped her hands to dispel the sudden melancholy. "Come on, let's get you cleaned up. Bring the dress."

Ronja disentangled herself from the sheets and followed the spritely girl out of the alcove, the gown tucked carefully under her arm.

Iris wove expertly through the pathways. Voices droned like auto engines, smiles were exchanged like cash. The air was thick with anticipation, the fumes of celebratory cigarettes and home-cooked meals.

Iris led Ronja down the short flight of steps to the tracks that once shuttled steamers. Ronja felt queer stepping onto the rails. She could not shake the fear that a train might plow her over at any moment.

"This way," Iris called over her shoulder, sensing she had stopped.

Ronja hurried after her guide as she made for the left-hand tunnel, which was obscured by a sheer yellow curtain. When she reached the mouth of the tube, Iris threw a smile over her shoulder and disappeared in a swish of vibrant cloth. Ronja stepped forward cautiously and brushed aside the silk.

Strings of electric lights drooped from the arching ceiling like sagging vines. Dim oil lamps dangled from hooks on the walls, accenting the glow. The air was humid and heavy with the scent of water and flowers. The noise of the Belly was inexplicably muted, though only a thin cloth separated the alcove from the platform.

In the middle of the wide-set tracks stood a massive stone bath. Three drenched plywood steps led up to the long, wide pool. Women of all ages lounged inside. Some sat on the lip scrubbing their feet. Others had submerged themselves completely, cleansing the oil and dirt from their hair. Candles, slumped from the heat of their wicks, stood on the rim of the tub, their wax pooling in the water.

"Welcome to our bathhouse," Iris said, putting her hands on her hips.

"Wow," was all Ronja could think to say.

"Clean ground water comes in through that tube over there," Iris pointed at a wide-mouthed faucet spitting water into the tub. "And the dirty water goes out through a drain at the bottom."

"Isn't it freezing?" Ronja asked.

"Nah," Iris said, grinning widely. "Some of our techis rigged up the pipes from the closest working station to bring in the steam."

Ronja shook her head wonderingly. Some of her dirty curls escaped from her bun and fell in her eyes. She swept them away absentmindedly.

"I'll stay with you, if you want," Iris offered. "I'm nearly ready."

"Thank you," Ronja said gratefully. She shrugged off her thick jacket and folded it in the corner, then kicked off her boots and placed them atop the coat like paperweights.

She paused before slipping out of her sweater and trousers. Her body was pockmarked with scars. A discolored lump on her abdomen marked the afternoon she was stabbed with a pencil in the sixth grade. The puncture wound was never treated, and the lead was still burrowed beneath her flesh. A small white moon beneath her ribs recalled the night an Off had decided she had looked at him funny. She'd paid at the end of a stinger. A particularly nasty laceration at her left collarbone memorialized the day Layla had smashed a vodka bottle against the table and flew at her.

Ronja shuddered.

For better or worse, there was no Music to mute her memories now. If she thought too hard, they would consume her again.

Ronja took a deep breath and peeled off her woolen sweater and her pants while Iris pretended to examine her nails. She folded the articles atop her growing stack, then marched toward the bath with her chin raised.

No one stared or cringed in disgust as Ronja mounted the steps and slid into the pleasantly warm water. Relief ballooned in her chest. She sighed as the water crested her shoulders, her heavy hair fanning around her in a dark halo.

"Warm enough?" Iris asked, sitting on the side of the tub and dipping her feet into the steaming water.

In response, Ronja slipped beneath the surface, sending up a stream of air bubbles. Laughter broke out above the liquid seal.

Then the hum began, rippling around the catacomb like a breath of wind. Ronja surfaced, wiping the pearls from her eyelashes.

The collective thrum emanated from deep within the women's chests. It rose and fell like a bird riding air currents. Ronja turned to Iris for answers, but the girl was part of the buzz. She winked, licked her lips, then spoke.

I once knew a boy with river-stone skin
Smooth from the water, hard from the past
With my marble heart we seemed akin
But when he looked at me I saw we could not last

I once knew a boy with eyes of coal
They glowed through his lids, bright as gold
I thought perhaps they would spark my soul
Still somehow his gaze was cold

Iris spun the words like threads, pitching her voice higher and lower as she followed some intangible instructions. The words were just like those Roark had spoken during her amputation. They seemed to writhe with emotion, taking on their own lives when they hit the air. The women continued to hum beneath Iris's fluctuating voice.

Ronja listened, her jaw slack.

I once knew a boy with a birdsong tongue
He woke each morning with the rising sun
With keyboard teeth and a heart like a drum
But when winter came he was on the run

When winter came he was on the run
When winter came he was on the run

Iris fell quiet. She leaned back on her palms and let her eyes fall shut. Her feet dangled limply, their forms shivering in the water. A wave of applause flitted around the bath. Ronja joined in, though she did not understand exactly what she commending.

The chatter and bustle resumed, littered with the gentle shiftings of the pool.

"What . . . was that?" Ronja asked.

"That," the girl replied, her eyes snapping open. "Was a song."

22: WAR PAINT

Despite Ronja's repeated inquires, Iris refused to explain her bizarre performance. Swishing her feet back and forth, the redhead jabbered on about a string unrelated of subjects. Ronja did her best to follow, but it was difficult to hear over the ferocious hammering in her chest. She could not shake the lingering effect of . . . whatever it was that had just occurred.

The strange ritual filled her both with striking melancholy and inexplicable joy. The images that accompanied the words still played like a moving picture on the backs of her eyelids. The steady hum still rang in her ear each time she dipped her head below the water.

Iris told her that she needed to hurry, so Ronja washed her body quickly with the slab of homemade soap. When she was finished, Ronja stepped from the tub, shivering. Iris tossed her a towel and she wrapped it around her torso hastily. The heat drew out the color in her scars.

Reveling in the rare gift of total cleanliness, Ronja slipped into her boots and undergarments while Iris conversed with a group of women on the edge of the pool. Ronja slid into the dress Roark had given her. Iris drifted back to her to assist her with the buttons that scaled her spine.

A surge of unprecedented excitement swelled in her throat as she looked down at herself. The soap had softened her parched skin. It seemed to glow against the emerald dress, which accentuated what few curves she possessed. The rich fabric cascaded to her mid-thigh in uneven waves. It looked as though it had been purposefully shredded. The skirt shimmered dully when she moved. Her neckline did not plunge as Iris's did, but revealed the crests of her freckled shoulders. Best of all, most of her blemishes were hidden.

"Looks like chiffon—do you like it?" Iris asked, snapping the last button into place at the base of her neck.

Ronja nodded, though she had no idea what chiffon was.

"Turn," Iris demanded.

Ronja spun, the skirt billowing around her. She had never felt so feminine. It was not an unpleasant sensation.

"Gorgeous" Iris dubbed her, clapping her hands together.

"Thanks," Ronja replied, itching her nose rather forcefully.

Iris jabbed a ringed finger at her face. "Makeup."

Ronja blanched.

"It's not what you think," Iris promised. She grabbed Ronja by an exfoliated hand and dragged her deeper into the tunnel.

There were no homes in the dimly lit cavern, but there was plenty of furniture. Threadbare sofas, armchairs, and pillows huddled around small fires. Stacks of books as tall as Ronja lined the walls. Women and girls of all ages lounged among the stacks. Some read, others spoke in soft tones.

"Only girls are allowed back here," Iris explained as they walked. She pointed left, where about a dozen stalls stood against the wall. Through the mesh of voices, Ronja heard the unmistakable sound of water whooshing down pipes. "We managed to set up indoor plumbing a few years ago, which is fantastic. You wouldn't believe the smell when we had latrines."

Ronja wrinkled her nose at the thought.

"The boys have the same thing set up on the other side," Iris continued, jabbing her thumb over her shoulder.

"How did you get all this stuff down here?" Ronja asked, fixating on a particularly large couch that could not possibly fit in the service elevator Roark had pointed out.

"One of the tunnels used to be open, but Wilcox decided to have it closed off for obvious reasons. Although, it would be nice if we could get a new—"

"Who's Wilcox?"

"The only guy who outranks Ito," Iris explained, switching gears fluidly. "He and his team have infiltrated a whole bunch of Off stations around the city, so they're gone most days. Wilcox has worked all the way up to sergeant in the core. He might even meet The Conductor some day soon. Good day for us, bad day for him. Here we are."

The tunnel had come to an end in a hulking wall of rubble. The debris filled the tube from floor to ceiling. Scarcely a ribbon of air could snake through it. A makeshift salon had been erected in the shadow of the impregnable barrier. Encircled by dripping candles and several powerful oil lamps was a sagging dresser, complete with a cracked mirror. Several girls roughly Ronja's age were crowded around the mirror, applying color to their faces.

"Evie!" Iris called.

Ronja missed a step.

Evie whipped around and beamed at Iris. She was nearly unrecognizable. Her cropped hair was sleek, her skin free of grit. She wore a pair of billowing, rust-colored pants and a shirt that revealed her muscular stomach. What was most remarkable about her appearance, however, was her face. It was not smeared with makeup as Ronja had expected, but with bold streaks of black and white paint.

War paint.

Ronja jumped half a foot when Iris rushed past her and lunged at Evie with a reverberating whoop. She tackled the girl with such ferocity Ronja wondered if a fight was about to break out. Instead, Evie laughed and lifted the redhead in her arms. She spun Iris once, then planted a kiss firmly on her mouth.

Ronja blinked.

"Ronja, this is my genius girlfriend, Evie," Iris said, slipping her hand around the taller girl's waist. "She's the best techi in the Belly, the only reason we have a stable stream of electricity around here."

"Psh," Evie waved her hand as if she were swatting a fly. "She's exaggerating."

Ronja eyed the techi anxiously, fumbling with her reply. She did not want Iris to know about her collapse; she would fuss incessantly.

"Nice to meet you, Ronja," Evie said with a wink.

The movement had been so quick and subtle, Ronja wondered if she had imagined it. "You too," she said, her voice cracking.

"You clean up nice, mate," Evie complimented her with a grin.

"Your accent . . ." Ronja had failed to notice the girl's rhythmic inflection in the midst of her anxiety attack, but it was certainly not

Revinian.

"My parents came from Arexis," Evie explained, her lilting accent bobbing in the humid air.

"Arexis," Ronja repeated. "Across the sea?"

"That's the one. Hope I get there one day, if we ever get out of this place."

"All right, enough," someone scolded them, emerging from the shadows to nudge Evie in the ribs.

Ronja felt her heart hit the floor. It was Terra.

"We have our work cut out for us," the blonde said with a deliberate glance at Ronja's untamed hair.

Terra looked savage. Her face was decorated with a geometric design of black, red, and blue. Bangles clinked hollowly on her wrists as she swiped her hair from her face and offered Ronja a bitter smile.

"Yes," Iris said excitedly, evidently taking Terra's words as enthusiastic.

Ronja was sat on an overturned crate. Terra and a girl named Darren, whose dark skin was adorned with strips of white paint, did her hair.

Darren was gentle with her unruly curls, but Terra was vicious. She heaved and yanked her locks as if she were searching for riches in the knots. Evie and Iris dyed her face, arms, and chest varying shades of black, blue, and green. At one point, Iris slipped away and returned some time later, her porcelain skin now embossed with violet and white.

The smell of the paint was biting, but it was cool and refreshing against Ronja's skin. It dried quickly and crusted on the planes of her face, chest, and arms. As the four girls worked to alter her appearance, she hung in a strange place between tranquility and discomfort. As much as she wanted to be a part of whatever tradition was about to take place, she was highly unused to being labored over.

"Keep still," Evie snipped, steadying her jaw with a labor-hardened hand.

"Sorry."

"Didn't your mother ever do your makeup?" Iris asked.

"No," Ronja said shortly.

Iris flicked her eyes toward Evie, but neither commented on her sudden harshness.

Lean fingers brushed over her slowly healing wound. The touch seared the forming scar tissue, but Ronja refused to flinch.

"It's healing well," Terra commented. The words were benign, but her tone was acrid. "Any dizziness?"

"Not anymore," Ronja replied, craning her neck so she could look Terra in the eye.

"Lucky you. It took me a month before I could walk straight."

The girl shoved back a curtain of pale hair to reveal an ugly scar as long and wide as her pointer finger.

Ronja swallowed dryly. She turned back to Iris and Evie, her stomach flopping like a fish on a deck.

Terra did not speak again, and did not soften her technique. Evie and Iris made up for her silence twofold, chattering about things Ronja could not begin to comprehend. Darren chimed in occasionally, but seemed to be relatively introverted, which Ronja could respect.

"That should do it," Iris said, finally stepping back.

"Nice work," Evie cooed.

"Do you want to see?" Iris asked.

"Of course, she does," Terra snapped, shoving Ronja off the upturned crate.

Ronja stumbled, then whipped around, her tongue curling into a nasty insult. Before she could get the first syllable out, Iris was tugging her toward the mirror, bouncing up and down like a child.

"Look," the surgeon coaxed her.

Ronja allowed her eyes to drift up to her reflection. She could not hold back a quiet gasp when her eyes greeted their twins.

Her hair fell in soft, rich curls to the base of her ribcage. The right half of her crown was braided, the triplet plaits running horizontally across her skull. Black ribbons were woven seamlessly into the braids, clearly displaying her sutures. Ugly as it was, Ronja found she was not particularly self-conscious, not when others shared the mark. Her eyes were luminous against the brilliant hue of the dress.

But what truly shocked her were the patterns painted on her skin.

The meandering designs were mostly black with blue and green shadows highlighting the bold strokes. A string of green dots decorated her left cheekbone, and a bold branch of black swooped down from her hairline, ending in a curling hook above her right eyebrow. Her collarbones were highlighted black and blue, and rings of color ran up and down her bare arms.

Just below her left collarbone was the insignia of the Anthem.

"This is . . . " her fingertips hovered over the damp, concentric circles.

"Brilliant," Iris finished for her.

Ronja nodded dumbly.

A horn, not unlike the blast of a steamer, exploded though the tube.

"It's time!" Evie crowed. She snagged Iris's arm and tore back down the tunnel, whooping like a maniac. They were swallowed by the crowd working toward the platform.

Ronja was about to jog after them when Terra shouldered past her roughly, smearing several lines of paint on her arm.

"Watch it, *mutt*," Terra growled in her ear.

The girl stalked away, Darren trailing in her wake, seemingly oblivious. Ronja was left with her trembling reflection in the mirror.

23: THE JAM

"You look fantastic."

The voice jolted Ronja from her stupor. Somehow, she had managed to find her way back to the platform, though she did not remember the trip. She looked around, vaguely bemused.

A large space had been cleared on the stone floor, making way for a swelling throng. Everyone was adorned in paint and chattered excitedly.

Roark stood before her in the midst of the gathering crowd. He was barefoot, as were the rest of the Anthemites. His arms and face were streaked with black and gold. The Anthem's crest was tattooed over his heart, a more perfect rendition of the one wrought beneath her own collarbone.

"Thanks," Ronja replied absently. "You too."

"Was that a compliment?"

"I didn't want to bruise your feelings."

"Sorry, what was that?" Roark cupped his ear to hear her over the growing cacophony.

"I asked what was going on."

Roark grinned and gestured widely at the high ceilinged chamber. "This, love, is a jam."

"Like a traffic jam?" Ronja asked with mock politeness.

"Close. Tell me, in the short time you have been here, have you heard a song?"

"Iris did something with her voice, but I don't understand it."

"I suppose you wouldn't," Roark replied.

"What's that supposed to mean?"

"Not you personally, anyone in your situation."

"My situation?"

"Ah," Roark held up a finger.

As if in response, a hush settled over the knot of Anthemites.

The boy smiled down at her crookedly, his dark eyes gleaming like pools of oil. Ronja felt her heart falter. For once it was not from fear.

Silence reigned. The electric lights clicked off in droves until only the natural light of the fires remained, casting flickering shadows across the soaring walls. Ronja held her breath, though for what she did not know.

A deep, thundering beat began, like patterned footsteps stomping on hollow ground. Ronja felt a shiver scale her spine. The rhythm twined with her heartbeat and filled her lungs. A mountain range of gooseflesh erupted on her arms, though she was not cold.

"Come on," Roark whispered, grasping her hand.

He began to pull her forward through the crush. The Anthemites grumbled at first, but hushed when their eyes fell upon Ronja.

Roark halted when they reached the lip of the crowd, then reached back and tugged Ronja in front of him. She stood quite still, Roark at her back, and stared.

The quiet mob had formed a ring around one man. His skin was stained black, gold, and green. His eyes were closed, wrinkled in concentration. From a thick leather strap around his neck hung a wooden tub sealed with a swath of taut animal skin. With his palms and fingers, he hammered on the face of the skin, producing the thundering sound that shook Ronja's bones.

"That's a drum," Roark breathed in her ear.

Ronja did not know if it was his closeness, or the echo of the drum that made her skin tingle.

She whipped around when a new sound struck up behind her. A cheer went up from the crush, and Ronja grinned despite her lack of comprehension. Evie was moving toward them through a gap, swaying in time with the drum. In her hands was the strangest object Ronja had ever seen. It resembled a golden pipe, and was as long as her arm. Evie's lips were wrapped around its end, and her fingers flew across a series of valves along its flank. From the basin at the base of the pipe, a fluid sequence of sounds streamed, meshing with the pulse of the drum.

Evie winked at Ronja as she passed, then stepped into the center of the ring.

"That's a saxophone," Roark whispered in her ear.

Saxophone. Drum. Saxophone. Drum.

"Trip!"

Ronja turned as a boy about Cosmin's age appeared at Roark's elbow. He clutched an oblong black case in his arms nervously, as if it might explode at any moment.

"Thanks, Barty," Roark said fondly, rumpling the boy's hair and taking the odd case by its handle.

Ronja eyed it curiously, but Roark offered no explanation.

Cheers ballooned as another man joined the two performers. He carried a small wooden apparatus lined with a circle of tiny metal plates. Roark called it a tambourine. The sound was jarring, but electrifying.

The crowd opposite them split. Ronja raised her eyebrows as a man wheeled an oak machine into the clearing. It was roughly the size of a table, and possessed two rows of interlocking black-and-white levers. He left it at the center of the ring, then filtered back into the throng. A girl with auburn hair and rice-paper skin took his place. Her eyes were milky white. She was blind, Ronja realized with a jolt.

"Her name is Delilah, and that"—Roark pointed at the bizarre apparatus—"is a piano."

Delilah's disability did not seem to hinder her as she took her place before the piano and touched her svelte fingers to the plain of levers. Ronja looked on in unbridled fascination as the girl rolled the kinks from her neck, waved at the audience (much to their jubilation), and began to pound out patterns on the black and white levers.

Ronja inhaled sharply.

The clear sound released from the piano was more beautiful than the bells that tolled from the clock tower in the core.

Ronja felt tears prick the corners of her eyes. She brushed them away, checking around to see if anyone had noticed her, but it appeared that all were entranced by the performance.

"Excuse me."

Roark brushed past her gently, carrying the strange box with him. He crouched on the edge of the clearing and flipped the clasps on the lid. Ronja craned her neck to see what was inside, but his shoulders obstructed her view.

Roark rose swiftly, something roughly the shape of the case and the length of his arm in his left hand, and a thin rod in his right. He shot Ronja a grin over his shoulder. "And this is a violin."

The boy stepped into the clearing. A roar flared in the mob. The drum sped up and the piano, saxophone, and tambourine followed. Roark placed the wooden instrument on his shoulder, pressed the finely carved rod to the bundle of metal cords on its face and . . .

It was as if the voice of the violin sparked the wicks of each individual soul, jolting them from sleep.

As Roark's hand, continuous with the rod, flew across the strings, Ronja began to move. It could have been her emotions that ignited her muscles, or the way the other bodies moved around her. Stamping their feet, slapping their hands against their thighs, against their chests, friend swinging around friend and lover around lover like moons orbiting planets. Ronja could not know for sure.

All she knew was that she was moving, she was grinning, she was crying, she was breathing, and it was not because anyone was tugging at her ear telling her to do so.

She was moving because it felt right. She was grinning because there was no other way to be. She was crying because she had never heard anything so beautiful, or felt something so profound. And she was breathing, because for the first time in her life, she wanted to.

When it ended, Ronja was not prepared.

It seemed both a lifetime and a fraction of a second had passed since the jam began, and she did not want it to end.

Ronja still rocked on her heels long after the violin had released its last breath.

"Easy there," laughed a familiar voice. A slim hand touched her back. Iris stood next to her, her hair frazzled, her eyes bright. Her paint was flaking away, corroded by her salt sweat. "How was your first jam? Wasn't Evie fantastic? And Delilah? Roark was okay too, that pitcher."

"I . . . I . . . "

"Give her some space, Iris," Roark called from behind her.

Ronja spun to find him crouching on the floor before them, packing the violin away in its snug case.

She bent down, paint-smudged fingers outstretched. The rich wooden face of the violin gleamed in the firelight. The strings were dusted with white, as if a soft snow had fallen on them while he played.

"Oi, don't touch her," Roark snapped.

"Her?" Ronja asked, drawing her hand back warily.

Iris snorted when Roark failed to answer. "He's very particular about Sigrun," she said, hiding a mischievous smile behind her fingers.

"I don't understand," Ronja admitted, looking from Iris, to Roark, to the instrument.

"It doesn't matter," Roark said hastily, shutting and locking the lid. He got to his feet, his wicked grin firmly in place. "What matters is, what did you think?"

"It was . . . " Ronja riffled through her vocabulary, trying to find a word that suited the jam. "I don't think I have the words for it," she finally said. "It felt strange, sort of like . . . like a dream I had once."

Ronja let slip the confession before her lips could block it. A blush peeked between the strokes of paint adorning her cheeks. To her surprise, neither Roark nor Iris was laughing.

"What happened in the dream?" Iris probed.

"I was running through a field," Ronja said. Her eyes trailed something far away, just out of her line of sight. "I was running, and it was quiet. My Singer was broken, or gone. I couldn't hear The Music, but I could hear everything else."

"I wouldn't describe a jam as quiet," Iris said with a chuckle.

Roark was silent, searching her face.

"I don't get it though," Ronja said, her voice twisted with frustration and wonderment. "What *was* that?"

"Music," Roark replied. He spoke the word the way a child might cradle an injured bird. His eyes were as soft as feathers. "That was *real music*."

24: SKIN DEEP

The Anthemites filtered back to their homes, yawning and stretching the night from their muscles. A sleepy sort of comfort settled over the Belly. Voices were muted, fond goodbyes shared. Everything was bathed in the soft glow of the oil lamps, cook fires, and candles.

Ronja sat before one such fire next to Iris and Evie. Darren, two older boys named James and Elliot, and a younger girl called Kala sat across from them, sharing a quiet joke. A bottle of whisky was passed from hand to hand, the brown liquid steadily disappearing into their stomachs and heating their veins. Evie warned her it was strong, but evidently Ronja had inherited Layla's tolerance. She scarcely felt flushed.

Following the jam, Ronja had been introduced to a whirlwind of Anthemites. Everyone wanted to touch her forehead, and no one asked her probing questions about her origins. One boy barely higher than her hip asked her what The Quiet Song felt like, but he was swatted on the back of his curly head.

No one stared at her wound. No one turned their nose up at her. They wanted to know her, to hear her speak, to hear her laugh. It was both exhilarating and exhausting.

Her dark memories did not puncture the euphoric bubble.

"You were really good, Evie," Ronja now said, glancing up at the techi and away from the hypnotic flames.

Evie looked down at her fondly through her curtain of black hair. Iris was now snoring softly in her lap.

"Thanks, mate," Evie said, taking a swig of the liquor, then offering it to Ronja. "My mum taught me how to play."

"Play?" Ronja asked, grasping the dusty bottle and taking a gulp. She winced as it scorched her throat, then took another sip.

"Play the saxophone. She was really good. Better than me, but not by much."

"Is she here?"

"Nah, she died a few years back. Flu. Ridiculous, huh? Survived The Music, survived the riots, got taken down by a glorified cold."

"I'm sorry."

"No worries. Besides, I've got this one," Evie glanced down at her girlfriend, who was mumbling something in her sleep. Even with her jaw dangling and her hair crusted with sweat and paint, she was beautiful.

"You haven't said anything," Evie said suddenly.

Ronja shifted to better view her face. The shadows splayed across her features by the fire were severe, but her eyes were warm.

"About?" Ronja inquired.

"Me and Iris."

Evie snapped her gaze to the ceiling, and Ronja followed it. Beyond only a few meters of stone, Revinia was churning like the gears of a massive timepiece. Ronja thought she could hear the click of its gears through the shielding rock.

"I hadn't thought about it much," Ronja replied honestly. She cocked her head to the side, considering. "I've never met a girl who was in love with another girl, but I don't see why it would be a problem."

Evie contemplated this. Iris shifted in her lap. "It's more common than you'd think," Evie said. She brushed a wayward curl from Iris's forehead. It fell back into place stubbornly. "But you've never met anyone like us because The Music shuts down that part of them."

"You mean—?"

"The Music is just a mirror of The Conductor's preferences," Evie cut in, rolling a kink out of her neck. "If he doesn't like something, all he needs to do is plant the notion, and people turn against it."

"Strange, how easy it is to change our minds," Ronja commented after a pause.

"Soon as I got my Singer off I ran smack into this one carrying a stack of books about as tall as she was," Evie said, smiling down at Iris, whose snores had deepened. "It was right out of a picture show, I swear. I picked up her books, and when I looked into her eyes, I was gone."

"I'm glad you found each other," Ronja said, and found she truly meant it.

She turned back to the arching ceiling, tracing patterns in the stones. She felt safe underground, but she missed the dull flare of the stars in the smog-choked skies.

"What did you think of it?" Evie asked after awhile.

"Of the jam? It was incredible."

"See, that's real music. Not *The Music*. Just music. Plain and simple."

"It doesn't seem so simple to me."

Evie snapped her fingers and pointed at Ronja, who started. "*That's it.* That's the thing about music, it's whatever you want it to be," Evie said. She shifted to better look into her seatmate's face. "I might think a song—"

"What *is* a song?"

"I'll tell you one thing, it ain't The Day Song or the goddamn Quiet Song. Those are all made up. Stolen. A *song* is a piece of music about this or that, like a chapter is to a book. Anyway, I might hear a song and think it's about one thing, and you might hear it and think of something totally different."

"So, music is whatever you want it to be," Ronja repeated, kneading the concept in her mind.

"Bingo." Evie snapped her fingers again.

The dark-haired girl switched her attention to Iris, who was still comatose in her lap. Evie prodded her shoulder gently, and the surgeon twitched awake. Sighing loudly, Iris disentangled herself from her partner and clambered to her feet. She stretched her lean arms toward the arching ceiling, her eyes closed. Evie stood, smirking, and grabbed Iris by a porcelain hand.

"You've got company," Evie alerted Ronja, nodding to their left.

Ronja followed the gesture to Roark, who was approaching at a leisurely pace. He had washed the swaths of paint from his arms and face, and his sweat-stiffened hair was pulled into a knot.

"G'night, mate," Evie called, leading Iris down one of the paths. Ronja waved, then turned back to Roark.

"Evie's great, isn't she?" he asked, coming to a stop beside her.

"Yeah, seems like it," Ronja replied, offering him the bottle. He accepted with an arched brow.

"Seems?" he asked, taking a generous gulp. He dropped down beside her on the bench, his shoulder brushing hers lightly. Darren and her friends were breaking apart across the fire. They whipped good natured insults over their shoulders as they went their separate ways.

Ronja twisted to face Roark, her spine abruptly stiff. "This all seems just a little too good to be true, know what I mean?"

Roark shook his head.

"I just . . . " She paused, unsure of how to convey her thoughts.

Ronja leaned forward, pressed her elbows into her knees. Her eyes swam as they fixated on the shuddering flames. Her memories were returning in the afterglow of the jam, battering her skull from the inside out. Spurred by her thoughts, she shot to her feet and whirled to face Roark. His regal features were jagged in the firelight.

"Can you keep a secret?" Ronja blurted.

A crease formed between Roark's eyebrows, but he nodded. The whiskey stood beside him on the bench, forgotten.

"I ran the package because my family was going to starve within a matter of weeks," she said. "I'm the only provider for my two cousins and my mother, who's completely . . . disabled."

Roark's face was impassive. He waited patiently for her to continue.

"When I was fourteen I had to drop school," she continued. "I tried to finish on my own, but it was hard. I'm not book-smart any more than you're poor, but I understand things. I always have."

The words were spilling from her, and there was no dam in the world that could stop what she was going to say next.

"Since I was a kid I've been forced to the outside of everything because of stupid, skitzing prejudice. I have one friend, two cousins, and a mother who treats me like shit. You know what that gave me? Perspective."

Her hands trembled now. She clasped them behind her to calm them. Her voice had pitched an octave higher than she thought it could.

"You keep saying The Music alters your perspective, makes the bad seem normal. It put me in a lot of pain, skitzed up the way I saw myself, but . . . I don't think it ever really worked on me. I was too miserable. Nothing could have convinced me that everything was okay."

Ronja fell silent, gathering her scattered notions as she sank to the seat. A disintegrating piece of plywood shifted among the flames. Clumps of ash peeled away from it with sleepy sighs. The girl rubbed her aching temples.

"What are you saying?" Roark asked after a long moment.

Ronja rolled her fingers into fists. The room was tilting on its axis, the ceiling was rotating, but her soul felt as still as a stagnant lake.

"Thank you," Ronja heard herself say. "Not for showing me that The Conductor was evil, because I think I always knew that, even if I could never say it. Thank you for freeing me from my Singer, and for letting me know that . . . "

"What?" Roark reached forward and grabbed her balled fist, unfurling her fingers with his cool touch.

Thank you for letting me know that I'm not a bad person. Thank you for showing me there's something better out there. Thank you for showing me music. Thank you for setting me free.

"Nothing. Just, thank you."

Roark looked like he was burning to ask her more, but he just smiled and nodded softly. "You're welcome."

Suddenly it seemed as though the air between them had evaporated, the space compressed. The boy tightened his fingers around her curled fists, pulling her gently toward him. A thousand thoughts whipped through her mind, but they all led in one direction: Roark.

"Trip!" a man called.

Roark leapt to his feet, stepping around her hastily. Ronja rose and spun on her heel, her heart in her mouth. A gasp tore from her chest and she stumbled forward into the bench. The whisky bottle tumbled from the rickety seat and shattered on the floor, spraying her bare calves.

"Offs," she choked.

A small knot of Offs strode toward them, their trench coats fanning behind them and their stingers gleaming at their hips. The Conductor's bleached insignia scowled from their lapels. Ronja snatched Roark by the arm, but the boy was standing at attention, his spine rigid.

"Roark?" she breathed, tugging at his arm. The boy glanced down at her curiously, but did not budge. "We have to run."

"Run?" the head Off asked. He came to a stop before them, and his team followed suit. His buzzed brown hair was peppered gray, and his eyes were the color of steel. Canyons carved by stress branched across his forehead, and he was four days late for a shave.

"Who is this girl, Trip?" the man inquired, turning to the boy.

"This is Ronja. She arrived a few nights ago," Roark replied.

"Was she cleared?"

"By Ito, yes."

"I see," the Off raised a gloved hand to Ronja's face, and she jerked away, a chunk of glass crunching under the heel of her boot. Surprise flickered across the man's weathered features. "I'm not going to hurt you—I just wanted to see if you had a Singer."

Her heart wriggling in her chest, Ronja clenched her jaw and tilted her head so he could see the puckered scar where her ear used to be. The man appraised the newly freed flesh with a satisfied nod.

"So what was this, then?" Ronja asked, keeping her voice low so it did not tremble. "Some sort of test? A trick? Seems like a lot of trouble for one skitzer from the outer ring."

The Off cocked his head as he mulled over her words. "I'm not sure what you mean," he finally admitted.

"Couldn't give me a peaceful death, huh?" Ronja asked, her voice caustic. "So, what's it going to be? A new Singer? Stingers? Or are you finally going to finish what you started with my mother?"

The man looked to Roark now, a thick eyebrow arched. For a moment the boy appeared just as baffled as the older man. Then he slammed his palm into his forehead.

"Oh!" Roark exclaimed. "You're in your Off uniforms!"

Ronja froze. Silence fell.

The team burst into a fit of rumbling laughter. The ringleader cracked a wry smile, though he did not join in the loud guffaws. Ronja gaped at them, jaw slack.

"I'm so sorry, love," Roark said, swallowing his own laughter. "They're—."

"Infiltrating the Offs," Ronja muttered under her breath, ducking her chin to hide her mortified blush. She had completely forgotten Iris's explanation.

"They won't hurt you," Roark went on, trying heroically to smother his chuckles. "Although, judging by your expression, you might need another day or two to recover."

The gray-eyed man stepped in and extended his hand for Ronja to grasp. "Apologies, Ronja . . . "

"Zipse," Ronja replied curtly. She grasped the offered hand and matched his viselike grip. "Ronja Zipse."

"An interesting name," the man replied, pulling his hand away rather quickly. "I'm Tristen Wilcox."

"Nice to meet you," Ronja said icily.

"I'm sorry we frightened you, it was not our intention," Wilcox apologized. Ronja's lip curled, but she did not respond. "What do you think of our operation?" the man went on.

"It's fine, I suppose," Ronja replied curtly. "I could have done without the kidnapping and mutilation, but it's nice to have the buzzing out of my head."

"Ah."

Wilcox glanced at Roark, who wore a blank mask in place of his trademark grin. The man turned back to Ronja, who regarded him levelly.

"I assume you're staying in the medical wing. We can find you some permanent housing tomorrow."

"Thank you," Ronja said. "I'll need space for my family as well."

"Your family?" Wilcox asked, arching a silvery brow.

"Ito said they could stay," Ronja said, crossing her arms defensively.

"I have the final say in all matters," Wilcox replied in a clipped tone. "You look like you're from the outer ring, there are many large families out there. How many siblings do you have?"

Ronja felt her remaining ear grow hot.

"Zero," she replied flatly. "Two cousins, and my mother."

"Wilcox," Roark said, stepping forward, his hands raised placatingly. A fragment of glass crunched under his boot. "She was heavily resistant to The Music."

"Is that so?" Wilcox peered at Ronja, vague curiosity sparking in his iron gaze.

"It is," Ronja replied, swelling with unexpected pride.

Wilcox chewed on his words. A muscle bulged in his cheek.

"Your family is welcome among us," Wilcox finally said. "It was a pleasure, Ronja." He spun and marched away, his coat trailing him like a black storm cloud. His team followed, chattering among themselves.

"That," Roark said, "was fantastic."

"Yeah, sure," Ronja muttered. She turned her nose up and stalked away, realizing faintly that she had no idea where she was going.

"Oi!" Roark shouted, jogging after her. "Are you really upset about that? Wilcox is harsh, but he's like that with everyone."

"No," Ronja lied. "But I have to go now. My cousins need me."

"We're going to get them tomorrow, don't be ridiculous."

"I have to make sure they're safe."

"One night isn't going to change anything."

"You don't know that."

"Ronja, what's going on? Three minutes ago you were thanking me. Why are you so upset?"

"I . . . "

Ronja slowed her pace, then stopped, fixating on her boots.

She did not know, precisely. Wilcox was undeniably harsh, but she was not one to quail in the face of a blunt personality, especially when it matched her own. Perhaps it was seeing the Offs and thinking the worst. It had shaken her to the bone. Ito and Roark had promised her that no harm would come to her family, but mutts were monitored far more closely than the average Revinian. What if . . .

Panic burgeoned in her mind.

What if she had been deluding herself? She wanted desperately to believe this place was a haven for herself and her family, but what if Roark and Ito were wrong? What if there were real repercussions for her family? She would not put it past the Offs. Even if Georgie, Cosmin, and Layla swore they knew nothing of her actions, would it be enough?

Ronja stared up at the stone barrier that encased them. It seemed to fold in on itself. The walls of the fabric homes inched closer. The dying fires hissed back to life behind her, fueled by her fear.

"I have to make sure they're okay" she muttered, her voice low.

"Don't be—"

"*Roark.*" Ronja glanced around like a frightened rabbit. The narrow walkway was empty, save for an old man stoking a fire several huts down. All the bones they had ever broken, all the bruises they had inflicted, all the insults smeared across her skin, were begging her not to tell.

She took a deep, shuddering breath. "Roark, why do you think they played The Quiet Song for me as soon as I got down here?"

Roark furrowed his brow, shifted on his feet. "The Music responds to changes in your emotions," he said. "Too much fear, too much doubt, too many questions and it builds. When it peaks, it rolls over into The Quiet."

"But you'd never seen that happen to anyone that quickly, right?" Ronja asked, knowing the answer.

"No, but—"

"My family's Singers are different."

She waited for Roark to respond, but he said nothing. His expression was impassive, but she could see the curiosity lurking behind his eyes.

I wonder how he'll look at me after this.

"My—my mother's a mutt."

Roark stiffened. Ronja felt her bones turn to dust, yet somehow she remained standing.

"Oh, skitz," Roark whispered. His eyes were glazed, blank. Ronja could see herself reflected in them, frail and terrified.

"I'm so sorry I didn't tell you," she croaked. "Please don't . . . you have to understand I'm not really a mutt. I'm still—"

"We have to go, *now*," Roark said mechanically.

He seized her hand and tore off down the walkway, dragging her in his wake. Ronja followed as fast as her recovering legs would allow.

"What's happening?" she gasped.

Roark ignored her, continuing to pull her across the platform. When they reached the west end, he yanked her around a corner and into a tighter wing of the station, where gaggles of hawkers and merchants once sold their wares. There were only half a dozen tents in the compact alcove, but they were larger than the ones on the main floor.

Roark released her and ducked into one of them. The cloth door flapped shut behind him. Ronja folded her arms over her chest, trying to soothe her trembling hands. She listened as the boy rummaged through his belongings. After a moment, he reappeared, dressed in his black coat and boots that crested his knees. His riding goggles ringed his neck.

He carried a black-muzzled pistol trimmed with thin ribbons of gold.

Ronja swallowed, eyed the gun fearfully.

"Can you shoot?" Roark asked, drawing a plainer pistol from the holster at his hip.

Ronja reached for the weapon cautiously. A chill lanced through her when her fingers brushed the handle, but she grasped it firmly. Roark released the gun to her. It was heavier than she had expected.

"No," she admitted, examining the weapon. "Why would I need to?"

"Why didn't you tell me?"

Ronja let the pistol fall to her side, disbelief plastered across her face. "Why would I?" she hissed. "It's not something to be proud of. Anyway, as far as I know I'm not really a mutt."

"I can see that," Roark growled. "But your mother is, correct? That means your entire extended family has mutt Singers."

"Ye . . . yeah."

"We need to get to your house. Fast. How well do you know the streets?"

"Like the back of my hand."

"Good, because we don't have any time for dawdling."

Roark reached for her arm, but she tucked it behind her and took a tiny step backward.

"First, tell me what's going on," she demanded.

Roark glanced about anxiously. Panic simmered in his eyes. "When someone becomes a mutt, their entire family feels the repercussions."

"No skitz," Ronja muttered.

"Their entire family is outfitted with new Singers in case the disobedience is genetic."

"Do you have a point?"

"Their Singers are *connected*. If one person hears The Quiet Song . . . "

"Everyone else hears it too," Ronja breathed.

"Not exactly," Roark corrected hastily. "The link is like an echo. They just get a taste of it, enough to put them in a temporary coma. But . . . "

"But?"

"After that they're usually taken in and . . . reconditioned."

"Reconditioned. You mean—"

"Ronja, I'm so sorry. I had no idea."

"No . . . no . . . no . . . " Ronja dropped the gun. It clattered to the floor, cartwheeling over her laces. She crumpled to her knees, dragging her fingers through her hair.

"*Ronja*, listen to me," Roark crouched down and grasped her bare shoulders with his gloved hands. She blinked up at him hazily. "There is still a chance. The coma lasts for days if undisturbed. Sometimes the Offs in the outer ring are slow. Your family might not be gone yet, but we have to go now."

Ronja sucked in an electric breath of air and grabbed the pistol. She staggered to her feet.

Faster than her brain could track, she was sprinting down the platform toward the service elevator. Roark's footsteps commenced behind her, powerful and lithe.

25: SPILLED MILK

Ronja's mind was numb.

A moment ago her thoughts had been on fire. Thoughts of Georgie, of Cosmin. Thoughts of them strapped down, tortured, twisted into mutts. Of their insides being scooped out and flooded with mangled DNA and the endless wrath of The Music. Thoughts of Layla, even. She was already a mutt. Would she simply be killed?

Then, when Roark told her there might be hope, there was nothing.

Her mind was void. Her muscles were wracked with adrenaline. She ran.

The huts blurred past. Snatches of quiet conversations studded her hammering footfalls. She knew where she was going. No matter how foreign it looked, the blueprint of the Belly was identical to all the rest of the stations. The elevator crouched on the left hand side of the atrium toward the edge of the platform.

Ronja skidded around the corner of a canvas tent and barreled blindly forward, Roark on her heels.

She almost missed the sliding iron door. It was painted with a sprawling geometric design of green and white that made her eyes swim. She blinked, then jammed her finger into the button to call the lift.

There was a distant shriek of gears, followed by a familiar, steady thrum. Neither Roark nor Ronja spoke; both breathed heavily as their exit ambled toward them.

There was a final, muffled thud followed by the polite tinkling of a bell, and the elevator door slid into the wall. The inside of the compartment was unaltered. When she crossed the threshold into the nauseous green light, it was like stepping into her past. She slammed the only button on the panel and the metal door rolled shut on the Belly.

There was a shudder as the elevator prepared to ascend. Then, with a lurch, they began to move.

Ronja kept her eyes on the reflective face of the door. She was twisted, blurred by the scratches and dents in the steel. She was still covered in war paint, which was smeared by her cold sweat. Her hair was wild, her stitches protruding like brambles from behind her exposed temple.

With shaking fingers, Ronja began to unknit the plaits that drew her curls away from the raw injury. Roark looked on silently as her locks fell in quick succession, his gaze solemn.

"Wait."

Ronja looked over at the boy, her eyebrows knit together and her jaw clenched. Roark shrugged off his overcoat and tossed it at her. She caught it with a snap of leather.

"Wear this, put the hood up," he ordered.

Ronja complied and slipped her twig arms through the sleeves. She had to fold them back twice to free her hands. The coat stirred about her ankles—it would have brushed the floor if not for the slight heel on her boots. She tugged the deep hood over her untamed curls.

There was another mannerly ding, muted by her fabric halo, and the elevator came to a shivering halt.

The door slid open on a dimly-lit aboveground chamber, its numerous windows crisscrossed with boards. The floor was littered with smashed tiles. Copper wiring had been ripped from the drywall. Plain chandeliers without light bulbs dangled precariously from the waterlogged ceiling.

Ronja shivered as she and Roark stepped from the elevator. The place made her skin crawl.

"Evening, Samson," Roark said, lifting his hand in greeting.

Ronja jumped, her heart high in her throat.

What she had thought to be a bundle of rags was in fact a man, hunched beneath one of the obstructed windows. His shoulder-length hair was matted and greasy, and a thick layer of grime caked his skin. He was wrapped in multiple layers of filthy rags, and Ronja got the sense that he was considerably smaller than he appeared. However, this did little to comfort her.

Samson grinned. His teeth were white as fresh snow.

"It's actually morning, Trip," he replied.

Roark shook his head with a fleeting smile. "It isn't morning until the sun comes up."

"Where are you two off to?" Samson asked from his place on the floor, trying to catch a glimpse of Ronja beneath the hood.

"Oh, just a late night stroll, nothing anyone needs to know about," Roark said with a cheeky wink.

Samson released a barking guffaw, shaking his head. He shifted, and Ronja could have sworn she heard something metal rap against the tiles.

"Be careful out there," Samson warned, abruptly somber. "There was a surge in Off activity a few nights back."

Ronja blanched, and was glad of the shadows hugging her face.

"We won't be on the streets for long," Roark said with a laugh, hooking Ronja by the elbow and tugging her close. "See you around, Sam."

Ronja gave the sentry a halfhearted wave as Roark led her across the eerie room to the stooped exit. He opened the door for her, flashing his teeth, and ushered her out into the steady rain. She only breathed when he had shut the creaking door on Samson, who had recommenced chuckling.

"Are we not allowed to leave?" Ronja asked, descending a flight of sopping wooden steps into an alley.

"We are," Roark said, locking the door. "But this isn't exactly a typical late-night excursion. We don't want anyone knowing about this until we're certain."

Ronja nodded absentmindedly, then peered around the dank backstreet.

The familiar gray and brown brick buildings grew from the cobblestones. The night sky growled with thunder. The alley was lined with tin trash bins and soggy crates. It smelled of rotting fish and vegetables, far more putrid than she recalled. It was freezing, even with the protection of Roark's overcoat.

Ronja plodded forward and peeked around the corner into the sprawling outer-ring avenue. The army of gas lamps strained heroically to light the street for a crowd that was not there. Only a handful of insomniacs and sap addicts milled about the gaslit roadway. A solitary truck advertising a meat-packing business rumbled past, spewing foul fumes.

The girl turned back to the side street, attempting to breathe through her mouth.

Roark had moved to the back of the alley and was working to shift a stack of wooden crates from the back wall. Ronja approached hesitantly as a large structure cloaked in an inconspicuous tarp was revealed. The boy grasped the canvas and yanked it back sharply. Ronja raised her eyebrows.

Gleaming dully in the dim light was a sleek black motorbike. It was by far the finest piece of machinery she had ever seen, untarnished by time and rust. Roark took it by the handlebars and began to wheel it past her toward the mouth of the alley. At the lip of the road, he popped the kickstand and spun back to her.

"What's your address?" he asked, drawing a cap from his pocket and shoving it over his rain darkened hair.

"756 Turner Street."

Roark pulled his scarf up around his nose and mouth and slapped his brass rimmed goggles over his dark eyes.

"Ever ridden a motorbike?" he asked, straddling the waiting vehicle, which dipped beneath his weight.

Ronja shook her head, approaching tentatively. She did not want to tell him that she had never even ridden inside an auto.

"Get on behind me and hold tight."

Ronja did as Roark told her, hoping she appeared at ease. Once she had plunked down on the leather seat, she curled her arms around his chest and tucked her head against his back to avoid the rain.

Roark adjusted his goggles, inhaled deeply, then gunned the engine. They shot into the street, drawing a shout from a bum pawing through a trash bin. Quiet houses whizzed by. The rain pelted Ronja's bare hands. Her hood flapped around her curls like the wings of a startled bird. She squeezed her eyes shut, fighting nausea she had not experienced since she had been freed of The Music.

"You all right?" Roark yelled over his shoulder.

Ronja nodded against his spine, but could not bring herself to speak. They drove for some time in silence, the gale whistling in their ears, the tires screeching with each turn. Through her sealed lids, she watched the world switch between night and day as they passed between the periodic lamps.

"What street did you say?" Roark called back to her.

"Turner!" Ronja cried, forcing her eyes open against the sting.

The deli on the corner of Turner and 23rd screamed into view. She gasped and punched the motorist in the bicep.

"Skitz! Here, *here!*" she bellowed into the wind.

Roark swore and careened around the corner, narrowly missing an elderly woman who had stepped from the curb. The old woman disappeared around the deli before Ronja could see if she was all right.

The driver eased his foot onto the brake and the world slowed. The engine slacked, grumbling quietly beneath them. Ronja turned her head sideways, watched the monotonous houses float past.

746 . . . 748 . . . 750 . . . 752 . . .

"Just up here," she said softly.

Roark angled the bike toward the curb. He flipped a switch and the engine died. The bike sagged toward the ground. The rain softened its blows.

"We don't want to draw more attention to your house than we have to," he explained, swinging his leg over the side of the bike and tugging down his scarf and goggles.

He offered Ronja his hand, but she ignored it and slipped from her seat gracelessly. Her nausea receded as soon as her soles struck the ground.

House 756 appeared the same as ever, lethargic and devoid of color . . . but there was something off about it, something Ronja could not place. She halted before the haphazard steps leading to her doorway, too unnerved to be self-conscious about the state of her home.

"Do you want me to go first?" Roark asked.

"No," she replied distantly. "But something's . . . " She trailed off as her eyes latched onto the clay pots lined beneath the kitchen window.

Georgie's vegetables were far past ripe.

Ronja let out a sound like a wounded animal and sprinted up the steps. She rammed her shoulder into the doorway. She expected it to resist her, but the lock was broken. She tumbled through the portal and collapsed into the gloomy hallway.

"Georgie? Cos? Layla?" she called, her voice cracking when it hit the empty air.

Ronja clambered to her feet. The room tilted. The ceiling traded places with the floor. Roark was saying something behind her, but she could not hear him. She lurched into the kitchen.

A fog had settled over the room, accompanied by a bone-deep hush. Time flowed sluggishly as Ronja paced around the table. Three plates picked clean waited patiently before their chairs. Two congealed glasses of milk stood guard by the dishes.

The third was smashed on the floor, the milk a clumpy stain amid the fractured glass.

"GEORGIE!" Ronja screamed, tugging her fingers down her face. "COS! LAYLA!"

"Ronja," Roark intoned from the kitchen doorway.

The girl shoved past him and stormed up the staircase. She burst into Georgie and Cosmin's bedroom. The tartan drapes fluttered hauntingly in the window. Their beds were made. Cosmin's books were stacked neatly on his desk. His reading lamp was on, the bulb flickering weakly in its socket. Ronja turned tail and thundered down the steps.

Roark was waiting for her on the landing, his expression telltale. "Ronja, I'm—"

"Shut up!" she screamed.

She wrenched open her bedroom door and flew down the steps blindly. Panting, she felt her way to her desk and ignited her oil lamp with a brutal twist of the knob. The flame coughed to life, and she looked around desperately.

The basement walls stared back at her lamely.

Ronja crouched before her bed and peeked beneath the dangling comforter. Part of her expected to see Georgie and Cosmin huddled beneath the bed, waiting for her, but she was greeted only by a bulbous spider.

Ronja let the blanket fall. Her whole body ached, but she barely registered the pain. Her mind had been severed from its anchor and was floating somewhere far above.

"Ronja . . . ?"

The uncertain voice sent her crashing back into her body. Her head snapped over to where Roark stood, his arms outstretched in consolation.

"You *bastard!*" she shrieked.

She flew at the boy and tackled him around his torso, sending them both crashing to the ground in a plume of dust. She was punching him, slapping him. All she wanted was to feel his bones break. He did not fight back or move to restrain her, but crossed his forearms over his face protectively.

Ronja wrenched her arm back abruptly. Her war paint had been washed away, but her knuckles were black and blue. Roark cracked an eyelid. They locked gazes for half a moment, one livid and one dejected.

Ink bled into the corners of Ronja's vision. Her muscles gave way beneath her. She crumbled to Roark's chest, her forehead pressed against his sternum. Her eyes stared blindly into the knit fabric of his sweater. She wanted so badly to cry, as if it could drain the blackness away, but her ducts were dry.

Roark made no move to console her, nor did he try to shift her away. He did not even try to wipe the blood from his eyes or to access his cracked nose.

His wounds had started to crust over by the time Ronja could move. She peeled herself from his chest and rose unsteadily, not daring to look at his face. Roark followed her tentatively, as if she were a skittish animal he did not wish to frighten.

"Where will they be taken?" Ronja asked hoarsely, her eyes trained carefully on her desk.

In her peripheral vision, she saw Roark touch his broken nose and wince.

"My best guess? A facility outside the wall called Red Bay Rehabilitation Clinic. They call it a clinic, but it's more of a prison. The same place your mother was turned into a mutt."

The oil was evaporating from the scorched glass chamber of

her lamp. The slit of a window she had worked so hard to keep clear was polluted with sludge.

"How do I get there?" Ronja asked.

"You can't be serious."

"I am." Ronja turned and looked Roark directly in the face, forcing herself to view her work. Upon seeing his battered features, a morsel of guilt grew in her chest. She crumpled it. "I am going to save my family, and you're going to help me do it."

"Red Bay is one of the most heavily guarded facilities in Revinia. You can't just waltz in."

"I can't, but I bet you can, *Victor Westervelt III.*"

The boy stiffened. Ronja nodded brusquely, her suspicions confirmed.

"I thought so," she murmured under her breath. "I *knew* I recognized you from somewhere. You used to appear in *The Bard* all the time when you were a kid, then you dropped off the face of the planet. I hear you spend half your time on Adagio with shiny heiresses from the core . . . " Ronja broke off, shaking her head at the dirt floor. Then, she lifted her chin, directing her words at Roark again. "Your father runs WI. Your grandfather was *the creator of The Music.* You're first in line to take over the company."

Roark seemed incapable of speech for a moment, but eventually he mustered a reply. "I'm a double agent for the Anthem," he said, raking a hand through his thick hair. "I bring them intel on my father, on the company, even scraps of information about The Conductor. Roark really is my middle name, though."

"Oh," Ronja gave a bitter laugh. "Glad you were honest about *something.*"

"You're one to talk."

"That is *not* the same thing."

"How?" Roark asked, spreading his hands pleadingly. "You wanted to be judged on your character, not a stereotype. I wanted the same."

"You know, there were portraits of your father and grandfather hanging below The Conductor's in my school. I kept wondering when yours would join them."

"I remember when they sat for those."

Ronja pushed on, ignoring him. "I used to look at them and think about my mother, how it was their fault she was turned into a . . . a monster." Ronja spat at his glossy boots. "You're just as bad as them."

Roark flinched.

"This is your fault," she continued unrelentingly. "You took me without thinking, and before you say you were just protecting your people, I already know and I don't give a damn. Now, you're going to help me get my family back, even my mutt mother, if she's still alive."

Roark observed her stoically. A patchwork of bruises had begun to form on his face, and his left eye was swelling shut. "I swear on the Anthem I will do everything in my power to return your family to you and to protect you.

"I don't need your protection," Ronja snarled, turning her back on the heir. "I need your name."

26: SNAPSHOT

Roark waited in the kitchen while Ronja collected her belongings. She had little to gather. She had left her bag on the train the night Roark abducted her, and her cap and coat were still in the Belly.

Ronja shed her damp, flimsy dress and wiped the remaining paint from her arms and face with a cloth. Shivering, she redressed in a thick gray jumper that fell past her knees and her warmest boots and stockings. She found a faded scarf in the bowels of her drawer and tied it around her head, wincing as the fabric chaffed her wound. She hoped her stitches would hold; the last thing she wanted was to attract attention to her ear, or lack thereof.

She borrowed Cosmin's knapsack and tossed in her pocketknife, lighter, and various other objects that seemed worthy of bringing on a rescue mission.

Ronja stood in the nucleus of her room for a moment, her bag slung over her shoulder. Something was tugging at her consciousness, something she was forgetting.

The epiphany struck her like a bottle smashed over her head, and she nearly yelped. She bounded back to her bed and lifted the thin mattress. It flopped against the wall, freeing a lifetime of dust from the stuffing. Coughing, she bent down and retrieved the photograph of her mother and father from its hiding place. She folded it in half and crammed it into her bag, as if to prove to herself that it was not a treasure.

Roark was at the kitchen table when she reemerged from her bedroom. He had borrowed a rag to wipe the blood from his face and looked marginally better. His left eye was sealed shut, however.

An apology built in Ronja's mouth, but she choked it down. "This is yours," she said instead, offering him his overcoat.

"Keep it," he waved her off.

Ronja continued to dangle the coat before him. He sighed

wearily and took it back. An awkward, heavy silence built between them. The girl was distinctly conscious of the purplish bruises blooming on his face, the blood turning brown on his sweater.

"Well," she began, clearing her throat.

"We can't just leave straight from here," Roark said, sliding back into his jacket. "You need new papers. We'll need fake Singers, supplies."

"That could take days," Ronja said, her voice creeping dangerously low.

"I have a friend who can forge them in three hours, and getting the supplies will just take a few minutes."

"Fine." Ronja whipped around and started toward the door, but Roark caught her wrist and spun her back around to face him. She narrowed her eyes and wrenched her arm away.

"What?" she snapped.

"This is the single stupidest thing you have ever done in your life."

"You barely know me."

"This is the single stupidest thing *anyone* could *ever* do in their entire life. If you want to survive, you need to trust me."

Ronja paused, searching his face for a trace of a lie. She found none—or it was hidden by the patterns her fists had left behind.

"Fine," she said tersely.

She adjusted her scarf and made for the front door, Roark following behind like a scolded dog.

The rain had slowed to a languid drizzle by the time they got outside. The storm clouds were snaking away over the distant walls, and dawn was seeping through the avenues. As Roark descended the steps to the sidewalk, Ronja paused to shut the door behind her. It left a pit in her stomach; she knew she would likely never reopen it.

She flipped the lock, remembered it was broken, then flew down the stairs after Roark, who was already revving his motorbike down the road.

Ronja climbed onto the back of the bike in silence and wrapped her arms around the boy stiffly, prickling with discomfort. His spine was equally rigid.

Roark revved the engine and they exploded into the empty road, the wheels spraying sludge behind them. He drove less frantically than before, so Ronja was able to watch the outer ring roll by.

The early risers were trickling into the streets, along with a handful of rusted autos. She watched the pedestrians shuffle from task to task, though it made her nauseous. They all seemed so frail compared to the vibrant Anthemites. They were bent, crumpled, like discarded paper dolls.

Ronja knew she had been like them not long ago, and wondered how much she had really changed since then.

Roark ferried them back to the alleyway adjacent to the abandoned subtrain station and parked behind the wall of crates and rancid trash bins. Ronja stood guard at the mouth of the side street, but there was scarcely a soul in sight. Mostly, she was looking for any excuse not to look at Roark.

"We'll get your papers started first," Roark said, plodding toward her. "My guy isn't far from here."

"Who is he?" Ronja asked as they stepped into the just stirring avenue.

"My friend, more of a brother, really. We met when we were children."

"He's a member of the Anthem, then?"

Roark tilted his head thoughtfully.

"Third generation. His parents and grandparents were avid members, but he's a bit more reserved with his time. He's our forager and our contact in the outer ring."

"Have I met him?"

"No, he doesn't come down to the Belly anymore."

"Why?"

"His mother and father were killed on a mission when he was just a child. I suppose he doesn't need the reminder."

"Oh."

They fell into another charged silence. Roark had a long stride, and despite Ronja's anxiety she found herself wishing he would slow down. He kept the brim of his hat pulled low over his face and his chin tucked into his scarf. At first Ronja thought he was cold, but then she realized that if she had recognized him, others might too.

"We're here," Roark said suddenly, scraping to a halt.

Ronja followed his line of sight. Her jaw went slack.

"No way," she muttered.

"What?"

"No *way*. You've got to be *pitching* me."

"What—?"

Ronja had already launched up the steps and was pounding on the front door with a balled fist. She rammed her thumb into the doorbell repeatedly and heard the echo ricochet around the house.

"What the hell?" Roark asked, materializing behind her.

The door swung open and a boy appeared in the frame, his mouth poised to shout. He froze, his eyes flicking between Ronja and Roark like a rapid pendulum.

"*Ronja?*"

"Henry!"

Ronja leapt at the boy, who barely managed to remain standing when she slammed into his chest. Her arms could not fully encircle his torso, so she clung to his shirt and inhaled his familiar scent. She shook violently, her dammed tears desperate to flow. She bit them back, held on tighter.

Henry took a moment to recover, then wrapped his burly arms around her in a bone-crushing hug. He stroked her damp curls as she trembled.

"What the hell, Roark?" Henry growled, his chest vibrating with rage.

Roark stepped through the doorway delicately and closed it behind him, careful not to graze Ronja in the process. "I was about to introduce you to my new friend, Ronja, but it appears you two are already acquainted," Roark said lightly.

"You could say that," Henry replied tersely. "I suppose it was you on the receiving end of the package, then."

Ronja heard Roark shrug, his leather coat crinkling.

"You are such a *skitzing freak*, shiny," Henry said, tightening his grip around Ronja. He pulled his head back and Ronja looked up at him, her eyes in danger of overflowing. With an apprehensive hand, Henry reached out and brushed a chunk of her hair away from her bulky stitches. His face contorted.

"Was this your choice?" he asked softly.

"I didn't have one, I was about to die. Though I wouldn't have been dying in the first place if he hadn't kidnapped me," Ronja said, glowering at Roark over her shoulder.

"Okay, I thought you were an Off," Roark said, rolling his eyes. "Not to mention, I apologized."

"You're going to do a hell of a lot more than apologize," Ronja said with a humorless laugh.

She pulled away from Henry. They clutched each other's forearms as if afraid to let go. "They have my family at Red Bay," she told Henry. "Roark is going to help me get them out, but I need new papers."

Henry's jaw bulged. His gaze flicked toward Roark. "Ronja, I'm sorry," he said, returning his attention to her. "If they've gone to Red—"

"They're either dead or mutts. I've heard the speech. Can you get me the papers or not?"

Henry's grip tightened around her arms. His nails would have dug into her skin if not for the thick fabric of her dress. He gazed down at her with his quiet, searching eyes. She matched his stare unflinchingly.

Finally, Henry sighed, his willpower slumping. He released her forearms and ran a hand through his coarse hair. "I'll get you the papers, Ro," he told her. "But I can't come with you."

"I didn't ask you too," she clarified quickly. "I know you can't leave Charlotte."

"You're my family, too," he countered uncertainly.

"I'm not your blood, and I'm not helpless."

"Roark's a pitcher, but he won't let anything happen to you, if only to preserve his pride."

"Oi," Roark grumbled.

Ronja and Henry ignored him.

"And if he does let something happen to you, I swear I'll kill him myself."

"I used to kill spiders for you." Ronja reminded him, her mouth quirking into a fleeting smile.

"But I never had any trouble killing rats," Henry replied, shooting a scalding look at Roark.

Ronja chuckled as Roark rolled his eyes again and huffed exasperatedly. "I'll be fine, Henry," she assured her friend, squeezing his forearms. "Especially if I have papers."

Henry nodded, as if he were trying to convince himself.

"I'll get started right away," he said.

Henry disappeared into his bedroom, which apparently served as his office. Roark fell into an unsteady slumber on the parlor couch, a bag of ice perched atop his eye like a tiny cairn. Ronja helped herself to the fresh loaf of bread sitting on the countertop and a glass of milk from the icebox. The Romancheck fridge had always been fuller than her own, so she felt no guilt.

As she chewed on the dark bread, her mind and eyes wandered, flashing between memories and bleak predictions.

She saw her cousins, strapped down, needles jutting from their veins, pouring the carrier virus into their bloodstreams, disintegrating their bodies along with their humanity. She saw her mother, limp and heavy, her limbs twisted at impossible angles, shoveled into an oven, burned to ash. Mutts and their families were not allowed proper burials. They were cremated, then used to fertilize the fields.

Ronja was buoyed into the past.

She was nine. It was her first day of fourth grade. She had snagged the most remote desk she could find, then pushed it even further away from the others. It was almost pressed against the wall. She still received disdainful looks from her peers as they filtered in. She focused on her book, burying her nose deep in its worn pages.

"Hi."

Ronja pretended not to hear, fearing the worst.

"Do you mind if I sit here?"

Ronja peeked over the lip of her novel. Her muscles coiled as she prepared to run or fight.

A boy stood before her, tall for his age, with a face scrubbed raw and freshly trimmed hair. He wore a patched sweater and a wide, genuine smile.

Ronja jerked her chin at the desk to her right. The boy sat. She plunged her nose into her book again. The words blended before her eyes as she waited for the insults to fly.

"I hear we got Mr. Erickson," the boy said. Ronja scooted closer to the wall. "Could have been worse, right? Could have gotten Woods. I hear her mole got bigger. Do you think she'd let us dissect it in class?"

Ronja snorted involuntarily. She lowered the dense volume slightly and peered out at the boy, who was still smiling. His eyes were soft.

"I'm Henry," he said, sticking out his hand for her to shake.

Ronja stared at the extended arm for a moment. It was the first time anyone had offered to shake hands with her. She grasped his fingers lightly and shook.

"Ronja," she said.

Ronja plummeted back into the kitchen.

It all made sense now. Of course Henry had shown her kindness. He was free of The Music, free of the ceaseless voice in his ear that implored him to treat mutts like something stuck to the bottom of his shoe. What about the handful of other people who had shown her kindness throughout her life? Were they free, too, or were they just less malleable?

"Is there any food around here?"

Roark appeared in the doorframe, yawning and stretching. He had shed his coat and boots, and his long hair was mussed from sleep. The skin around his eye was now a blend of red and violet, but the swelling had receded somewhat.

Ronja nodded at the bread resting on the cutting board. Roark shuffled forward sleepily and began to saw at it with the serrated knife.

They were silent for a while. Roark crunched on his stale bread, cringing slightly at the tough texture.

Ronja finally broke the hush. "Can I ask you a question?"

The heir inclined his head as he chewed.

"Do I look like a mutt to you?"

Roark set his crust on the countertop slowly. He flicked a stray morsel to the floor with a long forefinger. "Do you know how mutt Singers work?" he asked, staring after the suicidal crumb.

"They're stronger than normal—"

"No," Roark cut her off, shaking his head. He ran his fingers through his black hair, then leaned toward her over the counter. "They send out waves that alert humans to their location and their status. If I were to wear a mutt Singer, everyone with a normal Singer would think I was a mutt, no matter how handsome I may be."

Ronja was silent. The icebox hummed from the corner. The tires of an auto squealed outside the window, followed by a good deal of muted swearing and shouting.

"I don't know what to make of it, but to answer your question: No, you do not look like a mutt. You look beautiful."

Ronja put her face in her hands. The world was shredded through her splayed fingers.

"I'm sorry," Roark said quickly. "I didn't mean to offend—"

The girl shook her head, her curls bobbing. Memories were corroding her vision, swallowing the black of her fingers and the pieces of the kitchen. "I grew up thinking . . . you know . . . I knew I wasn't, but . . . everyone said . . . "

"No one should have to endure what you and your family have gone through," Roark said quietly. "I'm sorry for what my father and The Conductor have done to you."

"I didn't mean what I said about you," Ronja said through her hands.

"You did in the moment, and I deserved it."

Ronja took a great, shuddering breath and let her mask fall. Her face tingled. Her lungs were too small. Roark was watching her intently.

"Talk to me about something else," she demanded, massaging her temples briskly. "Anything."

"What do you want to know?"

"How did you and Henry meet?"

Roark beamed. He picked up his crust again and bit into it, spraying crumbs across the countertop. Ronja swept them into the bin with her sleeve.

"You wouldn't believe me if I told you."

"Try me."

"Well, I met him in the Belly after the Anthem kidnapped me. I was twelve. They drugged me, and I woke up cuffed to a chair—same one as you, actually."

"No pitch?"

"No pitch."

"So, basically what you're saying is that you're projecting your childhood trauma onto me?"

Roark punched her arm lightly across the countertop, and Ronja mustered a snort of laughter.

"Why did they take you?" she asked.

"I was bait."

Ronja cocked her head.

The boy sighed, as though he had already recounted the story a thousand times. He moved closer to her across the surface.

"The Anthem got intel that a shipment of improved Singers was going to be delivered to a WI warehouse just outside the city. It was a huge shipment, half a million units. My father sent most of his private Offs ahead of our auto to guard the warehouse. The Anthem was going to raid it, but they needed to get the Offs out of the way. They thought that if I were taken, my father would send all his Offs after me, and the warehouse would be left unguarded."

"Did it work?"

Roark paled considerably beneath his bruises.

"No. The entire strike team died that night, including Henry's parents."

"He told me they died in an auto accident," Ronja breathed.

Roark shook his head. "The Anthem found their heads in the factory that night. The warehouse was swept clean, too—all the improved Singers were already gone."

Bile rose in Ronja's throat. She gulped it down. "Why did you stay with the Anthem? Did you have a choice?"

"Well, Wilcox was all for killing me, but Ito saw my value. Once I learned what was really going on in the city, and I met Evie, Iris, and Henry, I begged to stay. It didn't hurt that my father was a skitzing monster."

"What?" Ronja asked with a dry laugh. "Did he give you two ponies for your birthday instead of three?"

"Not exactly."

Roark rolled up his sweater sleeve to reveal a constellation of small, round scars. Cigarette burns. "One for each time I spoke out of turn," he said. "I . . . " he broke off, staring at her forearm, which was sheathed by her dress. "I did the same to you."

Ronja shook her head, hid her arm behind the countertop.

"Forget it," she said. "I've had worse." She shoved back her curls, revealing a thin gash in her hairline. "Layla gave me this when I hid her whiskey. This"—Ronja tugged down her collar to reveal the white scar across her chest—"was from when I woke her from a nap. She smashed a bottle of vodka on the nightstand and stabbed me. I was picking out glass for hours."

Roark closed his eyes and took a slow breath through his nose. The wall clock trudged through the seconds as the pair sifted through their memories.

"It's funny," Ronja went on after a lengthy pause. "They always told us The Music counteracted violence, but honestly I think it just made things worse."

"It stops people from being violent toward the *government*. They don't care about what we do to each other."

"Guess not."

Roark reached across the table and took her small hands in his own. "I'm sorry, Ronja," he said softly, gazing at their interlocking fingers. "I know you don't want to hear it, but—"

"What's done is done. Stop apologizing."

"I hoped that—"

"Yeah, me too. It's my fault too, though. I should have gone to check on them sooner. I was selfish. I was happy for the first time in my life, and—"

"No."

Roark released her hands and cupped her cheek with his warm palm. Ronja flinched, but did not move away. His gaze held her in place. She had never noticed how much gold there truly was in his brown eyes. They did not seem dark at all.

"You don't get to blame yourself for this."

Ronja smiled ruefully. "Just get me to Red Bay," she said. "Then I'll go about forgiving you and myself."

"I'm going to need to take your photograph."

Ronja jerked, looking to her left.

Henry stood in the doorway, his arms folded over his chest, a thunderous expression plastered across his face. He looked like he might grab Roark by his shaggy hair and ram his head against the wall.

Repeatedly.

It was only then that Ronja realized how close she and Roark had grown. They were barely a breath away from each other, and his hand still rested on her cheek. Ronja made a small noise of shock and reeled away. Roark chuckled and scratched the back of his head with mock humility.

Henry motioned brusquely for Ronja to follow him and disappeared around the corner. She did so with her head drooping, like a dog caught sneaking scraps from the table. Roark tried to say something in her ear as she slunk past, but she ignored him.

Henry's room was at the end of the hallway. He was already inside, but had left the door ajar. Despite the warm light that spilled through the crack, Ronja felt cold entering the familiar space.

The boy was waiting for her behind a monster of a camera, which was propped up on groaning wooden stilts. He was busying himself preparing the shot. He fiddled with the lens and checked the spotlight that loomed beyond the contraption.

"Shut the door, would you?" he asked, sounding far too casual.

He twisted the light bulb in its socket, and the electric lamp glowed brighter.

Ronja closed the door softly, pressed her back to the wood.

"I never knew you had a camera," she said, trying to fill the yawning gap between them.

Henry nodded without looking up.

"I forge everyone's papers, make sure they stay under the radar."

"I always thought of you as so straitlaced. I was always the one getting in trouble, but here you are, Singerless. Did you *ever* have one?"

"No."

"Wow," Ronja murmured, perching on the edge of the pristinely-made bed. "It looks so real," she commented, motioning at his false Singer. "How does it stay on?"

"It's pierced," he explained, still not meeting her eyes. "All Anthemites that spend a lot of time aboveground get them pierced in. I got mine so I could go to school up here."

"Why?"

Henry shrugged.

Silence bloomed between them again. Ronja punctured it.

"You could have told me, you know," she said.

Henry's hand twitched, nearly knocking the camera from its perch.

"About the Anthem? You wouldn't have been able to resist telling someone," Henry gestured at the wound on the side of her head, the gravestone for her Singer.

"I wouldn't have ratted out my best friend," Ronja replied.

"You don't know what you would and wouldn't have done," he countered stiffly. "Doesn't matter now. I did what I thought was best."

"Why don't you go down to the Belly anymore?"

"I do sometimes," he shot back defensively.

"But you live up here."

"This is where I'm useful," he said with a shrug. "I'm not a spy, or a solider, or a leader. I'm good with forgeries, so that's what I do."

"Are you sure it's not because of what happened to your parents?"

Henry went rigid. He had been adjusting the lens with his back to her, but now he turned on his heel slowly, his eyes aflame. "You don't know what you're talking about," he hissed.

Ronja wilted. "I'm sorry. You're right. I was out of line."

Henry deflated. The embers behind in his eyes smoldered, then died. Exhaustion creased his dark brow. He looked far older than his age.

"It was a long time ago, Ro," he said with a voice that matched his countenance. "I never wanted you to get mixed up in this pitching mess."

Ronja felt her pity dissolve. "What, so you were just going to leave me to rot from the inside out?" she asked, her long-suppressed rage sparking. "Starving? Drowning in The Music? They used to torture me between classes, you know. The other kids."

"I was there. I was the one who saved you."

"Not always!" Ronja leapt to her feet. "Not often enough! Not when they . . . " Ronja gnashed her teeth together. Flashbacks came crashing through the roof of her mind, so potent her knees nearly buckled. They were bitingly clear, almost tangible.

She could still feel their hands tearing at her clothes, roving across her skin.

"When they what, Ronja?" Henry asked softly.

"Nothing," she said gruffly, dropping back onto the mattress. "Forget it."

"No," Henry reached forward and snatched her hands. "Tell me what happened."

Ronja shook her head mutely.

They left her in the alleyway on her hands and knees, her clothes torn and her face bloodied. She did not cry. She was empty. Her shell flaked away, piece by papery piece.

Ronja put her face in her hands, gazing blankly at her palms. "What's happening to me?" she asked to no one in particular.

"It's okay, you're okay," Henry murmured, sitting down beside her and rubbing her back briskly. "You're seeing your past as it was for the first time. It sometimes helps to talk."

"No," she said too loudly. "No . . . not now."

She uncurled from her hunched position and slapped her cheeks, hoping to work some of the feeling back into them. "Weren't you going to take my picture?" she asked briskly.

Henry considered for a moment. The radiator beneath the window grumbled. Ronja breathed in deeply, bracing herself.

1-2-3

2-2-3

"Yeah," Henry finally said. "Stand against that wall."

27: TOO FAR GONE

As hard as he tried, Henry could not coax her mouth into a smile. Ronja stood with her hands clasped, her shoulders back, her lips pursed, and her eyes vacant.

Ronja had only been photographed once in her life, for her official mutt documents. It was the only picture she was allowed to have of herself. She had been ill that day, her skin wan, her cheekbones sunken, her hair matted and greasy. She tried to cover the snapshot with her thumb each time she was required to produce her papers, but most Offs required her to show it. Their noses wrinkled with disgust each time.

"Three . . . two . . . "

A blinding flash and a satisfying click. Ronja blinked rapidly. As her vision settled, she caught sight of a plume of smoke rising from the body of the camera.

"Did my face break it?" she asked.

"Surprisingly, no. That's supposed to happen," Henry replied.

He plucked the camera from its tripod and tucked it carefully under his arm. "I'll develop this and print it. You and Roark can go get your stuff from the Belly."

"Okay," Ronja said.

She reached out toward Henry for a tentative embrace, but he shook his head, smiling slightly. "I'll see you soon, understand?"

Ronja nodded, dropping her arms and scratching her nose to mask her disappointment.

"Ronja, are you coming or what?" Roark called from the hallway.

Ronja rolled her eyes at Henry, who responded in kind. She stalked to the door and threw it open. Roark was standing outside, his fist raised to knock again.

Ronja shouldered past him with a pointed look. He huffed and fell into step behind her.

"Well, that was unexpected," Roark said as they descended the cracked stone steps to the sidewalk.

"You're telling me," Ronja said, skipping the final crumbling step and landing on the bricks with a thud. "Henry was the most compliant person I knew. Then again, he was pretty much the only person I knew."

"He's a convincing actor," Roark agreed.

They walked in silence for a while. The sun was rising in earnest now, and the streets were packed with Revinians on their way to their respective pubs and places of work. Roark wore his hat low and kept his face angled toward the ground.

"Is there enough food to go around in the Belly?" Ronja asked after awhile.

"Plenty, why?"

"Henry and Charlotte struggled last winter."

A crease formed between the heir's dark brows.

"He should have told me," Roark muttered, jamming his fists into his pockets like a petulant child. "I would have helped."

Ronja shrugged. "Henry never really talks about himself," she said, sidestepping a woman lugging a careworn briefcase. "He gives his all and asks for nothing in return. It's part of what makes him such a good friend . . . incidentally, it's also why I hate him."

Roark shot her an amused look beneath the shadow of his cap. "Why is that?"

"Because he never lets *me* help *him*."

They reached the vacant subtrain station and slipped into the alleyway. Ronja much preferred the side street when it was robed in shadow; in the glow of the rising sun, every droplet of sludge and piece of rotting fruit could be seen in full detail.

Roark unlocked the door and ushered Ronja inside. He followed quickly, slamming and sealing the entry behind him.

"Morning, Samson," Roark called.

Samson did not appear to have moved since they left him. His eyes flashed open, but Ronja doubted he had truly been sleeping. His dirt-caked lips parted as he drank in the Roark's bruised face.

"Trip!" he exclaimed, starting to get to his feet.

Roark threw up a hand, grinning through his bruises.

"It's a fantastic tale of ex-lovers and daring deeds, but I have a hangover to sleep off, so if we could do this tomorrow, Sam?"

Samson gaped at Roark for a tense half moment, then broke into a fit of uproarious laughter.

Roark beamed and slung his arm around Ronja's shoulders, shepherding her toward the elevator. He jammed the button with his knuckle, still chuckling along with Samson. Ronja remained silent, her mouth pinched into a smile masquerading as a grimace. She was a horrible actress. Relief flooded her when the bell rang politely and the door opened on the green-tinged compartment.

It was surreal, descending back into the subterranean city. When Ronja had returned to the surface, her time spent below ground had seemed like a dream, too good to be true.

And it was.

She had selfishly chosen to stay with the Anthem, and now her family had paid the price.

"I *will* save them," Ronja muttered to herself as the bell announced their arrival.

The door sidled into its recess and the pair stepped into the Belly, which was already flush with activity in the early morning.

Ronja was about to ask Roark what their next step was when he clamped his hand over her mouth and yanked her into the shadows.

She shoved his hand away roughly. "What?" she snapped.

"There's something I should tell you," Roark muttered.

"What, did you get my father arrested from beyond the grave?"

"Mutts aren't allowed in the Anthem."

Ronja paused. "Why?" she finally asked in a dangerously calm voice.

"It's complicated," Roark said, tugging at his collar agitatedly.

"Simplify it."

Roark craned his neck to view the ceiling, as if he was sorting his thoughts on the plane of bricks. Ronja narrowed her eyes.

"Think about it," Roark said, snapping his gaze back to her. "You got scared *once* and triggered The Quiet. You were almost dead in five minutes, and as far as we know you aren't even a real mutt. Imagine what would happen if we brought a full-blooded mutt down here. We would never be able to cut their Singer off in time."

"Have you tried?" Ronja asked bitterly.

"Yes," Roark replied gravely. "We did. One man survived the operation as well as The Quiet Song. He lived here all of two days before he tried to escape to inform The Conductor of our location. We barely caught him in time. The next year, another mutt, a woman, survived the operation. Three days later we caught her trying to escape with her Singer in her pocket."

"She wanted it back," Ronja said softly.

Roark nodded.

"What about mutt families? People without the genes? Can they live here?"

"I don't know," the boy said honestly, raking a tan hand through his hair. "It's never been done. That's actually the second reason we stopped trying to save the mutts. If we save a mutt and they go into The Quiet . . . "

"Their family pays the price."

"Exactly."

"What about me?"

"What about you?"

"I'm not . . . I mean I don't look or act like a mutt."

Roark's eyes roved across her face. A subtrain roared through a nearby tunnel, shaking dust from the arching ceiling.

"You're certain your mother gave birth to you post-serum?"

"Positive."

"But you aren't a mutt."

"I don't think so."

"I don't know how to explain your condition, but I'm sure we can convince Wilcox and Ito to let you and your cousins stay."

"What about my mother?"

Roark was silent. It was answer enough.

Ronja pressed the heels of her hands to her eyes, attempting to trap her swarming thoughts. Splotches of color danced across the backs of her compressed lids, and for a long moment she watched them.

"My mother is a pitcher, but she is also my responsibility. I will *not* abandon her," Ronja finally said, peeling her palms from her face. "If we can't stay in the city, and if we can't stay with you, then there's no place for us here. We can flee into Arutia, cross the sea if we have to."

Every book Ronja had ever read maintained that Arutia crumbled in the wake of the war, but Ronja guessed that it was not entirely true. Even if Arutia had fallen, there were other countries they could hide in, free of The Music.

Roark maintained his silence for a long moment.

"If that's what you think is best I will help you get out," he finally said, his voice heavy. "But first, we have to get your family out of Red Bay and cut their Singers."

"They'll be just as sensitive as me," Ronja said, itching her nose nervously. "We need to be fast."

Roark gave a ghost of a smile.

"I know just who to ask."

28: DOPPELGÄNGER

Ronja followed Roark through the maze of huts, keeping her face angled toward the ground, as if her dormant mutt genes would suddenly burst through her human facade.

The Belly was swarming with activity. Individual songs peppered the station. Ronja strained to catch snippets of the music, cupping her remaining ear to amplify the sounds.

Little watcher, little waiter
Little seer, little lion with your
Claws torn out . . . out . . . out . . .

A young woman sang from a bench as she knitted a blanket. Her voice was flawed, it cracked on the high notes, but was soothing all the same. A boy not much younger than Georgie played around her ankles. He hummed along with the tune, sketching pictures on the floor with a lump of charcoal. Ronja craned her neck to view the drawings, but found they were mostly squiggles. Still, they did not appear to be meaningless. They were continuous with the melody. When it crescendoed, the boy turned his chalk sharply to make a wicked edge. When the pitch fell, he created a softer curve.

Ronja hoped that there would be music wherever she was bound.

Roark came to an abrupt halt and spun on her. "Get your things. I'll get my stuff and find our surgeon," he said quietly, gesturing toward her room. Ronja had not noticed they had arrived back at her curtained chambers. She nodded and ducked inside wordlessly.

Her quarters had been tidied since her departure. The cot was made with military precision. A single flower bathed in water stood beside the amber bottles on the nightstand. It was a lily, the first she had seen in years. Three petals had fallen from it, their edges bruised brown. They curled in on themselves as if in pain. Her scarf, hat, and overcoat had replaced the saline drip on the coatrack.

Ronja donned her belongings methodically. By the time she had laced her boots and buttoned her coat, she felt almost whole. She swiped the medications from the table and dumped them into her knapsack.

She shouldered her bag, the pills rattling like rain on a tin roof. She made for the exit, but something stopped her. Ronja peered back over her shoulder.

The burgundy drapes seemed to breathe with her. When she had first awoken in the chamber, she had feared for her life. Now, all she wanted to do was curl up on the cot and let the musty walls embrace her.

Mutts were not allowed in the Anthem. Even if they could verify that the virus did not run in her veins, nothing but time could prove that her loyalties did not lie with The Conductor, that The Music did not continue to hold her though it had been silenced. Even if the Anthemites allowed her and her cousins to remain in the Belly, Layla would doubtlessly be sent away.

Layla.

Ronja's eyes slipped from focus. Her bed, the coatrack, the lily approaching its twilight, doubled.

Layla was not long for this world. Her mutated genes were eating away at her mind as well as her body. She would never again be the woman in the photograph. Still, a part of Ronja had hoped that if, by some miracle, they could free her from her Singer, her mind might come wandering back. That she might finally get to meet even a shade of the woman cradled in the faceless man's arms . . . but she was gone.

Layla was chained to The Conductor indefinitely. It went beyond The Music. It was engrained in her DNA.

Ronja heaved a sigh, blinking rapidly. The blurry doubles snapped back into place. She whipped back around and swept the curtain aside.

"Okay, let's—"

Her boots scuffed against the flagstones.

"Where do you think you're off to, mutt?" Terra snarled.

Terra stood behind Roark, who was stiff beneath his bulky

pack. The leather handles of two matching chrome stingers jutted from the open mouth of his bag. His fists were bleached white at his sides. He locked eyes with Ronja, then glanced down to his right. She followed his line of sight. Her jaw clenched.

Terra held a wicked blade with a serrated edge. Its jagged tip poked into Roark's stomach.

"Get back inside, *now*," Terra commanded.

Ronja nodded passively and backed into the room, her hands raised. Terra shoved Roark roughly, and he tripped through the entrance. Ronja caught him by the forearms, but Terra yanked him back by his ponytail, forcing him to look up. The tendons in his neck strained, but he did not make a sound.

Ronja dropped her pack, raising a mushroom cloud of dust from the floor.

"This has nothing to do with you," Ronja said in a low voice.

"It has *everything* to do with me," Terra barked, twisting the knife deeper into her hostage's stomach.

Roark sucked in a sharp breath through his bruised nose, but did not cry out. A droplet of sweat loosed itself from his brow.

"We need Roark," Terra continued icily. "I can't allow a mutt to drag him into Red Bay—it's suicide."

"He'll be just as dead with a knife in his gut," Ronja pointed out.

Terra tightened her grip on the hilt of her blade. Roark hissed as red bloomed beneath the honed metal, seeping through the fabric of his pullover.

Ronja stepped forward cautiously.

"She told Wilcox," Roark said, his voice strained.

Terra yanked his hair again, arching his back and forcing the tip of the knife deeper into his abdomen.

Ronja took another step forward. Terra was trembling, but it was not from fear. Rage crackled just beneath her tanned skin.

"You're biding your time," Ronja realized.

"Wilcox will be here any second," Terra replied.

"You knew before. How?"

"Roark never should have brought you here," Terra spat, ignoring her question. "You should have stayed in the pitching slums where she left you."

"Who—?"

Crack.

Terra's hazel eyes spread wide, flickered, then rolled back into their sockets. Her fingers slackened around the blade. Ronja lunged and snatched it just before she collapsed, dragging Roark with her.

They plummeted to the ground, a tangle of limbs and blood. Ronja looked up in shock.

Iris, her red braids frazzled, a canvas duffle slung over her shoulder, stood above the fallen pair. She brandished her otoscope over her head like a club.

29: RUSE

Ronja hooked her pack with one hand and grabbed Roark by the back of his coat with the other. He staggered to his feet and narrowly missed stomping on Terra.

"Figures," Roark grunted as he righted himself, brushing dust off his knees. He shoved his hair from his eyes with a huff and scowled down at Terra's crumpled form. "She must have heard me and Iris talking. She was always eavesdropping."

Ronja ignored him and lifted the hem of his sweater frantically. She sighed with relief. The slit in his abdomen was only a flesh wound, far from life threatening. All at once Ronja was acutely aware of the warmth radiating from his brown skin. She had not realized how muscular he was beneath his thick clothing. She forced his jumper back down hurriedly and backed away, unbraiding herself internally. Ronja refused to look at Roark directly, but she could have sworn she saw a slight smile flash across his face in her peripheral vision.

"We need to go!" Iris said shrilly, waving her otoscope around madly.

Roark hoisted his knapsack higher on his back, his elegant stingers clinking like empty bottles. He stepped over Terra carelessly and held the heavy curtain aside for them to walk through. Iris and Ronja looked at each other for a split second, then ducked through the opening in quick succession. Roark followed them out, letting the curtain fall over the unconscious girl with organic nonchalance. He scanned the Belly with calculating eyes. Ronja followed suit.

No alarms were blaring, no one was sprinting toward them with weapons and voices raised.

Yet.

Roark grabbed Ronja by her right elbow and Iris by her left. He began to drag them deeper into the Belly, away from the elevator. Ronja opened her mouth to inquire, but the boy spoke first.

"Follow my lead," he hissed through the side of his mouth. Ronja looked up at him. He was smiling, but his eyes were flat. He offered a friendly nod to an elderly man hobbling past. "Talk about something."

"You look constipated," Ronja whispered.

Iris and Roark both laughed with a shred too much force. Ronja winced internally, but joined them.

They made their way through the village as quickly as they could without attracting attention. Iris spewed her every thought, though this was far from abnormal. Ronja felt sweat beading under her arms. Her jaw ached from smiling. She could have sworn she felt eyes locked onto her back, but each time she glanced around their tail was empty.

The Anthemites moved about them like a well-oiled machine, oblivious to any cracks in their ruse. They called out greetings to Roark and Iris, and some offered Ronja genial nods. She returned the nods with as much grace as she could muster. Her head buzzed; her wound throbbed in time with her pulse.

"Almost there," Roark muttered in her remaining ear.

Ronja felt the fine hairs on the back of her neck stand on end. She peeked over her shoulder, pushed her curls out of the way to view the meandering walkway.

Her stomach hit the floor. A pin dropped in the halls of her mind.

Ronja parted her lips to scream.

"WESTERVELT!" Wilcox bellowed.

"Run!" Roark bawled.

Before Ronja could launch into a sprint he was dragging her forward like a rag doll. Iris darted ahead, her duffle clanking like a suit of armor.

"Sorry! Sorry!" the surgeon cried as she barreled through the crowd of unassuming Anthemites, her palms out to clear their path.

Cries of shock flew up as the group plowed through the throng. Wilcox's thundering footsteps studded the bewildered babel, drawing steadily closer. Ronja pumped her arms harder to keep up with Roark and Iris, who were as lithe and swift as stray cats. Ronja thought she could feel Wilcox breathing down her spine.

"Left!" Roark yelled.

Ronja torqued her body, following Iris's bobbing plaits. Her toe caught on an uneven stone and she flew forward. Before she hit the floor, Roark yanked her backward by the elbow. Gratitude built on her lips, but he was already pulling her onward.

Ronja squinted ahead. Roark was leading them to his tent. She could see it twenty paces ahead, warm light bleeding through its linen walls.

"Why—?!" Ronja yelled.

A scream and a series of ringing clangs tugged her attention backward, but Roark shoved her into his tent just as a reverberating crash and a bellow of pain filled the air.

"What was that?!" Ronja shouted.

"Hurry up!" Iris shrieked, batting a hanging lantern out of her face.

Ronja glanced about wildly, her heart in her mouth. Roark's tent was overflowing with strange and beautiful objects, half of which she did not recognize. Books of every color and size lined the walls floor to ceiling. A hammock stuffed with a red and gold duvet and several fat pillows swayed gently, suspended from the low ceiling. Everything seemed to have its place, and there was not a speck of dust in sight.

Roark crashed to his knees and slid aside a luxurious, patterned rug, revealing a plywood panel. Before Ronja could ask, he flipped the board aside. A yawning, black hole with craggy edges had been drilled into the stone floor.

"Jump," Roark commanded.

Before Ronja or Iris could so much as flinch, he leapt into the hole and was swallowed by the blackness. Ronja felt her breath catch for a split second, then she heard him land with a wet splash.

"Come on!" his voice echoed from below.

Iris looked at Ronja, her pink mouth tight and her shoulders stiff. Ronja glanced over her shoulder at the rippling cloth wall. Sprinting footfalls were building beyond it. She turned back around in time to see Iris's red braids flash and disappear down through the escape hatch.

Ronja sucked in a deep breath, laced her fingers through the straps of her knapsack, and jumped.

Before her toes could kiss the darkness, a staggering force bowled her over. Her head struck the velvety carpet, rebounded. Electric blue splotches bloomed before her eyes as she tried to breathe through the immense weight crushing her ribs. She blinked away the pulsing light show. Wilcox's snarling face greeted her. His brawny forearm was pressed to her neck, squeezing the life from her.

"So, The Conductor thought he could fool us with a pretty face, hmm?" he hissed, his breath hot and foul in her face. Ronja kicked madly, trying to strike him in the groin. Wilcox pinned her legs with his own, pressed harder on her neck. "I knew I didn't like you, *mutt*."

Bang.

A shot from below sliced through the air, narrowly missing Wilcox's knee. The hulking man whipped around, loosening his grip on her by a hair.

It was just enough.

Ronja shook her leg free and slammed her knee into her attacker's groin. He roared in shock and agony. She rolled out from beneath him, then scrambled toward the exit on her hands and knees. Wilcox lunged and caught her around the waist, wrenching her back. Ronja screamed in frustration, curled her fingers around the jagged edge of the manhole.

"You won't get a—"

Ronja lashed out with her booted foot. She felt rather than heard her opponent's nose crack. Wilcox howled and lost his grip. The girl shimmied forward and plunged headlong into the gaping black hole.

A damp wind struck her face. The blackness rushed past her. She closed her eyes, preparing for her skull to crack against the stone floor.

A pair of strong arms knocked the wind from her. Ronja and Roark crashed to the sodden floor with a wet splash. Ronja cracked a tentative eyelid, but found she was blind. Roark had tucked her head into the crook of his elbow. Her face was pressed into his sweater. Even in the dank sewer, he still smelled like himself.

"Now!" Roark yelled.

Metal shrieked against metal, louder than the screech of a vulture. White lights burst in the darkness as the sound scorched Ronja's remaining ear. There was a resounding clang and a shout of fury.

Then two hands grabbed her by the shoulders and yanked her to her feet. "Thank . . . you," Ronja wheezed, looking up through her curls, expecting to see Iris in the dim space.

Instead, Evie grinned down at her, her white teeth flashing in the light of an electric lantern. A hulking black rifle half her height was strapped diagonally across her back.

"What the hell did you do to him?" the gunslinger asked, squinting up at the round portal. Ronja followed her gaze, expecting to see Wilcox crouching in the bright space. Instead, she found the source of the screeching sound. An iron gate had been slammed over the portal. A long chain dangled from it, squeaking quietly as it swayed back and forth. "He's probably gone around the other side," Evie went on, her hands on her hips. "I think . . . "

The rest of the sentence was lost on Ronja. Roark snatched her by the hand and barreled down the storm drain, kicking foul water in her face. The two Anthemites followed. Iris was for once stoic. Evie howled like a maniac, her war cries bouncing off the curving stone walls.

30: TRAITOR
Terra

"Terra?"

The voice pricked her foggy brain. Terra blinked rapidly and squinted through her throbbing migraine. A pale face loomed above her. She could not make out its features but would know Ito's fiery mane anywhere.

Roark.

Terra shot up with a gasp, throwing wild punches at the air. Ito grabbed her forearms with viselike fingers and forced her back down.

Terra looked around wildly. The fight leached from her when she absorbed the familiar fabric walls of her home, her stacks of dog-eared novels, and her oil lamp, which swung like a pendulum from the low ceiling.

"Easy, easy," Ito hushed her. "You have a concussion."

"Ito," Terra gasped. "Did they get out?"

"Roark and the others?"

"Did they escape?"

Ito released her and pulled away slowly, her dark eyes full of inquiry. "Yes, they got out," she admitted levelly. "Roark had a secret hatch in his quarters. It doesn't bode well for him."

"No," Terra said, rocking her head back and forth against her pillow ferociously. She winced. It felt like her brain was slamming against the walls of her skull. "No, he isn't a traitor, but . . . I might be."

Ito narrowed her eyes to slits. Terra felt her mouth go dry. Her heart stuttered. She clenched her sheets with her weak hands, trying not to squirm beneath her mentor's scorching gaze.

"What do you know?" Ito asked carefully.

"I made a mistake," Terra breathed, her eyes trained on the shivering flame of the oil lamp.

"Care to elaborate?"

"There isn't time," Terra pleaded, struggling into a sitting position. Ito did not assist her, but observed her distantly, calculatingly. "All you need to know—"

"I'll tell you what I need to know and what I don't," Ito cut her off, a warning rumbling in her tone.

Terra dipped her chin, closed her eyes.

"I lied to Wilcox about Ronja," she heard herself say.

"You lied to Wilcox," Ito repeated icily. "He told me you said Ronja was a next generation mutt and that she had tricked Roark. Is that not true?"

Terra shook her head, rubbed steady circles into her pulsating temples. Her skin was cold and clammy beneath her fingertips.

"I can't tell you right now," Terra insisted. "If we get them back, I swear I'll explain everything."

"You know where they're going."

It was not a question.

Terra bobbed her aching head in confirmation, snapped her eyes open. Ito regarded her with a mixture of rage and determination.

"I know where they're going," Terra said, climbing to her feet haltingly. Ito followed suit, hunching slightly to avoid the linen ceiling. "We're going to need an airship."

31: TIES

They exploded to the surface five blocks from the elevator, startling a flock of pigeons into flight. They clambered to the street one by one, silent save for the sounds of their hands and feet scraping against the bricks. Evie exited last and shoved the manhole back into its crevice with the toe of her boot.

She and Roark bolted to the back of the alley and together lifted a sopping wooden crate with a mutual grunt. They worked smoothly, seamlessly. Ronja wondered how many missions they had completed together, and how many of them had been illicit. She wondered how many times they had been accompanied by the child of a mutt.

They let the crate fall over the rusted iron manhole with a reverberating thud. Murky water sprayed across their boots. Iris exclaimed in disgust, the first noise she had made in some time.

Then they were running, weaving through the knotted crowds like a needle through fabric.

Every few feet, Ronja shot a furtive glance over her shoulder, but they were not pursued. Their hatch may have barred Wilcox, but he would doubtlessly lead a team through the main exit. He would catch up to them sooner or later.

Fear fueled her steps, but by the fourth block, Ronja was winded. Years of malnourishment had destroyed her natural stamina. She would have envied her companions' strong bodies if not for the ink bleeding into her vision and the fire in her lungs.

"Keep up, love!" Roark called from far ahead.

Ronja narrowed her eyes at his back. She swallowed a sharp retort and plunged forward.

They did not wait to knock when they reached Henry's door. Roark vaulted up the steps three at a time and burst through the entrance, which Henry had miraculously left unlocked. Evie, Iris, and Ronja shot through the portal like train cars trailing a steamer.

"Henry!" Ronja gasped as she threw the door shut behind them. She crouched, clutching her sides. Evie sidled past her and locked the door. "Henry!"

Thundering footsteps commenced. A pair of almost comically large boots flooded her vision. Ronja raised her chin. Henry stood above her, a canvas knapsack swinging back and forth in his hand. He was dressed for the cold and rain.

The boy shrugged when he saw Ronja's bewilderment. "I sent Charlotte to our grandmother's across town. I've got to take care of *all* of my family."

Ronja climbed to her feet, swaying like a sapling in the wind. Henry reached out to steady her, but he never got the chance. Ronja threw herself at him, wrapping her arms around his neck and burying her face in the thick folds of his coat. He smelled like home and memories she would not mind reliving in their fullest form.

"We'll get them back," he whispered into her hair.

Ronja screwed her eyes shut to dam her tears. She could always hear the lie in his voice. She pulled away, blinking quickly.

"I assume by your rude entrance that Wilcox didn't take kindly to your shiny ass running around with a mutt?" Henry asked Roark, as if the situation was commonplace.

"Right, I could use some clarification there," Evie cut in. Iris made a noise of agreement. "Terra called you a mutt. Ronja, how could that be?"

"Well," Ronja sucked in a rattling breath and turned to face the rest of the group. "It's complicated."

Evie gestured for her to continue, rolling her wrist like a wheel around its axis.

"Well . . . my mother's a mutt, but I'm not. At least, I don't think I am. When I went into The Quiet, the . . . what did you call it . . . ?" Ronja asked, looking to Roark.

"The echo effect," he replied absently, peeping through the drapes that shrouded the street-facing window.

"The echo effect hit my mother and cousins. Roark thought they might still be at my house, but when we got there . . . " her voice cracked.

Ronja raised her fingers to her lips in an attempt to coax her tale forward. Henry clapped a warm hand on her shoulder, silently encouraging her. She took another unsteady breath and dropped her fingers. They twitched against her sides, so she tucked them into fists.

"When we got there they were already gone. We think they've been taken to Red Bay. My cousins will be turned into mutts and my mother . . . Layla . . . will be killed."

Silence greeted her tale. Evie was the first to break it.

"Red Bay," she repeated under her breath, shaking her head. She blew a soft whistle through the gap in her front teeth. "Skitz."

"Skitz is right," Iris said blackly. "Roark, what were you *thinking*?"

Ronja blanched. Roark rounded on the redhead.

"How many times have we gone down that hatch together, even when Wilcox ordered us to stay put?" he asked. "This isn't the first time we've gone rogue."

"No," Iris replied, advancing on him. She planted her feet firmly and lifted her chin to hold his gaze. "But it *is* the first time we've shot at him and run away with a mutt."

"I'm not—" Ronja spoke up tentatively.

"It doesn't matter what you are," Iris waved her off without taking her eyes off Roark. "Wilcox thinks you're a mutt, and that's all that counts."

Ronja paused her lips. She dropped her gaze to her boots. Henry gave her shoulder a reassuring squeeze.

"This is suicide," Iris went on, her voice abruptly hushed. "You knew we would follow you anywhere, Trip. You took advantage of that."

"Aren't you always saying we need to do what's right, no matter what?"

"Not when it'll get everyone I love killed!"

"Do you really think I would ask you to come with me if I didn't have a plan?" Roark reached out and clapped his hands to her slender shoulders. Iris buckled beneath the weight, but maintained her snarl. "Have I *ever* let you down?"

Iris looked away, her teeth gritted.

" 'ris?" Roark probed, trying to catch her gaze.

"We'll explain everything to Wilcox when we get back," Evie reassured her levelly. "He'll understand, and if he doesn't, Ito will."

The surgeon peered over her shoulder at her girlfriend, who leaned against the front door with her arms folded stoically. Iris opened her mouth, a retort prepared, but someone beat her to it.

"Listen for the deaf, sing for the mute, fight for the powerless."

All eyes turned to Henry, who had spoken so quietly they thought they might have imagined it.

"Our mantra," he went on more audibly, fixating on Iris. His gaze was firm, but not angry. "We have the duty to defend those who can't defend themselves."

"You think I don't know that?" Iris snapped.

Henry shook his head. "You know it better than most," he replied. "But neither of us has ever experienced The Music, and *none* of us knows what it's like to be a mutt . . . except Ronja."

Their collective gaze shifted to Ronja, who felt the rest of the blood leave her face. "I—I don't think I have the words for it," she admitted gruffly, her eyes trained on the scuffed floor. "All I know is, I've watched my mother waste away for nineteen years, and if my cousins—if they—"

Ronja broke off. She swallowed the lump rising in her throat.

"I barely know you, Iris," she said softly. "But I am *begging* you. Please, help me save my family. I'll do anything. I'll—"

Iris marched forward and drew her into a fierce embrace. Ronja was so shocked that she was paralyzed for a moment. Then she wrapped her arms around the petite surgeon. She was so slight, so frail. For a split second Ronja was transported back to her kitchen, back to the morning not so long ago that she had held Georgie in her arms . . .

Iris pulled away abruptly. She shouldered her bag, not looking at Ronja, and made for the back door without another word. Evie followed swiftly, her rifle thudding against her back.

"Wait," Henry called, reaching a hand out as if to grab the retreating girls.

"What?" Iris snapped. She scraped to a halt, but did not turn back. Her slight form was rigid. Evie looked at Henry over her shoulder, a brow arched in warning.

Henry smiled, his dark eyes flicking between Evie and Iris. "You two might want to consider washing off your war paint, or you'll have a lot of explaining to do at the checkpoint."

Evie snorted, reaching up to touch the remains of the crusted paint on her cheeks. She had evidently forgotten it was there. Though Iris still did not turn around, Ronja thought she saw her shoulders relax slightly.

Without a word the fiery girl made a left into the back hall, her boots clacking against the hardwood. Evie trailed her. A moment later the squeak of a rusted tap and the hum of running water filled the air.

"Do you have the auto?" Roark asked, turning to Henry.

Henry dipped his chin.

"In the garage, a few blocks down."

32: THROUGH

The auto was tucked away in a storage locker beneath a massive swath of brown canvas. It was the newest model on the market, Roark informed them, and the fastest. Fresh from the Westervelt Industries Auto Factory. It was as dark as oil, and roofless, with a thick glass windshield. Golden switches and levers adorned the polished oak dashboard.

"How was this not stolen?" Ronja asked dubiously as she climbed into the leather passenger seat. She ran her calloused hand along the sleek doorframe, then drew her fingers back gingerly, worried she might tarnish the beautiful machine.

"Luck and brainwashing?" Henry guessed as he opened the driver's door.

"Whoa, whoa, whoa," Roark said, raising his hand. "I'm driving."

"Hey, you entrusted this baby to *me*," Henry rebuffed him, leaning across the windshield toward Roark.

"To babysit, not to drive."

"I know how to drive!"

"Subtrains don't count."

"Don't you have a chauffeur, Roark?" Evie asked dryly from the backseat. She was reclining against the headrest with her fingers laced behind her head. An unlit cigarette was pinched between her teeth.

Roark jabbed an accusatory finger in her face, which she swatted away like a gnat. "No smoking in my car," he growled.

Evie clicked her lighter in response, cupping the shivering flame to the cigarette. She inhaled unhurriedly, then hissed out a lungful of smoke. Ronja's nostrils stung, but she had to fight a smile.

"I'm risking my life to help you and your girlfriend," Evie said, tapping the ashes over the side of the car. "I'll smoke if I like."

Ronja was suddenly glad it was dim inside the storage locker.

"Are Ronja and I the only ones who are serious around here?" Iris asked loudly, dropping her duffle into the backseat with a reverberating clang.

"It's called deflection, and it's a highly successful coping mechanism," Roark replied stoutly. "Right, love?" Ronja shot him a scathing look, but it was lost in the dimness of the garage. "*Anyway*," the boy went on. "If you would just step aside, H—"

"Ugh, move *over*," Iris ordered.

She stalked forward and wrenched open the door, then yanked Henry out of the front seat by the back of his jacket. The boy stumbled into Roark, who shoved him off with an exasperated grunt. Iris slid behind the wheel gracefully. She twisted the key in the ignition and revved the engine. Iris looked out at the two boys expectantly, a pristine brow arched.

"Get in, pitchers," she commanded.

Henry and Roark shared a look, then climbed into the back compartment without further argument. Evie continued to smoke in silence. Ronja appraised Iris in vague awe. The pixieish girl ignored her, but a faint smile dusted her lips.

The driver cracked her knuckles, then placed her hands on the leather steering wheel.

"Where are we going?" she called back to Roark.

"Out of the city, north gate," he replied.

Iris nodded, then moved to put the auto in gear.

"Wait," Roark said.

Ronja and Iris twisted in their seats. Roark was digging through his pocket. After a moment, he withdrew a handful of glinting silver devices.

False Singers.

Roark held them out for everyone to take. Ronja reached to grab hers, then retracted her hand, embarrassed.

"Actually, I have something else for you," Roark said.

The boy thrust his hand into his coat again, and withdrew something white and red. He tossed it at Ronja. She caught it gingerly. It was a blood-drenched cloth.

"Why . . . ?" Ronja trailed off, letting it dangle by a red tip.

"It's not real blood," Roark assured her. "It's tomato paste and glue."

Ronja wrinkled her nose dubiously.

"You're my girlfriend," Roark said, poking a finger at Ronja, who tensed. "You were riding on the back of my motorbike and we got in an accident, which explains my face, and your ear. You wanted to go to the hospital, but I knew that Red Bay was the best place for you."

Ronja bobbed her head in understanding, breathing an internal sigh of relief.

"Who are we?" Henry asked.

"Friends. We're dropping you off at my country home."

"There's just a slight problem with all of this," Henry cut in reluctantly. Roark glowered at him sidelong, daring him to put a kink in his plan. "I didn't have time to finish her papers."

Roark groaned loudly and looked to the ceiling for answers.

"It's not my fault you came back three hours early," Henry said defensively.

"Okay," Roark said with exaggerated exhaustion, kneading his temples. "I'll think of something—just follow my lead."

"Are we done here?" Iris asked impatiently. She was staring out the windshield, her knuckles whitening around the steering wheel.

"Yes," Ronja said.

Iris wrenched back a lever and slammed down the accelerator. Tires squealed against the concrete, and Ronja was pinned to her leather seat. She clawed for her safety belt and did not breathe until it was clicked into place across her lap.

The wind whipped her face and stung her wound as they tore out of the storage compound and onto the motorway. Pedestrians gawked as the glossy black car wove through the maze of rust-eaten junkers and livestock trucks.

Iris was a fantastic driver, smooth and self-assured, but Ronja could not help but feel queasy with each hairpin turn she made. Even Roark's motorbike was better than this powerhouse. She missed the steady hum of the subtrain.

As they zoomed toward the edge of the outer ring, the brick buildings gave way to shantytowns, the cobblestones to mud and sewage. The murky brown sludge sprayed behind them as they roared forward. Ronja pressed herself toward Iris, hoping to avoid the wayward flecks of crud that leapt up from the wheels.

The great wall of Revinia expanded before them, four stories high and crowned with obsidian watchtowers. The gray stones between the towers blurred with the smog-choked skies, making the barrier appear without end.

A sense of foreboding built in Ronja's gut as they approached the north gate. She had only read about the outside world, and the information she had been fed was doubtlessly flawed. Every book she had ever read told her the world beyond Revinia was a terrible place brimming with sporadic warfare. That much of the land was arid due to the ravages of battle. That civilization had never reemerged in the once-powerful Arutia.

Ronja did not know what to believe anymore, but realized with a jolt that she soon would. There was nothing for her in Revinia any longer. She and her family would have to leave the city-state and commence a new life in Arutia, or beyond. The possibilities were as endless as they were terrifying.

The girl peered back over her shoulder at the drab slum, at the slick road growing thinner in their wake, at the golden clock tower glittering in the distance. The city had brought her nothing but suffering for nineteen years.

So why did her throat constrict at the thought of leaving?

An image of the Belly flashed in her mind, and at once she understood her hesitation.

"Okay love, get ready to act," Roark called over the gale.

Ronja turned back toward the windscreen. The enormous northern gate loomed before them like a mouth with its teeth slammed shut. Two trucks headed to the fields idled before the sealed exit.

"It wouldn't hurt if you screamed a bit and thrashed about. It'll make them gloriously uncomfortable," Roark went on from behind her.

Ronja grimaced, but nodded.

Iris eased her foot off the gas as they came up on the gate. Half a dozen Offs paced around the truck nearest the exit. As they rolled to a stop, one of the sentinels shouted and waved at the nearest tower. There was a bang like a gunshot followed by the steady crank of gears. Ronja craned her neck around the second truck as the gate was retracted like paper sliding into a scroll. She fidgeted in her seat. Her view of the open land was choked by the black smog from the tailpipe of the second truck.

Another earsplitting crack, and the whir of machinery. The iron door eased back into the ground. The remaining truck inched forward, then came to a shuddering halt. Ronja hunched over and clutched the rag to her ear as the Offs wrapped around the hood of their car to access the canvas covered truck bed. She watched through her eyelashes as two of them jumped into the hooded compartment, searching for a whiff of illegality. The remaining Offs interrogated the driver. Ronja could hear their stingers crackling even over the hum of the engines.

"Clear! Let him through!"

Ronja squeezed her eyes shut. They were next.

Bang.

Ch . . . ch . . . ch . . .

The truck coughed into motion. Smog prickled in her nostrils as it chugged forward.

Bang.

Ch . . . ch . . . ch . . .

"Next!"

"Keep it up, Ronja," Iris whispered as she eased the auto toward the exit.

Ronja pressed her chest to her knees. She hardly had to fake a pained countenance. Though the medication muted the sting, her injury still throbbed, not to mention her persistent motion sickness and her jarred nerves.

"Here we go," Iris muttered.

Heavy boots sang across the bricks. The crunch of leather as an Off came to a halt beside Iris. Ronja could not see him through her tangled curls, but judging by his breathing he was nearly as fat as Wasserman. Slow, but powerful.

Kneecaps, eyes, throat. Kneecaps, eyes, throat, Ronja reminded herself frantically.

"Papers," the Off demanded in a guttural voice.

A collective rustle as the occupants of the auto handed over their documents. The Off took them and began to leaf through them lazily. Ronja breathed shallowly, as if it would somehow diminish her presence. She clenched both of her hands to the discolored cloth.

Ronja flinched when the sentry smacked the wad of papers against his leg.

"I count four," he growled.

Ronja felt her stomach plummet, but she said nothing.

Kneecaps, eyes, throat.

"My girlfriend lost her papers earlier this morning," Roark intoned from the backseat. "We were in a motorbike accident, as you can see."

"Hospital's the other way."

"Red Bay is this way."

The Off was momentarily stunned into silence, then he barked an echoing laugh. Ronja counted her heartbeats.

"Red Bay?" he rumbled. "The prison? Why the hell would you punkass kids want to go there?"

"It is also the most advanced hospital in a thousand miles. My personal physician resides there, and I want nothing but the best for my girl."

Ronja twitched uncomfortably. She hoped to pass it off as a spasm of pain.

"Only way you're getting into Red Bay is in chains, which may just happen if you don't turn around now."

"You may want to check my papers more carefully, *sir*," Roark said, executing the final word like a jab to the gut.

The man snorted.

A rustle of paper. The hum of the engine. The babel of the slums. Ronja's own heart like the propellers of an airship.

The Off cleared his throat.

"My . . . my sincerest apologies, Mr. Westervelt. I wish your . . . friend a full recovery."

Rubber scraped against stone as the man turned on his heel and waved the gate open.

Bang.

Ch . . . ch . . . ch . . .

"Drive," Roark ordered tightly.

Ronja heard Iris snatch the papers from the guard. Then she was thrown back into her seat as the auto roared forward, its wheels screeching like a startled bird. She brought her head up as they shot through the yawning portal.

Ronja opened her eyes.

33: CRICKETS

I t was better than the books.

The colored photographs in *Flora and Fauna*. The hoarded magazines she had poured over, searching for snippets of information on the outside world. All paled in comparison to the real thing.

The first thing Ronja noticed was the air. Her lungs could not get enough of the crisp, sharp wind. It was so light, so rich with oxygen, unburdened by smoke and smog.

The sky roiled with bruised thunderheads. A vast prairie wandered below them, stretching as far as the eye could see. The grass was tinged silver and an eerie shade of green beneath the gray sunlight. Flowers peppered the grassland like vibrant birthmarks on the skin of the earth. Irises, poppies, ragweed, daisies. Violet, red, yellow, white.

Ronja whipped around, swiping her hair from her face to reveal a massive grin. The walls were already growing smaller in their wake. The way back was already shut, its black teeth clenched. From far away, Revinia seemed nothing more than a toy, a model. Benign.

Just like that, Ronja was out.

Her smile faded as quickly as a cloudburst. Her family's faces were reflected in the landscape. *They were here,* she realized, her gut oscillating with something other than motion sickness. *They were unconscious. They wouldn't have seen this. What if they never see it?*

Ronja turned back around to face the windshield, her mouth a grim line.

Roark directed Iris down the meandering dirt road. Evie pitched her cigarette over the edge of the car with a dejected sigh. It was impossible to smoke in the howling wind.

They drove for thirty minutes in silence. Ronja stared through the glass, oblivious to her numb cheeks and watering eyes. Her awe and pain wrestled ceaselessly.

"Here come the fields," Evie finally called from the back seat, breaking the hum of the engine and the gusting of the wind.

Ronja craned her neck. Her itching eyes widened as they crested a hill.

The wild prairie morphed into a sea of golden wheat that stretched far past the horizon. Dozens of hulking trucks, their beds sagging with the crop, idled along the road. Pinprick white splotches studded the monotonous field.

As they drew closer, the bright flecks morphed into people. They were garbed in stained white uniforms and carried wicked-looking scythes they were using to reap the wheat. They worked mechanically, reminding Ronja of the workers in the outer ring library.

"How are there shortages with this much land?" she shouted over the gale.

"Most of the food's going to the core," Evie replied with a voice that could cut steel.

Ronja felt her stomach cinch.

All those winters spent trudging to soup kitchens for meals. Pawing through garbage bins in search of half-eaten leftovers. Swiping fruit from stalls. Things had improved when she quit school and took on a second job, but her family had never left the edge.

Ronja clenched her teeth, rolled her fingers into fists in her lap. Her head began to throb ominously. It felt not unlike the start of one of her migraines, which she'd hoped she had left behind with her Singer.

"After we take down The Conductor, we'll open the fields to everyone."

Ronja swiveled to face Roark. He had shoved a gray woolen stocking cap over his dark locks. His nearly black eyes appraised her from behind escaped strands of hair.

"Why are you smiling?" Roark asked.

"Forget it," Ronja replied, twisting again to face the front. "It's just, you're not so bad for a shiny."

Night was bleeding into dusk by the time they reached their destination.

Part of Ronja had hoped they would be headed straight for Red Bay, but of course that did not make any sense. They had no plan that she knew of. Without one, they would be killed before they could take one step into the compound. Still, she had to fight a scream of frustration when they pulled into the driveway of a quaint whitewashed cottage.

"What is this place?" she asked instead as they clambered from the auto, working the knots from their muscles.

"My family's summer cottage," Roark replied, unlatching the trunk and yanking his bag from the deep compartment. "My father never comes here."

"Bit plain for a Westervelt," Ronja commented.

The house was only one story. It possessed a single square window of distorted glass and a squat red door with a brass knob. Ivy snaked up the pale walls, and a copper roof stained with turquoise corrosion flared in the dying light. The tall grass hugged the base of the cottage. The air was full of cricket songs, tranquil and jarring all at once.

"I like my house, thank you very much," Roark said stiffly.

"Yes, yes, we know it's simple chic," Iris sighed, shoving the boy away from the trunk with a bump of her hip.

The surgeon heaved her duffle out with a dainty grunt. She shouldered the bag and returned her attention to Ronja.

"The Westervelt estate is all the way south of the territory, about as far away from here as possible."

"As well it should be," Roark interjected darkly.

"Won't the Anthem follow us?" Ronja asked, glancing uneasily at the horizon.

"The only people that know about this place are here now," Roark assured her, starting to shuffle backward toward the door. "As long as they still buy that you're a mutt, they'll expect you to go straight to the nearest Off station, anyway."

"Wilcox *definitely* believed it," Ronja muttered, brushing her tender neck with the tips of her fingers.

She was not eager to appraise herself in a mirror; she imagined her neck was a network of bruises. The dread in her stomach sparked a memory, and a question.

"What do you think Terra told Wilcox?" she asked. "He called me a mutt, but he was acting like I was a spy."

Roark scraped to a halt and gave an exhausted sigh.

"Terra," he began, massaging the bridge of his nose with his free hand, "is a master manipulator. She could get him to believe we were all aliens if she had the time."

"You think she told him we were traitors?" Iris asked, a twinge of hysteria creeping into her voice.

Roark shook his head slowly, contemplatively.

"No, I doubt it," he said. "If Wilcox really thought we were traitors, he would have just shot us on the spot."

"You think Terra told him we were duped," Evie cut in, slamming the auto door and sidling up to the trio, her hulking rifle slung over her shoulder.

Roark shrugged, his stingers tapping together in his pack as his muscles bulged.

"That makes the most sense. The question is, why?"

"She hates me," Ronja said morosely.

"Roark!"

The quartet glanced toward the auto. Henry had popped the hood and was leaning over the engine, scratching his head. A trail of smoke snaked from the innards of the vehicle. Ronja did not know much about autos, but was fairly certain that was not supposed to happen.

"What did you do?" Roark growled, dropping his pack and stalking toward the boy.

"Terra doesn't even know you," Iris scoffed, ignoring the interruption.

"Tell me about it," Ronja replied.

"That girl had better come clean. I am *not* going to die a traitor."

Iris whipped around and marched toward the cottage, her clanking bag drowning out the crickets.

"Don't mind her," Evie implored, pulling another loose cigarette from her coat. She coaxed her lighter to life, then pressed it to the rolled paper. "She isn't really mad at you, she's just scared."

"You sure about that?" Ronja asked with a humorless laugh.

"Iris lost her family when she was twelve," Evie said, watching the smoke slither away to join the clouds. "We're all she's got."

"I don't want anyone to get hurt because of me."

Evie barked a laugh, startling Ronja.

"Don't take this the wrong way, but we aren't here for you."

Ronja flushed. The black-haired girl flicked her cigarette into the dirt, then stomped on it with her heel.

"Well, maybe Roark and Henry are," Evie amended with a considerate tilt of her head. "But Iris and I, we're here for those pitchers skitzing up the auto over there. Wilcox may be in charge, but Roark is our leader, has been since we were kids. If he wants to go staggering around Red Bay for a girl he just met, you bet your ass we're going to be right there with him."

Ronja looked down at the gravel, nudged a clump with her toe. What must it have been like, growing up in the Belly? Dangerous, certainly, but to grow up free, to be raised among such loyal, unyielding friends . . .

"Not that we don't like you," Evie said hastily, misunderstanding her downcast eyes. "Actually, Iris wouldn't shut up about you, but—"

"You don't really know me," Ronja finished, raising her chin. "I understand. Thank you."

"Roark! Where's the skitzing key? It isn't under the rock!" Iris screeched from the front door, stamping her foot petulantly.

Evie smiled, her nose crinkling.

"Coming, coming," Roark placated from the auto. In a lower voice, he added, "I told you to set traps, H. *Pitch* me."

The two boys slammed the hood and jogged toward Iris, loathe to keep her waiting. Evie and Ronja followed at a slower pace, their boots crunching the rocks in time.

When he reached the cottage, Roark withdrew a ring crowded with several dozen keys. He pawed through his vast collection methodically, then settled on a large, brass one. He unlocked the door with a clunk of tumblers.

"Shoes at the door," he ordered as he crossed the threshold, stepping out of his heavy boots and kicking them onto the rug beside the door.

Henry, Iris, and Evie shared a knowing look, then removed their shoes. Ronja followed suit quickly.

Roark flicked on the electric lights, and Ronja sucked in a breath.

The cottage was small, but far from stifling. The walls were whitewashed like the exterior and adorned with a handful of small paintings hung from wooden pegs. Twin red sofas squatted comfortably around the brick hearth. A coffee table sat before the couches, stacked with several dozen books. A pinewood shelf housed more volumes, some stacked and others standing. Two stooped doorways opposing the fireplace led to a bathroom and a bedroom, Ronja assumed. Adjacent to them was a kitchenette with an icebox, stove, oven, and brass sink.

The rebels were already dropping onto the sofas like stones. Roark had moved off to his bedroom. Ronja could see him through the cracked doorway, shedding his coat and stretching toward the ceiling. The hem of his sweater climbed up, revealing his chiseled abdomen.

Ronja reddened and turned away. She collapsed onto the empty cushion next to Henry, who was supporting his head with his hand. She allowed her own head to sag onto his shoulder while Iris and Evie conversed in hushed tones. Henry reached around her shoulders absentmindedly and gave her a reassuring squeeze.

Ronja must have fallen asleep. When she opened her eyes, the room was swathed in the glow of a merry fire. She lay on her side on the couch, wrapped in a knit throw. She sat up quickly, sweeping her unruly hair from her brow and blinking her surroundings into focus.

Iris sat cross-legged on the hearth with her chin in her palm, staring numbly into space. She looked up at Ronja as she disentangled herself from the blanket. The surgeon appeared slightly less agitated than before, and Ronja thought she could read a trace of an apology on her heart-shaped face.

"She's awake," Iris called.

Ronja rubbed the sleep from her eyes and peeked over the lip of the sofa. Evie, Roark, and Henry stood in a semicircle in the kitchen, talking quietly.

"Good," Roark said in a louder voice, clapping his hands together. "Let's begin."

34: TWENTY ON THREE

"Over the past few months, there's been a massive upswing in the number of prisoners going into Red Bay, and a considerable decrease in the number of mutts coming out," Roark began.

They had filtered back into the parlor. Unsurprisingly, Iris and Evie sat together again. Henry sat by Ronja with his elbows on his knees, his fingers knit loosely. Roark stood before them all, leaning against the warm bricks of the chimney. Firelight played across the facets of his tawny face, highlighting his dark freckles and high cheekbones.

"Why?" Ronja asked, though she was not sure she truly wanted to know the answer.

"We don't know, but I actually don't think it's a bad sign."

Ronja shared a look with Henry, who was stony-faced.

"Red Bay is as much a lab as it is a prison," Roark continued, scratching his stubble-shaded jaw contemplatively. "They're constantly experimenting with everything from genetics to The Music. If your cousins were already mutts, they'd have been sent home by now."

"So, what do we think is going on, then?" Evie asked.

"That's the catch," Roark said grimly, folding his arms across his chest. "Nothing good ever happens at Red Bay."

"So, they're either dead or being experimented on," Ronja inferred flatly.

Roark inclined his head, respecting her enough not to sugarcoat his answer.

"How are we going to do this?" Evie asked after a moment of silence.

"Bishop Street."

A collective chuckle rippled through the Anthemites. Even Henry shook his head with a vague smile.

"Bishop Street?" Ronja asked, looking from face to face inquisitively.

"Our first rogue op," Evie said with an inappropriate air of fondness. "Bishop Street was the location of an intelligence office with direct links to The Conductor."

"Or so we thought," Iris cut in.

"It was a trap, the office was empty," Henry continued the tale. "We were a team of twelve. Iris was our medic, Evie our sniper, Roark was on the ground, and I was running surveillance."

"Eleven of us got out, but Ito was left behind," Roark picked up. "Wilcox ordered us to leave, but the four of us went back later that night. We saved Ito before she was forced to pop her cyanide. She was a little beaten up, but Iris patched her up just fine."

"Okay, so it was a rescue mission," Ronja concluded. "What does that have to do with saving my family?"

"Same strategy, larger scale," Roark explained, surveying them with calculating eyes. "At Bishop Street, I used my name to get us inside to save Ito. We'll do the same thing here tonight."

"We can't walk in through the front door," Evie pointed out. "You'll attract too much attention."

"No," Roark agreed. "But I can phone Dr. Berik and have him let us in through his apartment."

"Dr. Berik?" Ronja asked.

Roark gave a thin smile. "I wasn't lying when I told the Off my personal physician resided at Red Bay. Among other things, he leads the team that oversees mutt procedures."

"And you think he'll just let us in, no questions asked?" Henry inquired dubiously.

"He owes me a favor, not to mention he's a bloody coward. Even The Music can't obliterate cowardice."

Henry considered this, then motioned for Roark to continue, his brow scrunched in incredulity and anxiety.

"I'll phone Berik tonight and tell him that a friend of mine is in need of his assistance," Roark said, starting to pace purposefully back and forth across the luxurious rug. "We'll tell him Ronja is ill, and he'll take her to his private office. In all likelihood, he'll leave us in his living quarters."

"What if he sees my ear?" Ronja asked.

"He won't have time. As soon as he closes the door, you'll jam this into his neck."

Roark stopped pacing and dug into his pants pocket. He withdrew a folded silk kerchief and tossed it at her. Ronja caught it ungracefully and dumped the contents into her palm. It was an unprogrammed stingring coated with dully gleaming gold.

"The shock is enough to knock him out for several hours," Roark went on. "Once you've stung him, come find us outside. We'll break the lock and trap him so he can't call for backup."

Ronja nodded, scrutinizing the tiny weapon, then slid it onto her right index finger. She winced as the metal grew hot, syncing with her skin. The burn faded quickly and left a firm sense of security in its wake.

"Evie." Roark turned his attention to the techi.

"Hilltop?" she inquired with a slightly manic grin.

"Hilltop," Roark confirmed. "Wouldn't put you and Lux anywhere else."

Evie shot a fond glance at Lux, her long-range, over the ridge of the couch.

"What happens after Ronja takes Berik down?" Iris asked.

"We make for prison control. They should keep a list of every prisoner in the compound. Once we find them, we'll sedate Ronja's family so they don't roll into The Quiet, and get the hell out."

"And if we're seen?" Ronja prodded.

"We shouldn't have a problem if we look the part."

"And who are we going to look like?" Iris asked, her eyes narrowed dubiously.

Roark grinned.

"A surprise inspection crew from WI, led by Mr. Victor Roark Westervelt III himself."

There was a pause filled only by the incongruently cheery crackling of the fire. Then Evie barked a sardonic laugh, going so far as to slap her knee.

"An inspection led by four teenagers in the middle of the night? Shall we take bets on how quickly this will go south? Anyone?"

"Twenty on three minutes," Iris muttered.

"My father has been known for his eccentricity," Roark said with a withering glance at the couple. "Frankly, I'm sure it won't be the first late-night inspection."

"Led by his philandering, gambling-addicted son?" Evie drawled.

"Not my fault *The Bard* doesn't have anything better to talk about than my cover life," Roark said defensively.

"Oh please," Evie laughed. "Don't act like you don't enjoy strutting around with those shiny ninety-pound numbers from the core on your arm."

"Guys," Henry and Iris sighed at the same time.

"Wait," Ronja said, throwing up a hand. "That's it? *That's* the plan?"

The somber atmosphere was reinstated as Roark mulled over her potent question.

"Sometimes the simplest plans are the best," he replied. "Less can go wrong when there are fewer moving parts."

"No," Ronja said sharply, standing and fixing her gaze on him. "No," she continued in a lower voice. "This won't work."

"I appreciate the vote of confidence," Roark retorted flatly. "But I don't think you fully comprehend the influence my family has. We are *built into The Music*. People are trained to want to please us, nearly as much as they are The Conductor. It *will* work."

"And if it doesn't?" Ronja asked, advancing on him until they nearly touched.

She had to crane her neck to maintain his gaze. She could feel three pairs of eyes, probably flown wide with surprise, drilling into her back. Ronja swallowed dryly. "I'm not saying it's a bad plan. I'm saying maybe Iris was right." She gestured back toward the surgeon, who shifted in her place. Ronja went on. "Answer me truthfully: has *anyone* ever escaped Red Bay?"

Silence was her only reply. It was answer enough.

"Exactly," she continued hollowly. "We can't do this. Iris was right, this is suicide."

A harsh noise of disgust caused Ronja to whirl. Evie was observing her with cinched brows and a snarl. "Are you *seriously* going to back down *now*?" she demanded.

"No, of course not! But I can't let you come with me. I won't let you risk your lives."

"You won't *let* us?" Evie released a ringing laugh. "Do you really think you have any control over what any of us do?"

"No, I just—"

"Being an Anthemite is about being able to make your own choices, even if they cost you. I don't know about the rest of you pitchers, but I already made my choice. I'm going to help you, and I'm going to protect my brothers."

Evie ended her speech with a decisive dip of her chin, then dug into her pocket and withdrew her lighter and another cigarette. Roark huffed quietly but had given up chastising her.

"What she said," Iris said with uncharacteristic brevity.

"You're all but my blood, Ro," Henry said quietly. "That means Georgie, Cos, and Layla are too."

"I skitzed up, I owe you," Roark said from behind her.

Ronja felt the world dissolve around her. She tried to think of something to do or say that could pay them back for their generosity, but no word in her vocabulary suited her gratitude.

They must have understood something in her expression, because Evie reached over and punched her in the shoulder, pinching her smoke in her free hand. Henry did not move to embrace her, but caught her gaze from the couch. It was just as good.

Georgie, Cos, Layla, I'm coming, Ronja whispered silently.

35: MORPHED
Cosmin

The first night was the worst. Cosmin awoke from his coma on an unforgiving concrete floor in a pool of his own vomit and piss. He never quite rid himself of that stench in the following days. His head had felt unnaturally cool and light pressed against the stone. It took him an embarrassingly long time to discover that his hair had been sheered away.

When he had collected his wits enough to stand, he'd paced the perimeter of his six-by-eight-foot cell, searching for a way out. There were no windows. There was a small air vent in the ceiling. Even if he could have reached it, he could not fit his shoulders through. The only viable exit was a steel door equipped with a small portal for food. The hatch had been opened only three times in the past five days. If they were trying to starve him, they would fail. Cosmin had been through worse. They all had.

At first he tried to sleep, curling his bald head into the crook of his elbow. He quickly realized it was useless. The cold and the hunger he could handle. It was the screams that kept him awake.

They were not screams of fear, anger, or even agony. It was as if the prisoners in the cells around him screamed for the sake of hearing their own voices, as if they were trying to drown something out.

Now, lying on his side, Cosmin reached up and brushed his omnipotent Singer with filthy fingers. It was unnervingly quiet.

He knew where he was, though he did not know why.

They had been eating dinner. Layla was awake, but hardly cognizant. He and Georgie were talking about something irrelevant; then they were falling. Shattered glass. A hard floor. A barrage of keening notes. His last thought was to wonder what they had done wrong.

Now he realized, his vision blurring as he stared at the scratches on the impregnable door, that he already knew the answer.

They had done nothing wrong.

A part of him had always known that mutt Singers were connected. When Georgie was upset, his Music swelled too. When Ronja was stressed, he felt the repercussions. It did not take a genius to figure out (though Cosmin knew he was one).

Ronja had not returned for her dinner break the night they were taken. She rarely missed a meal. That meant something had happened to her. That meant something had gone wrong in her Singer. She had triggered something, whether she intended to or not. Was she here in the prison? Was that her screaming in the cell adjacent to his? Or did they kill her outright, as she was the catalyst?

Cosmin knew what would happen soon. He and Georgie already had the Singers. Now it was time to get the genes.

He was asleep when they came to his door. He leapt to his feet and pressed his back to the far wall as the guards fumbled with the lock. His Music flared, manifesting as searing lights in his vision. Fear clawed at his throat.

He did not try to fight when the Offs barged through the door. He put his hands behind his head. Still, they stung him until he pissed himself, until his skin and voice were equally raw. They dragged him down an endless corridor, their stingers flashing in the electric lights. Finally, they dumped him in a room only slightly larger than the one from whence he came. Cosmin rose on quaking legs and found himself staring into a glass wall.

He yelled and flew at the barrier, bombarding it with his fists until they were black and blue.

Georgie was on the other side. Though he could not hear her, he knew she was screaming. She had been clawing at her Singer. Ribbons of blood ran down her face and neck.

When Georige's eyes rolled into the back of her head, The Day Song morphed in Cosmin's ear. His screams were not nearly enough to drown it out.

36: THE MOOR

"Where did you get all this stuff?" Iris asked as she emerged from the washroom, struggling to loop the button at the back of her neck.

She was laced into a starched cream corset and sweeping lace dress. Her chestnut boots rose past her knees, and her strawberry-blond hair was tugged into a severe knot at her crown. Her false Singer gleamed proudly from its perch, bitingly cold among her constellation of soft gold jewelry.

Evie, dressed in heavy black gear, moved to help her with the clasp.

Roark laughed from his place on the couch.

"I try to keep my house stocked, in case there comes a time when a girl might desire some fresh clothes."

Iris darted over and swatted Roark on the shoulder. He feigned agony, clutching his arm and groaning. Ronja felt vaguely ill as she gazed at the elegant stack of garments folded in her hands.

"Your turn," Evie said, tapping her on the shoulder and nodding toward the bathroom.

Ronja ducked into the warm, tiled washroom without a word and shut the door firmly. She jiggled the brass knob to make sure it was locked, then pressed her spine to the wood.

She was not partial to wearing clothes Roark's one-night stands had worn, but she forced the undesired thoughts away as she shed her gray dress and stockings.

The new clothing fit her better than she could have hoped. Despite her initial qualms, Ronja had to admit she did not look half bad.

She could have easily come from the core, if not for her gaunt features. She wore an intricate, high-necked cape embroidered with gold ivy. Her full-skirted dress, which ended above her knees, was woven of black silk to match the cloak. It shimmered and rustled when she moved. On her feet were a pair of high-heeled ankle boots studded with gold. A raven feathered hat angled to cover her wound was pinned to her curls.

Ronja almost smiled at her reflection, then she remembered why she was garbed in such beautiful attire.

"Okay, I'm all set," she called. She turned her back on the mirror and exited the bathroom hastily, her heels clacking loudly.

"Wow, Ro," Henry breathed, his eyes widening. He got to his feet and worked his way around the couch. Ronja raised her eyebrows in surprise. Henry wore a black suit and matching tie and looked wildly different from the boy she had known in the outer ring. "You look—"

"Perfect," Roark finished for him, flicking the light switch as he exited his bedroom.

Ronja turned to the boy, clasping her hands behind her back to still them. Roark was gazing at her with an odd expression. He wore a tailored, high-necked jacket studded with ornate bronze clasps and black slacks to match. He had combed his hair into a loose knot at the back of his head, and he looked startlingly handsome.

Ronja looked down and away, fixating on a clump of dust peeking out from beneath the sofa.

"If you two are done making bedroom eyes," Evie quipped from the kitchen, where she was gnawing on a piece of jerky.

Ronja nodded briskly, begging her face to regain its sallow hue.

"I rang Dr. Berik while you were changing," Roark said, abruptly businesslike. "He'll open the side door to us at 1:00 this morning."

Ronja checked the clock that hung on the kitchen wall. "That's two hours from now," she noted accusingly.

"We'll leave in an hour to set Evie up on the perimeter," Roark said, ignoring her impatience.

"I can see a hair up a nose a hundred meters out with Lux," Evie bragged, gesturing proudly at her rifle, which leaned against the wall by the front door. "A bunch of fat Offs should be no problem."

Ronja swallowed dryly. It was not the idea of killing that bothered her—she had even more reason to hate the Offs than the average Anthemite. Still, the notion of Evie shooting someone unsettled her. Up until this moment, she had thought of their mission purely as a rescue operation. Now, she realized she had stumbled into a war.

"Can't we leave now?" Ronja begged, tugging at one of her curls anxiously.

"The longer we're in the vicinity of Red Bay, the better chance we have of being caught," Iris said, plunking down on the couch next to Henry.

"Should we go over the plan again?" Henry wondered aloud, picking a piece of lint off her shoulder.

"I think we all know our parts," Evie replied.

"I have an idea," Roark said suddenly.

He held up a finger, signaling for them to wait, then disappeared back into his room. They waited in curious silence as they listened to him rummage about. With an audible grunt of effort, his weighted footfalls recommenced.

Ronja cocked her head as Roark reentered the parlor, bearing a leather case in one hand and two slim parcels in the other.

Iris and Evie exclaimed happily. Even Henry managed a weak smile at the sight of the box. Roark bowed low and passed the thin slabs to Evie. He placed the box near the hearth and knelt before it. Evie hurried over from the kitchen and plopped down on the free sofa. Ronja took a seat by her and observed Roark with growing curiosity.

The walls themselves seemed to bate their breath as the heir opened the case, but Ronja's confusion only waxed when she saw what was inside.

The box housed some sort of machine with a large, smooth wheel at its center. Two dials labeled **P WER** and **TONE** orbited it. Ronja assumed **P WER** stood for **POWER**, but that the letter had been rubbed away by time and use. A metal arm jutted from the interior, tipped with a silver needle.

"What is it?" Ronja asked, leaning forward slightly.

"An old Anthemite tradition before battle. Technically

speaking, a record player," Roark told her with an offhand smile. "Actually, it's the reason we met for a second time. It seems fate has a sense of humor."

"Or maybe death does," Iris muttered.

"I haven't heard this one," Evie said, holding up one of the slabs for Roark to see.

Ronja craned her neck to view the thin package. It was painted, she noted with surprise. It depicted a girl standing atop a hill. Her hair and skirts were caught in the wind. She shaded her eyes from the damp glow of the sun beyond gathering anvil clouds. There was not another soul in sight, nor any sign of civilization. Two words were scrawled across the darkening sky in pale calligraphy.

"The Moor," Ronja tested the words on her tongue.

Evie offered her the painted package, and she took it warily. Its weight and dimensions were familiar.

"This is what I delivered to you," Ronja realized with a start.

It was not a question, but Roark answered anyway.

"Yes," he said, taking the parcel back with careful hands. "A record."

Roark pried the paper open carefully and drew out an obsidian disk lined with hundreds of faintly ridged rings.

Ronja reached for it curiously, but he snatched it from her as if she were a child reaching for a delicate vase.

"They're fragile," he apologized. "Never touch a record on its face, hold it by the edges, like this." Roark showed her how to pinch the rim of the record with the very tips of her fingers.

"What's it made of?" Ronja asked as Roark placed the record on the wheel. "Stone?"

"Vinyl," Roark replied, twisting the **P WER** dial with the tips of his long fingers. There was a hollow pop, followed by a spray of static. To Ronja's surprise, the record began to rotate steadily on its axis, rocking faintly as it spun. "Come here, love, I want you to drop the needle."

"What?"

"Here, see this?" Roark pointed to the metal arm that brandished the thick needle.

Ronja slipped from the couch onto the plush rug. She shuffled toward the machine on her knees, cautious.

"Yeah," she said uncertainly as she came to a halt next to Roark.

"Raise it up right here, exactly. Now move it to the edge."

"Here?"

"Yes. Now very carefully, I want you to drop the needle on the outermost ring."

"Won't that hurt it? I thought you said they were fragile."

"Just trust me."

Cringing, Ronja let the arm fall.

There was a mournful squeak, and for one horrible second Ronja thought she might have ruined it.

Then music graced the air.

37: VINYL

The song began slowly, the way a tired engine creaks to life after a long period of stasis. A drum was thudding between the fluid notes of a powerful instrument Ronja did not recognize. Beneath the rhythm, a piano was being played gently, as if the musician was afraid they might wake someone. The song was issued from the speakers on the sides of the box, but to Ronja it felt as though it was born of the air itself. It was so pure, unpolluted by the incongruous shouts and footsteps of the jam. It was more personal than that, which made her feel as though she was connected to every person around her.

This music, this song, felt as though it was for her ears only.

Chills scampered along her spine, erupting on her skin as gooseflesh. Her lungs felt as though they might burst, inhaling wave after wave of the intoxicating beat. When the rhythm accelerated, her pulse followed. She shut her eyes, allowed it to sweep her away.

Then, a woman began to sing.

> First day you saw me I was way down low
> With my hands in my pockets and nowhere to go
> You were standing on my neck just to reach so high
> Sifting for those diamonds in the sky
>
> Blood in my veins and you say it's cold
> But if you cut my skin it will come out gold
> The brain waves are crashing on the shores of my mind
> And if you stare too long then you may go blind
>
> I got little wars
> Little wars in my head
> Telling me wrong from right
> Out of mind, out of sight

Little wars
I am a warrior

The voice wove through her mind, becoming a part of her before she could understand how or why. It seemed as if the song had always been with her, as if she already knew what the woman was going to say before she said it.

Though it came from a machine, it did not flatten her emotions the way her Singer did. It heightened them, dredging up her rage, terror, and determination. She could see everything before her and everything behind, every possible outcome of their mission, but only one that was acceptable.

Now I know I seem strange when I'm walking alone
But I'm laced in my thoughts and I'm lost in my soul
I got love for the rest and the best of you
But I'm leaving in the morning for a different view

I got words in my belly and they keep me high
I got voices in my head and they never lie
I got feathers in my ribs and I'm gonna fly
I got two little words and they're "good" and "bye"

I got little wars
Little wars in my head
Telling me wrong from right
Out of mind, out of sight
Little wars
I am a warrior

The song faded out on the wings of the piano, and was replaced by the crack and hiss of the needle tracing its cyclical path. Ronja opened her eyes. The room felt unfamiliar, the dim lights too bright. Her skin was foreign, as if she had abandoned it for a spell.

"Who was—?" Ronja started to ask.

The ethereal voice stole her breath again. She leaned forward eagerly, entranced by the way the whirling disk shed sound like a snake shedding skin.

> *When the day shakes beneath the*
> *Hands of night*
> *When your page is ripped*
> *From the Book of Life*
> *When your knees crash*
> *Into the ground*
> *And your desperate lips*
> *Won't make a sound*
>
> *When you're all alone*
> *And the night is deep*
> *When you're surrounded*
> *But you want to weep*
> *When the morning comes*
> *And it's all but bleak*
> *When you want to scream*
> *But instead you're meek*
>
> *Sing my friend*
> *Into the dark*
>
> *Sing my friend*
> *Into the deep*
>
> *Sing my friend*
> *Into the black*
>
> *Sing my friend*
> *There and back*

There was a soft click. Ronja allowed her eyelids to flutter open. She did not realize she had closed them. The mechanical needle scooted away from the record, which had ceased its revolutions. The vinyl glimmered dully in the firelight.

"Is it over?" Ronja asked, unable to mask her regret.

She felt clean, raw, exhumed. Her emotions were more powerful than ever. Not long ago this would have terrified her, but these were somehow manageable. As if she were in total control, had some sort of weapon at her fingertips.

"There are two more songs on the other side, but we should get moving," Roark said, taking the disk from its axis and flipping it thrice between his palms. "It helps, doesn't it?"

Ronja bobbed her head, her eyes still locked onto the now static record player.

"Why did The Conductor call it The Music?" she asked, brushing the edge of the leather case with the rough pad of her finger. "Real music, it's nothing like His."

Evie, Iris, Henry, and Roark shared a knowing look.

"I was hoping you would understand that," Roark said, gently moving her finger from the player and shutting the lid with a hollow click.

"It was a trick of sorts," Evie explained, getting to her feet and stretching toward the ceiling with a groan. "Bullon and the original Westervelt thought people would be more susceptible to their manipulation if it went by a familiar name."

"That's awful," Ronja burst out, surprising herself.

"Looks like we have an audiophile on our hands," Evie said with a chuckle, moving to collect her rifle.

Ronja looked around for answers.

"A lover of music," Henry explained.

"Well," Roark said, climbing to his feet, the record player swinging from his hand by its grip. "According to Anthemite tradition, we're now prepared to kick some ass. Shall we?"

38: RESPONSIBILITIES

O nce Roark had stowed the record player, Henry insisted on performing an inventory on their supplies in his coffee-stained notebook. It was a nervous habit he had developed as a child, but it made him feel in control.

Roark rolled his eyes melodramatically at the proposal, but emptied his knapsack and pockets onto the carpet without further complaint.

He had brought along his gold-embossed pistol, two black radios with extendable antennas, his twin stingers, another pistol, a drawstring bag that clanked with bullets, and a roll of documents tied with a cord.

Iris had packed a different kind of arsenal. Her bag was busting with surgical tools, bandages, and enough pills to last a lifetime.

"She has two cousins, darling, not twenty," Evie reminded her, eyebrows high on her forehead.

"You never know," Iris replied stoutly, plunking down several amber canisters of pills. "What if I need to remove their Singers on site? What if they're sick? What if—?"

Roark clapped a hand to her shoulder and flicked his gaze toward Ronja, who was staring into the low fire with glassy eyes.

Iris was silent after that.

Evie had packed only Lux, a pair of plain stingers, a spyglass, and a knife with a wicked, serrated edge. Henry quickly scribbled down a list of her belongings, then she was free to do as she wished. As the inventory continued, she sat cross-legged on the hearth, scrubbing the barrel of her gun with a long, thin brush.

Ronja was embarrassed to admit that she carried almost nothing of value. It was unanimously decided that she would leave her pathetically small pocketknife behind, along with her knapsack, and would be outfitted with one of Evie's stingers in addition to her newly-programmed stingring.

Henry had not brought much in the way of weapons or medical supplies. Instead, his bag was stuffed full of several dozen rolls of paper. Ronja drew out one such scroll and laid it out on the lush rug.

"Blueprints of the compound," he said, eyeing the detailed map over the lip of his notepad. "I don't know how old they are."

"The ink looks old," Roark commented, kneeling next to Ronja to appraise the documents. "Are you sure they're accurate?"

"If you prefer we could just flip a coin at every intersection," Henry replied blandly.

Ronja ignored them both and bent closer to the blueprints. Even on paper the prison was a maze. It put knots in her stomach.

"Don't worry," Roark reassured her, sensing her apprehension. He gave her a lopsided smile, which did little to unlace the hitches in her gut. "I was inside a few times as a child. I have a pretty good memory."

He tapped his skull with a long finger. Ronja nodded and changed the subject quickly. "How the hell are we going to get this stuff inside?" she asked, lifting one of his elegant stingers and examining it by the dying light of the fire.

"Under our coats. But the truth is, we could walk in guns blazing and no one would say a word. No one would dare question a Westervelt," he replied.

"You sure about that?" Henry growled.

Ronja looked over at her oldest friend. He stood near the hearth, his notepad open in his hand, his pen tucked behind his ear. His dark eyes roved across the spread of weapons and medical supplies uncertainly.

"Quite," Roark said with undeniable finality. "You satisfied, H?"

"*Quite*," Henry replied, his tone dripping with vexation.

Iris and Roark repacked their belongings in silence. Evie continued to scrub the barrel of her gun, a fresh cigarette dangling from her lips. Henry closed his notebook and stared blankly into the failing embers. There was something off about him, something other than the obvious strain of the situation. If she did not know better, she might say Henry was . . .

"All right, are we set?" Roark broke her musings.

He got to his feet and shouldered his pack, peering around the room expectantly.

Iris and Ronja stood as one. Evie gave no indication that she would be moving any time soon, and Henry continued to mull over his fresh notes.

The two girls followed Roark from the cottage and into the night. The air was brimming with sound, though it was not jarring the way it was in the city. The crickets, the rustle of the grass, all melded into a single, ceaseless rhythm. It was a bit like a song itself, Ronja thought, as she threw her head back to view the winking constellations. She had never seen them so clearly. There were more stars than she could have imagined.

It was somehow comforting to know they had always been there beyond the sheet of smog and light pollution.

Ronja hoped she could show them to Georgie and Cosmin.

Iris and Roark dropped their burdens to the gravel as the boy fished for the keys in his coat pocket. Ronja stood by, watching with solemn eyes.

"Hang on, I forgot something," Iris exclaimed abruptly.

She took off back toward the cottage, her red curls bouncing in the moonlight.

Roark popped the trunk, and Ronja reached down to retrieve the surgeon's duffle. A hand, dark and strong, intercepted her own.

"Ronja," Roark began in her ear.

"Please don't," she breathed, gazing blindly at their crossed fingers. "I know they're probably gone, but I have to try. What if it was Henry, or Evie, or Iris?"

"I was just going to say, I would have helped you even if it wasn't my responsibility to do so," Roark replied. "And that I'm sorry you can't stay. We would have been lucky to have you in our family."

"Oh."

In an instant his arms were around her, and she was transported back to her room in the Belly, where he had lifted her from the floor. Back then he had held her as if she might break at the slightest touch. Now, he crushed her to his chest with such ferocity she thought she might snap in two.

Ronja breathed in his scent. Fresh rain, gasoline, cigarette smoke.

Not a day ago she had beaten him within an inch of his life. She did not regret the bruises she had left him with, but she found she wanted to touch him in a different way. She wanted to leave a different sort of mark on his face.

Ronja pulled her head away from his chest, looking up at him with her heart in her throat. Roark looked down at her as if he were looking up at the night sky.

He leaned down toward her, lips parted. She rose on her tiptoes.

"Are we ready, then?" a gruff voice inquired.

Ronja sprang away from Roark, touching her lips where his had almost brushed.

Henry was standing not two yards from them, his thick arms crossed, his expression thunderous. Ronja had not even heard him approach.

"Yeah," Roark said easily. "All set."

"Yeah," Ronja reiterated sharply.

Henry's interruption infuriated her. Before she was freed of her Singer, she had believed it to be sacrilegious for a mutt to be romantically involved with anyone other than one of their own. She was not a mutt anymore. Perhaps she never was. Should she not be able to kiss who she liked without someone breathing down the back of her neck?

I can't do this now, she realized, unbraiding herself internally.

"Let's go," she said, stalking away from the two boys with her shoulders set and footsteps sure.

39: DEAD LIGHTS

T he drive was predominantly silent save for the rush of the wind
and the guttural hum of the engine. Roark drove this time, as he
was the only one who knew the route to Red Bay. Ronja sat in the
passenger seat again, and the rest crowded into the back.

Ronja did not know if it was her fear or the motion that made
her so nauseated, but either way she was miserable. At least the sting
of her wound was muted by a fresh dose of pain-killers.

She stared up at the wandering night sky as they drove onward.
She would have found it beautiful were she not so terrified. The stars
were nearly as dense as the swirling prairie grasses whizzing past
their wheels. They glinted fiercely, as though they were desperate to
be alive.

"You know they're all dead?"

Ronja twisted around. It was Henry who had spoken. He too was
looking up with dull eyes.

"The stars?" she prompted.

"Yeah," he confirmed, switching his gaze to her face. "They've
been dead for millions of years. Their light is just reaching us now."

Ronja mulled this over for a time, then spoke. "At least they left
a mark."

Out of the corner of her eye, she saw Roark crack a half smile.

No one uttered another word until they crested a mammoth
hilltop. Roark slowed the auto, then cut the ignition and the
headlights. They rolled to a silent stop at the summit. Ronja half rose
from her seat, straining against her safety belt.

In the distance, the lights of Red Bay flickered.

It was far more vast than Ronja had hoped, dwarfed only by the
black bay to its left. The bay filtered into the ocean, she supposed, but
she could not see where it ended or began.

The compound itself crouched low between two great hills and spread like a plague across the grassland. It was stark white, but glowed reddish orange beneath an army of floodlights. It was enveloped in three layers of wire fences. The outermost barrier was dotted with gargantuan watchtowers, almost as high as those that encased Revinia.

Ronja felt the blood drain from her face.

Roark clicked his safety belt and spun around to view their companions. Ronja followed suit, scrambling to master her expression.

"Evie. You're going to set up at the edge of the tree line between those two towers," Roark pointed at the twin towers on the south side of the prison. "Stay in the woods when you travel. The lights sweep the land every thirty seconds."

"Shouldn't we be anywhere but the top of a hill, then?" Henry hissed.

"Blind spot," Roark replied shortly. He turned his attention back to Evie. She was clutching her rifle between her legs. When she sat, it rose far above her head. "Are you ready?"

Evie grinned. "Skitz yeah!"

Roark smiled broadly, but quickly whisked it away. "Get out there then, and take this." He reached into his pocket and withdrew one of the black radios. A pinprick of red light on its face indicated that it was live. "Don't call unless you have to, they might intercept it."

Evie took the device with a nod of gratitude. She kissed Iris on the cheek smartly, patted Henry on the shoulder, and hopped out of the car.

"See you in a few hours," she said, slinging her weapon over her shoulder and starting toward the trees.

"Evie," Ronja called softly.

The black-haired girl spun around, gravel hissing under the heel of her boot.

"Thank you."

"Any time, mate," Evie replied, offering her a sloppy, one fingered salute. "May your song guide you home."

"May your song guide you home," Ronja replied in the customary format. The words felt undeniably right on her tongue.

Evie turned back around with an easy smile and was swallowed by the dense mob of evergreens.

Iris released an unsteady breath. Henry began to rub her back briskly. Ronja started to apologize, but Roark spoke.

"No more talking," he ordered.

Roark gunned the engine and started down the hill toward Red Bay. Although the compound was deep in the valley, Ronja felt as though it loomed far, far above.

40: BERIK

They ditched the auto in a blind spot between two towers about a hundred yards from the outermost wall, then veiled it in a tarp cross-stitched with green, brown, and black threads.

"Berik said he would leave us a master key at the outer gate," Roark said as they crouched behind the vehicle, Iris hefting her long skirts to keep them from brushing the damp grass. Ronja wobbled in her heels and steadied herself against Henry. "He told the guards a surprise inspection crew would be coming in through the side door, but he was not to give my name. We shouldn't have any trouble getting in."

"*Shouldn't?* Iris hissed, hiking her train higher still, revealing the three syringes of sedative strapped to her thigh. The rest of her equipment, which combined weighed almost as much as she, remained stowed in the trunk.

Roark shrugged. "Never say never."

"We should go," Henry interjected, squinting at his watch in the pale moonlight. "We have 7 minutes."

"Walk fast and casual," Roark commanded them, getting to his feet.

Iris and Henry rose and began to stride toward the first gate. Ronja was about to follow them when Roark caught her arm and pulled her back.

"What?" she demanded.

"You should know," he said. "I may have told Berik you were . . . "

Ronja raised her brows, rolled her wrist, prompting him to go on.

Roark cleared his throat, shifted uncomfortably. "Pregnant."

"*Excuse* me?"

"It made the most sense," he said throwing his hands up defensively. "It fits my reputation and explains our need for secrecy."

"That's the *best* you could do?" Ronja groaned, slapping her forehead.

"I told him we want to end the pregnancy," he went on with a sheepish air that did not suit him.

"Okay, okay," Ronja exhaled deeply, tugging her hand down her face. "*Fine.*"

Roark grinned fleetingly and offered her his elbow. "Shall we, love?"

Ronja shook her head, a faint smile dusting her lips.

"If we get out of this . . . " She trailed off, not daring to consider the future.

"Yes?"

"Never mind."

Henry and Iris were waiting for them with their backs pressed to the chain link fence. Iris was gnawing on her fingernail. Henry might have looked at ease if not for his hand, which rested on the pistol in the waistband of his trousers.

"Berik told me the key would be around here somewhere," Roark said, disentangling his elbow from Ronja's and crouching again in the cool grass. "I just hope . . . ah!"

The boy grinned triumphantly and brandished a silver key as long as one of his slim fingers. He stood, brushing off his silk-covered knees. He tossed the key into the air, caught it, then inserted it into the lock with a flourish. With a screech that drew a wince from Ronja, Roark pushed open the gate on Red Bay.

The quartet stood rigid for a moment, peering into the mouth of the enemy.

A fine gravel path led up to the compound. It was surrounded by a pristinely-manicured lawn, so different from the wild prairie just beyond the barrier. Searchlights roamed the expanse like specters. No alarms blared when the lights passed over them, but still they flinched each time their skin blazed abruptly white.

They crossed the threshold in pairs, first Iris and Henry, then Ronja and Roark. It seemed as if the music of the night faded away, though the forest was only a few paces behind. Only the sound of their crunching footsteps and thudding pulses could be heard in the unnaturally still air.

Halfway across the first enclosure, Iris reached out and took Henry by the hand. Ronja had to hide her own inside her cloak to keep from doing the same to Roark.

Despite the chill, they were all steeped in sweat by the time they reached the second gate. Roark fumbled with the key and dropped it into the shadows.

"Pitcher," Henry whispered.

Roark cast his friend a scathing look as he bent to retrieve the key. Iris was fidgeting with her dress. Ronja heard the soft clink of glass when the syringes tapped together beneath the cascading lace.

Roark scooped up the key and jammed it into the lock with trembling fingers, for a split second breaking his tranquil facade. The gate opened at his touch, and they bolted though as quickly as they dared.

Time moved sluggishly as they approached the final obstacle between them and the compound. Up close, Red Bay was more massive than Ronja had realized. It was so still, so quiet, so without expression, it reminded her of a gravestone. There were no windows, no doors that she could see.

There was no escape.

Ronja felt her throat tighten. She stumbled, and Roark caught her by the elbow. She looked up at him gratefully, but he was already pulling her forward, his jaw set.

With a few more steps, the click of a lock, and the rattle of chain link scraping against gravel, they were through.

They were inside Red Bay.

Roark wasted no time. "This way," he said, moving to the front of the group.

"Two minutes," Henry warned, falling into step beside him.

"We're not far," Roark replied, his eyes fixed dead ahead.

The wall seemed to stretch on for miles. Two minutes felt like twenty. Ronja was ready to scream by the time the heir came to a halt before a nondescript white door.

"This is it," he said as they fell into line behind him.

Roark straightened his coat and combed his fingers through his hair. Ronja adjusted her hat, touched the feathers to make sure they remained in place.

"Would you do the honors?"

Ronja glanced up. Roark was watching her expectantly, his hand motioning toward the sealed door. She nodded. Forcing down her dread, she rapped four times on the blank face of the portal. Each knock sounded like a gunshot.

The door sprang open immediately, forcing her heart into her throat. Ronja reeled back and Roark caught her by the shoulders firmly. She wrenched free of his grasp, observing the man in the doorframe.

It was difficult to see Dr. Berik. There was little light both in and outside his apartment. He was dressed in a simple button-down, a white lab coat that brushed his knees, and a hastily knotted tie. His hair was colorless and slicked into a greasy comb-over. He wore thick bifocals, behind which his gray eyes shivered and roved ceaselessly.

"Mr. Westervelt, sir," the doctor greeted Roark. His voice was high and reedy. It matched his shifting eyes and oily scalp. "What a pleasant surprise."

"Hardly a surprise, I phoned hours ago," Roark replied flatly. His voice was firm and low, darker even than when he had spoken to the Off at the edge of the city. Berik quelled, quivering like a rat in a maze.

So this is Victor Westervelt III, Ronja thought.

"Of course, sir, of course. I only meant that the hour and company were a bit . . . " the doctor squirmed as he searched for the right word. "Unorthodox."

"You would do well not to question my companions, *Wilfred,*" Roark growled.

He seemed to grow taller with each word. Berik shrank toward the floor.

"Of course, sir, of course," Berik amended hastily. "Come in, come in." He jumped aside with surprising agility, bidding them to enter with a few sweeps of a liver spotted hand.

Roark went first, exuding authority. The rest followed rapidly. Ronja adjusted her hat to make sure it covered her wound, which itched insatiably.

Berik's apartment was spartan. It was furnished with a

threadbare pastel sofa, a low coffee table, a dining table with two spindly chairs, and worn shag carpets. No photographs or paintings decorated the beige walls. Three identical doors dominated the far wall. If Roark was correct, one of them led to the physician's examination room.

Ronja stroked her newly programmed stingring reassuringly.

Just like with a pitched subtrain rider, she reminded herself. *Besides,* look *at him.*

Berik was even more pathetic in the lamplight. His skin was creased and spotted with age. His cheeks were skeletal, and his coat appeared several sizes too large.

"Who is my patient, Mr. Westervelt, sir?" the old man asked in his ragged voice.

Roark stepped toward Ronja and slipped a strong arm around her waist. She felt herself blush, and was for once grateful. She was posing as his lover, after all.

"As I mentioned over the phone, Ms. Mills and I are in a slight predicament. We would like you to take care of it."

"Of course, of course," Berik mumbled breathily. "Who are your other companions, may I ask?" he said, motioning with a limp hand at Iris and Henry.

"Insurance," Roark said, smiling tightly. "I am to be a business man, after all."

Ronja glanced back at the two other Anthemites. Henry was six-two and muscle-bound. He crossed his arms imposingly, reminding Ronja of the tattooed guard posted outside the Office. Iris was less foreboding at first glance, but it was difficult to misinterpret her expression.

Berik blanched. For a moment, Ronja wondered if he had lost all the blood in his body.

"Right this way, Ms. Mills," the doctor said weakly.

He hobbled toward the center door on the far wall and began to fumble with the key ring at his belt. Ronja trailed him cautiously. She came to a halt behind Berik and watched over his shoulder as he chose an unassuming silver key and inserted it into the lock with shaking fingers.

Ronja glanced back at her three companions as the

hunchback held the door open for her.

Right when he closes the door. Ronja reassured herself as she crossed the threshold. *Right when . . .*

Berik shut the door behind her and flipped on the lights. Ronja blinked, peering around. The examination room housed a large leather table covered in a swath of sanitary paper. There was a quaint wooden desk opposite the table and a large, plain countertop with three sets of drawers at the far end of the room.

"Ms. Mills," Berik began with a sigh, shuffling toward the countertop. "I must tell you that I—"

Ronja crossed the room in three long strides and smashed her open hand into his liver-spotted neck. Berik did not even cry out when he crumpled to the floor, landing face down on the tiles with a sickening thud.

Ronja looked down at him for a moment, her face an emotionless mask. Then she let out a puff of air she had forgotten to release.

"Roark," she called, turning on her heel and starting toward the door. "Berik is—"

The girl froze, her hand on the knob. Her nose twitched. She drew a tentative breath. The air scorched her.

Ronja cried out, clamping her hands over her nose and mouth, and threw her back against the door.

The air around the vents shivered as the compact room was flooded with gas. Her eyes watering, her cognition wilting, Ronja whipped back around and jiggled the knob. It would not budge.

Tucking her face into her elbow, Ronja began to slam her fist into the face of the door.

"Ronja?" came a muffled, familiar voice.

The knob rattled as Roark attempted to enter.

"Ronja!"

The girl continued to pound on the exit. The gas was thick in the air, shuddering like a mirage, bathing her senses in honey. Her knees buckled, her hand screeched down the iron face of the door.

She needed to warn them. They might have only seconds. Her brain hovered above her skull, attached by a single, groaning thread. Her mouth was numb, her tongue like cotton.

"Roark . . . " she tried to scream, but it came out as a rattling gasp. She pressed her forehead to the iron as her eyelids flickered shut. "They know."

41: THE OLD METHODS
Roark

R onja was utterly silent behind the door. Her frantic knocking was replaced by the sound of his heart throbbing in his ribs.

"Henry," Roark said, whirling. "Do you have your tools? We have to get in there."

Henry, who was staring at the sealed doorway with vacant eyes, never got the chance to answer.

Time froze when the pair of Offs busted through the apartment door.

Roark's body lurched into action before his mind could react. He grabbed for the stingers holstered at his sides, but his first adversary was already upon him. Roark lashed out with his fists, but it was like striking steel with his bare knuckles.

The Off was twice his size. He wore a matte black Singer. Roark had been raised in the shadows of men and women with such onyx Singers. They lived only to fight and serve his father and Bullon. They could not be bought or reasoned with; their minds were beyond resurrection.

Skitz.

The heir spun fluidly and vaulted over the couch. He landed with a shuddering thud atop the low coffee table. He whipped out his stingers and flicked them to life. They buzzed in his hands like angry wasps.

"Come on, pitcher!" he bellowed.

His opponent appeared utterly unmoved. With an animalistic grunt, he shoved the sofa out of the way as if it weighed nothing. It struck the far wall and cracked the plaster.

"Now you're just showing off," Roark grumbled.

"Trip! He—!"

Iris's plea was cut short when the Off she and Henry were

battling smashed her into the floor like a rag doll. Roark lunged at her, but his own adversary flooded his vision.

The Off hit him with the full force of a steamer, knocking the stingers from his hands and the breath from his lungs. He heard his ribs crack. The Off shoved his knee into his gut and pressed his thick forearm to his neck.

"Henry!" Roark wheezed. "Help Ir—!"

The only response was the sound of a stinger flaring against skin and the unmistakable thud of a limp body striking the floor.

Ronja was still quiet beyond the locked door.

"Ro—!" Roark rasped.

"You have seen better days, son."

A familiar dread settled over Roark like a toxic fog. It consumed the pain in his ribs and the fire in his lungs.

The Off released him abruptly. Roark rolled backward, then sprang to his feet, fighting a scream as his fractures spread. Still, he had known worse. Worse was standing before him now, smiling slyly.

"I long suspected you of treachery," Victor Westervelt II purred. "All I needed was a shred of proof, but instead you offer me this bounty."

He stood in the open doorway, his hands clasped behind his back and his chin high. Two more dead-eyed Offs with black Singers flanked him, just as large as the first pair. Victor's colorless eyes flickered like a moving picture as they drank in the image of his son. His thin lips curled in disgust.

"You always did take after your sister," Westervelt continued.

Roark smashed his teeth together, but refused the bait. His stingers had rolled in opposite directions across the carpet. He would have to dive to reach them.

"The years have eased my rage. I have come to realize I may have given up on her too hastily," Victor mused, stroking his sharp jaw with a spindly finger. "Perhaps you can be redeemed, with the right persuasion."

Victor inclined his head. The four Offs converged on Roark, their electric weapons snapping like watchdogs. One took a pair of handcuffs from his belt.

Roark snarled and lunged at the closest of the four. He was deflected like a gnat. Before he knew it, he was pinned again, arms twisted and cuffed.

"I'll see you soon, Victor," his father called.

The Offs dragged him from the apartment and into the bleached corridors of Red Bay. They passed scores of identical doors Roark knew led to prison cells. Pathetic moans threaded through the cracks in the doorways.

Roark assumed he would be forced into one such cell. To his surprise, the Offs hauled him into a dimly lit observation room that overlooked one of the cells. The cell beyond the one-way glass was empty. The floor and two of the walls were concrete and were stained with splotches of brown Roark knew had once been red. The left-hand wall of the cell was also a window, identical to the one Roark gazed through. It looked into another vacant prison cell.

Roark did not struggle as the sentries chained him to the steel chair facing the window. A dashboard full of blinking lights and brass knobs only Evie could make sense of sprawled beneath the glass, just out of his reach.

When he was secure, the Offs left without a word.

As soon as they disappeared, Roark began to fight against his shackles, clinging to the vain hope that the craftsmanship would be shoddy. It was not, of course. If there was one thing he appreciated about his father, it was his commitment to quality.

Roark stilled himself, his hopes bleeding away.

He waited.

Nearly two hours passed without so much as a whisper from his captors. Roark was a breath from nodding off by the time the door flew open on the opposite side of the glass.

He shot to his feet, but was yanked back by his chains.

Two Offs stood in the doorway. One wore his hair in a greasy black ponytail that matched his startlingly unattractive face. The other was entirely bald, with a hooked nose. Their Singers were black, and they were just as large as the guards Roark had fought.

Between them was a scrawny prisoner in a thin, white shift. Her head was shaved, revealing the healing scar on the side of her head. Electricity burns marred her skin, and blood gushed from her nose. Still, she raged. He could not hear her through the soundproof glass, but her lips formed a string of vile oaths.

Ronja.

Roark swore and strained against his unyielding restraints.

The guards threw Ronja to the ground, and she skidded across the concrete. She immediately sprang to her feet, her twig legs trembling. She raised her fists before her and wiped her bloodied nose with the back of her wrist.

The guards laughed. Roark could imagine their nauseating guffaws. Ronja took advantage of their amusement and bolted for the door. The Off with the hooked nose caught her and smashed her back into the ground. Her head ricocheted off the concrete. Roark was glad he could not hear the sound of her skull cracking.

Ronja blinked sluggishly, attempted to rise. The bald guard kicked her in the stomach. His partner gripped him by the arm. For half a moment, Roark thought he was going to suggest restraint.

Then he gestured to Ronja, said something Roark could not hear, but innately understood. The two sentinels shared a ghoulish grin. The black haired Off reached down and grasped Ronja by the neck. He dragged her to her feet and pinned her to the wall with a single hand. The other he began to trace up her inner thigh.

Ronja trembled. Her eyes were utterly blank. Her bare feet danged an inch above the floor, twitching.

Roark was screaming, hurling the foulest words he could think of at the glass. The Offs could not hear him, but they knew he was there. The one with the crooked nose smiled sickly, winked in his general direction.

Roark's shackles bit into his wrists and ankles, drawing blood.

The Off holding Ronja began to fumble with his belt buckle.

Roark did not hear the door open behind him, nor did he register the lazy footfalls sauntering toward him. Victor appeared out of nowhere at his side. His son twisted around and looked up at him desperately.

"Stop this!" Roark demanded hoarsely.

"My Offs work hard, they deserve a reward," Victor responded absently, watching the scene unfold calmly.

"Please—"

"Do you swear to answer my questions truthfully, no matter what they may be?"

"Yes! Stop them!"

Victor leaned forward with infuriating lethargy and pressed a button on the dash. The intercom screeched to life inside the cell, and the men froze. Ronja looked around wildly, panic dissolving the fog in her eyes.

"Havarland, Bayard, retreat to your quarters."

The dark haired Off let Ronja fall without a second thought. She crumbled to the floor. Her eyelids fell shut like curtains on a terrifying opera.

Roark closed his own eyes, exhaled slowly. He sank back into his chair, which was slick with his sweat. Pain came crawling in through the slits in his wrists and ankles, but he ignored it.

"You called her name," his father noted.

Roark opened his eyes, dread welling up inside of him.

"Ronja, was it?"

"Let her and the others go, and I'll tell you anything you want to know," Roark bargained.

"I think not."

Victor perched on the edge of the dashboard, gazing down at him with shrewd, gray eyes. Roark had not seen his father for several months. When he was not in the Belly or on a mission, he spent most of his time at his flat in the core, stoking the rumors that kept his traitorous double life under wraps. In their time apart, it seemed age had started to creep into his father's brittle features, so different from Roark's own.

"You've rather shown your hand, son," Victor said, bringing him back to the claustrophobic chamber.

"Does it matter?" Roark snarled. "Aren't you just going to stick Singers on all of us anyway?"

Victor cracked a deadly half smile. "Many are surprised to learn I prefer the old methods of persuasion to the new. Progress can and will be made at any cost, but when it comes to my family, I prefer a more personal touch."

Roark spat in his father's face.

Victor blinked rapidly as a glob of saliva dribbled from his brow into his eye. He reached into his pocket and withdrew a silk kerchief. He cleansed his face methodically, then tossed the cloth to the ground.

"Your comrades are your pressure point, this girl in particular," his father said, nodding toward the window as if nothing had happened. "Why would I waste my time with a seven-hour-long procedure when I can make you talk right now?"

Victor peered over his shoulder at Ronja. She had not moved since the Offs had left. Roark felt his stomach sink as a grin split his father's mouth, his polished teeth glittering in the bluish backlight.

The man rose abruptly, pursed his lips into an unreadable line. He began to pace steadily, just out of his son's line of sight.

"How long have you been working for the rebels?" Victor asked.

"Since I was taken as a child," Roark replied, his eyes locked onto Ronja.

"What do you do for them, precisely?"

"I bring them information on you, on The Conductor, on the company."

"How long did it take them to bend you to their will?"

Roark barked a harsh laugh.

"This might be difficult for you to understand, but they actually got me to help them without the use of torture. Strange, isn't it?"

Victor was at his back in an instant, his breath startlingly cool on the his neck. He clapped his hands to Roark's rigid shoulders and learned toward his ear, the one that would soon be crowned with a Singer. "You were always an insolent child, even with my guidance," Victor whispered.

"Guidance," Roark snorted disdainfully, keeping his eyes fixed on the glass.

"How many of my own Officers are traitors?" Victor asked, changing the subject.

"More than you'll ever be able to weed out," Roark taunted through gritted teeth.

That was a lie. 52 Anthemites were situated in various Off stations throughout the city, but Revinia employed over ten thousand.

"I want names," Victor said, a twinge of vexation coloring his tone.

Roark clenched his jaw, switched his gaze back to Ronja. He could see her eyes roving behind her papery lids. He wondered if she was dreaming and hoped she was somewhere far away.

"Bayard and Havarland did not go far," Victor reminded him softly.

"Smith," Roark said through his clenched jaw. "Joshua Smith."

"Smith was killed in an auto accident half a year ago," Victor said sweetly. Roark could not see his face, but could hear the vindictive smile on his mouth. "I can smell the lie on you, Roark Westervelt, that is what you call yourself now, is it not? Tell another falsehood and she will pay dearly for it."

"Harriet Fairbanks," Roark said after a moment.

Harriet was currently on leave from her post in the core with her new infant daughter. She would be safe in the Belly.

"If that is the extent of the Anthem's infiltration, I am far from impressed."

"Agatha Morrison. Brendan Tan. Cynthia Link."

Morrison and Link were currently suffering from influenza in the quarantine ward. Cynthia had broken her leg the week before on a mission. All three were protected underground.

For now.

"Is that all?" Victor asked.

"All I can recall," Roark replied levelly.

"You are lying."

It was not a question.

"Believe whatever you like," Roark retorted vehemently. "I'm in the inner circle of the Anthem, far more valuable than any of my comrades. Let them go. You only need me."

Roark felt his father's eyes drilling into the back of his head. He heard his fingers slide together like cogs meshing. His footsteps commenced, and Roark heard the door open. Stark white light flooded the room. Ronja was obscured in the violent glare.

Victor paused. Roark held his breath.

"I believe I heard one of our guests calling out for Ronja during an experiment. I am certain, however, that this was merely a coincidence."

Roark closed his eyes as his father shut the door with a polite click and the muted rattle of a knob.

42: THE IMPOSSIBLE

Ronja awoke with a hoarse cry, her cheek raw against damp concrete. She struggled to her feet, which were bare and filthy. Her fine clothes had been stripped and replaced with a flimsy hospital gown. She crossed her arms over her chest, peering around self-consciously.

Her breath caught in her lungs.

Two walls of her suffocating cell were stone, crusted with mold and dried blood. One was mirrored. The other, glass.

Ronja could not take her eyes off the girl that had hijacked her reflection.

Angry burns peeked out from the collar of her gown. Her wild curls had been shaved, leaving behind a sparse stubble. Without her hair to cover it, her scar was even more grotesque, and looked infected.

Her face was a patchwork of purple and black. Had she been in a fight? Hazy memories laced with her screams hovered on the outskirts of her mind.

Two men. Their hands. She could not move. Could not fight. Could not run or scream or cry. Could not . . .

Ronja shook her head viciously. She massaged her temples as if she could smooth the disjointed memories away, but they were wedged firmly in place.

She refocused on her reflection.

Lopsided. Monstrous. Disgusting.

Mutt.

The word lanced through her, followed by a familiar sting. Movement through the window caught her eye. She switched her gaze to the side. A scream built in her throat, but died on her tongue.

Beyond the glass wall was a room identical to her own. On the floor, crumpled like an old newspaper, was a boy. His back was turned to her, his head was shaved, but there was no mistaking him.

Ronja flew at the window. She pounded on the glass with her fists. It shuddered and stilled maddeningly. She backed up and threw her weight at the barrier. She was deflected like a fly against a windshield.

The noise stirred Cosmin, and he rolled over sluggishly. His eyes blinked slowly.

Once.

Twice.

This time, Ronja's scream managed to break through her lips.

Cosmin's eyes had sunken deep into their sockets. Bruises faded to the color of rotting bananas peppered his face, but they seemed several days old. Why? What had changed? Had he stopped struggling? Had he given up?

Ronja pressed her palms to the cool glass.

"Cos?" she whispered, as if his name could shatter the window.

The boy stared at her blankly, his eyes dull and flat. Blood had crusted in and around both his ears. Ronja leaned her forehead on the glass. Her breath fogged, temporarily veiling her cousin's—her brother's— frail form.

"*Cos?*"

The boy blinked mutely. Could he even see her? If he could, did he even recognize her?

Ronja felt faint. Her knees buckled, but she refused to fall again. She did not want them to see her broken. She knew they were watching her. She had read about one-way glass in the library. She wanted nothing more than to run at the mirror and hurl her rage at it, but knew it would do no good.

She inhaled.

Exhaled.

Inhaled.

Cosmin was alive. He was right next to her. He was broken, but his heart still beat. If he was alive, that meant Georgie and Layla might be too.

Ronja pressed her sweat-drenched back against the transparent wall.

Roark. He *had* to be alive. Red Bay belonged to his father.

Westervelt would not murder his own son, would he?

Iris and Henry. If she had been spared, had they also been? Would they all be turned into mutts? Tortured for information? Or would they be forced to undergo whatever hellish experiments the scientists had concocted? What about . . . ?

Ronja froze, her finger hovering over the bridge of her nose.

Evie.

Red Bay might not know about Evie. She might have gotten away, gone back to the Anthem and explained the situation. She could have gone on foot, or gone back for the auto. No, she would not have taken the risk. Not when the Offs were on such high alert. She would have run.

Ronja's ascending heart plummeted.

The Anthem would not come for her, a mutt. Even if Evie could convince them she was human, Terra would be there to extinguish any budding doubts Wilcox had. For some unknowable reason, she wanted Ronja gone. Perhaps even dead.

The Anthemites will come for their own though, right?

Even as Ronja weighed the question, she knew the answer.

Iris had said it herself. No one who entered Red Bay ever came out human, if they came out at all. Wilcox would not, could not, risk any more lives. They would not come.

Iris.

Ronja closed her eyes. She had begged the surgeon to help her save her family. Now, everything Iris had said was coming true. Their mission had failed. They would be killed because of her inability to protect her own family.

Ronja opened her eyes and looked back into the mirror. Her own ghastly reflection stared her down like a starved wolf.

If the Anthem would not come for them, she would get them out herself. There had to be a way. Over the past week, the impossible had been proven to her time and time again.

An entire culture free of The Music thriving beneath the streets of Revinia. Her Singer, ripped from her head to make way for a barrage of emotions and memories. Men, women, and children who looked at her and did not assume the worst. Black disks that weaved stories by spinning around a silver finger. Voices that could call up the best and worst of times. *Real* music. Something to live for. Something worth fighting for. A chance at freedom and grace.

There had to be a way out.

She would find a way. She owed it to the Anthem. She owed it to Iris and Evie, to Roark and Henry. Most of all, to her family.

Ronja paced the perimeter of her cell, trying not to look at Cosmin's crumpled form. He had closed his eyes again. His mouth sagged and drool pooled beneath his cheek.

She searched methodically for something to use as a weapon, but found nothing. She attempted to break the mirror with her bare heel, and was not surprised to find it impossible. The walls were pure concrete, so there were no loose bricks or stones she could tear out to use as blunt weapons. Her stingring had been stripped of course, but her nails were still long and sharp.

They would come for her soon, and she would be ready when they did.

43: RUSH
Evie

The radio went dead at 1:03 A.M. in a rush of static.

Evie had wanted nothing more than to scream. Instead, she crushed her own radio with the heel of her boot and buried it beneath the dank foliage.

She waited on her belly among the trees until dawn broke like a yolk in the sky. Roark had warned her that if they were not out after an hour, they were dead or worse.

Still, Evie could not bring herself to leave.

Lying flat on her stomach, she concocted a series of fantastical explanations for their tardiness.

They had decided to free the entire compound. They had discovered a portal to an alternate universe. They had met The Conductor, and it turned out he wasn't such a bad guy, and they were sharing tea and crumpets.

Each successive theory was more outlandish than the last, but they kept her distracted from what was really happening in the basin of the valley.

Evie got to her feet when the sun was hovering just above the horizon. The grass had carved pressure patterns in her elbows and stomach. She slung her rifle over her shoulder and stared down at the white compound, which glowed red in the swelling light, almost as if it was bleeding.

Before her brain could halt her legs, Evie took off down the slope, her rifle thumping painfully against her back. She caught it in her hand and poured on more speed.

Movement in the nearest guard tower caused her to throw herself onto the dew-crowned hill. She tumbled several yards before catching herself on a deep-rooted thistle. She held her breath while the Off paced behind the window, as if he could hear her from two hundred yards away.

The movement subsided.

Evie curled her thistle-stung palm into a fist. She sucked in a deep breath, then scrambled back up the hill. She did not exhale until she plunged into the tree line, safe among the shadows and pines.

She sat heavily on the forest floor, trying to control her breathing.

Evie had watched through her scope as her friends made their way through each successive gate. It felt as if she were watching them march into hell. She kept her eyes trained on Iris's brilliant curls, and breathed when she touched the wall of the compound. Then, the group disappeared around the corner.

Three minutes later, the radio sputtered and died.

It was then that all but Evie's last shred of hope faded.

They had been betrayed. Discovered. Captured. Whatever the case, Iris, Roark, Henry, and Ronja were in the hands of Red Bay. Maybe in the hands of The Conductor himself. The capture of four members of the Anthem was a goldmine, especially when one of them was a high profile figure like Roark. Would that be enough to draw The Conductor to the compound?

Evie could not sneak into Red Bay herself. She could not retrieve the auto. If they had found her friends, they had certainly discovered their vehicle. She could go back to the Anthem, but would they help? Possibly, if she could explain the situation without getting shot. She was a loyal member, had grown up in the arms of the resistance. Her parents had been valued fighters before their deaths. Did that not earn her some credit?

Yes, but Wilcox won't risk lives for a lost cause.

Her desperate hopes withered before they matured.

The Anthem would not come for them. She could not go in alone—she would never find them in time. There were only two ways out of Red Bay: as a mutt or as fertilizer. Evie slammed her fist against the ground in a sudden fit of rage.

How could she have been so stupid? She could have stopped Roark. He would have listened to her. He *only* listened to her. Without Roark, Ronja would not have dreamed of getting into Red

Bay. She would have been devastated for a time, but she would have recovered. They had *all* lost people, it was an occupational hazard. Ronja would have joined the Anthem, gotten her tattoo, and become a part of their family.

Everyone would have been safe.

Iris. Roark. Henry. Ronja. *Iris.*

Where were they now?

Dead?

Tortured?

Strapped down, needles pumping the mutt virus into their veins?

No.

Evie gritted her teeth and rose on one knee, glaring down at Red Bay through salt-stained eyes.

She would find a way. She always did. She was Evie Wick. Trusted member of the Anthem, unparalleled marksman, techi, child of Ella and Norman Wick. She was . . .

"Don't tell me. You're going to storm the gates with a rifle and a stinger."

Evie shot to her feet and cocked her weapon, aiming the heavy muzzle at the owner of the disdainful voice. She squinted into the dull dawn. Her jaw dropped, and her rifle fell with it.

"*Terra?*"

44: LOST

Ronja tried to count the seconds as they passed, but lost track somewhere in the mid-thousands. She switched to staring down whoever might be observing her beyond the mirror, but grew unnerved by her reflection and had to look away. She tried to wake Cosmin by pounding on the glass and shouting, but he did not stir again. He only moved to breathe, a pained, ragged motion that clawed at her heart.

It was too bright and cold to sleep, so Ronja began to pace. Four steps across her cell, four steps back. She wondered how much time had passed since her incarceration. Her memories were still hazy. She tried to sort through them, but something was blocking the events. Her own psyche, perhaps.

She had almost given up pacing when her cell door flew open.

Ronja leapt into a fighting stance, her fists raised to protect her middle, her back foot pivoted to steady her.

The Offs who had dragged her to this cell stood in the entryway, a door in themselves.

Ronja felt her throat constrict.

Her gaze flickered to their hands, which still burned against her waist and thighs. She still heard the clink of the sentry's belt buckle, felt the weight of what had almost happened pressing on her skull, making her dizzy.

The black-haired Off reached to his hip and unclipped a pair of handcuffs. He held them out for her to see, then tossed them to the ground. They landed with a rattling clang several feet from Ronja.

"What, you expect me to cuff myself?" she asked, her voice pitching up an octave.

The men did not reply, nor did any emotion crack their apathetic masks. They simply waited, their dead eyes fixed on her.

Ronja regarded the handcuffs glinting on the damp floor.

Every fiber in her body was begging her to run, but she knew she could not fight them both. If she refused to restrain herself, they would doubtless do it for her.

She did not want to be touched by them again.

Ronja bent down reluctantly and slapped the cuffs onto her wrists, tightening them with a dramatic flourish of her fingers.

Her guards stepped off to either side of the doorway, unmoved by her silent sarcasm. The bald one motioned for her to step forward. Ronja did as she was bid, slowly. Her bare arms tingled when she brushed between their twin barrel chests. She breathed a sigh of relief when she emerged in the spacious corridor.

"Wait."

Ronja halted, partially due to shock. "It speaks," she gasped wonderingly, spinning on her heel.

The vocal guard, the bald one, did not reply. Instead, he moved to stand in front of her. She felt the other Off breathing down the back of her neck. The fine hairs there prickled, and a shiver rippled down her spine.

"Walk," the anterior guard commanded, his wide back to her.

Ronja sighed to mask her fear and started forward. Both Offs followed suit, their footsteps beating in time across the tiles.

It was almost like a drumbeat.

The thought knocked a shocked grin onto her mouth, reopening the cut in her lip that had just started to close. It seemed that music was infectious, found even in those vaccinated with Singers.

Without thinking, Ronja began to hum. No one had to teach her how. It was as natural as breathing.

"Shut up!"

Her posterior guard shoved her forward by her sheered head. Ronja faltered. Her voice hitched, but she continued to hum along with the booted footfalls.

The record spun in her mind. She could see its obsidian face speckled with shards of firelight, could hear the pop and hiss of the needle. She could feel the song on her skin. It was as if it had never stopped playing.

Sing my friend

There and back

The guards halted in unison. In one rapid motion Ronja was pinned to the wall. The black haired Off tried to stuff a rag into her mouth. The girl swallowed her music and bit down on his fingers. He swore profusely as blood gushed from his digits. Ronja gagged, but refused to let go until he cuffed her across the cheek.

They dragged her the rest of the way, each of them gripping one of her bony arms. She screamed through the putrid cloth the entire length of the corridor, the song lost to her rage. When they finally reached the end of the hall after what felt like miles, the Offs forced her through a nondescript doorway. Ronja crashed to the floor, catching herself with her palms.

She spat the disgusting cloth out, along with a watery glob of blood, then scrambled to her feet.

The Offs stepped in after her and closed the door behind them. They watched her mutely, arms stiff at their sides and mouths rigid. The guard with the ponytail still bled profusely, Ronja noticed with a rush of sick satisfaction.

"You better get out of here, you sick skitzers, or I swear I'll bite your fingers clean off!" she screeched.

"My, my," a humorless voice intoned over an intercom.

Ronja whipped around.

"Roark!" she exclaimed, a grin spreading across her face.

Her budding smile dissolved when she saw that Roark was lashed to the wall of the unfurnished room. His short chain prevented him from standing straight, so he stooped near the expressionless wall. He was barefoot, stripped down to his undershirt and slacks. A pair of massive headphones were strapped over her ears, connected to socket in the wall by a spiraling, black cord.

"Ronja," Roark began, his voice rusty.

"Please do not speak to my subject, son. You cannot hear her replies anyway," the voice continued over the loudspeaker.

Ronja turned toward the featureless room's glass window, her breath wilting in her lungs.

A man stood in the semidarkness of the observation room, his hands tucked behind his back. He might have been handsome in his youth, but age was creeping into his sharp features. His black hair was crowned with gray, and deep crow's-feet adorned his colorless eyes. He wore no Singer, but Ronja sensed this was a gesture of loyalty rather than rebellion.

"Victor Westervelt II," Ronja said flatly.

"Ms. Zipse. I wondered if I might meet you one day. Cosmin and Georgie were so certain you would come for them."

Ronja snarled, blood spraying from her mouth. "What have you done to them?" she roared. "Cosmin is barely breathing."

"But not a mutt," Westervelt said, raising a manicured finger warningly. "You might thank me."

"Forgive me if I don't."

"Forgiven."

"Pitch you."

"Roark, I do believe we will have to teach this one manners."

Roark looked at his father, panic flaring like a match in his eyes. Evidently his headphones were linked to the intercom.

Victor nodded toward the Offs behind Ronja. She spun and started to back away, but they made no move toward her. In fact, they did not even look at her. Instead, they withdrew identical pairs of black headphones, similar to the ones Roark wore.

The girl felt a chill settle in her bones.

Roark could not hear her through the headphones. If the devices were intended to block out sound that meant . . .

Ronja glanced over her shoulder at Roark. He was watching her helplessly. She had never seen him look anything but fierce and arrogant. The way he flinched each time his father spoke, despite the barrier that separated them. She could see the constellation of discoid burns on his forearms even across the room.

The girl gnashed her teeth together.

"Father, I already gave you the information you asked for," Roark pleaded, speaking much louder than he had to. "You promised you would leave them alone."

No.

"Ah yes, but your information was full of holes," Victor replied. He clicked his tongue scoldingly and shook his head. "It appears you may need a bit more persuasion."

"Don't—"

Westervelt pressed a button on the dashboard.

Ronja did not even scream when The Music burst from the speakers. She collapsed to her knees, then folded onto her back. Her spine arched in agony. Her vision scattered. Her fingers contorted into jagged claws. The Music ripped the air from her lungs, tore at her muscles, hammered on her skull.

Somewhere far away, Roark was screaming.

It was over as quickly as it began.

Her pupils gathered sight and her lungs oxygen. Her fingers relaxed, the angles softened. She tried to climb to her feet, but her limbs failed.

"Impressive—you managed to remain silent."

Ronja rolled over on her side and glowered at Victor through the glare of the glass. She could only see his silhouette from this angle, but she could hear the patronizing smirk in his voice.

"Are you ready to answer my questions honestly, son?"

"I—" Roark began.

"No!" Ronja shouted.

She climbed to her knees gracelessly, ignoring the ballistics that popped in her vision. She disregarded the senior Westervelt's loathing stare, and held Roark's terrified gaze in her own. She shook her head fiercely.

"Don't give him anything else," Ronja implored, hoping her intentions would reach him through the headphones. "He's already—"

This time Ronja could not hold back a shriek of agony. The Music was louder now. It felt like someone was jamming shards of glass into her brain.

Victor halted The Music again.

Ronja lay on the floor. She did not remember falling, nor did she know how long the Song had been playing. Something warm and wet dripped from her working ear, splashing to the tiles in a symphony of nauseating plops. Through the dense fog in her eyes, she could see the horror plastered across Roark's face.

"It's a new form of The Music we've been working on,"

Westervelt explained over the intercom.

He spoke as though they were discussing the weather. Each word felt like the tip of a needle on her eardrum. Ronja attempted to press her palm to her ear, but her arms were leaden.

"Obviously, it does not require a Singer to be transmitted. In the past we have used The Music as a salve for troublesome emotions, but recently I realized that if we can pinpoint the emotional sectors of the brain, why not control the pain receptors? Like so."

Ronja braced herself, slamming her eyelids shut on the white room. She choked on her screams as the high-pitched keening again ruptured her brain.

Westervelt stopped it quickly.

"I was thinking of calling it The Lost Song in honor of the lost souls it will help tame. What do you think?"

"Pitch . . . you," Ronja wheezed from the floor.

"Victor . . . Father," Roark pleaded. "Enough. I'll tell the truth, anything you want."

No.

Ronja opened her eyes, her pupils retracting painfully.

Roark would tell him everything. He would give up the Anthem, give it up for her. She could see the words collecting on his lips like rainwater in a gutter. He was terrified of his father, the boy who feared nothing.

He was afraid for her.

Something blossomed in Ronja's chest, uprooting the pain. A wisp of a smile dusted her cracked lips. Somehow, someway, Roark Westervelt had come to care for her. He was about to give up the Anthem, his family, his cause, to save her life.

She could not allow it.

Ronja rose on legs that should not have worked. The sounds drained from the space as she wavered on the spot, then took a step toward Roark. Her guards trailed her. Their footsteps and the hiss of their stingers could not crack her tranquil bubble. Her vision was abruptly sharp. Blood still gushed from her ear, but she did not feel it.

There was only Roark and his terror-struck face.

He was beautiful, she thought as she drew nearer. Ronja had noticed it before, but never stopped to appreciate it. She wanted the time to count each of his freckles, each odd gold fleck in his brown eyes. She knew she would never have it.

For a moment at least, she could pretend.

Ronja reached up with a bloodied hand and cupped his cheek. His skin was hot and soft beneath her rough palm.

"Save. Them." she mouthed.

Ronja stretched up on tiptoe and kissed Roark full on the mouth. For a moment his lips were still against hers. Then he kissed her back, and it was enough.

The Offs were at her back, she could feel their disgusting breath on the nape of her neck.

They were exactly where she needed them.

She whirled, grabbed a crackling stinger by its charged end, and drove it straight into her heart. Roark screamed. Victor swore. She heard neither of them.

Ronja died smiling, her lips still tingling from her first and last kiss.

45: LINGER
Roark

Ronja was dead.

Her blood was cooling on his cheek. Her body was limp. Her upturned palms were raw where she had seized the stinger. He could smell her burnt flesh. He could see the lower rim of her pale green irises peeking through her thick lashes.

The Offs were staring at her in vague shock. The one with the ponytail nudged her shoulder with the toe of his boot. Her head lolled to the side.

"DON'T TOUCH HER!" Roark roared.

The Offs scuttled backward, unnerved by his ferocity. Both sheathed their stingers, as if that could take back what had just occurred.

"Shame," Victor sighed from behind the window. "You were about to tell me everything. Smart girl, she knew."

A shard of grief lodged itself into Roark's numb soul. His father was right. If he had been stronger, more resolute, Ronja would still be alive. They could have found a way out together.

Anything but this.

Roark sank to his knees. He shuffled forward and bent toward her shell, his manacles pulling fresh blood from his wrists.

Beaten, shaved, tortured, she was still beautiful. He could see the ghost of bravery on her angular face. He could still feel her lips against his and knew he would for the rest of his life, however short it might be.

He would have found a way to make her stay in Revinia. Even as he promised to help her find a way out of the city, he knew he could not lose her. He would have found a way. Convinced Wilcox to make an exception for her mother, hidden the woman in the tunnels if he had needed to.

"Take her to the ovens," Victor ordered lazily.

"No!" Roark cried.

The guards advanced. Roark strained against his chains, but could not reach her body. The Offs snorted at him disdainfully. Each grabbed one of her limp wrists and dragged her across the tiles still slick with her blood. Roark watched her until she was tugged around the corner, her heels screeching against the floor.

"I'll leave you here to think about what you've done," Victor said.

He flipped the light switch as he exited, plunging the room into absolute blackness.

Roark did not notice.

46: SCORCHED
Evie

I f we survive this, I'm going to kill you."

Terra looked over her shoulder to glare at Evie, but the motion was lost in the utter darkness of the sewage tunnel. "Not if I do myself in first," she replied, recommencing the crawl up the claustrophobic shoot.

They were both on their stomachs, wriggling their way toward Red Bay through a thick film of feces and piss. They had been lucky so far. No new additions had been made to the concoction.

When Terra ambushed Evie on the hilltop, she thought for certain the blond girl was there to drag her back to the Anthem.

As it turned out, she was.

"Where are the others? I'm here to bring you back," Terra demanded, her automatic trained unflinchingly on Evie's chest.

"Even Ronja?" Evie asked, batting the weapon away. "How did you find us?"

"She'll be sent away immediately," Terra replied coldly, ignoring the second question and refocusing her aim on Evie.

"She isn't a mutt, you've gotta know that."

"If her mother has the gene, so does she."

"You can't seriously believe . . . hang on. How did you know it was her mother that was the mutt?"

The crickets whirred in the space after the question. Even in the dense shadows, Evie saw the color drain from her fellow Anthemite's cheeks.

"It's not important," Terra finally snapped, steadying her weapon with her other hand. She advanced on Evie and pressed the barrel of the gun to her sternum. "Where is everyone? Please don't tell me they've already gone in."

Evie looked at the ground as if it might speak for her. The brush whispered in the breeze, but said nothing of any consequence.

"*Where are they?*" Terra demanded again, enunciating each word with devastating precision.

"I don't know," Evie finally replied, keeping her voice low so that it did not shake. "They went in to get Ronja's family and never came out."

Almost an hour later, in the bowels of the sewage system, Terra had yet to cut Ronja any slack.

"If that stupid pitcher hadn't shown up with those skitzing doe eyes and that sob story, we wouldn't be in this mess," she huffed.

"If you want to blame somebody, blame Roark," Evie shot back, grunting as she plunged her elbow into a particularly large lump of excrement. "He was never one to turn down a pretty face."

"Is that what you call that half-starved squirrel?" Terra huffed.

"What is your *problem*?" Evie asked, the gears of her mind spinning in the stagnant, putrid air. "This is personal," she realized slowly. "You wanted Ronja gone for good—why?"

"We're getting close, shut up," Terra replied.

Evie opened her mouth to retort, but thought better of it. If they survived, she would force whatever Terra was hiding into the open.

They crawled on in silence.

Evie tried to hold Iris's face in her mind, to smell her perfumed hair rather than the nauseating odor of the sewer. The exercise failed. Each time she pictured her smile, Iris's countenance twisted into a mask of agony and terror.

"Almost there," Terra whispered from several feet ahead.

Evie nodded mutely, more to herself than her companion.

Terra struggled toward the gray light peeking through the thick slats in the sewer grate. Evie followed suit frantically, latching on to the threads of fresh air.

"I need to push off your shoulders," Terra said.

"Wha—?"

Terra slammed her booted feet into her shoulders with a wet slap. Evie grunted, but swallowed her complaints.

"Ready?"

Evie nodded again, her teeth slammed together.

"Three . . . two . . . "

"Ugh!"

Terra shot forward, her rubber soles digging into Evie's muscled shoulders. Metal shrieked against concrete as Terra dislodged the grate from its recess. A wreath of light poured into the tube, followed by a surge of fresh air. The blonde squirmed the rest of the way out, then turned to offer Evie a crud-slick hand. She grasped it firmly and was yanked from the tunnel.

"That was disgusting," Evie moaned quietly, wiping her hands on the seat of her pants.

Terra ignored her, scanning the room with her keen hazel eyes.

"Where are we?" Evie asked, glancing around.

They had emerged in a vast, dim room caked in concrete. Crates and boxes were stacked to the low ceiling, which was crisscrossed with leaking copper pipes.

"Under the prison wing, I think," Terra replied, drawing her sidearm from the holster on her thigh and cocking it resolutely.

"You *think*?" Evie breathed disbelievingly. "We can't go off assumptions here, Terra."

"I know more about this place than you do," Terra shot back darkly.

Evie paused, her eyebrows knit together as she regarded the other girl. Terra was in the process of twisting her hair into a knot at the top of her head. She drew her two red rods from her jacket and jammed them into her locks with expert fingers. Without so much as a glance toward Evie, she took off across the expanse at a slow jog. Evie followed without a word.

The basement seemed to stretch on for miles. By the time they reached the stairwell to the surface, Evie was ready to accept a life of wandering the dank cellar.

They mounted the stone steps in silence, highly attuned to their echoing footfalls and breaths. They eventually came to a rust-eaten door. Waves of heat poured through the cracks in the portal, accompanied by the ferocious glow of an inferno.

Terra paused and turned to Evie.

"We're coming out near the ovens. No one can have the time

to raise an alarm, do you understand?"

Evie nodded.

"I've killed before," she assured Terra.

They had been on a raid at a WI warehouse on the west side of the city. Evie was posted as a sniper on the rooftop across the street. It was bitterly cold, and sleeting. She had wanted nothing more than to go home to her bed, but forced herself to remain alert. Iris was with the team on the ground. She had been brought along as part of her medical training, but was left without a guard. She did not even notice the Off sneaking up behind her, his automatic aimed at her head.

Evie had shot him clear through his left eye from two hundred meters out and not felt a thing.

Terra wrenched open the door with a screech of its corroded hinges. She poked her head through, looking left and right. Terra nodded once, then slipped through the entrance. Evie followed cautiously. She choked as she drank in the polluted air. She felt she might wilt in the scorching heat. Evie blinked the smoke from her eyes and peered around.

She wished she had not.

Evie gagged again, but this time it was not from the smoke. She pressed her stained hands to her mouth, smothering a scream.

The room was dominated by a hulking, wide mouthed oven that issued gusts of unbearable heat and hungry, orange flames. An immobile conveyor belt was poised to feed the ravenous fire.

Bodies were stacked two deep on the broad platform, bald, naked, and sallow.

Evie made a noise close to a squeak and began to back toward the basement door.

"Focus, Evie," Terra commanded sharply, moving toward the door that led to the rest of the prison. "Don't think about it."

"How can I—?" Evie gulped, shaking her head violently.

"Close your eyes. Follow my voice."

Evie slammed her eyelids shut and began to walk toward Terra.

"Almost there," the blond girl called softly.

Evie felt her muscles seize.

If we aren't back in a few hours, we're probably dead.

Evie's eyes flashed open and she whirled on the spot.

"Terra!" she breathed. "What if they're here?"

Terra was at the doorway, her hand on the knob. "Then we can't help them."

"I have to know," Evie muttered, approaching the conveyor belt in a sort of trance. "I have to . . . "

She leaned toward the first body, a man in his mid forties who might have once been handsome. Evie reached down gingerly and gripped him by a bloodless shoulder. She lifted him up a few inches and peeked beneath his shell. A girl with a wide nose and glassy blue eyes rested beneath him. A bolt of relief went through Evie's heart, followed by a twinge of self-loathing. It was not Iris, or Ronja, but the girl was still dead.

"Help me, Terra, please," Evie begged. "We don't know when they're going to start the belt. I need to know."

Terra glanced apprehensively at the door, then back at Evie. She sighed deeply and gripped her weapon tighter. "Be quick."

Evie rushed toward the next stack of bodies, rifling through them unceremoniously, choking on her own vomit. They felt like cold fish beneath her fingers.

"Evie . . . " Terra warned from the door.

"I'm going as fast as I . . . "

Evie stilled, her fingers clamped around a girl's boney, freckled arm. It was still warm.

"Oh," Evie whispered.

"Evie?" Terra asked, moving toward her.

"It's Ronja."

47: SNUFFED
Ronja

Death was breathing down the back of her neck. His lungs were full of hot, foul air. It burnt holes in her skin, like paper licked by fire.

She was not dead yet, she was fairly certain. She could not move her body, but her mind still spun weakly. She had never believed in the existence of an afterlife, or a higher power other than The Conductor. If she was cognizant, she figured she had to be alive.

Not for long, though.

Her heart was coughing like a dying steamer. Soon its wheels would still and rust.

She had not wanted to die, but it had been the right thing to do. In her death, Roark might find the strength to resist his father. She believed that he would find a way to save her family, and their friends if they still lived.

Death was closing in. She felt his hot palms on her bare shoulders, tugging her gently toward a door she could not see, but knew was there all the same.

Soon she would step through it and leave her trust behind with Roark.

48: VIOLENT LIGHT
Evie

Terra and Evie hauled Ronja's body off the static conveyor belt, disentangling her from the arms of another victim, an old woman whose milky eyes were fixed on the ceiling. Ronja was as heavy as a wet sandbag. They laid her on the hard floor as gently as they could. Her head lolled to the side.

Terra rose and backed away, but Evie dropped to her knees next to the girl, her hands cupped around her mouth.

"What did they do to you?" she breathed.

Ronja was a patchwork of bruises and burns. Even her palms were scorched. Her beautiful curls had been shaved. Still, an inexplicable smile lingered on the corners of her mouth. Her eyes were closed, her face inexplicably peaceful.

Evie reached out hesitantly and placed her palm over Ronja's heart, where her tattoo might have been one day.

Her mother's life all but ended here, Evie realized. *She's come full circle.*

"She deserved better," Evie said quietly.

"A lot of people did," Terra replied.

Evie looked around at her comrade, her hand still resting against the Ronja's frozen heart. Terra glanced away quickly, her mouth a taut line and her hands clenched around her gun.

Beat.

Evie gasped and yanked her hand back as if shocked. "Terra!"

"What?"

Evie did not answer, but pressed her ear to Ronja's chest.

Come on, come on, she begged.

Beat.

Evie reeled backward, charged by adrenaline, and slammed her crossed palms into the girl's ribcage.

1-2-3

2-2-3

3-2-3

She counted the compressions, just as Iris had taught her.

"Evie, she's dead. We gotta go," Terra whispered urgently.

"I felt her pulse," Evie insisted without stopping the cyclical motion.

Terra advanced and grasped her by the shoulders, attempting to drag her away from the body. Evie shook her off wordlessly, ignoring the growing ache in her biceps.

"Evie—"

"Wait."

Evie leaned forward and pressed her ear to Ronja's chest again. She closed her eyes, listening for the telltale hum of life.

She was met only by the ravenous hiss of the fire to her right, and Terra's anxious shiftings to her left.

"Come on, please," Evie muttered, as if her words might coax Ronja back into the realm of the living.

The tongues of flame cast shadows across her bald head and battered face. Had the warmth Evie had felt rising from her skin been the heat of the fire? Had the heartbeat she thought she felt been a trick of her desperate mind?

Evie rocked back on her toes. The metal tip of her stinger clinked against the unforgiving ground. Suddenly, she did not want to own such a weapon. It looked as if Ronja had been at the mercy of one. Concentrated, circular burns decorated her stomach and chest. A particularly nasty burn had scorched the plane above her heart.

"This must have been what got her," she said softly, staring at the scorched flesh with glassy eyes.

"Electricity can give and take life," she recalled her mentor, Haverford, telling her as she ran her fingers across a newly-constructed circuit board.

"What do you mean?" she had asked him.

Haverford was gnawing on the end of an unlit cigarette, a habit he developed after his wife forced him to quit.

"Hope you never find out," he'd replied with a dark chuckle.

"I think I hear someone coming," Terra said, a thread of panic creeping into her typically cool tone.

Evie dropped like a stone back into reality. She took one last look at the body. She wished she had something of Ronja's she could give Roark, if he was still alive. She had seen the way he looked at her. She had never seen him look at anyone that way.

"Evie, skitz, we gotta go."

Evie stood, her ears ringing. She rested a callused hand on the hilt of her stinger.

Electricity can give and take life.

Her fingers reacted before the epiphany hit her. Evie flipped the switch on her stinger and it snapped to life. She raised the weapon above her head, and drove it into Ronja's chest.

The girl arched, flooded by the violent energy.

"Evie!"

Evie no longer heard Terra's pleas. She spun the nob at the tip of the weapon. The current flared white. She slammed it down again.

Ronja was thrust back into life with a retching gasp.

49: WALK

The air was choked with putrid fumes, but she craved it all the same. She thought her ribs might crack beneath the strain of her heaving gasps. Evie was grasping both her hands to hold her upright, enveloping her in words of encouragement.

"It's okay, you're okay, you're okay."

Ronja tried to speak, but her numb lips had forgotten how to form words.

"Get up."

Someone shoved Evie out of the way and gripped Ronja by her limp wrist. Her vision scattered to black when the hand yanked her to her feet.

"Here."

The weight on her shoulders made her knees buckle, but she remained standing. Ronja sucked in another deep breath and her sight gathered. Someone had draped a heavy coat around her. It fell past her knees.

"Thank . . . you . . . " she rasped, buttoning the clasps with clumsy fingers.

"Don't. I would have left you."

Ronja looked up. Her eyes popped.

Terra stood before her. Her mouth was pinched into a razor-thin line, and she was slathered with filth. Twin knives were strapped to her thighs, and she gripped an automatic with both hands. Her skin was blanched where it was not covered in muck.

Ronja turned around to thank Evie, who was also robed in sewage, but was distracted by the scene beyond. She stumbled backward, a scream bubbling in her throat. Terra caught her beneath her arms and smacked a hand over her mouth.

"If we don't leave now we will be caught, and you'll end up back where we found you," Terra hissed in her ear.

Ronja nodded mutely, unable to look away from the heinous sight. She could see the gap in the tangle of bodies that had been her grave. Terra let her hand fall cautiously.

"If they'd started the belt . . . " Ronja croaked.

"They didn't," Terra cut her off brutally. "Can you walk?"

Ronja nodded again.

"Then walk."

Evie and Terra supported her between them as they wormed through the sterile halls of Red Bay. The corridors zigzagged endlessly, but Terra seemed to know where she was going. Numbered steel doors stood like soldiers against the walls. Ronja shivered to think that she had been behind one not long ago. How long had she been out? She wanted to ask, but was too exhausted.

Her bones and muscles ached, and her burns stung almost as badly as her ear. She had never realized how warm her hair kept her. Even in the leather coat, she was freezing.

"How are we gonna find them?" Evie muttered to Terra over Ronja's bald head.

"Prison control isn't far," Terra whispered back.

"Oi!"

Ronja and Evie went rigid.

Terra instantly retracted her support from Ronja and whipped out a knife. She spun on her toes and flung it at the man who had spoken. Ronja heard a wet crunch and could not suppress a wince. The man fell without so much as a whimper.

"Someone will find him," Terra said, retrieving her knife with a sickening squelch. She wiped the stained blade on her pants. "We need to run."

"But . . . " Evie began, glancing down at Ronja anxiously.

Ronja eased her arm from her waist and steadied herself. Her stomach roiled and her muscles groaned, but she did not fall.

Terra nodded approvingly, then sprinted off ahead. Her boots barely made a sound on the tiles. Ronja still felt Evie's worried eyes on her, but she ignored them. She started after Terra with as much speed as she could manage. Evie followed half a beat later.

They weaved through the corridors in silence and did not

meet another soul. If Ronja had been able to think straight, this would have concerned her, but her only thoughts were of each successive step.

They passed scores of identical doors numbering into the high hundreds. The portals were as still as gravestones, but Ronja knew that many of the chambers were throbbing with The Music. New forms of it. Forms that could reach people without Singers. She could still feel The Lost Song burrowed in her head like a parasite.

If they made it out alive, she would tell them what she had learned, but she knew she could not burden them with the knowledge now. There would be no point in warning them, anyway. If The Lost Song reached them, there was nothing they could do to defend themselves against it.

"Here," Terra said, halting before an unremarkable white door.

Evie and Ronja sputtered to a stop next to her. Ronja leaned against the wall, struggling to keep from panting. The sounds of casual conversation and unhindered laughter bled through the keyhole.

"How do we get in?" Evie whispered.

Terra unsheathed one of her knives and offered it to Ronja, who took the weapon by its leather handle. It was heavier than she expected.

"Stay here," she commanded Ronja, jabbing an accusatory finger in her face. "Evie, with me."

Terra knocked loudly with the grip of her automatic.

Ronja wrapped both her hands around the knife.

The ruckus behind the door ceased. The sounds of guns cocking studded the hush.

"Who's there?" a gruff, male voice called.

None of the girls replied.

A pair of cautious footsteps approached the door. Terra raised her gun and Evie her stinger. Ronja pressed herself against the wall, gripping her knife like a life preserver.

The door flew open.

Terra fired once. The bullet hissed through the silencer and struck its mark with a wet splat.

A spray of blood lashed Ronja across the cheek. Terra flew at the man before he could topple and grabbed him by the front of his collared uniform. She grunted beneath his weight and fired three more times over his broad shoulder.

"Put down your weapon," Terra commanded over the slumped shoulder of her victim.

Ronja tried to peer around the doorframe to see who Terra was addressing, but Evie thrust her back protectively.

There was a sharp clang as a gun hit the floor.

"Kick it to me."

Metal screeched across the tiles.

"Hands."

There was a pause.

Terra let her human shield fall through the threshold with a nauseating thud. His dark blood dyed the tiles like dawn spreading across the plains.

"Evie, Ronja."

Terra stepped over the dead man nonchalantly. Evie jumped over him, then offered her hand back to help Ronja. She took it and hopped over the corpse gingerly.

"Get his feet inside," Terra ordered coolly, her gun still trained on her target.

Evie and Ronja bent down wordlessly and dragged the man the rest of the way through the portal. His blood-soaked form squeaked against the ground.

"Close the door."

Ronja shut it with a quiet click and locked it. She turned to see who Terra had taken hostage.

He was not what she had expected. The man was in his late twenties, gangly and pale. His dark brown hair was unkempt, and thick-rimmed glasses sat on the bridge of his long nose. He wore a white lab coat, the unmistakable sigh of a chemi. His spindly hands were raised. He looked almost relieved to have dropped his gun, a black pistol that did not suit his scholarly countenance.

Four corpses were losing their heat on the ground, their blood snaking into the cracks between the tiles.

"What's the likelihood that someone is going to disturb us?" Terra asked, visibly tightening her finger around the trigger.

The man shook his head frantically, his curls flopping.

"Low," he said. "Almost everyone is at the assembly."

"Assembly?"

"Victor Westervelt II is visiting."

"We know," Ronja snapped. "He's here for us."

"No," the man said, shaking his head again.

"Then why is he here?" Ronja asked rawly, taking her place next to Evie, her fingers curled around the borrowed blade.

"He's been here for days," the chemi said.

"Why?" Terra asked through clenched teeth.

"*Why?*" Evie repeated when the chemi failed to answer.

"The launch of the new Songs," he whispered, his fingers drifting up to his Singer.

Ronja blanched.

"No," she spat through her teeth.

"Ronja?" Evie asked, peering at her sidelong.

"Tell me he's not going to put The Lost Song in the Singers," she demanded in a low voice, prowling toward him.

The chemi backed into his metal desk, which screeched across the floor. A stack of papers tumbled to the ground, whispering against the tiles. Ronja grasped him by the front of his shirt and dragged him down to her level. He gulped audibly, his Adam's apple bobbing beneath his stubble.

"No, no, no," he stuttered, panic crawling into his voice and eyes. Ronja twisted the fabric of his shirt, pulling him close so that their noses nearly brushed. "No, The Lost Song isn't for the public, it's for the rebels."

Ronja released his shirt and shoved him back into the desk. The chemi caught himself, and adjusted his glasses with a trembling finger. Ronja put her head in her hands, trying to control her breathing.

"They can't use this . . . *Lost Song* on us," Evie said doubtfully. "None of us have Singers."

Ronja shook her head, her palms blacking out the room. "No," she heard herself say. "It can be played over speakers. Anyone can hear it."

"It looks like you've felt the effects," the chemi noted from his place on the desk.

"Ronja?" Evie asked.

Ronja let her hands fall and turned to Terra and Evie.

"Westervelt tortured me to get Roark to talk."

Evie closed her eyes, pain working its way across her face. Terra looked at Ronja blankly.

"He took me to a room and played The Lost Song over the speakers," Ronja continued, rubbing the bridge of her nose and eyeing the ground. "It was . . . it was bad."

"Is that what nearly killed you?" Terra asked emotionlessly.

"No," Ronja admitted, looking up at the two girls almost embarrassedly. "I . . . uh . . . tried to kill myself."

"Because of the pain?" Evie asked, shock rupturing her expression.

"No," Ronja said. She flicked her gaze to the tiled floor, her naked feet. She curled and uncurled her toes. "No. Roark was going to give up the Anthem to save me, to save us. I couldn't let him. So, I ended it."

Evie and Terra were silent, regarding her with a mixture of shock and admiration. Terra was the first to recover.

"When do they plan to use this Song on us?" she asked, returning attention to the chemi, who again threw his hands into the air.

"A few months, I don't know!"

"Does The Conductor know where we are?"

The chemi's lips parted silently, revealing a gold front tooth. Tears pooled in his wide eyes, and he shook his head vigorously.

"I—I—"

"DOES HE KNOW WHERE WE ARE?" Terra roared, stalking forward and slamming the muzzle of her gun into his temple.

The chemi began to sob. Terra looked disgusted, but did not retract her weapon. She grabbed him by his pointed chin and forced him to meet her gaze.

"Answer me," Terra commanded, her voice almost velvety.

Slowly, the chemi shook his head.

"Ronja, do you think Roark would have told him?" Terra asked, letting her gun fall to her thigh and stepping away from the sobbing man with a look of absolute revulsion.

"No," Ronja said.

"You," Terra barked at the chemi, who jumped, scattering more papers. "You got a name?"

"Maxwell," he whimpered, adjusting his spectacles again with a quaking hand. "Maxwell Wagner."

"We're looking for three prisoners, *Maxwell*. Iris Harte, Henry Romancheck, and Roark Westervelt. You're going to help us find them."

"Six," Ronja corrected firmly. "Layla, Cosmin, and Georgie Zipse."

Maxwell nodded hastily, his pupils dilated. "I know where they are."

"All of them?" Evie asked incredulously.

"I have perfect recall. Harte is closest."

Terra motioned for Maxwell to step toward the door with her automatic. He crossed the room, stepping over one of his fallen comrades, his sweaty palms still raised above his head.

Terra stepped behind Maxwell and jammed the muzzle of her gun into his spine. She stood up on tiptoe so she could whisper in his ear.

"Scream, call for help, and you'll be dead so fast you won't have time to say goodbye to your Conductor."

Maxwell bobbed his chin, then dropped his scrawny arms.

Evie opened the door cautiously, sticking her dark head into the hallway.

"Clear," she announced over her shoulder.

"Lead the way, Maxwell," Terra ordered bitingly.

50: UNSCATHED

"A re you ready?" Ronja asked Evie quietly.

They stood in a tight knot outside an expressionless doorway Maxwell insisted led to Iris. Ronja knew what they might find beyond it, and was not sure she or Evie were ready to face it.

"No," Evie admitted. She looked up at Maxwell, who was still trembling at the barrel of Terra's automatic. "Do it."

Maxwell reached into his pocket and withdrew a ring of keys. He chose a small bronze one and inserted it into the lock. It sprang with a click.

Evie reached around him and yanked open the door.

A blur of white burst through the portal, knocking Evie clean off her feet. Fists and curses flew as Iris whaled on Evie, who had been knocked onto her back.

"Iris!" Evie shouted as loud as she dared.

Iris paused, one fist still in the air like a club. She looked from Terra, to Maxwell, to Ronja, to Evie. Slowly, like fog lifting off a lake, the rage washed from her face. Tears budded in her eyes and spilled over onto her cheeks.

Iris laid her freshly shaved head down on Evie's shoulder and began to sob silently.

"Reunions later," Terra said. She nudged Maxwell with her gun, drawing a terrified squeak from him. "Take us to Henry."

Evie rose with a grunt, clutching Iris around the waist. Iris wrapped her arms and legs around Evie, ignoring the dry sewage caked on her front.

"Iris," Evie said softly, ignoring the dagger-eyes Terra was sending her. "I have to put you down."

Iris nodded, sniffled, and unwound her arms and legs. Evie set her down delicately. Ronja looked Iris over. She looked exhausted and shaken, but altogether unscathed.

"What happened?" Iris breathed when she laid eyes on Ronja.

Iris reached up a boney hand and brushed the cuts and bruises on her face. Ronja flinched away as pain flared beneath the featherlight touch.

"Later," Ronja said.

They flew down the curling corridors, following Maxwell, who was muttering to himself about The Music. The man ran comically, his feet flapping like a duck's flippers. They met no resistance. Maxwell had said everyone was at an assembly, but Ronja had not believed him until now.

"How long is this assembly going to last?" Ronja panted as they ran.

"Twenty more minutes, maybe," Maxwell huffed, peering down at her from behind his sweat-fogged spectacles.

"Hurry," Terra hissed.

"Here," Maxwell said quickly, thrusting a thin finger forward. "This door, right here."

They screeched to a halt before cell 453. Ronja tried to swallow her heaving breaths. Everyone except she and Maxwell seemed unfazed by the sprinting.

"Open it," Terra commanded, prodding Maxwell between the shoulder blades with the barrel of her gun.

Maxwell did as he was bid. He fiddled with his keys for a moment too long, drawing an annoyed grunt from Terra. He located the right key and inserted it into the matching lock. As soon as the tumblers clicked, Ronja shoved him out of the way and put her hand on the knob.

"Henry?" she called quietly, not wanting to be bowled over by a boy with at least one hundred pounds on her. "Henry it's us, we're coming in."

There was a pause. Ronja saw his shadow shift through the crack between the floor and the door.

"Ro?" came his raspy reply.

Ronja wrenched open the door, her heart high in her throat.

Henry stood at the back of his cell, his fists partially raised in preparation for a ruse. He was dressed in ill-fitting white scrubs. His right eye was swallowed by a ring of bruises, and circular burns decorated his chest, but he appeared to be in one piece.

"Ro . . ." he trailed off, dropping his fists and looking her over with darkening eyes.

"I'm okay," Ronja said hurriedly, waving him off. "I'm—"

Henry flew at her and wrenched her into a bone-crushing hug, squeezing the lie from her. He reeked of sweat, but beneath it Ronja could smell his familiar musk.

"Henry," she said weakly, patting his drenched back. "We gotta go."

Henry released her and straightened. He caught sight of Terra standing in the doorway and arched a brow. "Thank you," he said, as if the words did not taste right on his tongue.

Terra inclined her head sharply and gestured for them to move into the hallway.

"You," Ronja barked, jabbing her finger into Maxwell's boney chest. "Cosmin, Layla, and Georgie. Where are they?"

"A different block," Maxwell said, polishing his spectacles with the edge of his lab coat. He put them back on, covering the pink divots where they squeezed his nose too tight. "We need to hurry. If I'm seen with you—"

"What about Roark, where is he?" Evie cut in.

"If I had to guess, with his father at the assembly."

Ronja clenched her jaw, the image of the cigarette burns on Roark's arms surging into the front of her mind.

"How are we going to get to him?" Iris asked nervously, clutching for a hand to hold.

"One thing at a time," Evie said, taking her hand absently. "Victor isn't going to kill Roark outright, right?"

"I don't think so," Ronja replied, slowly shaking her bald head. "He wants to use him."

"So we get your family out first," Evie conceded. "Right, Terra?"

Terra scowled at Evie, but she dipped her chin begrudgingly.

"Lead the way, pitcher," Evie commanded Maxwell.

The chemi flushed behind his glasses, but his only reply was to jog forward on his behemoth, flat feet. They went after him swiftly and silently.

51: INCONSEQUENTIAL
Roark

Not ten minutes after Ronja was dragged from his life, the two Offs who had thrown her in the ovens returned.

Roark trembled with rage as they observed him indifferently, then tossed a bundle of clothing at his feet. A pair of dress shoes followed, their varnished faces reflecting the sterile lights.

"Dress, and meet your father outside," the bald Off ordered.

Roark did not reply, nor did he move to don the clothing.

"Do as you're told," the other Off commanded.

"I can't," Roark snarled, rattling his chains demonstratively.

The dark-haired Off dug into his pocket and withdrew a silver key. He lobbed it at Roark, who ducked. It struck his shoulder and bounced to the floor, landing several tiles away.

"Do as your told, or you'll be worse off than the mutt."

Roark lunged, but was dragged down by his chains. He hit the floor awkwardly, and bolts of pain shot through his wrist. He suppressed a wince and clambered to his feet.

The Offs left, their laughter dogging him until they slammed the soundproof door.

Roark looked from the key to the pile of clothing.

He could refuse, suffer at the hands of the two goons. He had endured worse. He knew, though, that his father would find a way to get him to cooperate.

And if he got out of this cell, he was one step closer to ripping out Victor Westervelt II's throat.

Roark reached for the key with a bare toe and dragged it close enough for his fingers to grasp. He inserted it into the first of his manacles, grunting when the metal snapped against his sprained wrist.

When the last of his cuffs rattled to the ground, Roark stretched.

He rolled the kinks from his neck, the wayward vertebrae popping like fireworks. He let his eyes fall shut, but opened them again quickly. Her face was still plastered across the backs of his lids. Having his eyes open was not much better. Her blood was turning brown on the floor.

Roark focused on dressing.

His muscles groaned as he stepped into the freshly-pressed slacks and shrugged on the matching top. Intricate gold clasps lined the high-necked jacket. The Conductor's emblem glowed white against the black backdrop, suffocating the record tattooed over his heart.

Roark slipped on the stiff dress shoes, steeled himself, and exited the room.

His father stood in the center of the corridor, examining a pristinely-trimmed fingernail nonchalantly.

"Ah, Roark," he said, letting his hand fall. "Looking much improved, though I wish my Officers had not touched your face."

"It wasn't them," Roark said, coming to a halt several feet from Victor. "It was Ronja, when she found out you'd taken her family."

"You always did have a taste for spitfires," his father noted, observing him keenly.

Roark rolled his fingers into fists at his sides, but refused the bait.

"Walk with me," Victor ordered, joining his hands behind his back and starting down the corridor.

Roark started after his father without complaint.

"I was somewhat confounded when you called out her name," Victor began, his voice rebounding off the walls of the empty passageway. "I had been hearing it for days on the lips of two of our guests. I asked the younger of the two who Ronja was, and she informed me that she was her cousin. Interesting, given that the children's aunt is also here. Even more intriguing was the fact that the aunt is a mutt."

Roark felt his father observing him as he processed the information.

"I would like to speak to the mutt about her offspring, but we have other matters to attend."

"Such as?" Roark asked through his teeth.

"A demonstration," Victor replied, flashing Roark a winning smile. "I thought you might be interested to see what your father has been working on these past months. You must have noticed the snow in my hair," Victor said with a chuckle, patting the white streaks that had crept into his dark hair. "I would like to show you what has caused me so much grief, and why it is entirely worthwhile."

Roark did not reply. They trekked the empty halls in silence, their footfalls disturbingly matched.

"How long have you suspected me?" Roark asked after awhile.

"Since before your sister died. I knew there was a possibility she might have swayed you."

"She wasn't part of the Anthem."

"No, she was far more dangerous."

"Yes. Yes, she was."

"Sigrun died bravely. I was proud."

"Don't you dare say her name," Roark spat, screeching to a halt. "She was no more your child than I am. Whatever blood we share is inconsequential."

Victor regarded Roark with flat eyes, his most dangerous expression. Roark braced himself, preparing to fend off an attack. Victor let his hands drop to his sides, his fingers twitching like pale earthworms.

The man spun on his heel and started down the hall again.

"You've grown bolder, son," Victor called over his shoulder. "You'll make a fine candidate for this presentation."

52: HEADPHONES

We keep mutts and their relations in a separate wing," Maxwell explained breathlessly as they ran through the vacant halls.

"Why?" Ronja asked.

"Different Music, different experiments."

Ronja chewed on her words, then swallowed them. She had to conserve energy. Her adrenaline was starting to fail her. She did not know how much longer she would last before her legs gave out.

Terra stopped ahead, throwing up her fist. The group staggered to a halt as one. The blonde pinned her back to the wall and peered around the corner. She whipped back around and swore soundlessly. She held up four fingers, then jabbed a gloved finger at Evie.

Evie drew her sidearm capped with a silencer. Now was no time for stingers.

Terra pointed at Henry and Iris in turn, then jerked her chin toward Ronja and Maxwell. Henry stepped forward and clapped a massive hand over the scrawny chemi's mouth. Maxwell trembled like a leaf, but did not struggle. Iris moved to stand in front of Ronja, a rather pointless act as Ronja could see clear over her head.

Any other time Ronja would have growled that she could take care of herself, but she was too busy breathing to argue. Ink bled into the edges of her vision, and it felt like someone was hammering on her skull.

Terra and Evie pressed their backs against the wall, keen eyes trained on the corner. Militant, booted footsteps approached.

Terra raised three fingers. She let one fall, then the second.

The girls burst out from behind the corner just as the pack of Offs rounded it.

Terra let one of her blades fly and nailed a man between the eyes before he could scream. She yanked the knife from his skull as he crumbled, leaving behind only a thin strip of red in his skin.

Evie vaulted over the man Terra had felled and shot a dark Off in the neck. He clutched at his spurting wound. Evie put him out of his misery with another shot to the temple. His comrade flew at her and wrapped a bulging arm around her neck. She twisted in his grip, pounding on his arm with no avail.

Terra whirled toward Evie and slashed the man across his bulging bicep. He cried out and released Evie, who fell to her knees, gasping. Terra used the man's confusion to plunge the blade into his heart, twisting it slowly and drawing an agonizing moan from him.

Pop.

Terra wheeled around, her hands empty and her eyes flown wide.

The last Off swayed for a moment, then crumpled to the floor. Blood gushed from the hole in her forehead. The knife she had been preparing to plunge into Terra's back skidded across the tiles, glinting sharply in the electric light.

Terra looked down.

Evie lay on her stomach, grinning wickedly, her smoking automatic aimed around Terra's left leg.

"Not bad, huh?" she drawled in her foreign lilt, raising her blood-splattered hand for Terra to grasp.

The blonde took the offered hand. She yanked Evie to her feet and slapped her on the back in a rare show of affection.

Ronja slipped out from behind Iris, her eyes fixed on the ring of fallen Offs. She padded through the spreading pool of blood. The warm fluid squelched between her toes, but she scarcely noticed.

"Ro?" Henry asked from somewhere far away.

Ronja crouched beside one of the Offs, her hands plastered to her knees. His eyes were wide, ogling the ceiling blindly.

"Headphones," Ronja murmured, touching the black device clamped around his ears with a tentative finger.

"Wha—?" Evie began.

"We have to get out of here," Ronja said, shooting to her feet and backing away. She slipped in the blood and caught herself, her arms pinwheeling through the air. "We have to—"

"What's going on?" Terra asked harshly.

"Those things keep The Music out," she said, pointing at the headphones. "They're going to play it over speakers."

"What do you mean?" Henry asked carefully.

"Breaking news, we no longer need Singers to hear The Music, lucky us," Evie said, clapping her hands together in an overwrought impression of an excited child. "And now they have a torture song."

"They know we're out," Iris gasped, her fingers flying to her prim mouth.

"No," Ronja said, some of her panic leaking away as logic took hold. "No, if they knew we were out they would have used it a long time ago. I think they're going to test it on someone at the assembly. Someone without a Singer."

"Roark," Terra said grimly.

Ronja locked eyes with the girl and nodded. "We should split up," she suggested. "Some of us will get Roark, the rest will get my family."

To her surprise, Terra agreed.

"Evie, Iris, take Maxwell and get Ronja's family," she commanded.

"Excuse me?" Ronja asked incredulously.

Terra ignored her, turning to Maxwell.

"I assume all three members of the Zipse family will be under the Recovery Song?"

"I would guess so," Maxwell confirmed, shifting from foot to foot.

"Good, so stinging them won't be a problem."

"What?" Ronja yelped.

Terra rounded on Ronja, one hand on her hip.

"The Recovery Song is barely a breath from The Quiet Song. If they become lucid and get scared, they'll be dead in minutes. Would you prefer them have one burn or your space in the oven?"

Ronja paled. She opened her mouth to reply, but Terra was no longer paying attention to her.

"Maxwell, you'll guide them to Ronja's family, then you'll accompany them out through the storm drain on the south side of the compound."

"That leads to the bay," Maxwell squeaked. "I can't swim."

Terra cocked her head to the side.

"I think you've mistaken me for someone who cares. As I was saying, you'll lead them out through the storm drain into the bay or you will die in agony. *Do you understand*?"

Maxwell flapped his lips uselessly. His spindly hand snaked up to clutch his Singer, which Ronja could almost hear inching toward The Quiet Song.

"Excellent," Terra said. "Get going."

"Hold up a pitching second," Ronja said, snatching Terra by the arm. "You expect me to abandon my family?"

"No," the girl replied, knocking her hand away. "I expect you to let your family get out first. You'll be no help to them in your condition, but you might be able to help Roark."

"How?" Ronja asked incredulously.

"Roark will fight for you, like you did for him," Terra said offhandedly, wiping her blood-slick knife on her pants and jamming it back into its sheath. "If he sees you're alive, he might even fight this Lost Song."

Ronja regarded the girl grimly, but could not muster a reasonable counterargument.

"It's settled then," Terra said with irrefutable finality. "Ronja, Henry, put on your headphones. Everyone grab a weapon."

53: THE NEW METHODS
Roark

R oark figured Victor was marching him to a laboratory of some sort, but this assumption proved incorrect. As they rounded a corner, Roark's footsteps faltered. His father glanced at him over his shoulder, though his pace did not waver.

Roark's eyebrows cinched, and a familiar sense of foreboding took root in his stomach.

"The atrium," he muttered under his breath.

The pair of double doors thrown open at the terminus of the corridor led to the central lobby. Even from afar, Roark could see the vast, sterile room was burgeoning with hundreds of loyal employees. Their words wove themselves into a bubbling hum. Roark fought the urge to run. His dread grew with each forward step.

He lifted his chin as they approached the entryway. His blood froze as he crossed the threshold, and he cringed when he heard Offs slam the doors in his wake.

Conversation spiked and plummeted in rapid waves as the employees laid eyes first on Victor, then on Roark. He kept his eyes trained on his father's back, but still saw people pointing at him like a zoo animal in his peripheral vision.

Roark could not blame them, he supposed.

His family was the second best-known in Revinia, and certainly the most gossiped about. Roark in particular was targeted by rumors. He often disappeared for weeks at a time on Anthem business, which understandably aroused suspicion. As far as The Bard was concerned, he had been murdered, addicted to the sap, addicted to gambling, and had slept with half of the core.

He let the rumors fester, even fueled them. Better to be branded as a philanderer than a traitor.

Now, it seemed, he might be regarded as both.

Victor escorted him to a newly-erected wooden stage at the far end of the hall. Roark's stomach twisted as he mounted the flimsy flight of steps to the platform. When he reached the top, he scanned the room.

The atrium had been converted into a theater of sorts. The stage looked out over a sea of folding chairs. Chemis, techis, Offs, and physicians of all ranks mingled among them. The makeshift theater possessed only one visible exit, the double doors through which they had entered. There would be no escaping that way. It was nearly thirty meters away and blocked by a tight knot of Offs.

If he ran now, he would be taken down. He did not care to discover if his demise would come in the form of a bullet or The Quiet Song. Could they reach him with The Quiet Song yet? Had it been converted?

"Showtime," Victor murmured under his breath.

Roark slid his gaze sidelong. Victor licked his thin lips and gave the audience a dazzling smile. He raised a silencing palm. The babel fizzled, then died as people took their seats.

"Devoted employees, citizens of Revinia, thank you for being here today," Victor began.

His voice swallowed the room, as if his words were their own Music.

"These past months you have poured your time and energy into fulfilling our Exalted Conductor's wishes. You have His personal thanks."

Applause gathered, then dissipated.

"Nearly fifty years ago Revinia was ravaged by civil war. We had severed ourselves from the world in hopes of avoiding such things, but ultimately the violence rose from the heart of our city. Seeing no end to the savagery, our esteemed leader Atticus Bullon looked for a way out."

"May the ages hold his name," the audience droned.

Victor inclined his head solemnly, then continued.

"Bullon came to my father with a simple question: Why continue to fight a ceaseless battle when other options may exist?"

Victor laced his fingers behind him and began to prowl the stage. The scalding spotlights deepened the branching lines on his face.

"The Conductor spoke of The Music, of course. At the time it was merely a nebulous concept, but my father saw the genius in it. With The Conductor's help, he created The Music that now guides us. We would not be the great city we are today without the notes in your ears right now."

The audience members bobbed their heads, touched their Singers affectionately.

"Unfortunately, The Music as we know it is no longer enough to snuff the disobedience so innate in human nature."

Roark felt his heart sputter in his chest. Victor's suited back was to him, but his smugness radiated.

"We have some special guests here today to exhibit your fine work. If you would bring them forth, Bayard."

Roark looked to his left, his gut plummeting.

Bayard, the Off with the black ponytail, emerged from the shadows. A length of cord was wound around his wrist. He checked over his shoulder and gave the wire a tug. Gasps rose from the crowd. A few people even stood. Roark craned his neck to see who the massive man led.

There were four of them bound to Bayard by their necks and wrists. The first was an elderly man whose mousy hair was coming out in chunks. His eyes were glazed and slightly crossed. After him came a young girl with stubble almost as fiery as Ito's. She peered around sullenly, her small nose wrinkled. After her was a wiry man with dark skin and a nervous tick in his fingers. All three wore Singers.

The final prisoner was a woman. A mutt, Roark quickly realized. Her fingers were clubbed, her skin sallow. Her features were coarse and her eyes yellow, but there was something about the shape of her mouth . . .

"Layla," Roark breathed.

The woman's head snapped up, her mustard eyes ablaze. She had heard him halfway across the auditorium.

"Bring them here," Victor commanded.

Bayard yanked the chain gang roughly, and they tripped forward like dominos. Someone in the audience guffawed loudly, but most chuckled under their breath. Roark swallowed the lump of anger in his throat.

The four prisoners were led to the center of the stage, where Bayard began to unchain them.

"Do not try to run," Victor intoned, strolling along the aisle of prisoners. "You will be gunned down before you reach the door. In but a moment, you will realize you do not wish to run."

The redheaded girl snarled. Roark eyed her curiously. Her Singer glinted proudly in the spotlight, doubtlessly imploring her to respect Victor. She appeared to pay it little mind.

Ronja's indignant face flashed in his mind. Their second meeting on the platform. Her migraines. Her curiosity. Her persistence. Her scarcely-veiled rage.

"The people of Revinia have developed a subtle deafness to The Music," Victor said, turning back to face the audience.

They observed him raptly. Their attention appeared genuine. Roark wondered if they would be so attentive if their Singers were removed.

"In some cases this tolerance is harmless," Victor continued in his silky voice. "For example, the outer ring recently created an office that offers impoverished citizens unapproved jobs. While not sanctioned by The Conductor, this organization is fundamentally benign. However," Victor raised a slim finger. "Far more serious rebels lurk in our city. They call themselves the Anthem."

Whispers thick with fear and revulsion gathered above the crowd. Roark felt his insides writhe. Cold sweat beaded on his forehead.

"These criminals hide like cowards in our midst, mutilating their members, *children*, by cutting off their ears as well as their Singers. They are barbarians in the worst sense of the word. They are the embodiment of the thing The Music strives to stamp out.

"Classically these criminals would have been turned into mutts." Victor gestured to Layla, who gave a soft growl. "But this practice is outdated and messy. If we were to mutate every wayward citizen, there would be more mutts than humans among us."

The audience shuddered collectively and exchanged hushed

words of agreement. Roark might have imagined it, but he thought he saw Layla lift her chin.

"Is it not more prudent to pull out the roots of this problem rather than to cut its branches?" Victor asked, spreading his hands peaceably.

A ripple of agreement passed through the hall, chilling Roark to the bone.

"We did our best to allow the public some leeway, but it would seem they cannot handle even an ounce of freedom."

"You call this freedom?"

Victor stiffened. He turned toward Roark slowly, his chest ballooning with rage. Not long ago Roark might have quelled, but not today. He could not allow himself the luxury of fear.

"Would you care to tell us what you mean?" Victor asked.

He spoke cautiously, as if his words might shatter glass.

"No one in Revinia is free," Roark said, moving to face his father. He had never realized that he was taller than Victor by a full three inches. "Not even you. You may be free of The Music, but you still serve The Conductor."

"By my own choice," Victor replied, smiling sweetly.

"Choice," Roark snorted. "Your choices are going to get you killed one of these days. I only hope I get to be the one who pulls the trigger."

The room erupted.

People leapt to their feet and jeered at him, screaming threats and throwing whatever they could get their hands on. Roark ducked as a clipboard narrowly missed his temple and cracked against the wall. Papers fluttered to the ground halfheartedly.

Victor raised his hands and calm descended.

"My son has been misled by the Anthem."

The audience loosed a collective gasp. Victor nodded calmly, then went on.

"They captured him when he was a child and reared him to be their spy. He was weak to fall for their trickery, but is not past redemption. I had hoped I might be able to sway him with my words alone, but the more I speak with my son, the more I realize how far gone he truly is."

Victor flicked a finger at Bayard, who had been standing inert at the edge of the stage. The behemoth lumbered forward and offered his master a pair of black headphones. Panic gripped Roark. Before he could bolt, Bayard was squeezing his shoulders with his meaty fingers, his foul breath on the back of his neck.

"You will find a pair of noise-canceling headphones beneath each of your chairs," Victor said, slicking back his peppered hair and donning his own. "If you would please tune them to channel one, you will be able to hear what I say."

"How do you know I'm not resistant?" Roark spat.

Victor smiled.

"Judging by the terror in your eyes, I do not think that will be a problem."

54: SIGHTLESS
Evie

They're just around the corner—we put the children in the same cell to save space," Maxwell said quietly. The boney man glanced behind them, his fingers flickering between his glasses and his Singer agitatedly. "We don't have much time."

"How can you live with yourself, experimenting on children?" Iris whispered bitingly as she peeked around the bend. Evie had given her girlfriend her stinger, which she now white knuckled. Iris motioned for Evie and Maxwell to follow her.

"This one," the chemi said, hastily pointing at a door labeled 649.

The trio came to a halt, glaring at Maxwell expectantly. He stood motionless, staring at the door with glassy eyes.

"Hurry *up*, pitcher," Evie growled.

She shoved Maxwell roughly and he tripped toward the portal, his key ring jangling in his clammy fingers.

Evie guarded the door while Maxwell fumbled with the keys. Iris shifted from foot to foot nervously, twirling the stinger between her middle and index fingers like one of her surgical tools. Charged by the adrenaline, Evie assumed. A part of her hoped that Iris would recover quickly from whatever she had endured. She had only been in Red Bay for a night; how much damage could they have done to her?

The image of Ronja's mangled body strewn across the conveyor belt flared in her mind, and her doubts were resurrected.

The lock clicked behind her.

Evie turned to find Maxwell opening the cell door. She pushed him out of the way brazenly and strode across the threshold. Iris followed, her bare feet whispering on the tiles.

They were engulfed by the foul combination of body odor, urine, and mold. Iris put her hands over her nose and mouth, but shock left Evie immobile.

She shook herself free from the grasp of horror.

"I'll put them under," Evie said.

"Be gentle," Iris implored from behind her.

Evie shot a wry glance over her shoulder, a smile lifting the corner of her mouth for a half second. "Right," she drawled sardonically. "I'll knock them out as gently as possible."

Evie turned back and crouched by the boy before Iris could berate her. His eyes, green shot with gray, were spread wide. They regarded the ceiling blankly, and she knew they did not truly see. He was dangerously thin, his face a map of yellowing of bruises.

"You resisted," she murmured under her breath. "You have her blood."

Evie suddenly realized she did not know either of their names. She had never stopped to ask Ronja. She reached to her hip and drew the stinger she had lifted from a fallen Off, twirling it between her fingers uncertainly. Could these two survive a shock of this magnitude? Evie wished Iris still had the sedatives, but of course they had been confiscated along with her hair and clothes.

Evie clenched her teeth, the stinger still dancing in her fingers. If the shock was too powerful the children would be killed. If it was not powerful enough The Quiet would doubtlessly consume them. When she had brought Ronja back to life Evie had not held back. She had flooded the dead girl with the strongest current her stinger could muster. This was a much more delicate process; one she was not certain she could handle.

"If they go into The Quiet they've got no chance," Iris said gently, squatting down next to her and clamping a firm hand on her shoulder.

Evie whistled out a steadying breath. "I'm sorry," she muttered, looking into the gaunt face of the boy.

She flicked the switch with her thumb and drove the weapon into his neck. He convulsed violently, but his blank eyes registered no pain.

Evie pulled back her stinger, holding her breath as she waited. Iris squeezed her shoulder reassuringly.

The boy's eyes rolled back into his head, and his vein-checkered lids closed over them.

Evie stood and backed away as Iris knelt beside him. She placed her fingers on his blotchy neck, just above the burn. Iris nodded after a long moment, and Evie released the breath she did not know she was still holding. She stepped around the boy delicately and knelt beside the girl.

She was free of bruises, but was frailer than her brother. Her skin was almost gray in the cold light, and her chest rose and fell shallowly. Her eyes were wide like her brothers and roved across the blank ceiling in search of something that was not there.

"Could you?" Evie asked softly, nodding toward the little girl.

Iris did not need to ask. She knelt next to the child's mousy, brown head. With careful fingers, she closed the girl's fragile lids over her wandering eyes, then touched two fingers to her brow.

"May your song guide you home," Iris whispered.

Evie flicked the stinger to life and pressed it to the girl's neck. She closed her eyes as the electric current ripped through her feeble body, and she did not open them until she wrenched the stinger away.

"That should do it," Iris said, feeling for her pulse. "That'll keep her down for awhile."

Evie got to her feet, pushing down her relief to make room for professionalism. "Maxwell," she barked. "You carry the girl. I'll take the boy."

"Are you sure you can manage?" Maxwell asked from the door.

"*You* certainly can't, so I can."

Maxwell blushed fiercely, then adjusted his spectacles in an attempt to hide it.

Gently as she could, Evie slid her hands under the boy's shoulders and knees. She hefted him into her arms with a grunt of effort. One of his arms flopped over her bicep, and his head lolled backward. His sightless eyes peeked out from beneath his thick lashes, unnerving her.

Maxwell maneuvered around Evie and her charge and squatted by the girl. He lifted her with awkward gentleness and curled her toward his chest.

"Which way?" Evie asked.

"Left," Maxwell said.

"If you're lying, I'll kill you."

"I expect so."

55: SURREAL

I t was surreal, watching the world rush by in utter silence. They met no further resistance as they hurtled down the halls, but Ronja still white-knuckled the large automatic she had stolen from the fallen Off. It was longer than her forearm, and she had to hold it with both hands.

Terra threw up her fist and Ronja slammed to a halt, her bare feet scuffing against the tiles. She felt rather than heard Henry screech to a stop behind her.

With an open palm, the blond girl gestured for them to wait then flashed a glance around the corner. She nodded over her shoulder, and for half a moment they relaxed.

Ronja reached up to her headphones and tentatively peeled away one of the cups. Hearing nothing, she swiped them off her head. The others followed suit.

"There's a door at the end of the hall that leads to an atrium. That has to be where Roark is," Terra whispered. "Six guards, all wearing headphones. Even if we can get past them, there's no way we can get to him inside. There are probably hundreds of people in there."

"Why bother now? We should just wait until they take him somewhere else," Henry suggested.

"We don't know what they're going to do to him," Ronja retorted angrily, rounding on Henry. "They could be torturing him, killing him for all we know."

Henry threw up his palms in surrender and blew out an exasperated breath through his nose.

"What's the plan, then?" Ronja asked, her vexation receding.

Terra smiled grimly and pointed at the lights buzzing overhead.

"Electricity," she said. "We need to take out the power grid, plunge the place into darkness. It should be enough of a distraction for us to get out."

Henry and Ronja nodded approvingly, and Terra went on. "Three corridors back the way we came and to the right is the main generator," Terra said. She turned to the boy, who raised his chin slightly. "Henry, I want you to skitz it up until everything goes black. Alarms will go off, everyone will panic. As soon as it goes dark, follow the corridor to the right, turn left once, then right, then go down the flight of steps to the basement. You'll see the storm drain. Follow it to the bay. Evie and the others should be there."

Henry bobbed his head.

Terra grabbed him by the wrist and tugged him several paces down the corridor, away from Ronja. She started to follow, but Terra shot her a warning look over her shoulder. Her blood simmering, Ronja leaned back against the wall while Terra pulled the boy down to her level and whispered something in his ear. He nodded, his eyes trained on the floor.

Terra clapped him on the shoulder bracingly, then slipped something small and black into his hand.

"Understood," he said, straightening and curling his fingers around the object. "Three corridors down, right, dark, right, left, right, down, bay," he repeated methodically.

Terra inclined her head. She reached to her hip and drew her spare sidearm. She held it out by the barrel for Henry to take. He scowled at the weapon, but took it without complaint.

The boy paused, looking from Terra to Ronja. "How are you getting out?" he asked.

"How *are* we getting out?" Ronja reiterated.

"Just trust me, *please*," Terra begged, sliding an exhausted hand down her face. "I've gotten you this far. Go, Henry. Now."

Henry jogged back to Ronja and roped her into a fierce hug, which she returned enthusiastically. She pressed her nose to his chest, memorizing his smell. Then the boy tore away and sprinted off down the hall, donning his headphones.

"What now?" Ronja asked when he had disappeared around the bend.

"We wait and hope no one finds us," Terra replied.

"Really, how *are* we getting out?"

Terra blew a breath through her nose like a bull about to

charge, then began to fish around in the pocket of her vest. Ronja craned her neck to see what she was doing, but Terra maneuvered out of her line of sight.

"But—"

Terra stowed whatever she had been fiddling with and put her headphones back on, effectively signaling that the conversation was over.

"How—?"

Terra started. She gestured wildly for Ronja to put on her headphones. Ronja fumbled with the apparatus and slapped it onto her head, wincing when the leather chaffed her wound.

" . . . is called The Lost Song."

Ronja froze. The world around her evaporated in a haze of terror as Victor's voice reverberated through her mind. She wanted to rip the earphones from her skull, but she could not move.

"This Song will be saved only for the most dangerous criminals. It attacks the pain centers of the brain and temporarily incapacitates the receiver. As I explained, it can travel through the air like radio waves. It does not require a Singer, so it may be used on the troublesome rebels. Bayard, if you would."

Silence reigned, but she knew Roark was screaming.

To her left Terra was gripping her headphones as if she could squeeze the hush from them. Her jaw bulged beneath the drying filth on her cheeks.

"Enough," Victor said delicately in her ear. "Get up."

Ronja gripped her automatic and stalked forward, prepared to fly around the corner. Terra caught her by the arm and wrenched her back.

"Again, louder."

Silence fell again, but Ronja knew that beyond her shield The Lost Song was blaring. She could still feel it burrowed inside her mind like a worm.

"Enough," Victor said. "As you can see it is highly effective, but only to incapacitate our most dangerous enemies. Our true weapon against emotion is far more refined. This is the Song that will be released to the public within the year. It can travel by air as well as Singer, and will replace all current forms of The Music. It is far from perfect, but it is merely a prototype. Bayard."

A high-pitched keening built in her remaining ear, but it had nothing to do with The Music.

Time slowed to a crawl as Ronja ripped her arm from Terra's viselike grip, cocking her automatic as she moved. She felt the girl reach out for her, but she grasped only air.

Her finger was clamped around the trigger before she placed it there. She was sprinting down the corridor before she could think to run. She was screaming beyond the bounds of her hearing, and the storm of bullets joined her chorus. She saw the guards fall like cans off a fencepost, their blood splattering the blank, double doors in great crimson arches. She saw through a sheen of red, as if the blood had splashed in her eyes.

Ronja stalked forward, shoving the knot of limp corpses out of her way with her bare feet. Vomit bulged in her throat. The lives she had extinguished were tugging at her, pulling her down, but she could not heed them. She refused their cries.

Ronja wrenched open the portal and lunged through, straight into the arms of her enemies.

56: FREQUENCIES
Henry

The speech flooded his headphones like a sudden downpour. He heard the words of Victor Westervelt II and finally knew the voice that haunted his friend, his brother.

The day Roark was freed from his tormentor as a child was the day Henry lost his parents. He remembered his brain going quiet when he received the news from Wilcox, remembered walking to the room Roark was being held in, planning to confront him, to put all the pain he was feeling into his fists.

When he arrived, he'd found a boy half his size with his head in his hands, sobbing silently in the corner.

Henry had sat down beside him. He did not remember crying, but when his mind wandered back he found his mouth was fuzzy and his eyes raw. He had looked over at Roark through glassy eyes. The boy was staring at him, his expression a blend of terror and rage.

Henry had risen unsteadily and left without a word. A week later, when Roark was allowed out of his cell, Henry was the first to offer him a meal. From that moment forward they were brothers, and never spoke of the tears they shed together.

As time passed, Roark improved. His wounds healed, both mental and physical, and he reveled in his newfound purpose. He spent six solid months in the Belly after he was taken, and in that time the Anthemites grew to adore him. They both understood the vital role he would come to play in the war and appreciated his antics. Henry introduced him to his companions Iris and Evie, and they became fast friends. Soon, the quartet was inseparable. It might have continued that way forever, if Henry had not begun to walk a different path.

As Roark healed, Henry deteriorated. He pulled away from his fellow Anthemites. His sister, Charlotte, was only a baby then. He was able to blame his increasingly lengthy absences on her. Iris, Roark, and Evie tried to coax him back to life, but he only retreated deeper into himself.

When Henry turned fifteen, he took Charlotte and moved out of the Belly and into the house of his late grandmother.

It was not as if he cut all ties, of course. He became the Anthem's primary forger . . . it was paramount that those posing as Offs and government employees had the proper documents. Roark, Evie, and Iris visited him as often as they could, but things were never the same.

Now, as he listened to the long gaps between Victor Westervelt II's words, the ones he knew were in reality filled with the screams of his brother, Henry wished he could rewrite time.

His instinct was to rip the headphones from his ears as he hurtled toward the generator room, but he forced himself to listen, as if his intangible presence might somehow alleviate some of Roark's pain.

Victor inhaled sharply in his ear, and Henry nearly tripped.

"Bring her to me," he commanded.

No.

Henry gritted his teeth and plunged forward, her name echoing in the halls of his mind.

Ronja.

The door to the generator room screamed into view on his right, labeled with large, stainless steel letters. Henry came to a halt, his bare feet screeching soundlessly on the tiles. The gun Terra had given him was slick with sweat, as was the radio. She had not told him who would answer if he called, only that it was better not to in case the line was tapped.

"I am rarely surprised, Ronja," Victor was saying, his voice wavering as a burst of static chewed on the radio waves. "I thank you for an intriguing day."

Henry felt his ribs tighten around his lungs like the laces of a boot. He reached for the knob but found it locked. He stood back, buried his face in his shoulder, and released two bullets on the lock. The gun kicked silently in his hand. He rammed his bare heel into the portal and it caved. A wave of heat engulfed him and he lunged into it, his weapon raised.

Two Offs, their ears crowned with black Singers, stood before a massive, whirring machine. Henry did not know much about electricity, but he was fairly certain it was *not* a power generator. It was nearly two stories high and criss crossed with wires and blinking lights. If he did not know better he might say it was a . . .

The Offs lunged at him as one, unnaturally lithe for all their bulk. Henry took aim and fired two consecutive shots. The guards managed one more step each before crumbling to the floor, identical bullet holes like blazing suns on their brows.

Henry had told Ronja he was not a soldier, but that did not mean he was incapable of being one.

Henry stepped over the corpses, trying not to look at the blood he had spilled. He gaped up at the machine, his jaw slack. After a moment, he pulled the headphones down around his neck and held the radio up to his lips, bristling in discomfort as the hum of the world greeted him once again.

"This is Cerberus," he said, using the name he had not used since Bishop Street.

The meandering of the static; then, a voice.

"Cerberus, this is Harpy."

Henry smiled.

"I should have known it would be you," he said into the microphone. "I have a plan. I can incapacitate this entire facility, but first I'm going to need you to make us an exit."

57: ON THREE
Evie

E vie panted as she ran, sweating beneath her charge's dead weight. She hefted his limp form higher in her arms, but he only slipped again, his head bobbing in time with her footsteps.

"You've got it," Iris coaxed from her side.

Evie glanced over at Iris, who now toted the automatic they had stolen from the Offs along with her stinger. The gun was as long as her arm. Iris had never been the best shot, but Evie figured anyone could fire an automatic.

"He—here," Maxwell panted ahead of them, his mammoth feet flapping to a noisy halt. The unconscious child drooped in his grasp, one of her pale arms swaying hypnotically.

Evie skidded to a halt before a door labeled "maintenance" in bold letters. She dropped to one knee, puffing beneath the strain of the boy's body.

"If you're lying about this, you're stuffed, understand?" Iris said, jabbing Maxwell in the back with her stinger, which was for the moment turned off.

The chemi tensed, but Evie saw the way Iris blanched at her own words.

"Open it, Iris," Evie said, struggling to her feet.

Iris moved in front of Maxwell and put a frail hand on the doorknob. She stood motionless for a moment, her shoulders rigid beneath her hospital gown. She leaned forward and pressed her ear against the pale face of the door, listening.

"Clear," Iris told them after a moment. "On three . . . one . . . two . . . "

Gunfire ripped the air.

Evie dragged Iris to the ground, shielding both her and the boy from the hail of bullets.

The pain never came.

Evie raised her head a fraction of an inch, peering around warily. The corridor was deserted. Maxwell had dropped to the ground and enveloped the unconscious girl in his wiry arms. Catching Evie's disbelieving gaze, he relaxed his grip on the child and rose to his feet unsteadily.

"It came from that way," he said, nodding back down the hallway they had come from. "Your friends taking down the Offs, I presume."

"I thought they were going to sneak in," Evie murmured. "They were supposed to do it quietly."

"We can't go back," Iris said softly after a tense moment. "They'll be on high alert. We take these two and we swim for shore. That's what Roark would want."

Evie gazed at Iris. She appeared even smaller than usual without her vibrant curls. Her eyes, though, were bottomless. Fierce.

"Okay," Evie said, trying to convince herself. "Okay."

Iris shouldered her gun and wrenched open the maintenance door. The hinges shrieked, but the sound and the semidarkness were all that greeted them.

Iris went first, her automatic raised before her awkwardly. Maxwell followed, cradling the girl to his chest carefully. Evie went last. She glanced over her shoulder at the gaping lights of the corridor. There was no more gunfire in the distance.

Evie closed the door with a sharp screech and stepped into the dim room.

Iron shelves stocked with cleaning supplies lined the long, cramped expanse. The floor and walls were concrete, and a single naked bulb dangled from the ceiling.

A manhole labeled "storm" was rooted in the asphalt.

Evie laid the boy on the floor tenderly and gestured for Maxwell to do the same. He placed the mousy haired girl next to her brother.

"Help me open this," she commanded Maxwell. "Iris, guard the door."

Evie and the chemi squatted on opposite sides of the exit and dug their fingers into the narrow slits around the rim of the cover.

"On three," Evie said, holding Maxwell's feeble gaze in her own. "One . . . two . . . "

With a grunt the two lifted the grate from its niche. Evie felt one of her nails spilt. She hissed air through her teeth as blood welled at her fingertip.

They tossed the cover aside with a dull clang.

Evie squinted down into the hole. The sickly light from the bulb glanced off the damp floor of the tunnel five feet below. The air filtering up to meet her was thick and humid, but was infinitely better than that of the sewage tunnel.

Evie jerked her thumb at Maxwell without looking up from their escape hatch. She knew Iris was watching her.

"Watch him," she said absently.

In her peripheral vision, she saw Iris nod and adjust her automatic.

Evie straddled the manhole, then lowered herself into the near total blackness. She hovered for a moment, her muscular arms trembling, then dropped into the tube. The cool air rushed past her for a split second, then she hit the ground. She landed in a crouch, splattering stagnant water across the curved walls.

Evie rose and looked up at Maxwell. His spectacles flashed in the naked light, obscuring his expression.

Evie raised her hands, gesturing for him to hand the children down to her.

Maxwell disappeared for a moment, his white sneakers scuffing against the grimy floor. Half a moment later he reappeared, cradling the unconscious girl in his twig arms.

"Easy," Evie warned as he lowered the child feet first into the dimness.

She wrapped her arms around the girl's jutting hips. Maxwell released her cautiously. The girl weighed almost nothing. Evie lowered her to the damp ground, then reached up for the boy. Maxwell already had him in hand, and dangled him over the gap, his arms quivering with exertion.

Evie grunted as Maxwell relinquished the boy into her hands. Her knees buckled beneath his weight, and she let them sink to the floor. She laid him down quickly, then stepped away from the hole.

"Come on," she called up to Iris and Maxwell.

The chemi looked over his shoulder wearily. Evie could almost hear The Music roaring in his ear.

"You'll be killed," Evie reminded him from below. "By us or Red Bay. Unless you get down here right now."

Maxwell let his eyelids fall shut for a moment, massaging his temples methodically. Even in the dim light, Evie could see the veins popping in his forehead.

"Forgive me," he muttered, looking up to the ceiling.

Maxwell took a deep breath and jumped into the gaping manhole. He landed awkwardly in the static water, arms flailing. Evie steadied him roughly.

Iris handed her gun down to Evie and leapt into the mouth of the hole lithely, landing in a deep crouch. She rose, wiping her dainty hands on her white gown and wrinkling her nose at her bare, soggy feet.

"Which way?" Iris asked softly, looking left and right down the dank tube.

Evie spit on her forefinger and raised it to the air. A faint, cool breeze kissed the saliva, and she pointed in its direction.

Maxwell lifted the girl again and Evie slung her brother over her shoulder.

They started down the tunnel away from the nightmarish compound, but Evie and Iris left their thoughts behind.

58: THERE AND BACK

The silence deepened when Ronja blew through the doors.

Countless pairs of disbelieving eyes locked onto her, their shock punctuated by their O-shaped mouths.

The lobby had been converted into a makeshift theater with a single wide aisle running down its center. At the terminus of the gap loomed a long, wooden stage.

Atop the dais stood Roark, tense and heedless of the blood gushing from his ears. His eyes were twin voids, his hands limp at his sides. Victor stood behind him, a leeching shadow. To their right were four prisoners crowned with headphones and garbed in grimy hospital gowns.

Layla was one of them.

Her matted gray hair had been shaved, emphasizing her rough features and hooded yellow eyes. She had wasted away. Her joints jutted dangerously from beneath her pasty skin.

Layla's gaunt eyes flashed toward Ronja. For a slice of a moment, their gazes locked.

Then the Offs were upon Ronja, tearing the automatic from her fingers and pinning her to the ground. She felt her nose crack against the tiles and coughed as blood pooled in her mouth.

Movement flared to her left. She struggled to see through the tangle of limbs around her. Terra was fending off a pair of Offs with her knives. She felled one with a slice to the throat, but the second put her in a headlock, forcing her to the floor.

"Enough."

The word broke the Offs' grip, and in an instant she was free.

Ronja leapt to her feet, wiping her oozing nose with the back of her wrist. She readjusted her headphones hastily, but her gaze never left Victor. He smirked at her from atop the stage.

"Bring her to me."

Two pairs of hands grasped her shoulders and started to force her toward the stage. She shoved them away, baring her teeth at the Offs in a silent warning. They hesitated, ready to catch her if she bolted.

Ronja stalked toward the stage, her naked feet leaving red silhouettes on the floor.

Victor's smirk morphed into a delighted grin, his mouth stretched too wide across his wolfish face.

Ronja halted at the foot of the platform, her neck craned back to regard the man.

"I am rarely surprised, Ronja," his voice intoned in her ear, disturbingly close. "I thank you for an intriguing day."

"Pitch off," Ronja growled.

"I apologize: this is a one-way stream. I cannot hear you, though I assume your words would have scorched my ears."

"What have you done to Roark?"

"Impressive, is it not?"

Victor turned to his son, clapped a hand on his shoulder. Roark did not seem to notice his presence. His gaze was trained on the opposite wall, his mouth faintly slack.

"It is far from perfect," Victor acknowledged with a thoughtful tilt of his head. "We are still refining it, but by the time this Song takes its final form, our city will be filled with innately loyal citizens, unhindered by emotion."

"Roark," Ronja implored, ignoring the senior Westervelt's exultation. She took a tentative step forward, rested her sweaty fists on the wooden stage. "Roark you have to fight it. Can you hear me?"

Roark blinked sluggishly, his eyes heavily lidded. He did not seem to recognize her presence.

"Roark," Victor said. "Look at me."

Roark snapped to attention and spun to face his father.

"Bow," Victor ordered lazily.

Roark swiped his hand behind his back and bowed low, his long hair sweeping forward to obscure his face.

"Rise."

Roark smiled vaguely as his spine uncurled.

"He is completely obedient," Victor said, shifting his attention back to Ronja. "There will be no question of loyalty in the future."

"Roark," Ronja repeated.

She could hear nothing but Victor's breathing, his quiet laughter. She could not even hear her own heart pumping in her remaining ear. The Music was clawing at her headphones, begging to be let inside. It was thick in the air, crackling like static electricity, kissing her skin with razor teeth.

"Roark, you can beat this."

Roark was gazing at his father with unmistakable reverence. If he heard her voice, he did not acknowledge it.

Ronja opened her raw palms on the rough stage and launched herself up. She rose quickly on her bare feet. She felt the Offs swarm behind her, preparing to take her down.

Victor shook his head subtly, and they retreated.

"Please, try to sway him," Westervelt invited her, splaying his hands. "It will make a good show."

Ronja snapped her gaze toward the audience. Most were on their feet, their expressions twisted with misplaced rage and terror. Terra was still ensnared in the beefy arms of a female Off. She locked gazes with Ronja and offered an almost imperceptible nod.

Ronja turned back to Roark.

"Roark," she said loudly.

She reached forward and grasped his stiff hand. The boy finally looked down at her, confusion briefly cracking his glassy stare. It faded quickly when he glanced over his shoulder at Victor, who gave him a reassuring nod.

Ronja twisted to view her mother. Layla was regarding her intensely. She had seen such a sharpness in her mother's eyes before, but this was different. Her expression was focused, potent.

"I was angry with you," Ronja said, returning to the shell of the boy she knew. "But I'm not anymore. You freed me from The Music—I won't let you fall to it because of me."

Roark blinked lethargically. His eyes tracked something nonexistent beyond her head.

"It is useless," Victor said almost gleefully. "He's—"

"When the day shakes beneath the hands of night," Ronja whispered.

Victor ceased breathing. Out of the corner of her eye, Ronja saw his smile falter.

Ronja raised her voice.

"When your page is ripped from the Book of Life."

She could feel the words flying from her mouth, though she could not hear them. She did not need to hear them. She could see them spark and pop when they struck the air, smoking and crackling against the electric wall of The Music.

"When your knees crash into the ground, and your desperate lips won't make a sound."

Ronja took Roark's stiff hands in her own. He was trembling. Sweat beaded on his dark brow, and his eyes glinted anxiously.

"Raise The Music," Victor ordered in her ear.

Roark shuddered and his vision stilled.

"When you're all alone and the night is deep," Ronja sang, tightening her grip on his still fingers. She pulled Roark down to her level, holding his bleak gaze in her own. "When you're surrounded but you want to weep. When the morning comes and it's all but bleak, and you want to scream but instead you're meek."

Roark blinked.

Once.

Twice.

There.

"Sing my friend into the dark."

She could see it all around her in her mind's eye. Her own voice, clashing with The Music in the air.

The Music was stark white with arms like whips. It was omnipotent, riding every air current, lurking in every brain.

Her own voice was black, exploding around her like dark supernovas and obliterating the tendrils of The Music.

"Sing my friend into the deep, sing my friend into the black, sing my friend, there and back."

There and back.

Ronja felt her breath catch in her ribs.

His lips had moved, reflecting the words only he could hear.

"Roark?" she whispered.

Ronja.

The room erupted in a soundless surge of white.

59: ON THE MEND

Ronja and Roark dove from the stage as the explosion ripped through the atrium. The force knocked her headphones from her ears, but when she lifted her rattled head all she could hear was a high-pitched keening, the aftermath of the eruption.

The boy wrenched Ronja to her feet, wound his arms around her head protectively. She pressed into his chest and wrapped her arms around his waist, peeking out from beneath his bicep.

Around them was chaos and sunlight.

Chunks of metal and concrete and wire littered the ground, smoking in the shafts of brilliant sunlight that tumbled through the gaping hole in the roof. Screams and cries of shock began to break through the shrill note that lingered after the blast. People scrambled, clambering over each other to get to the double doors, which were thrown open. Even the Offs seemed stunned.

Ronja looked around fearfully for Victor, but he was nowhere to be found.

"Roark!"

Terra was sprinting toward them, waving her arms and leaping over mounds of rubble.

Ronja felt Roark beam, his jaw perched atop her head.

"Terra!" he shouted, uncharacteristically overjoyed at the sight of the blond solider.

"We needed an exit!" Terra called through her smug grin. "She should already have picked up the others in the bay."

"She?"

Terra pointed toward the new skylight. Ronja and Roark followed her finger, but all they could see was an unusually blue sky.

A low rumble flooded the air. Ronja gaped as a behemoth, burgundy airship slid into view in the ragged portal. Its propellers glinted sharply in the midmorning light. The cold air lashed Ronja's raw skin, but she welcomed the sting. It cooled her burns.

A rope ladder spiraled down through the hatch. Terra caught it singlehandedly.

One moment Ronja was grinning. The next, the hairs on the back of her neck were standing on end. She whipped around, poised to shout a warning. Before the hail of could bullets riddle her, Roark dragged her to the ground behind a hulking slab of concrete. Terra dove to the floor beside her, her hands clamped over her own head.

"Skitz!" Roark bellowed over the shelling, his arm wrapped around Ronja. "What do we do?"

"Wait!" Terra yelled back.

"For what?!"

The gunfire stopped as quickly as it had began, the last shells singing against the floor almost cheerily. For a beat there was only the thrum of the propellers and the sound of their labored breathing.

Then, the screaming began.

Terra was the first to get to her feet, a twisted grin splitting her mouth. The wind whipping her hair, her eyes glittering, she looked terrifyingly beautiful. She craned her head back and released a ringing laugh, motioned for Ronja and Roark to rise.

They got to their feet cautiously, wincing as the gut-wrenching cries continued. Ronja peered around the chunk of rubble. Her mouth fell open.

The team of Offs was writhing on the floor, their black uniforms caked in white debris. Their bodies were rigid with pain, their fingers paralyzed with agony. Blood drained from beneath their headphones, dying the powdered concrete.

"We sent Henry to cut the power," Terra laughed, grasping the rope ladder with a strong, tanned hand. "He had a better idea."

"The Lost Song," Ronja realized with a breathless laugh. "He put it in their headphones."

"Come on," Terra called over the din, already several rungs above them. "We don't know how long it'll hold!"

"My mother!" Ronja gasped, spinning toward Roark and grabbing him by the forearms. "The other prisoners!"

She and Roark separated and whirled about. The stage was smashed to splinters, crushed beneath a hulking slab of concrete.

Ronja rushed forward, picking through the rubble. A debris-dusted foot caught her eye and she lurched forward. Roark came up behind her and ripped away several jagged planks of wood.

A skinny girl about their age emerged from the rubble, bleeding profusely from a gash in her forehead, but otherwise unharmed. Roark put a hand behind her back and helped her to her feet. Ronja ignored the girl and continued to search through the debris.

"Layla!" she screamed. "Mom!"

A twitch of motion to her right.

Ronja flew toward it and began to dig through the splintered planks. A hand shot from the pile, clawing at the air. The fingers were clubbed.

"I got you! Hang on!" Ronja cried.

She tore away the final few planks. Sunlight shot across her mother's coarse features. Her mouth was twisted into a grimace of pain.

"Mom, I—"

"Took you long enough," Layla grumbled, shoving a chunk of stone the size of an apple from her chest.

Ronja let out a laugh that was closer to a sob. She threw her arms around her mother and rocked her back and forth steadily.

"Ach . . . you're hurting me . . . " Layla grumbled.

"Ronja!" Terra screamed from above. "Get your pitching ass up here!"

Ronja drew back from her mother and yanked her to her feet, brushing tears from her eyes.

The rope ladder swung hypnotically in the bright air. The atrium was almost completely empty, save for the Offs who were falling silent in droves. The girl with red stubble and an old man with birdlike features were scaling the ladder steadily. Roark stood at the base, steadying it. His eyes were bright in the glare of the sun, his white teeth flashed.

Ronja's stomach twisted itself into knots.

We did it.

"Go ahead!" Ronja called. "I'll get her up!"

Roark nodded and leapt onto the ladder.

"Come on," Ronja said, ushering her mother forward.

Layla shooed her flustered hands away and jumped toward the ladder. She began to climb.

Pop.

Ronja blinked, squinting up into the sunbeams.

A drop of rain, warm and full of life, graced her forehead.

For today my friend
I promise you are on the mend,

The water sang, just as it had in her dream. By the time Layla struck the ground, she was long past the world of dreams and nightmares.

60: COULD HAVE

Her mother's eyes were still open. They gazed up at the waiting airship, the swaying ladder, the crisp, autumn sky. A wary smile hung on the corner of her Layla's perpetually swollen mouth. A politely tiny hole dotted the center of her rumpled forehead where the bullet had exited.

Ronja crashed to her knees, her hands limp at her sides. Roark was hanging off the top of the ladder, screaming for her to climb.

The tears would not come anymore. Her whole body was dry. Parched of blood. Starved of sensation.

When she got to her feet, her vision was clear. The Offs were as quiet as corpses, twitching occasionally in the debris.

Ronja looked around calmly in search of her mother's killer. A thin trail of smoke wormed through the air several paces to her right. She followed it to the shooter.

She knew who it was before she saw his broken form beneath a jagged wedge of concrete.

His breaths came out in rattling hisses. Blood gushed from his mouth, drawn from his crushed legs. A revolver lay smoking in his palm, empty of bullets. The sharp tang of the gunpowder mingled with the metallic scent of his blood. His headphones had been knocked from his head and lay nearby, cracked clean in half.

Victor Westervelt II choked a laugh as he regarded Ronja with manic eyes. "I was . . . aiming . . . for . . . Roark . . . " he coughed.

Ronja nodded.

"The Music . . . will get out . . . " he continued. "It doesn't matter if you kill me or not."

"I killed six people today," Ronja said quietly, drinking in the destruction around her. The bodies she had left in the doorway had been trampled by the escaping crowds. Their limbs were cranked into strange angles, but they did not bleed. "I pulled the trigger, but their blood is on your hands."

"Finish . . . it . . . " Victor choked out.

Ronja shook her head slowly.

"Zipse . . . " Victor rasped. "Finish it . . . "

She turned her back on him.

"I'm done taking orders from you."

Ronja strode away from the man, impervious to the rubble beneath her naked feet. She did not look back, even as his cries for mercy commenced.

Before she started to climb the waiting ladder, she stopped before her mother.

Layla looked peaceful in the morning light. The red on her forehead could have been war paint. She could have been on her way to a jam.

She could have been.

Ronja knelt by her mother, caressed her rough cheek. Westervelt's screams were dissipating in the background. His cries were almost childlike, as if they did not belong to him. Ronja ignored them.

"It wasn't your fault," Ronja said softly, shutting her mother's eyelids with her palms. "I know it wasn't. You would have loved me."

She pressed two fingers to Layla's jaundiced forehead, plugging the bullet wound.

"May your song guide you home," she whispered.

61: THE WEIGHT

Ronja had always wondered what an airship looked like from the inside. She had imagined luxuriating in a floating palace, garbed in fine clothes and sipping champagne as she watched the world turn far below.

Instead, she was doused in blood and draped in nothing but an ill-fitting overcoat. She almost chuckled at the irony as she scaled the writhing rope ladder, leaving her mother and the screaming silence of Red Bay behind.

When she emerged from the hatch in the belly of the airship, she was greeted by a hushed ring of her companions. Their gazes were heavier than the weight of the concrete that had crushed Victor.

Roark was there and so was Terra, both cloaked in debris. Iris and Evie, both drenched to the bone in the waters of the bay, stood side by side, their hands clasped tightly. Iris was crying silently, but did not seem to be aware of it. The two surviving prisoners, the redheaded girl and the old man, lingered on the outskirts of the semicircle. The man was clutching his skull and muttering to himself, but the girl seemed stable.

Someone was missing.

"Henry," Ronja breathed, getting to her feet. As if it had sensed her presence, the airship lurched and began to sail forward with impossible speed.

Roark bowed his head.

"I'm right here, Ro."

Ronja looked around wildly, her breath catching in her throat, a smile budding on her lips. But her comrades were not rejoicing.

Terra stepped forward, her face turned down, her hand outstretched. She was holding a small black radio.

Ronja reached out, her expression blank. She flinched when her fingers wrapped around the warm metal.

"Sorry," Henry said, his voice warped by the buzz of static. "I got held up."

"You stupid pitcher," Ronja whispered.

"Your bedside manner is terrible, has anyone ever told you that?" Henry inquired with a weak laugh.

A distant hammering drained the blood from Ronja's face.

"What was that?" she asked, clutching the radio closer to her cheek. "Henry? What was that?"

"I shoved a filing cabinet in front of the door, but it won't hold for long," the boy replied. His tone was frighteningly calm, resigned. "Turns out not all the Offs had headphones."

The persistent thudding continued as Ronja struggled to speak.

"Ronja, listen to me."

"No," she whimpered.

"Ro, please," Henry begged. "All of you, listen to me."

"We're here, H," Evie assured him in a thick voice.

"I will not let them take my mind, understand? The Anthem will be safe. You will all be safe."

"What do you mean? What are you talking about?" Ronja demanded, switching the radio from one hand to the other as if it burned her.

"I have one bullet left," Henry said softly.

Over the radio the click of the safety echoed. Iris let out a sob, clutched Evie tighter.

"Terra," Henry said.

The girl brought her chin up, her eyes unusually bright.

"This is not your fault, okay? It was my plan. But if you want forgiveness . . . then I forgive you."

Terra swallowed, screwed her eyes shut.

"May your song guide you home, Henry," she finally said, her voice low and steady.

"Roark, Evie, Iris."

The trio of Anthemites straightened when Henry addressed them.

"You were there for me when no one else was," the boy said, raising his voice to overpower the horrible drumbeat. "I should have stayed with you."

"You did what you had to," Roark said levelly. "You will always be our brother."

"Ronja."

Ronja released a wrenching sob, clamping her hand over her mouth, staring at the radio as if she could pull Henry from the speakers.

"Please find Charlotte, take her back to the Belly where she belongs. Be happy. Be free. You have a universe inside you. And Ronja . . . maybe the stars are alive after all."

"Henry—"

The unmistakable screech of metal against concrete as the filing cabinet was toppled.

Ronja felt rather than heard the gunshot. She knew she was screaming, but the sound had been sucked from the airship. Strong arms were around her, to restrain or to calm. She wrenched away, began to run, her bare feet slapping against the polished oak floorboards. She did not make it far before the unbearable weight slammed into her from above, forcing her to her knees.

Ronja wept until a dreamless sleep consumed her.

62: SEDATED

Ronja awoke with her cheek pressed to a damp velvet throw pillow. She peeled her swollen lids open, blinked the sting away. A blurred figure sat across from her on a gold-stitched sofa, his head in his hands.

"Roark," Ronja rasped.

Roark inhaled sharply and brought his hands down. His eyes looked as raw as her own felt. His nose was capped with red.

"Ronja," he said, his voice rusty. He leaned forward to touch her, but seemed to think the better of it and retracted his hand.

The engine chugged beneath the sofa Ronja lay on. Sunlight crawled across her skin, across the knit blanket wrapped around her, but she could not see its source.

"My cousins?" she finally asked quietly.

"Safe," Roark replied gently. "Sedated."

He offered her an olive hand. Ronja reached out to take it, then paused. Her hands were swathed in clean, white bandages. Beneath the linens her burns felt cool and damp, the agony muted by salve. She disentangled herself from her blanket to find she was garbed in a plain white nightshift.

"It was Iris," Roark reassured her. "She needed to clean your wounds."

Ronja nodded, then got to her feet, her knees knocking together.

Roark led her by the elbow from the side parlor into the central hall of the airship. Ornately carved wooden pillars lined the sprawling atrium. A massive chandelier cast golden light throughout the room. Lush sofas and armchairs were scattered throughout the forest of columns, accompanied by polished coffee tables and stacks of fine books.

"The chemi, Maxwell, is in the brig," Roark told her as they walked.

"Okay," Ronja replied.

"Ito and Terra followed us as soon as we left the city," Roark went on.

Ronja inclined her head without looking at him.

"Terra found Evie on the hilltop and helped her get in."

Ronja dipped her chin again.

"She wasn't completely certain she could trust you. That's why she didn't tell you Ito was coming."

Ronja did not respond, but kept her eyes fixed on the gleaming oak beneath her feet.

"Thank you," the boy said. "You saved my . . . you saved me."

"You saved me," Ronja pointed out, numbering the varnished boards as she passed over them.

"No, I almost got you killed. Twice. I thought you were dead."

Ronja stopped and turned to Roark. The hum of the engines crawled in through the bare soles of her feet, making her bones sing.

"You freed me," she countered.

"I just took off your Singer," Roark said. "Freedom is a state of mind."

Ronja nodded, cast her gaze to the ground again. She could feel his eyes drilling into her, but she could not meet them.

"Come on," he said, pulling her forward gently by her elbow.

Roark guided her down the rest of the hallway to a small arched doorway carved with ivy. Ronja paused before the door. She could hear nothing on the other side, no screams or cries of pain. Just silence.

Ronja closed her eyes, pursed her lips to keep them from trembling.

"What is it?" Roark asked gently, as though he did not know.

"Henry," Ronja whispered. "He was supposed to stay behind and now . . . "

Ronja sucked in a deep, shivering breath. "And now he's dead. My *mother* is dead. I hated her so much, but it wasn't her I should have hated. It was your father. Your grandfather. The Conductor. I spent my entire life hating her and now . . . "

She trailed off, her throat constricting.

"She knew you came for her," Roark said gently. "In the end, she knew."

Ronja exhaled slowly. She placed her hand on the cool, brass knob.

"Victor," she said slowly, looking back at the boy over her shoulder. "He's dead. Crushed."

"I know," Roark replied, his expression a tranquil mask.

"Okay."

Ronja took another breath and opened the door.

The room was tiny, but well furnished. Two twin beds with wooden headboards stood against the back wall, guarded by electric lamps with heavy shades. Colorful tapestries decorated the walls, and a small window crisscrossed with wooden slats looked out over the sprawling landscape.

Two sleeping forms lay on the beds.

Ronja covered her mouth with her hands.

"Georgie . . . " she breathed. "Cosmin."

Her cousins were laid out on their respective beds, the velvety blankets tucked up to their chins. Their heads had been shaved like her own, making them look even smaller than they actually were. Both were plugged into saline drips, and both were utterly still. Cosmin looked like he was simply sleeping, but a faint smile dusted Georgie's cracked lips.

Ronja padded forward, her hands still crossed over her mouth. She knew her cousins were in deep comas, but still she scarcely dared to breathe.

"Iris is going to operate on them as soon as we get back to the Belly," Roark said from behind her. "After we tell Wilcox what your voice can do, there's no way he can turn you away."

Ronja heard Roark speaking, but did not acknowledge him. She was staring at Georgie's wan face, her sunken cheekbones, the tiny mole near the right corner of her mouth.

Her hand trembling, Ronja reached down and cupped the girl's soft cheek. It did not melt away at her touch or ripple like a mirage.

Ronja drew her hand back.

She turned back to Roark with drowning eyes. The boy stood in the door, leaning against the frame with his arms folded.

He barely had time to unclasp them when Ronja lunged at him, wrenching sobs tearing at her throat. Roark lifted her from the ground like a child and allowed her to cry until she was empty once more.

63: ANTIDOTE

The early evening light was stretching across the horizon when they gathered in the silk-embossed lounge. The room was dominated by soaring stained glass windows that colored the sky a hundred shades of itself.

Ronja watched in dull fascination as the Technicolor shards danced across the white bandages that spiraled up her arms. Her eyes were bloodshot. She rubbed them with her palms, hoping to work some moisture back into them.

Roark sat beside her, his thigh brushing hers softly. He had been silent since her reunion with her cousins.

Evie was sprawled on a deep green sofa across from them, her newly clean feet propped on the coffee table. She clutched Iris to her side fiercely. The redhead had closed her eyes, but Ronja doubted she was truly asleep. Her muscles were coiled, her jaw pinched.

Terra perched on a stiff-backed chair, her elbows on her knees, her pointer fingers resting against her lips like the barrel of a gun. She had yet to bathe; her blond hair still caked with brown. She stared into space hostilely. Ronja thought it a wonder that her eyes did not burn holes in the patterned rug.

The two prisoners they had rescued from the demonstration lingered on the outskirts of the parlor. The elderly man refused to speak, but the girl had let slip that her name was Sawyer. Neither spoke now. Sawyer twisted her hands and peered out the stained glass window absentmindedly. The man tugged at his Singer, straining against the bombarding notes. Iris would have to attend to them soon, but so far neither showed signs of approaching The Quiet.

Ito stood at the nucleus of the room, her hands on her slender hips, her eyes caustic. "In all my years with the Anthem, I have never seen such startling stupidity," she began.

No one spoke; there was nothing to say. Ito continued.

"Thanks to you four, we have lost our only direct link to Westervelt Industries, and Henry is lost. If Terra and I had not shown up, you would have joined him."

Ronja stared at her thighs sightlessly, the brilliant face of her best friend swimming before her.

"You put hundreds of people at risk, weighed the lives of the few over the lives of the many. Do any of you have anything to say for yourselves?"

No one spoke. Sawyer coughed behind them. The engine hummed beneath them, and the wind rushed over the colored glass like waves over a sinking ship.

"What would you like us to say, Ito?" Roark asked tiredly. "We made a call. It had consequences. It saved innocent lives." Roark sat forward, holding Ito's blistering gaze in his own. "And also gained us invaluable information."

Ito narrowed her hooded eyes. Her nostrils flared, but she allowed Roark to continue.

"My father is dead," Roark said.

Ito drew a sharp breath. Roark nodded in confirmation.

"He was crushed by your dramatic entrance. Ronja denied him the mercy of a bullet, and he bled out on the floor. He tortured her in an attempt to get information from me."

"Did it work?" Ito asked somewhat desperately, her eyes flashing back and forth between the pair.

"Four agents were made," Roark admitted, turning to Ronja, who returned her gaze to her thighs. "Ones I knew were safe in the Belly."

"What matters is what we learned," Ronja broke in. "The Conductor is planning an attack on the Anthem. He's going to use a new form of The Music to drain your emotions completely. It can travel through the air—no Singer necessary. It's still a prototype, but—"

"I can promise you, it works," Roark finished darkly.

"He's going to put it in the Singers after he wipes out the Anthem," Ronja continued. "The entire city will be a shell."

"He has a torture Song, too," Roark added. "The Lost Song. Ronja felt that one."

Ronja waved Roark off. Her brain pinched at the fresh memory. "The chemi, Maxwell," Ronja said. "He reckons the attack is still three or four months out. You have time to get your people out."

"Or we could stay and fight."

All eyes looked to Roark. A ghost of his signature grin hung on the corner of his mouth.

"We can't fight The Music, Westervelt," Ito nearly growled.

"Actually, we can."

Roark turned to Ronja, who felt her stomach flip.

"We can fight it with her."

Ito was silent for a moment. Her gaze flashed to Ronja, who met it levelly. It took every ounce of her self-control not to crumble.

"Explain," Ito finally demanded.

"My father used the new Song on me, the one that drains emotion," Roark said, wincing visibly at the memory. Ronja felt driven to reach out and grasp his hand, but the moment was not right. She itched her nose instead.

"Ronja and Terra stormed in, guns blazing," Roark continued. "They were captured, of course. Then Ronja started to sing."

Ronja felt her face grow hot, submerging her freckles in a bath of red. She felt all eyes on her, but she kept her gaze trained on Ito.

"I was gone, Ito," Roark said. "Completely void. But when she sang, I woke up. Just like that." Roark snapped his fingers.

Ito chewed on his words, working her jaw. Shards of multicolored light sprawled across her regal features, but did little to soften her expression.

"What did you sing?" she finally asked Ronja.

"There and Back."

"How did you know to sing?"

"I didn't. I just . . . " She glanced around. Everyone watched her blankly, waiting. Roark touched her hand lightly, shooting electricity into her veins. She fought a shiver and continued in a stronger voice. "You fight fire with water, right? The Music and music are polar opposites. I didn't know it was an antidote, but it made sense."

To her surprise, Ito nodded thoughtfully.

"We need her, Ito," Roark implored. "Without her, we don't stand a chance. Her voice is . . . " He gestured at the air helplessly. "With the right training, she could be the best in a generation."

Ito breathed a heavy sigh, bringing her thumb and forefinger up to knead the bridge of her nose. "I could brand you all traitors," she muttered. "I don't care how noble your intentions were, you shot at Wilcox, ran an illegal mission—"

"Let's be honest, that was *not* the first time we ran our own mission," Evie said from the opposite couch. The girl was chewing on a toothpick, as she had been prohibited from smoking on the airship.

"Henry is dead," Ito continued as though she had not been interrupted.

She trailed off, looking at each of them in turn, her expression unreadable. The airship itself seemed to hold its great breath.

"You also gained invaluable intelligence and an antidote that could potentially save us."

Ronja emptied her lungs, and felt everyone else do the same.

"Ito," Ronja said, getting to her feet. Her sore muscles creaked in protest, but she forced herself to stand tall. "I'm sorry I put you all in danger. It was selfish, but I would do it again for my family. If my voice can protect you, if it can fight The Music . . . please. I am begging you. Let me fight for you."

Ito regarded her for a long moment. They watched her thoughts ticking like clockwork behind her hooded eyes.

"If you are a mutt you're the strangest one I've ever met," Ito said, her mouth quirking into a vague smile.

"She's not a mutt."

64: SINGER

The entire room rounded on Terra, who had risen from her seat. Her open hands trembled at her sides. She shoved them deep into her pockets and drew a steadying breath. The girl turned to Ronja, who moved in turn to face her.

"When I tell you this, I put my life in your hands," Terra began, her eyes on her boots.

Ronja nodded uncertainly, her heart pumping frantically.

Terra sucked in another deep breath and locked eyes with Ronja. "I knew you were a mutt from the start, long before I overheard Iris and Roark discussing your escape. You knew that."

Terra paused for Ronja to react, but she remained silent and expressionless.

"I also knew you weren't really a mutt."

Ronja felt her cracked lips part, but no sound came out. Roark and the others watched the exchange in total silence. Even the engine below seemed quieter.

"My mother worked at Red Bay," Terra continued. Her voice was steady, but she clenched and unclenched her pocketed fists in quick succession. "She was a scientist, one of the best. Victor Westervelt I sought her out for her work in gene splicing. He forced her to carry out his plans to turn rebels into mutts. It was the perfect plan, really. It was . . . "

Terra tilted her head backward, her gaze skimming the gold inlaid ceiling. Her eyes were unusually bright in the dying evening sun. "It was the perfect punishment," Terra continued without looking down.

Ronja flinched as if someone had struck her.

"A mark of shame that would live on through generations, one that would crush any chance of rebellion in the present and future.

"One day, a woman was brought in. She was pregnant. She was

supposed to be turned into a mutt. My mother was on duty. Just before the procedure started, the woman went into labor. She begged my mother to let her baby be born before she was turned . . . "

Terra swallowed. The skin on her throat glistened in the soft light. "My mother allowed it."

Ronja felt as though her chest had been punctured. The air was gushing from her lungs. The airship tilted though its course was steady.

"My mother outfitted the baby with a mutt Singer to avoid suspicion," Terra continued, her voice muffled by the dull roar in Ronja's ears. "She knew the baby would be treated as a mutt, since her Singer would emit the same signal, but at least she wouldn't die a slow, painful death. The next morning, my mother sent them to live in the outer ring under a new name. It all seemed fine, until a nurse ratted on my mother."

Terra was crying. Tears were leaking down her suntanned cheeks, bubbling over a thin, white scar on her cheekbone. She did not seem to notice them.

"She was killed in front of me," Terra whispered. "They used The Quiet Song, nice and slow. It lasted hours. Westervelt was there. Didn't bat an eye. They dumped me off in the outer ring. That's where Ito found me. I never saw the baby or the mother again, until Roark brought you in."

Ronja was disconnected. She heard the echoes of Terra's story distantly, as if through a tunnel. She was floating far above the room, far outside the airship, somewhere deep in the tangle of sun-dyed clouds.

"I knew it was you the moment I saw you," Terra said. "Your eyes were exactly the same, but I had to be sure. I dug your Singer out of the garbage. It was a mutt's . . . and right then I wanted you gone.

"You are the reason I lost my mother," Terra said, her voice cracking. "I know you didn't mean it, I know it wasn't your fault, but you were the reason. You reminded me of what I lost, and I wanted you gone. I hoped I could scare you away by calling you a mutt, but it didn't work."

The words were pouring from Terra now, coins tumbling from a purse and rolling away into the gutter.

"When I heard you and Roark were going to Red Bay, I knew it was suicide for the both of you. I wanted you gone, but I couldn't risk Roark."

Terra flicked her pleading eyes to the boy, who looked down at his knees, his expression inscrutable. She took a shuddering breath, withdrew her gaze, and went on.

"I . . . I told Wilcox that I'd found your Singer. That you were a new type of mutt, one that didn't bear the physical markers. That you had tricked Roark and were probably some sort of mole."

"He tried to kill me," Ronja rasped, her hands quivering at her sides. "He might have helped me get my family if he'd known I wasn't a mutt, if you'd just told the goddamn truth."

"You can't know that," Terra replied unsteadily. "You can't—"

"All this time, you knew," Ronja choked.

She stepped toward Terra, who in turn stumbled backward.

"My mother saved you," Terra sobbed. "She saved you, and she left me."

"You got Henry killed! You got my mother killed!" Ronja roared. "Because you couldn't tell Wilcox the truth! Couldn't tell *me* the truth!"

"I was selfish. Weak. I'm so sorry. I told Ito what I had done minutes after you left, and we came after you. To save Roark and the others, but also so I could make amends."

"Amends?" Ronja laughed hysterically. She put her hands over her eyes, ran her fingers down her bruised cheeks. Her face was wet. She had not realized that she too was crying.

Ronja sank into her place on the sofa and put her head in her hands. She viewed the world through the bars of her fingers. For a long moment, she simply breathed. The roar in her ear diminished like an auto rolling away.

Finally, she dropped her hands and looked up at Terra, who had wiped away her tears. She still trembled.

"I'm sorry about your mother," Ronja said in a low voice. "And I'm grateful for what she did for me. I understand why you did what you did, but I can't forgive you."

Terra swallowed, braced her jaw, then nodded firmly. She spun on her heel and strode away, her back as straight as a pin, her hands curled into fists.

For a long moment, silence reigned.

"Terra wasn't lying," Ito broke the hush. "She realized the error in her ways and sought redemption."

Ronja nodded wordlessly. Roark placed a reassuring hand on her back, but did not offer her any words of comfort. There was nothing to say.

"There is a place for you in our ranks, if you still want it," Ito continued. "If what Roark says is true, that your voice can counteract The Music, you would be our most valuable weapon."

Ronja rose again. Roark lifted his hand from her back, watching her with a ghost of a smile.

"I will be your weapon," Ronja said.

Ito held out her hand. Ronja grasped it firmly, her eyes ablaze and her blood searing.

"Welcome to the Anthem, singer."

EPILOGUE: THE PSYCHOLOGIST
Terra

The brig was adjacent to the engine room. The air trembled with heat, which the tiny slit of a window did little to alleviate. Terra sweated profusely as she stood before the metal cage, her bare arms crossed over her tank top.

"Warm enough?" she asked, raising her voice over the thrum of the engine.

Maxwell smiled tightly from his seat on the floor. He had shed his white coat, shirt, shoes, and socks. His wan skin was slick with perspiration, his dark hair was plastered to his forehead. He had removed his glasses, which were hopelessly fogged.

"I prefer the cold," Maxwell replied easily, as if they were acquaintances discussing the weather. "How are the children?"

"There's something that's been bothering me," Terra said, slipping her hands in the back pockets of her trousers.

Maxwell reclined against the gridded metal of his cell, an eyebrow arched inquiringly.

"Perhaps I can be of assistance," he said.

"Oh, I know you can be," Terra said, prowling toward the cage. She stopped a breath from the iron bars and glared down at the prisoner with calculating eyes. "I'd like you to tell me why I didn't have to kill you."

"Contrary to popular belief, psychologists cannot read minds," Maxwell said with a rueful smile.

"Psychologist," Terra said, bobbing her head. "That suits you."

"Thank you."

"It wasn't a compliment."

Maxwell's smile widened. His gold tooth snagged the dim light. "I sense your question was rhetorical," he said.

Terra did not reply right away. She leaned forward and wrapped her damp fingers around the rusted slats of metal, which were warm to the touch.

"I intended to kill you as soon as you rolled into The Quiet," Terra said. "You gave us information. You helped us free *six* prisoners. You should have gone under, but you didn't."

Maxwell sighed wearily. He reached up with his lanky arms and gripped the rods that crisscrossed the ceiling, then got to his feet with a groan. Terra watched with narrowed eyes as he rolled the kinks from his neck slowly, luxuriously.

"I helped save you, the filthy rebels, despite The Music in my ear that bid me not to," he finally said, padding toward her on the balls of his bare feet. Terra raised her chin to hold eye contact as he came to a halt three inches from her face. His eyes were bizarrely flat and dull, but their shape was familiar. Before Terra could place them, Maxwell spoke again. "What does that tell you?"

"I'm asking the questions," Terra growled.

"You already know the answer," the psychologist replied softly.

Terra did not reply. Maxwell breathed a laugh.

"Come on, Terra," he drawled, splaying his hands invitingly. "You're a smart girl. I saw the way you led your comrades. You're being groomed for command, I'm sure. I never had the luxury of being in charge myself, but I know a leader when I see one. So tell me," Maxwell pressed his face to the bars with a wicked grin. "Why didn't you have to put me out of my misery?"

"Because you were appeasing The Music," Terra whispered. "You wanted us to take you."

Maxwell jerked away from the bars and released a howling whoop, clapping his hands together gleefully. Terra took a step back, her hand on her stinger.

"Of course I did," Maxwell confirmed, abruptly toneless. "I knew you were Anthem as soon as you stormed in, I could smell your ego a mile away, no matter you were all Singerless."

"You're a spy."

"Psychologist," Maxwell corrected smoothly. "And I'm here to learn all about your pretty little heads for our Exalted Conductor. I had no idea I would get such a rare treat when I woke up this morning, but when you started waving that gun around I just couldn't resist tagging along."

"I'm not in the mood to play games," Terra said in a low voice, her fingers tightening around the weapon at her hip. "So unless you have any other secrets to spill, I'll just put your lights out now."

Maxwell clucked his tongue, waggling a long finger. "I wouldn't do that, lovely girl," he said, tapping his chin thoughtfully.

"Why?" Terra snorted, unsheathing her stinger and flicking it to life. The power hummed through her fingertips. She wanted more than anything to plunge it into his smug face.

"Oh, I suppose I forgot to mention," Maxwell said, tapping his skull with a little laugh. "I say I have perfect recall, but this heat must be overheating my circuits."

"Mention. What."

"That The Conductor will probably be missing his favorite, bastard son."

ACKNOWLEDGEMENTS:

There are so many people to thank. I could go on for pages, but I'll try to keep this short and sweet.

Mom, you are my primary editor and biggest supporter. You read draft after draft of this story. You poured just as much of your soul into it as I did. We shared so many laughs combing through my early drafts. I still can't write about airships without laughing. There is no way I could have done this without you. You are the strongest woman I know, and I could not be prouder to be your daughter.

Dad, you are my most logical critic. Science fiction is not your cup of tea, which makes your attentiveness to this project even more meaningful. You were always there to help when I needed to test out a tricky concept. You always listened, even when you didn't understand, even when you had other things that required your attention. That means more than I can say.

I would not have felt remotely comfortable sharing this book with the world without the guidance of my fabulous editor Katherine Catmull of Yellow Bird Editors. Kat, you polished this book with candor and warmth. You always went above and beyond. I am so lucky I found you.

Despite the old admonishment, nearly everyone judges a book by its cover. For that reason, I would like to thank Marta Bevacqua for selling me the picture that would become the cover of this novel. Seriously guys, trust me, check out her work. She is an artist of rare skill.

My beautiful betas. Maya. Ella. Lauren. Zoe. And Katie. You five are golden. You slogged through hundreds of pages of questionable grammar, awkward dialogue, and wonky spacing only to turn around and encourage me. I could not have asked for more.

I could not have asked for a better mentor than Heather Gudenkauf. Heather, you have supported me in my creative endeavors since I was fourteen. You were the first person outside my family to take my writing seriously. Thank you so much for believing in me.

Allie (A.K.A. Katherine with a K), we have been through so much together. I am so lucky to have a friend like you, and cannot wait to spend the next three and a half years together in the city that never sleeps.

Mackenzie, you brought *Little Wars* to life. It was more beautiful than I could have possibly imagined. Keep creating, keep singing, keep writing. You are incredible.

Grandpa Tom, Grandma Wanda, Grandpa Wayne, Grandma Sharon, Lisa, Tony, Jack, Aban, Darlene, Dani, Mica, Scout, Cameron, Bo, Arthur, Jim, Sam, Maria, Masha, Jeffrey, Nate, Rachel, Madeline, Jiaming, Annmarie, Zoe, Ashley, Patty, Margaret, Iyal, Aliyah, Sylvie, Lili Mae, Yeso, Marina, Emily, Caroline, and so many more. Thank you for supporting me, for listening to me, and for putting up with me. Thank you for loving me. You are my family, my friends, and I love you with all my heart.

To all my followers on Tumblr who have been there with me since before this book even hit the market, I love you.

And of course, I want to thank my readers. I love you all. Thank you for taking a chance on this little book.

Lastly, shout out to Diet Coke for keeping me propped up when my head was sagging into my keyboard.

Thank you all, and may your song guide you home,

Sophia

ABOUT THE AUTHOR

Sophia has been writing novels, short stories, and poems since she was still losing her baby teeth. Throughout her high school career she amassed an impressive 35 Scholastic Art and Writing Awards including two National Gold Medals for science fiction short stories. As a Scholastic alumnus, she joins the ranks of many great authors including Truman Capote, Sylvia Plath, and Joyce Carol Oates. Sophia has twice been accepted for publication in international young writer journals (*Polyphony HS* and *The Claremont Review*). She now resides in New York City as a student at her dream school, NYU. Sophia grew up in Iowa with two dogs and two fantastic parents. She is a 2015 graduate of Lake Forest Academy boarding school in Illinois. She loves dogs, books, and thunderstorms and hates racists, homophobes, and cantaloupe. She has a cactus named Nao because her dorm prohibits pets. Learn more at www.calidaluxpulishing.com or on Facebook at www.facebook.com/calidaluxpublishing .

CPSIA information can be obtained at www.ICGtesting.com
Printed in the USA
LVOW07s1757220216

476186LV00007B/575/P

9 780692 569832